**Praise for *USA TODAY* bestselling author
Emilie Richards**

"Richards's ability to portray compelling characters
who grapple with challenging family issues is laudable."
—*Publishers Weekly, starred review,* on *Fox River*

"[Richards's] characterizations are transcendent,
endowed with warmth and compassion."
—*Booklist* on *Wedding Ring*

"Magically interpreting the emotional resonance of
love and loss, betrayal and redemption
through luminously drawn characters...."
—*Booklist* on *Touching Stars*

Praise for bestselling author Janice Kay Johnson

"Johnson will hook readers with her
well-developed characters and emotional story."
—*RT Book Reviews* on *Someone Like Her*

"I can't wait to read more of [Johnson's] books."
—*Dear Author* on *Bone Deep*

EMILIE RICHARDS

Emilie Richards's many novels feature complex characterizations and in-depth explorations of social issues, a result of her training and experience as a family counselor, which contribute to her fascination with relationships of all kinds. Emilie, a mother of four, lives with her husband in Florida, where she is currently working on her next novel for Harlequin.

JANICE KAY JOHNSON

The author of more than eighty books for children and adults, Janice Kay Johnson is especially well-known for her Harlequin Superromance novels about love and family—about the way generations connect and the power our earliest experiences have on us throughout life. Her 2007 novel *Snowbound* won a RITA® Award from Romance Writers of America for Best Contemporary Series Romance. A former librarian, Janice raised two daughters in a small rural town north of Seattle, Washington. She loves to read and is an active volunteer and board member for Purrfect Pals, a no-kill cat shelter.

USA TODAY Bestselling Author

EMILIE
RICHARDS

The Trouble with Joe

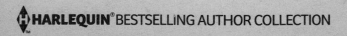

HARLEQUIN® BESTSELLING AUTHOR COLLECTION

Recycling programs
for this product may
not exist in your area.

ISBN-13: 978-0-373-18085-1

THE TROUBLE WITH JOE
Copyright © 2014 by Harlequin Books S.A.

The publisher acknowledges the copyright
holders of the individual works as follows:

THE TROUBLE WITH JOE
Copyright © 1994 by Emilie Richards McGee

SOMEONE LIKE HER
Copyright © 2009 by Janice Kay Johnson

This edition published by arrangement with Harlequin Books S.A.

For questions and comments about the quality of this book, please contact us at CustomerService@Harlequin.com.

® and TM are trademarks of Harlequin Enterprises Limited or its corporate affiliates. Trademarks indicated with ® are registered in the United States Patent and Trademark Office, the Canadian Trade Marks Office and in other countries.

Printed in U.S.A.

CONTENTS

Dear Reader,

It's always a pleasure to know a book with special meaning to me will find a new audience. *The Trouble with Joe* was a labor of love, as novels should be since authors live and breathe every story as we write it.

Adoption is a subject close to my heart. After two wonderful sons my husband and I chose to adopt what we thought would be our last child. Our daughter was six when she came to us from India. Fitting an older child into a family, especially one who doesn't speak the same language, is a unique test of patience on both sides. There were times when we looked at each other and wondered what we had done. The daughter *and* the parents.

Still day by day, month by month, she became ours in every way. When we moved out of the first house we had shared, we found her name written on the walls in places where furniture had long hidden it. Our daughter had made certain we all understood that the house and everything and everyone in it belonged to her, as well as to those of us who had lived there first.

She was absolutely right.

Now my six-year-old is an adult and a mommy, too, and she is utterly devoted to her own husband and beautiful daughters. I look at all of them and know how much our family would have missed if one day my husband and I hadn't said: "You know, this time around, let's offer a child who's already out there a home."

I hope you enjoy the story of Samantha, Joe and Corey, and the way a small child can steal your heart and never, never give it back.

Happy reading,

Emilie

THE TROUBLE WITH JOE

USA TODAY **Bestselling Author**

EMILIE
RICHARDS

PROLOGUE

NOTHING WAS HOTTER than a summer day in Sadler County, North Carolina. And even if the calendar said it wasn't quite summer, the mercury on Sadler County thermometers hadn't been informed.

In the worst part of the afternoon Joseph Giovanelli stood in the heart of a grove of pines and felt waves of heat shimmer over his body. His white shirt was already wet, and an interior voice reminded him that he would have to change before he returned to school.

He wasn't sure where he would find the vitality to go back at all. He had come home for something he had left behind, a list of new students who would be attending the high school in the fall. Due to a colleague's absence, the task of assigning the students to home rooms had fallen to Joe. That wasn't unusual. Historically rush jobs fell to the first in command. And as principal of Sadler High, the buck always stopped at Joe's wide-open door.

He hadn't minded the extra work. He had done it last night, finishing after midnight. These days he relished working late. He had always been an active man, happiest when he was busy. Now there was a manic quality to that activity; he was as aware of it as everybody else. But work was the only thing that made Joe feel alive. And if a man didn't feel alive at least some of the time, he might as well be dead.

Overhead a crow cawed his displeasure at Joe's presence in the woods. Joe told himself that the crow was right. He needed to get back; he did not need quiet woods or disquieting contemplation. Despite that, something urged him forward. His feet passed down a well-traveled path, one he had lined with wood chips from the trees he had been forced to take down when landscaping near the house.

He had made good use of the rest of the wood, too. One hundred yards down the path he stopped in front of a small log cabin whose wide shadow stretched to the calm blue of a one-acre lake.

There were ducks swimming near the shore, and at Joe's approach a goose, like a white-feathered watchdog, honked a warning. But the warning was drowned out by voices in Joe's head, the voices he had come to hear.

Joe, you know you're crazy, don't you? Nobody, but nobody, builds a playhouse for children they don't even have yet. Not before they finish the house they've got to live in every day. There's no floor in our dining room and not a cabinet in the kitchen. I'm tired of cooking from cardboard boxes. Let me repeat... Joe, put me down! No, I will not be a party to this. Not here. I don't care if the playhouse has walls, Joe. There aren't any doors. Yes, I know it's getting dark. Yes. Oh, Joe, you idiot! You wonderful idiot!

He stared at the cabin and saw the ghosts of two people with their lives stretching in front of them, good lives, happy lives. He saw his wife, Samantha, as clearly as if she were really standing there, as clearly as he had this morning when he watched her drive off to her job at Foxcove Elementary School. Blonde, reserved Sam, with the china-doll complexion and the lake-blue eyes. Eyes that hid so well the passion only Joe had known.

Sweat poured down his back and beaded his forehead. There were other ghosts here, too. Ghosts of children who would never run along this path or play in this cabin. Ghosts of grandchildren who would never know the beauty of this lake, the peace of piney North Carolina forests.

He couldn't hear their voices or their laughter. He had never heard them and never would.

In the stillness the crow cawed again, as if he had followed this strange upright animal to ask what he planned to do next.

"I plan to go back to work," Joe whispered. "What in the hell else is there to do?"

He turned his back on the cabin, on the lake and on a lifetime of dreams.

When the crow cawed again, there was no one there to hear it.

CHAPTER ONE

ROSES FADED. ROSES wilted. But to Samantha Giovanelli's knowledge, roses never turned into something else entirely. Not unless they had a little help.

Or a little helper.

Sam had walked by her desk three times that afternoon and never noticed that flawless white rosebuds had turned into wilting yellow dandelions. Now she could ignore it no longer. Long stems had been exchanged for those just long enough to fit into a child's grubby fist. And the delicate white porcelain vase that had been delivered with the roses had a sizable chip in the rim.

Sam supposed she was lucky the vase wasn't leaking water all over the papers piled on the desk, papers collected after a year of teaching twenty-six first graders how to read, 'rite and resist clobbering each other. In three years as an educator she had learned to appreciate the smallest things—and people. Now as she rummaged through her wastebasket she told herself that the dandelions were a symbol of what the year had meant to one little girl. They were a sign that Sam had succeeded in an impossible task: civilizing Corey Haskins.

Not that the task was finished.

At the bottom of the wastebasket, piled high with papers, used-up workbooks, melted crayons and lumps of clay were six formerly perfect rosebuds. The stems were crushed and the petals bruised. Sam lifted them carefully—although care at this stage was a sign of terminal optimism—and trimmed the stems to two inches with blunt-end scissors from her desk drawer. Then she filled the sink on the other side of the room and immersed the flowers in the cool water.

If she couldn't have a bouquet, at least she could have a corsage.

"Sortin' your trash now, Sammy? If we were all as organized as you, this school would run like a four-legged dog in a three-legged race."

Sam turned off the water and weighted the ends of the stems with a rock so the roses wouldn't float to the top. She flashed a smile at Polly, the first-grade teacher from a room down the hall who was standing in the doorway. "A four-legged dog in a three-legged race?"

"Think about it," Polly drawled. She wandered into the room at the same speed as her words. As always, Polly seemed in need of a jump start. "You did know your trash was higgledy-piggledy all over the floor?"

"I know." Sam dried her hands and headed for the wastebasket again. She began to stuff the trash inside.

"And you do know that this is the last day of classes, and you're supposed to be doin' flip-flops up and down the corridor?"

"Anybody who could do flip-flops in this heat deserves a gold medal."

"Mind tellin' me what you're doin'?"

"Did you see the man from Allen's Florist in the hall earlier?"

"Yep, I did."

"Well, Joe sent me roses. Six gorgeous white roses."

"Joe can put his sneakers under my bed just any old time he chooses."

Sam laughed. Polly was ambling toward fifty, and along the way had picked up an extra pound for every single year. Her hair was bottle red and her clothes most suitable for a church rummage sale. But Harlan, her husband of thirty good years, still thought she was the most wonderful woman in Sadler County, and so did their eight children. Sam didn't have a thing to worry about.

"So why do you have the world's poorest excuse for dandelions in this vase if Joe sent you roses?" Polly ran her finger over the chipped rim and shook her head. "Next question's why you have this vase at all?"

Samantha finished the trash and began to straighten her desk. "It was minus the chip when the roses came in it. Apparently one of my students decided that dandelions would look better and switched them sometime after class. Probably when I was up at the office. Then she threw the roses in the trash and covered them up well. I just found them."

"She." Polly hadn't missed the pronoun that eliminated fully half of Sam's classroom. "Corey?"

"Probably," Sam admitted.

"I'da stuck that little gal in the closet if she was put in my class this year."

"Sure you would have." More often than not when Sam walked by Polly's classroom door, some child was settled in Polly's ample lap or arms receiving either a dose of TLC or the gentlest of reprimands. She was Miss Pollywolly Doodle to all the first graders, and she would no more raise her voice or hand to a child than she would take up running or go on a diet.

"Why do you suppose she did it?" Polly asked.

"I guess Corey wanted me to remember her."

"Like anybody here could ever forget her."

Sam couldn't argue. Corey was unforgettable. She lifted the framed class photo from her desk and her eyes went right to Corey in the back row. Corey was shorter than most of the other children, but the photographer had taken one look at her and relegated her to the back, where her clothes would be covered by the heads of other children.

The maneuver had been only partially successful. There had been no way to hide Corey's chopped-up blond hair and scratched-up face. Sam had tenderly washed that little face herself, but Corey had been mauled by an alley cat—she had probably tormented the poor thing—and under the usual dirt had been railroad-track scars that showed clearly in the picture.

"What will she do this summer?" Sam asked.

Polly took the photograph from Sam's hands and set it firmly back on the desk. "Now, you listen here, Sammy. First off, that little girl is now a second grader. By the grace of God, maybe, but still a second grader. She's somebody else's problem now, because she sure can't be yours anymore. There's nothing you can do. She's got a mama, and the county says her mama is fit to raise her."

"Does a fit mother send a child to school in filthy bedroom slippers?"

"You know we can't take a kid away from her mama just because she's poor."

Poverty wasn't the issue, and Sam and Polly both knew it. There had been other poor children in Sam's classroom; Sadler County, North Carolina was full of poor people. But most of the time their kids were clean. Those kids came to school with something in their stomachs, even if it wasn't Sam's idea of good nutrition. And the parents showed up for teacher conferences, or took the time to fill out forms so that their children could receive free lunches.

Corey's mother could learn a lesson from any of them.

There were people all over the world who longed desperately for a child; Sam knew that all too well. And then there were people like Verna Haskins who had a child and cursed the day that child had been born.

"I know I can't be her teacher forever," Sam said. "But it's hard to let go."

"Better learn."

"Do you know how many phone calls I got this year about Corey?" Sam forced a smile. "Thirty-two. I kept track. All from angry parents wanting to know what I was going to do about her. You'd think I'd be doing those flip-flops you were talking about."

"While you're at it, don't forget the time old Ray Flynn tried to have her put in a special needs school and you threatened to quit your job over it."

"If Joe wasn't the high school principal, Dr. Ray would have forced me out."

"Yep. Joe can make things tough on folks who go after what's his, that's for sure."

"Is that right?"

The deep voice from the doorway caused both women to turn. Sam felt the impact of her husband's presence just as she always did. It started somewhere deep inside, curled and crept through her until she was smiling.

And hoping that he would do the same.

"What are you doing here?" she asked.

"I just came to see how you managed on your last day."

"I'm headin' out." Polly started toward the door. She patted Joe on the cheek as she passed. He took her hand and gave it a courtly kiss before she vanished down the hall.

Sam didn't move. There had been a time when she wouldn't have had to. Joe would have strolled over, lifted her off her feet and whirled her around the room. But the Joe lounging in the doorway was a different man. So many things had changed in the past six months.

"I got the roses," she said. "They were beautiful. I was so surprised."

"*Were* beautiful?"

"Well, there was a tiny accident. I'll be wearing them on my dress at the party tomorrow."

He pushed away from the doorjamb and came over to the desk. She rose on tiptoe to kiss his cheek. His arms closed around her and she rested against him.

"How was your day?" he asked.

Questions behind a question. She knew what he really wanted to know. Was the last day of school particularly hard this year? Was it painful to leave the children behind? Was she going to make it through the summer without the sound of childish laughter?

"All right," she said. "How about yours?"

"The seniors trashed the lawn and poured ball bearings in the hallways. Sometime this week somebody spelled out Dean Lambert Sucks on the football field. In herbicide. The grass died today."

"That's it?"

"If we're lucky."

She slipped her arms around his waist. Joe had a quarterback's physique—long muscular legs, trim hips and waist and broad, broad shoulders. He looked equally good in a suit or bathing trunks, but he looked his very best in nothing at all.

She leaned back so she could see his face. His features were striking and strong, straight off the steamship from northern Italy, with only a Slovenian grandmother to dare reconfigure the Giovanelli gene pool. His hair was shining black and his eyes as dark as his most secret thoughts. When he smiled his face came alive. Or it had once upon a time.

"Thanks for taking the time to come over here," she said.

"It was either this or chopping out sod on the field. I thought Lambert should chop, since he's the one who enrages the kids."

"Al wouldn't know what side of a hoe went where."

"Actually, he's got all the juniors who still owe detention hours doing it."

"Great. That way he can be sure the same thing will happen next year when *they're* seniors." Reluctantly she moved away. They couldn't stand in each other's arms all afternoon, no matter how good it felt. "I've still got next week to finish cleaning the room. Do you have to go back to school, or can you come home with me?"

"I'll follow you back."

She was so surprised that for a moment she didn't know what to say. "Well, fine," she said at last. "Maybe it'll be cooler there."

"Don't count on it."

"We can stand under the ceiling fans and drink iced tea."

"Do you need help with those?" He nodded toward two cardboard boxes beside the door.

"Just a few little things to keep me busy this summer. Some new textbooks to look over. The workbooks the board's decided we'll be using next year. Some music to learn, since the music teacher's been cut to half-time and now we'll be teaching music as well as everything else in the classroom."

"Overworked and underpaid."

"The definition of a teacher," they finished together.

"I'll get the boxes," he said. "Do you need to stop by the office?"

She nodded. "I'll meet you in the parking lot."

He started toward the door.

"Joe?"

He looked over his shoulder.

"The roses were the loveliest thing to happen to me in a long time."

His smile was brief and lopsided. But it was a smile. Hope stirred inside her. He had been gone a full minute before she collected herself and started for the office.

JOE FIT BOTH boxes in the trunk of his car. It was an American sports car, shiny black and low slung with more horsepower than the North Carolina blacktop could handle. He had bought it six months ago without consulting Sam. When he'd brought it home she had said all the right things, but her expression had told him what she really thought.

He didn't know what had possessed him to buy a car that every boy in the high school would sell his soul for.

He had seen it in the lot, a visible symbol of everything masculine and powerful, and he had signed the papers that afternoon. The psychology behind that decision was perhaps best left unexplored.

Killer—Sam's name for the car—bounced when he slammed the trunk. Joe had parked under a magnolia tree in full bloom, and a welcome breeze waltzed the scent through the air. A piano tinkled through an open door to the cafeteria, and children's voices sounded from the playground on the other side of the school. He leaned against the car and crossed his arms. Despite the sensory attractions even the short wait made him restless.

He scanned the school yard for something to look at. A squirrel attempted the leap from one tree to another and managed admirably. A mockingbird squawked at the intruder, then made a faulty dive bomb when the squirrel didn't take the hint. Just beyond the school grounds a car pulled from its parking place and drove down the empty street.

Joe tapped his foot and drummed his fingers against his arms. Pressure built inside him. He was so seldom idle that now he felt as if someone had tied him, hand and foot. He thought of a million things he needed to be doing, and wished he could do them simultaneously.

Suddenly a small figure crawled from behind one bush to another under the windows of the classroom closest to the parking lot. The landscaping was overgrown, and there was almost no room between the flourishing juniper and holly and the brick wall. At first Joe wondered if he had fantasized the child as an antidote to unaccustomed inactivity. He took off his sunglasses and squinted at the bush where he thought the child had gone. Nothing moved, but there was the tiniest scrap of red visible between one evergreen branch and another.

He started forward.

"Joe?"

He held his finger to his lips, but Sam, coming toward him from the other side of the building with a loaded box topped with a vase of wobbling dandelions, didn't see.

"Joe, grab this vase, will you, before it falls?"

He abandoned hide-and-seek and went to meet Sam. Twenty-five yards from the car he took the box and let her carry the vase.

"There's a kid hiding in the bushes over by the sixth-grade classrooms," he told her.

"Why?"

"Who knows? It's been a while since I was a kid."

"I don't see anybody."

"This kid knows how to hide, you've got to give her that."

"Her?"

"I caught a flash."

"What exactly did you see?"

"Blond hair. Red shirt."

"Corey." Sam set the vase on Killer's hood and started toward the bushes. "Corey," she called, "come on out and meet Mr. Joe. You're going to get all scratched up back there."

There was no telltale rustle. "Corey?" She moved closer, but not quickly. Joe guessed that Corey was easy to spook. Sam would know from experience.

"Come on, Corey," she said softly. "Nobody's mad

at you. We just don't want you to get hurt. That's no place to play."

There was a flash of red at the far end of the row, three classrooms and more than two dozen scratchy evergreens away. Sam straightened. Joe turned his head just in time to see a little girl dressed in a long-sleeved shirt and corduroy pants—too worn to be appropriate any time of year—crawl out from behind the last bush. She stood and stared at him. Even from a distance he detected suspicion in the dark eyes that took up half the child's face. Then she turned and made a run for the sidewalk in front of the school. She disappeared around the corner before Sam could say anything else.

"So that's Corey." Joe went to stand beside her.

"That *was* Corey. I'm sorry. I've talked about her so much I wanted you to meet her."

He stuffed his hands into his pockets. "After all the stories I've heard, I can wait until high school before I'm forced to get to know her."

She smiled, but he saw the tinge of sadness in her eyes. "You just might like her, Joe. The two of you have some things in common."

"Yeah?"

"You both love me."

He wanted to touch her hair, to tell her that Corey obviously had exquisite taste, but instead he shifted his weight to his heels, not quite moving away from her. "What else?"

"Neither of you has the slightest idea how to cope with your feelings."

He stared at her. The remark was so unlike Sam that for a moment he was at a loss for words. "What brought that on?" he asked at last.

She looked away. The breeze lifted a lock of her long blond hair and blew it against her cheek. He had always loved her best like this, when something unexpected ruffled her calm exterior. Now he wanted to tuck the hair back in place—almost as much as he wanted to insist she take back her words.

"I'm sorry." She didn't elaborate.

"So it has been a tough day," he said.

"Yes."

"I know you hate to say goodbye to your kids."

"Not *my* kids, Joe." She sighed. "I really am sorry. It's just that it's hardest of all saying goodbye to Corey. She has such potential. Her IQ is so high Dr. Ray went back and hand-graded the test after the results came in. Nobody but me believed she could be that smart."

"You're going to have a Corey every year in every class."

"And is it that easy for you to stay distant? It never used to be."

"You learn."

"You know what? I hope I don't. I hope my aptitude for cutting myself off from people is so low the psychologists have to hand-grade my results, just to be sure."

She had managed a smile, but he couldn't make himself smile back.

"I guess I need to get out of the sun," she said. "Let's go home and have that iced tea. I'll make something special for dinner tonight. How about your mother's manicotti?"

He looked at his watch. "No dinner for me. I've got Kiwanis tonight."

She searched his face. "Is it really important? We haven't had a night together in a long time." She moved a little closer. "We could test out the pond and see if it's warm enough for swimming. And if it's not…"

He knew the rest of the sentence. They could keep each other warm.

"I'm sorry, but I promised to give a report, so I can't skip." He looked at his watch again, as if it might help something. Anything. "And I hate to say it, but I didn't realize it was getting as late as it is. I'm not even going to have time to go home first. I've still got some work to do at school before the meeting."

"Can't it keep?"

"I wish." But he didn't, because he didn't want to go home anymore. He wanted to be busy. He wanted to do a thousand things at once.

"Why, Joe?"

He pretended he didn't understand. "Why what?"

"Why did you come here this afternoon?"

"I came to see how your day had gone."

"I think the part that's already finished is going to be the best part of it." She started toward her car, parked several rows from his.

"This is always a busy time of year," he said.

"Which makes it the same as every other time."

He caught up with her. "We've got all day tomorrow."

She stopped. "We have a houseful of people coming for our housewarming."

"We'll find some time alone."

"No, we probably won't." She stopped beside Killer and got the vase she had left on the hood. The dandelions had shriveled in the sun until they were nothing more than stems.

"Go home and get some rest." Joe leaned over and kissed her cheek. For one moment he was close enough for anything, for kissing or shaking or sobbing in her arms. Then he pulled away. "I'll try to get home early."

She didn't answer. She just turned and walked away.

CHAPTER TWO

SOMETIMES THE SILVER-LINING theory of human existence had merit. Sam and Joe's house was a perfect example. One hundred years before, it had been a general store, weathered wood and flapping tin roof, with a wide front porch where customers could practice spitting tobacco or watermelon seeds into the ragtag bushes below. From those days of relative prosperity it had fallen onto harder times. The proprietors had departed soon after the advent of the automobile. There hadn't been a need for a store on Old Scoggins Road when everyone could go into Foxcove for a wider variety of merchandise.

Over the years the store had been used sporadically as a community center, then a storage barn for hay. Most recently it hadn't been used for anything except marking the halfway point for anyone looking for the Insleys, residents of a prosperous farm just a half mile farther south.

Turner Insley, the owner, hadn't seen much need for tearing down the store. It was too far away from anything to be a danger. If it collapsed in the dead of night, chances were good that no one would be nearby to notice. Tearing it down cost good money, and there was always a better use for that. Over the years the store had grown a little more dilapidated, a little sorrier, but nobody had minded much.

Not until Joe Giovanelli.

One afternoon Joe had been driving past the store on his way to see Turner about his youngest granddaughter. Nesta Insley was the most vivacious, flirtatious sophomore in a school of close competitors. Southern charm was common enough to be ho-hum in Sadler County, but one flutter of Nesta's eyelashes and Rhett would have abandoned Scarlett. Nesta had successfully wrapped every teacher around her pert little fingers, but Joe had been immune. Behind Nesta's vitality and charm he had seen a scared little girl who was cheating her way through school and life in general. Since her parents had claimed to be too busy to meet with him, Joe had been on his way to explain the situation to Turner.

He'd been a hundred yards past the store when he had applied his brakes and backed up to stop in front of it. In nearly a hundred years no one had seen the store's potential. But Joe had looked at the old building with the rusting tin and the sagging porch and called it home.

Conducting himself like the professional he was, Joe had waited until he and Turner had come to an understanding about Nesta. Turner was no fool; all he'd needed was Joe's professional opinion of his granddaughter and a few observations of his own. He had assured Joe that Nesta would be taken in hand. They had agreed on tighter curfews, supervised study hours and attention to weekly progress reports. Turner's word was still law in his family. If he told his son and daughter-in-law to shape up, they would.

Then the two men had gotten down to real estate. No, Turner didn't need the store, and he didn't need the land around it. There was a nice spring down behind the store, so he couldn't let the land go for nothing. No, sir, not for nothing. On the other hand, all he had to sell was the land, because nobody in his right mind wanted the store. Tearing it down was an expensive proposition. Yes, sir, a mighty expensive one, which was why it was still standing.

So they had bargained for the land. And after the two men had shaken hands on six acres, Joe had told Turner that he planned to renovate the store and make it his home. Turner had seen him out, laughing all the way to the car.

Sam had been the next hurdle. Now as Sam neared the store-turned-home she remembered the first time Joe had brought her here.

He had been sheepish, which for Joe meant that he was only half as cocky as usual. He had promised her a drive in the country. Their apartment in town was cramped, and getting out for the afternoon had seemed like a good idea. They had driven south, and Sam had assumed their destination was a lake near the county border. When Joe had turned onto Old Scoggins she had been mildly curious. When Joe had stopped in front of the store and suggested they take a walk she'd been curious.

When Joe had told her he had bought the store and land she had been furious.

It had taken a full month for Joe to persuade her they could turn the store into a home. Joe wasn't an easy man to say no to. He was domineering and brash. As a senior in high school the verbal score on his SATs had been high enough to garner scholarship offers at three different colleges. Polly always said that when Joe was fired up he could wear a body down so completely they'd do just about anything to make him go away.

But Sam had remained firm. She and Joe were opposites in many ways, but she was no less stubborn when something really mattered to her. Living in the store mattered. She hadn't been able to imagine that even fifty years of hard work would turn it into a home. Joe had looked at the store and surrounding land and seen a paradise. She had looked at it and seen heartbreak.

In the end, both of them had been right.

Today as she turned into the dogwood-shaded driveway, sunshine glinted off shiny tin and fresh white paint. Ivy and petunias spilled out of bright red window boxes flanked by spruce green shutters. A porch swing and three oak rocking chairs with blue calico cushions waited patiently on the front porch for someone to while away the evening sunset, and a hummingbird darted over the trumpet vine that screened one trellised end.

The scene was idyllic. There was enough sun to grow flowers and enough old trees to provide summertime shade. Red brick framed the flower beds and crisscrossed a walkway to the porch. The grass was soft and green, perfect for barefooted children to romp over. There were no children, but there was a bevy of kittens. Tinkerbelle, an aging calico who was old enough to know better, had presented Sam and Joe with her first and only litter just a month before.

Despite the kittens, despite Tink's greeting rubbed lovingly against Sam's leg, despite the cheery petunias and the newly flowering roses, Sam felt an oppressive loneliness.

A glass of iced tea, a shower and a change into soft knit white shorts and T-shirt did little to improve her mood. She picked at a muffin and tried the afternoon newspaper, but neither held her attention.

Finally, with the kittens frolicking at her heels, she started toward the pond. On its shore she reassured Attila, the watch-goose who had never learned to tell the difference between friend and enemy. The sun was dropping too slowly to suit her, but she settled on the soft grass at the pond's edge and watched its slow descent. There was no reason to go back to the house, no business there that couldn't wait.

The night she had first met Joe had been a little like this one. It had been late spring, but hot, anyway, so hot that she had spent the day drifting from one air-conditioned room or vehicle to another. Until she had met Joe, her life had consisted of nothing but slow, graceful passage from one comfortably colorless moment to the next.

Now, despite all the problems that confronted them, she remembered that night. And, despite everything, she smiled.

"Oh, SAMANTHA, NOT the red tonight. It's too bright and too low cut. I'll never understand why you bought something so unsuitable." Kathryn Whitehurst surveyed her daughter as she spoke, assessing her hair, her tasteful makeup, as well as the dress in question.

Samantha watched her mother silently tick off the details of her appearance. The red, a muted watermelon shade, was perfect with her pale blond hair and alabaster skin, and the sweetheart neckline just highlighted the subtle swell of her breasts. But it wasn't worth an argument. Kathryn had rigid standards for everything, but particularly appearance. As long as Samantha conformed, she and Kathryn could pretend they were the perfect mother and daughter. Samantha could be the flawless pearl bracelet to her mother's flawless double-strand choker.

"I'll wear the blue dress you bought me in New York," Samantha said.

"Well, hurry." Kathryn's tone implied that changing was Samantha's idea entirely. "Your father will be here in a few minutes, and you know how he hates to wait."

"I'll just be a minute."

In her room Samantha tossed the red dress onto her bed and found the blue in the back of her closet. It was the insipid hue of a cloudy sky, and once it was on and she surveyed the effect, she scolded herself for giving in to Kathryn's whims. She was twenty-one today, and she still couldn't stand up to her mother—or her father, for that matter. In fact, after twenty-one years of doing exactly what was expected of her, she couldn't stand up to anyone. She was a well-bred child turning into a well-bred woman. She had nothing but a well-bred future to look forward to.

Back in the living room she watched her mother's expression darken. The red silk flowed under her fingers as she held it out in apology. "The blue dress needed cleaning. I'd forgotten. But I softened this with the Hermès scarf you gave me. Don't you think it's better?" She smiled, encouraging her mother to compromise, too.

"I think you look very nice." Fischer Whitehurst came through the door just in time to hear her. "Imagine. You're twenty-one today." He didn't hold out his arms for a hug, but to his credit he didn't extend his hand, either. He just smiled—distant, reserved, eternally polite Fischer Whitehurst who, of Samantha's two parents, was slightly the colder.

"Our reservation is for seven. We'll have to hurry." Kathryn turned toward the door. "There's still time to change your mind, Samantha. We could eat at the club if you'd rather."

"Oh, let's try La Scala," Samantha said, looking toward her father for support. "I'm really in the mood for something different."

He held out his arm. "It's your birthday."

It was her birthday, a momentous one, and because it was, she had dutifully agreed to let her parents celebrate it with her. They had offered a party, something tasteful—and abysmally oversize—at their country club, with a band, champagne and a midnight supper buffet. She had countered with a plea for a small family dinner at a new restaurant in Georgetown.

Kathryn rarely set foot in Washington. Chevy Chase was already too close to the sprawling, brawling heartbeat of the nation. She still longed for her childhood home in proper suburban Charlotte, as she had for every day of the thirty years of her marriage. She could pretend she was still living in the genteel South if she didn't have to get too close to the purpose of Chevy Chase's existence: Washington, D.C., the city where her bank-president husband oversaw a financial empire that had weathered two hundred years of political wars and rainforest summers.

Now Kathryn gathered her jacket and tightened her lips into a line. She was obviously unhappy about Samantha's choice, but she would go, because it was expected.

Samantha was touched by the route their driver took

to get to La Scala. Melwin, the friend and confidant who piloted her father's limo, drove past national monuments lit by floodlights and along the Potomac where falling cherry blossoms littered the ground like drifts of snow. The route he'd chosen added twenty minutes to the trip, but she shushed her father when he tried to complain. Samantha knew the trip was Mel's present to her, and she was enchanted.

She and Mel had made this trip before—often, in fact—throughout the lonely years of her childhood and adolescence. To her parents Mel was simply an employee, a poorly educated but trustworthy nobody. To her he was the grandfather she'd never known, the fantasy caring uncle who brought her silly gifts or tickled her under her chin.

Mel had always done what he could to brighten her life. In his second week of employment he had taken one look at her long face and promised a treat if she would smile. Her dancing lessons had mysteriously slipped away that day—her parents had never known—in favor of a drive like this one. Melwin had told her stories about the city he loved, and in the process brought history to life for her.

That trip had been the first of many. Through the years they had eaten ice-cream cones at shabby neighborhood groceries, fed pigeons—and the occasional vagrant—in downtown parks, watched fireworks on the mall and traced tear-stained fingers over the name of Melwin's son on the Vietnam memorial.

Now Mel was trying to teach her something again.

By the time they arrived at La Scala, Samantha felt renewed. By Mel's subtle rebellion, his carefully plotted course, he had reminded her that she could have a different, more colorful future. She was officially an adult. Their trips to Washington no longer had to be secret, nor did her thoughts and feelings. She could be the woman she wanted; she could be free if she gathered a little courage.

He winked at her as she got out of the limo, and she winked back. Mel was retiring soon to go live with a daughter in California. She was going to miss him.

"I'll have a drink," she said, after the maître d'—who obviously recognized her father's name—had settled them at the nicest table in the house. The restaurant was subdued by her standards, but wildly frenetic by her parents'. Roman pillars flanked the cavernous marble-paved room, and despite the use of wooden beams and dark Oriental carpets, laughter and high-volume Puccini echoed off every surface. The cuisine was Mediterranean, with an emphasis on herbs, olive oil and garlic. The air itself was a fragrant enticement to eat heartily, to experiment and savor.

"Champagne?" her father asked. "Dubonnet on the rocks?"

"Bourbon. Straight." She didn't look at her mother. "Make it a double."

A male voice responded. "Only our best bourbon. We age it in casks Davy Crockett nailed together right before he left for the Alamo."

She looked in her mother's direction and saw a man looming larger than life at her side. He was dressed in black with a pleated white shirt that was so bright against his olive skin it almost hurt her eyes. He smiled at her, as if he understood exactly what kind of statement she had been trying to make. Something warm and liquid curled lazily inside her.

For a moment she couldn't respond. He was long and lean, and he stood like a man so confident in his own powers that serving others was nothing more than a small, thoughtful gift of himself.

"Make it a triple," she said.

He laughed, and the sound sparkled through her bloodstream, like the bubbles of the champagne she had refused. "Only if you promise to let me drive," he said in a low, distinctly dangerous voice.

Her mother made a small, distressed sound. There was a clear line between the server and the served, as clear to Kathryn as the difference between Chevy Chase and inner-city Washington. She spit out her own order and her husband's without asking his preference, then she waved the man away. "I don't know where you heard about this restaurant, Samantha." She massaged her forehead, as if she could erase the past few moments. "But it's really not our kind of place."

Samantha sat back. She felt alive; she felt daring. She felt bratty. "I don't think *we* have a kind of place. This is *my* kind of place. You have *your* kind of place. I was in the mood to share." She smiled her sweetest, most innocent smile. "Loosen up, Mother."

By the time she was halfway through her bourbon, her parents were speaking only to one another. Since she found she preferred it that way—and wondered why she had never realized it—she was free to sweep the room with her gaze in search of Joe. He had introduced himself with impressive flair when he returned with their drinks, and rattled off a history of La Scala, along with a varied list of special appetizers. He hadn't deigned to look at anyone but Samantha during his entire recitation.

She hadn't known that white bean soup with anise-spiced sausage could sound like an aphrodisiac, but it had, coming from Joe's lips. Words like calamari, risotto and tortellini had taken on the cadences of poetry. She had wanted to dance to them, twirl her Hermès scarf in wild gypsy abandon from a vacant tabletop as he regaled her with phrases like Provençal bouillabaisse and Casablanca couscous.

"Samantha, you're making a fool of yourself over that waiter!"

She noted the way her mother hissed her name and wondered if this was new, or if she was just aware of it now because of the fire of fine Kentucky bourbon and a stranger named Joe in her bloodstream.

"How can I be making a fool of myself?" she asked. "I'm sitting here listening to you and Daddy talk."

"You're watching everything that man does!"

"Well, he's a gorgeous male animal, and any woman worthy of the name would do exactly what I'm doing." She smiled lazily. "Watch him yourself, Mother. It's better than cardio."

"I think you'd better stop at one drink, Samantha," her father said.

"I think I need another."

She had several, each time smiling more seductively at Joe as she gave her order. His eyes were midnight velvet, a dark caress against her bare arms and throat and the hint of flesh just under her primly tied scarf. His teeth were a white slash against his skin, and they flashed only for her—and often. She was deeply in love before the salad and desperately in love by the time the bones of her oregano-scented lamb had been whisked away.

Her wrist and the side of her breast tingled where he had brushed them as he delivered her salad. Her heart sped unevenly because he had stood beside her, close, so very, very close, when he had taken the same salad away.

"I'd like dessert," she said when her father prepared to signal for the check.

"Your behavior has been disgraceful." Kathryn pushed her chair back, as if she might leave before they paid.

"I am having dessert." She pronounced the words slowly. She was immediately impressed with her own vocabulary. Her statement seemed to hang in the air, like the words of a comic-strip character. She tried another. "I am having a life, too." She liked the sound of that one. "My own life. I am twenty-one today."

Her father put his hand on hers. It was an uncharacteristic gesture, and there was no affection in it. She knew he was upset, and somehow, that pleased her. "Come on home now, Samantha. We'll talk about this tomorrow."

"Tomorrow it won't be my birthday." She leaned toward him and found that the room shifted subtly. "Today *is* my birthday," she said gravely. "I've been good for twenty-one years, and it's been such a burden."

His voice grew even colder. "You've had too much to drink. We're going home."

"You're going home. I'm staying for dessert."

"Just how are you planning to get back?"

"In a taxi." She considered. "Or I might not come back." She shrugged. "I don't have to, do I? Amazing. I really don't have to."

"*We'll* take a taxi." Her father stood and signaled

Joe. "We'll leave the car here for you. But I'm telling Melwin not to let you leave unless it's with him. Do you understand? You can stay here and make eyes at that…" He stopped himself, possibly just on the verge of an ethnic slur.

"Nice young man?" She narrowed her eyes. "Take this." She fumbled with her scarf and threw it clumsily to her mother. "And tell Melwin I might be very, very late. I might eat two desserts. Maybe even three."

Joe arrived at the table. "I'm sorry. Is there a problem?"

Her father thrust a credit card at him. "Take this, add your tip and whatever else she orders to the bill. If the card doesn't come back with my daughter before midnight tonight, I'll have you fired and investigated. Do I make myself clear?"

Samantha watched Joe's expression freeze. She was horrified, but before she could find the right words, Joe was towering over her father.

Joe found the right words with no problem.

Her father turned white, as if the suggestion for what he should do with his credit card had been meant literally. The rest of the exchange was a bourbon haze in Samantha's head. The maître d' arrived; the maître d' left with her parents, apologizing profusely as he went. The maître d' returned before she could form the words to apologize to Joe, who still looked frozen with rage. The maître d' told Joe to gather his things and never darken the front door again.

She began to cry.

"Come on, sweetheart." She looked up and Joe was bending over her. "You're coming with me."

It was the best idea of the night. She wondered why

she hadn't thought of it herself. Her tears stopped immediately. "I've led a very repressed life," she said.

His face unfroze, inch by inch. In a moment he was howling with laughter. He put his arm around her and helped her stand. She leaned against him and realized that she fit as if she had been measured for this position by a master tailor. "I don't think I'll be very good at sex," she confided. "I'm too upper class. You know, saltpeter in the boarding-school food. Too many perfect marble statues of David in Rome and Paris. A real man probably looks deficient."

He hugged her more tightly. "You're going to have some morning tomorrow. What's your name?"

"Samantha. Samantha Whitehurst."

"Yeah, I know the last part."

They were outside, and she didn't know exactly why and how. She only remembered a sea of shocked and fascinated faces, parting, as if by Moses' command. "I think I love you, Joe."

"I had the bartender water your drinks, Sam. Not a one of them was a double. You've only had three drinks tonight. That's all."

"Would you kiss me?"

He stopped in the shadows just outside the welcoming glare of La Scala's floodlights. Around the corner traffic roared down Wisconsin Avenue, and not too far in the distance she saw Melwin standing beside the family limousine.

"Is that the three drinks talking?" he asked.

She remembered that she had thought his voice was dangerous. Now it was even more so. "No."

"Are you slumming tonight? Because I know who

your father is. I was told in no uncertain terms back there, just before Gino fired me."

"Slumming?" The word had no meaning.

"Why do you want me to kiss you?"

"Because…" She looked up at him, and suddenly the world stopped spinning. She rested her hands against his shoulders. They were broad, and as solid as the earth. "For twenty-one years I've done what everyone else wanted me to. For the next twenty-one I'm doing what I want."

"What if I tell you that for the next twenty-one years you're doing what you want…with me?"

She didn't answer. She didn't have time to. He brushed her lips with his, as if giving her time to change her mind. He was warm, and his scent was as provocatively male as his smile. Her lips parted immediately, pleading for more. He pressed against her with the same passion that had been building in her all night.

She wasn't frightened, and she wasn't repressed. She wasn't even herself. The woman who kissed Joe back had never been to boarding school and never seen a statue. She was the woman inside Samantha who had known, from her first glimpse of Joe Giovanelli, that she had found the man for her.

CHAPTER THREE

"THERE WON'T BE enough food. I could roast a steer and twenty suckling pigs, and there wouldn't be enough food." Sam fussed over the dining room table, which groaned under the weight of casseroles she had made and frozen over the past month and platters heaped with deli meat and cheese.

North Carolina sunshine lit even the darkest corners of the room and bounced off brightly colored balloons and streamers. Last night Sam had stored everything precious and fragile in closets and locked the laundry-room cupboard and medicine cabinet. The house was ready for a family party.

Joe lounged in the doorway. "Mama's bringing a turkey, a vat of spaghetti and ten pies."

"You didn't tell me that."

"*She* didn't tell me that. But I know my mother. And everybody else in the family will bring food, too."

"It still won't be enough."

"You've never understood. It's always enough. It's just that the Giovanellis eat everything in sight. It's a custom. You put out too much food, we eat too much food. It's simple."

She stood back from the table and pretended to study it, but she studied Joe from the corner of her eye instead. He wore dark shorts and a madras sport shirt unbuttoned at the neck. His black hair hung straight and sleek over his forehead, and her fingers itched to brush it back. Not because she didn't like the effect, but because she wanted to touch him, yearned with everything inside her to touch him with that kind of casual we'll-always-be-married confidence that until six months ago she wouldn't have thought twice about.

"I wish my parents could have come," she said. "It would have been good for them. Rose always sets my mother on her ear. By the time she leaves one of these gatherings, Mother acts almost human."

"They'll come when they can."

"Maybe for the Fourth or Labor Day. They should be back from Europe by then. Maybe we should have another party."

He didn't respond. Joe, who lived for parties, for family gatherings, for excuses to celebrate, remained silent.

"And maybe we shouldn't." She felt her shoulders slump in defeat. "Maybe we shouldn't even have this one."

"Don't start, Sam." His voice was so restrained it seemed charged with emotion.

She was immediately contrite, but there was no point in apology. Both of them knew there was more that she hadn't said. "I'm going to change."

Their bedroom at the head of the stairs was large, filled with plants and faded antique quilts. A king-size bed loomed from a corner, an altar to sex that had once been so perfect Sam had half expected to die in Joe's arms. Now she avoided the bed as she gathered her clothes, just as she avoided thinking about what had just passed between them in the dining room. She was learning to avoid everything except the moment. Yesterday's retreat into memory had only made Joe's late arrival home last night that much harder to bear. Thoughts of the future were too painful to consider.

She heard the first horn honking as she stepped out of the shower. Some of Joe's family lived more than four hours away, so she knew they must have left home at dawn. By the time she started downstairs again wearing the new dress she'd bought for the occasion, the house was filling up with people.

She greeted Joe's brothers and sisters, his nieces and nephews and the occasional cousin as she pushed her way into the kitchen where Rose, Joe's mother, was already holding court.

"I brought a few things. Just a few, don't you dare say a word, not one," Rose warned. "Just some spaghetti. And Johnny shot a turkey for me last fall that was taking up too much room in my freezer."

"And pies?" Sam asked.

"How'd you know?"

"Lucky guess." Sam threw her arms around Rose and held on for dear life. There was a substantial amount to hold on to. Rose was large, not plump but big boned and rangy like her son. Her hair was a salt-and-pepper bristle that stood out from her rawboned face like a halo. Everyone who knew her thought she was beautiful.

"Just think, you and my Joey been married now for four whole years. And this house." Rose squeezed harder. "This house is something, Sammy. Something like out of some magazine. Teddy was just saying it ought to be written up somewhere, weren't you, Teddy?"

Samantha looked over Rose's shoulder at Johnny's wife, red-haired, long-legged Teddy, who had been a Giovanelli long enough to roll with the punches. "Something very similar," Teddy said.

"And all that food on the table. You're a regular cook, Sammy. A real Giovanelli woman. I've had to slap hands already. Two times already. We've gotta get somebody to guard the table till everybody else gets here, or there won't be nothing left. Nothing." Rose frowned, as if she had just announced the end of civilization.

"I'll guard, Mama," Teddy said.

"You, you'll eat yourself silly and not gain an ounce for evidence."

"Watch me." Teddy stationed herself in the doorway, but she didn't say a word to the herd of children who snitched a slice of cheese apiece as they raced through the room.

More family streamed in, followed by friends and neighbors. Reluctantly Sam separated herself from Rose. Joe was one of seven children, the second oldest boy of three. Francis was two years older and Johnny two years younger. Behind the boys, as if they had waited to make a more impressive entrance, one girl had arrived each year, each as stunning as the next. Now the Giovanelli tribe had grown to such proportions that Sam had to keep a written list so that no one was forgotten on holidays. All Rose's children had married young and presented the world with more just like them.

All except Joe and Sam.

The din increased as the day wore on, but Sam relished the noise. Surrounded by family, by neighbors and close friends, she could almost forget that all was not well in her marriage. She saw Joe at the edge of a group of adults, Joe spiking a volleyball over a net strung between a magnolia and a pine, Joe chatting with Polly and other teachers from both Foxcove Elementary and the high school.

But the places where she didn't see him were the most significant. She never saw him with his sisters' babies in the crook of each arm as he crooned lullabies in the front porch rocker. She didn't see him passionately arguing politics with Francis, or holding a weeping Teresa, whose husband, Jeff, had just shipped out on a naval destroyer. He hovered at the edge of real involvement. Most important, she never saw him anywhere close enough to touch.

Not until Rose declared it was time.

A corner of the living room was heaped high with housewarming gifts. One of them was a ship's bell, a gift from Teresa and Jeff to hang on the front porch. Rose took it outside and tested it herself, and when everyone had gathered around, she called Samantha and Joe to stand beside her.

"I guess I'm the family matriarch," she said. "Joe's papa should be here to say these things, but he's watching from up above, I know. So here goes. Joe and Sam have been married four years today. And in those years they took a terrible old store with rats and mice and broken glass and hay and dirt and—"

"Enough, Mama," Joe said.

Everybody laughed.

"And everything there shouldn't have been," she continued. "Everything! The stories Sammy could tell. Anyway, they made this out of it. Now I know that anything is possible." She turned to Sam and beamed. "And while I can, I want to say something about their marriage."

Sam didn't move, but she stiffened with dread and

her smile felt as if someone had painted it on her face. Then she felt Joe take her hand. She wove her fingers through his to keep him beside her.

"First time Joe brought Sam home, I didn't know what he was getting into," Rose said. "She didn't weigh ten pounds soaking wet. And she didn't know how to hug. And she didn't know how to yell at anybody, especially my Joey. Now she hugs and yells, and I can swear she eats a little, sometimes. This marriage doesn't work out, I'll marry her off to somebody else in the family. She's as good a Giovanelli as anybody born with the name, and I'm proud to call her my daughter."

Rose opened her arms, and Sam went into them to the applause and hoots of everyone gathered there. Someone turned up the music, and their carefully cultivated lawn became a dance floor. Francis came up to swing his mother into a slow dance right on the porch, and Sam turned to Joe.

"Will you dance with me?"

He held out his arms, and she stepped into them as courageously as she had the first night they'd met.

He waltzed her down the steps to catcalls and hoots, then he pulled her closer. "You look terrific in that dress."

She flushed with pleasure. "Short enough for you?"

He ran his hand down her side. "Nearly."

Her entire body reacted to his touch. She was like a starving woman who had just been thrown a crust of bread. "Are you having fun?"

"It's a great party. All your hard work shows."

"You were right about the food. There was enough for an army, and now it's almost all gone."

"When I was a kid we were never sure where our

next meal was coming from, but we were always sure when it came we'd enjoy every bite."

Sam moved a little closer. "The party should be breaking up soon. Most of your family's got a long way to drive, and some people are moving on to the Warwicks' at seven."

"Were we invited?"

"Sure. But we're not going."

"We're not?"

"I'm not. This is all the partying I can manage for one day. Unless somebody suggests a private party for two."

"We can take a bottle of wine out to the lake."

"Pond."

It was an old argument. "Lake."

"Either one'll do if I get you all to myself." She thought he tensed, but she couldn't be sure. "Joe, I've missed you. If I was out of line yesterday, that's the reason."

"I'm sorry I've been away so much. It's been a busy year."

"It's been a tough year." She searched his face. "For both of us. But it's going to be tougher if we don't come through this together."

"We're together."

She couldn't argue; this wasn't the right place. And besides, she wanted him to be right. She wanted to believe that they were together, that the events of the past six months hadn't destroyed their marriage, that they could come through their hard times stronger, closer, happier.

"I *always* want to be together," she said.

Another couple appeared a few feet away. Sam realized Johnny was closing in with Teddy in his arms. He was a shorter, heavier version of Joe, and although he looked a decade older, she saw with a sinking heart that his best younger-brother leer was firmly in place.

"You two look at each other in bed like you're looking at each other now, you'll make Mama a grandma again." Johnny winked. "Got to pass the Giovanelli genes along, Joey."

Sam forced a smile. "Teddy, make your husband behave."

"Listen, you married one just like him. You tell me if Joey does anything you say," Teddy said.

"Hey, a man's too well behaved, he can't make babies," Johnny said. "Mama's not getting any younger. She told me to tell you, she wants a grandbaby for Christmas."

Sam answered before Joe could. "Well, you'll have to tell Mama she asked too late. We already bought her a nice new set of towels. Now go away so I can make eyes at my husband."

"Just so it leads to something." Johnny swung Teddy away, and Sam and Joe were alone again.

She didn't know what to say.

"Johnny ever presses his legs together, he won't be able to think," Joe said.

She felt Joe's rage and shame in every inch of flesh that touched hers. She tried to pull him closer. "It's not Johnny's fault. Every one of you kids was raised to think you were God's gift to the next generation."

"The music stopped."

It had, and people were beginning to drift away. Desperately she tried to think of something to cheer him, something that would make him stay by her side. She thought of the fort, Joe's pride and joy, and the battle royal that was undoubtedly being staged right now by their nieces and nephews. "Do you want to walk down to the pond and see if any of the kids are still there?" she asked.

He looked at her as if she had asked him to strip naked in front of their guests. She realized with horror that perhaps she had done just that. She put her hand on his arm. "I'm sorry. I didn't realize…"

He shrugged off her hand. "I'm going to say good-bye to Chuck and Sally."

He didn't run, but he was gone before she could reply. She watched him stride away, a lithe, male animal with the broken heart of a little boy. She listened to the shouts and laughter of the people she loved most in the world, and she wondered how she could feel so alone.

JOE HAD ALWAYS loved parties. He had never longed for silence as a child. He was comforted by laughter, by loud music and voices raised in argument. Now he could hardly wait for the rest of his family and guests to go home.

Except that then he would be left alone with Sam.

He said goodbye to Teresa and her brood and turned to the next car. Johnny had drunk too much, something he only did at occasions like this one when he knew Teddy would drive him home. As Joe watched, Johnny hung his head out the passenger window and crooked his finger. His eyes were too bright and his grin too cocksure, but he was still Johnny, Joe's little brother, the Johnny he had fought for and fought with all the years of his childhood.

Joe approached warily. Erin, Shannon and Patrick

fought in the back seat of Johnny's green sedan. With a surname like Giovanelli Johnny and Teddy had chosen Irish names for their kids. It was a family scandal.

"You had too much to drink. Go home," Joe said.

"'Member what I said." Johnny's smile widened.

Joe started to turn away, but Johnny had never learned when to stop. "You get busy on that baby, Joey boy. You don't know how to do it, I can give you a tip or two." He gave a broad wink.

Joe twisted Johnny's shirt collar in his hand before he realized what he was doing. He saw Johnny's smile die and awareness make a slow return to his eyes. He twisted harder. "What Sam and I do is our business," he said softly. "You remember that, and you practice keeping your mouth shut. Understand?"

Joe heard a gasp behind him and knew who it had come from. He dropped his hand, and Johnny fell back in the seat. It had all happened so quickly that the kids were still fighting and pushing, oblivious to the front-seat version of the same thing.

"Johnny, I'm sorry," Sam said, stepping around Joe. "It must be the heat. Who would believe it's not even summer yet?" She was smiling a perfect finishing-school smile. "Now you have a safe trip home, and thanks so much for coming. It wouldn't be a party without you." She stepped away and Teddy, every bit as refined and tactful, raised her hand in a wave. In a moment the sedan shot out of sight.

"Joe—"

"Don't say it. Don't say a damn thing." He stalked away, covering the ground to the house in a long stride that got him there in record time.

There was no one inside. His mother had been the

first to leave, and the rest of the family had drifted away afterward, with Teresa and Johnny the last to go. A few neighbors and friends still strolled the grounds, but Joe knew that Sam would say his farewells.

In the bathroom he stripped and stood under a cool shower. The house wasn't air-conditioned. There was still work to do on the wiring—one of his summer projects—and the heat made him regret that he hadn't completely updated it before he sanded floors and built cabinets. Sam insisted that she didn't mind, but *he* minded. He was a powder keg waiting for the right match to set him off. Today it had been his brother; tomorrow it might be something as simple as a thermostat one degree above what he considered acceptable.

He hung his head and let the water sluice over his hair. The sight of his own body disgusted him, and he closed his eyes. But even with his eyes closed he knew he was the picture of youth and masculinity. He ran five miles every morning and worked out in the afternoons in the weight room at the high school gym. His muscles were well-defined, his legs and chest covered with silky, dark hair. In graduate school he had posed nude for a senior-level art class to help with finances, and he had seen in charcoal renderings exactly how he appeared to women.

And none of it mattered.

Out of the shower and dressed once again he took his time going downstairs. The house was absolutely quiet, and the only noise from outside was the trilling of a mockingbird. He called Sam's name and received no reply. For a moment he wondered if she had left, too, if she had finally gotten tired of his absences and his anger and his silence. Then he realized where she had gone.

The path to the lake crunched under his feet. Under the trees just at the forest edge he stood and watched her picking dandelions. Her new dress was the color of spring grass, a clear meadow green with sprigs of flowers dancing over it, and her golden hair floated behind her in the light breeze.

"Sam?"

She straightened and turned. "You look cooler."

"You ought to give it a try."

"I was considering a swim, so I waded. But the water's still ice-cold. None of the children were able to get in, either."

"We have a houseful of flowers. What are you doing with those?"

Sam looked down at the dandelions. When she looked up, he had moved closer. "Actually, I was thinking about Corey."

"What for?"

She sat on the grass and patted the space beside her. He joined her, even though it felt like a trap.

"I was watching your brothers and sisters with their kids today. The way a child is raised matters so much. Nobody here today was a perfect parent. Francis yells too much, and Magdalena is spoiling Sarah rotten because she has asthma. But they're good parents. They care, and their kids know it. The kids come first with all of them."

"What does this have to do with Corey?" He felt her shift beside him and knew she was looking at him, but he kept his eyes straight ahead. He knew what he would see if he turned: the most beautiful woman he had ever known.

"What happens to kids when they don't have that

kind of devotion, Joe? What happens when nobody loves them, and nobody puts them first? How do they feel about themselves when they grow up? We've got prisons full of people like that, prisons and other kinds of institutions. When are we going to learn?"

"You can't change the whole world. You're a professional. You know what happens. Some parents grew up in homes like you're describing, and they don't know how to give love. They expect it from their kids, and when they find out what being a parent is really like, they abuse or ignore their kids altogether."

"I know, but it's one thing when I'm talking about kids I've never seen and another when I'm talking about a child I care about."

"You shouldn't."

"Shouldn't what?"

He leaned back so he could see her face. He wanted to pick a fight with her. He realized it, but he felt completely powerless to stop himself. He wanted distance from her pain, more distance than he had been able to put between them in six months.

"You shouldn't care. For God's sake, you're a professional. You're going to have kids like Corey in every class you teach. If you go around and let your heart bleed over every one of them, you won't be any good to anybody. There won't be anything left of you."

She was silent for so long that he thought she was considering his advice. Then her gaze found his. "And what would that matter? There's nobody else who needs anything I have to give."

He had wanted a reaction; he had wanted distance. But when she got up and started toward the house clutching her ragged bouquet of dandelions, he cursed his own selfishness and insensitivity. He adored her; he had since the moment she had sat at the best table at a restaurant called La Scala and stared longingly at him with her dreamy, silky-lashed eyes. He had known that night that they would have a life together, a life full of ups and downs and sinfully acute pleasure.

He remembered the afternoon that life had really started. He had no desire to wallow in the memory, but it seemed he was powerless to stop himself from anything self-destructive today. As Tinkerbelle's kittens romped in the long grass, he sank back with his head pillowed in his hands and watched the sun descend.

CHAPTER FOUR

SAMANTHA WHITEHURST, BLUE-BLOODED, hot-blooded and possibly his. Joe had thought of nothing but Sam all morning as he fried eggs and flipped pancakes. He had seen her image in the shining chrome of the coffee-shop toaster, in incandescent soap bubbles and shimmering steam clouds. After only a few short weeks he knew her so well that he could see Sam in anything.

She still looked away sometimes when she talked to him, as if she was afraid he might think she was too silly or not quite bright enough for a Bryn Mawr coed. He loved it when she turned her head and cast her sapphire gaze to the ground. He loved her profile, the graceful curve of her chin, the subtle lift of her eyebrows, the way her pale skin stretched over bones sculpted to perfection by a hundred years of scrupulous Anglo-Saxon breeding.

Unfortunately there was nothing about Sam he didn't love. Not the touch of shyness, the sophisticated reserve, the way she fought against the passion that threatened to overwhelm them both. In the two months since he'd met her Joe had found nothing about Samantha Whitehurst that didn't make his blood sing and the most masculine part of him swell with longing.

Today he carried flowers to their meeting place. She deserved pale, perfect hothouse roses. He had settled for brilliant red and yellow zinnias, orange marigolds, deep purple heliotrope so fragrant and feminine that it almost embarrassed him to hold it in his hands. On his way to work that morning he had picked the flowers in three different yards, choosing only those blossoms that had nodded at him between fence posts. He'd taken a second, but no more, to rationalize his theft. The flowers had been doomed to be crushed by the next pedestrian.

Samantha was twenty-one, but the meeting place they had arranged was not her home. Her parents knew that she was seeing him, and in their few face-to-face encounters with Joe since La Scala, they had been coldly polite. It was he, not Sam, who had asked that she meet him somewhere away from the ice shower that was Kathryn and Fischer's warmest welcome.

He would have braved anything for her, stood up to any dignitary or defended her against the worst dragons of Chevy Chase. But he couldn't stand to see what Sam's parents did to her self-esteem. When she was with him, she was funny, bright and passionate, with only the occasional endearing moment of shyness or uncertainty. When she was with her parents, each moment was a fight for dignity. It was a battle she would never win until the outcome no longer mattered to her. In the meantime he didn't want to watch.

He crossed the street against the light, darting with city aplomb between honking cars. The afternoon was already scorching, with humidity like descending dew. The temperature was no hotter than his thoughts or the blood coursing through his veins. He had only to think of Sam these days and he was no different than a stag in rut.

He spied her hiding behind a tree at the east end of

the pocket park where they had agreed to have lunch. He wished he could afford to take her to one of the city's best restaurants, to lavish champagne and the finest cuisine on her, fill her hands with diamonds and roses and her ears with the strains of a string quartet.

Unfortunately sandwiches, cola and the trash-strewn grass of a downtown park were more his speed. The restaurant that had hired him after his dismissal from La Scala was not in Georgetown, and not the trendiest hot spot. He was lucky if his tips covered his rent. Last week he'd begun to work the morning shift as a short-order cook at a downtown coffee shop so he could save some money.

He approached the tree as if he didn't know she was there. He whistled off-key—the only way he knew how—then sidestepped and trapped her neatly between his body and the tree.

The part of him touching her responded immediately. He edged away and tried to joke. "Mine at last, me proud beauty. Scream if you must, but it will do you little good." He fondled a nonexistent mustache.

"You've never heard me scream."

He couldn't help himself. He moved a little closer again. "But I have heard you moan."

She blushed, something she did with regularity and intensity. He loved to watch the color wash over her cheeks and creep up her neck. Usually she averted her eyes, too, but today her gaze was fastened on his. "Not as much as you'd like me to, I bet."

"That goes without saying." He kissed her then because he couldn't wait any longer. Her lips warmed to his immediately. He felt her body warming, too, warming and clinging and moving in an age-old rhythm to the beat of his. He thought he was dying.

When he finally pulled back, her lips were an unnatural red and her eyes were clouded with desire. "I thought we were just having lunch."

"I do everything with passion."

"I can't speak to that. There are some things I haven't seen you do."

He smiled, a lazy, self-assured grin that covered up the way his heart had just dropped to his kneecaps. "Name the time and place."

"Now. At your room."

He stared at her, digging deep for the humor in her offer. "Before lunch?"

"I've been eating for twenty-one years. There are other things I've never done."

He touched the knuckles of one hand to her cheek. Her skin was as smooth and soft as the petals of the bouquet he hadn't yet given her. He traced the curve of her lips with his thumb as he watched the expression in her eyes. He wondered if she could feel his hand tremble. He wondered if she knew how much he wanted to pull her to the grass right here in front of office workers, homeless men and a trio of small children playing in a flower bed.

"I don't think so," he said at last.

"Why not?"

He straightened and moved away so he could hold the flowers out to her. They were a barrier of sorts. He needed armor. "I'm a good Catholic boy. I drink, but not much. I don't smoke and I don't do drugs. I don't want any hopeless addictions. And the first time you climb into my bed, that's what you become."

She stared at him and didn't raise a hand. "Hopeless?"

Desire smoked up his voice. Even to his own ears he sounded brusque and unfeeling. "Look at us, Sam. My old man sold salami and pepperoni in a Brooklyn meat market. Yours manipulates the world financial markets. You think you want me now, but one morning you're going to wake up and realize it's Italian bread and black coffee every morning for breakfast because that's all I can afford. And it's not going to get much better. I'm a teacher, someday maybe I'll be an administrator. I've never wanted anything different, and I never will. I'd give you anything I could, but that's not saying much. It's not saying enough."

She slapped the palms of her hands against his shoulders and pushed him. It happened so quickly he stumbled backward. By the time he recovered she was yards away.

He knew he should let her go, but he caught up with her and grasped her shoulder. "You know I'm right!"

She whirled. "What about that first night? You said we were going to spend the next twenty-one years together."

"I was as drunk as you were, only it was your damned perfect face and body and that innocent smile that had me going!"

"And now you're tired of me?"

He closed his eyes. "No. I'm besotted." He didn't know where the word had come from, but it was perfect. He dropped his hand and opened his eyes. "Damn it, I love you. And if I make love to you, it'll kill me when you see how impossible this is. What else do you want me to say? I love you. I can't sleep with you because I love you!"

He watched her expression melt by slow degrees. Then she was laughing. She threw herself into his arms, and he, fool that he was, held her tightly against him, stabbing her back with the wiry stems of zinnias.

"You can't sleep with me because you love me? That's perfect. That's priceless, Joe. I love you, too! I love you! And I want to sleep with you forever! I don't care about Italian bread and coffee. And I love you because you teach. I'd hate you if you were a stockbroker or a banker or an investment counselor. We can teach together. We can live together. We can sleep together." She pushed away so she could see his face. "Let's sleep together, Joe."

Resolve began to disappear. He told himself she was offering herself freely. He told himself that she knew what she was getting into, that he had clearly warned her. He told himself that he would survive if she changed her mind.

He wouldn't survive.

"Not unless you marry me," he said.

She stared at him. "Marry?"

He wasn't sure where the words had come from, but he knew they were right. "That's it, Sam. Marriage or nothing. You want me in your bed, you marry me first."

"What century is this?"

He grabbed her shoulders. The flowers fluttered to the ground. "You marry me, or else. That's it."

"You're going to withhold sex unless this is blessed by a priest?"

"I'll settle for a justice of the peace. I can compromise. I can't wait until you convert."

"Until…I convert?"

"I want us to be a team. I want our kids to see us at Mass together on Sundays. I want you holding my hand when they make their first communion."

"Kids?"

"Kids are part of the package. I want a lot. Little girls with blond hair, boys with black. A laughing, brawling, pack of sassy, mouthy kids. No lonely little princesses in castle towers. Dirty little kids with scraped knees and runny noses."

"I don't know. There's genetics to think about. We're bound to have at least one kid with brown hair."

He stared at her. Her eyes were laughing. The rest of her face had collapsed into shock.

"I can't be what I'm not." He had to lay it all on the line for her. He knew that this was his only chance because he would never find the courage to do this again. "I won't be rich, and I can't be Protestant. I can't settle for a lifestyle that's foreign to me. I know I'm asking you for everything and giving you nothing. And I don't expect you to say yes. I'm just telling you everything so it'll be easier to say no."

"Nothing's easy to say with you going on and on. Take a deep breath and shut up!"

He had run dry, anyway. There was nothing left except all the good things—and those would sound like pleas. He could tell her how much he would cherish her, help her, support her. Tell her about a lifetime of stolen bouquets and stolen moments, Italian bread and coffee brought to her in bed, nights spent rocking their babies so that she could get some sleep, days spent thinking of ways to tell her how much he loved her.

She drew a finger down his cheek. "I don't care what

church we go to, as long as we go together. I don't care
how many children we have, as long as they're yours.
I don't care how much money you make, as long as I
have some say in how we spend it. But I do care that
you don't trust me to love you enough. I care that you
don't see that I want exactly and only what you can give
me. You're not my adolescent rebellion. You're not some
three-bourbon fantasy, Joe. You're the man I love, the
man I'd like to love for the rest of my life if you'll just
stop laying down ultimatums."

He wasn't sure he had heard her right. But in a moment he knew his ears hadn't betrayed him, because
she spoke again.

"Now," she said softly, "shall we go to your apartment?"

His apartment was one room above a paternal uncle's
grocery store on a noisy corner of northwest D.C. that
was half an hour's bus ride away. He spent an hour's tips
on a cab that took ten agonizing minutes to get there,
minutes spent in back-seat purgatory.

They took the steps two at a time. The smells of
cabbage from the garbage bin drifted upstairs with the
fumes of traffic, but his room had never seemed so
welcoming.

"It should be more special," he said in the doorway,
giving her one more chance to back away.

"It couldn't be more special, could it?"

"Did you mean it when you said there were some
things you'd never done?"

"I've been waiting for you."

He told himself it didn't matter, and he knew that
it did. Virginity was a standard he hadn't been able to
meet, and he didn't expect more of Sam than he had ex-

pected of himself. But her answer had told him so much about the woman, her fears, her commitments. Most of all it told him about her decision today.

He clasped her to him and buried his face in her hair. He'd had just enough women to know what the fair sex thought of his sexual prowess, but apparently he'd had too few to get him past this moment. He felt like a virgin, too, a clumsy, bumbling oaf who knew only the most basic features of sex and none of the embellishments. He doubted he would have the skill or control to make this easy for her, much less pleasurable.

"You should have married me first," he said, his voice already harsh with desire.

"Why?"

"Because then it would be harder to scare you away."

She was braver than he. She laughed a little and her hands slid along his spine, fanning out like butterfly wings. "You can't scare me, Joe. I've seen movies. I've read books. Even my big, bad Italian stud won't be any surprise."

Judging by the way his body was reacting, he was afraid she was going to be surprised, anyway. He tugged her blouse from under the waistband of her slacks and kneaded her bare skin. She shuddered against him, and shuddered again when he unhooked her bra.

He had caressed her before, but never with unbridled longing. Always he had kept a part of himself in check with her. Now there was nothing kept in check. He explored her as she stood against him, savored the silky smoothness of her skin, the pillow softness of lush breasts that had seemed so refined and model perfect when covered by clothes.

She helped him unbutton her blouse, blushing

proudly when it was on the floor beside them. He was so overcome with desire that the signals in his brain were hopelessly crossed. He couldn't taste and touch and see her all at the same time, and one need thwarted another until he thought he might go crazy with longing. He slid his hands under her waistband and eased her pants over her hips. Desire poured—hotter, heavier— through him, pounding in his ears, roaring through his bloodstream until each sense blended into the others.

He wasn't sure how they got to the bed. He thought maybe Sam had led them there, because he wasn't at all sure that he was capable of independent movement. She unbuttoned his shirt—he knew that much because the aching purity of her hands against his chest was crystal clear. She unzipped his jeans and smoothed his pants over an arousal that should have frightened her witless.

She gasped when he pulled her naked body tightly against his own, then just as he was gathering control, she pressed herself against him.

They fell to his bed together. He had just enough sense not to take her immediately. He filled his senses with her scent, his lips with her flesh, his hands with her breasts and the seductive, sensuous curve of her hips. He parted her legs with one knee and she eased them wide apart in invitation.

Finally he sank into her like a man going home.

He felt her tense, then relax as he held himself still. He could do that much for her. She was small boned and fragile; he was not. He eased himself slowly deeper, re-citing the alphabet, stanzas of poetry from high school, lists he had memorized in catechism class. At last he rose on his forearms to look at her face, and the fragile control he had gained was almost lost.

She was crying.

"Sam." He wanted to cry, too. Worse, so much worse, he wanted desperately to finish what they had started. He wanted to sink into her again and again, and it was only the sight of her tears and a thread of decency that kept him still.

"Oh, Joe, I love you so much."

The thread broke. He gathered her in his arms as he never had another woman. He held her against him so tightly that there was little room for movement. He thrashed against her and felt the answering call of her body. And when his control was exhausted he raised himself higher and filled her with the love he had saved only for her.

It wasn't a masterly performance. When it had ended he wasn't sure that his audience was appreciative. He took her with him when he rolled to his back, afraid that he had disappointed her terribly. He caressed her, traced the curve of her hip with his palm. Then, because he couldn't wait any longer for the review, he spoke.

"It's not always great the first time. I sort of lost it there. I'm sorry."

"That wasn't great."

He shuddered and shut his eyes. Then he realized that she had said the words as a question. "I mean, sometimes it's not," he said.

She giggled. It sparkled through him. "Are you asking me if I had an orgasm?"

"I was trying to be a shade less clinical."

"I'll be a shade less clinical. I saw stars. Is that good enough?"

"Four or five?"

"How many was I allowed to see?"

"A universe." He turned her so he could see her face. "Did you see a universe?"

"I saw infinity." Her cheeks were still wet. "Joe, please don't tell me it gets better."

"I think eventually I get a little more skilled and you get a little less tender."

"It was perfect." Her gaze ran the length of his body and back to his face. "*You're* perfect."

"I'm in love." He framed her face. Her hair fell over his fingers like spun silk. "I'll always love you, Samantha Whitehurst. And I'll do everything a man can do to make your life easy and joyful."

"Joyful?" The expression in her eyes sparked an answer inside him. "I understand joyful, I think. Better than I did a little while ago."

He pulled her close. He couldn't give her joyful again. Not in the next few minutes, anyway. But he could give her all his love and the promise of joy.

As he held her, every fear he'd ever had that their life might not be perfect fell away.

SAMANTHA STEPPED OUT of the shower and into her robe. Joe still hadn't come back from the pond despite the fact that twilight trembled in the air. She doubted he would return until it was completely dark and the fireflies could light his way back home. Then he would find another excuse to avoid her, a project he had to work on, a friend to visit, some unfinished detail at the school that he had suddenly remembered.

She was tired of pretending right along with him. She was tired of a lot of things, of sleepless nights when Joe lay awake and silent beside her, of lovemaking that was increasingly rare and always unsatisfying, of conversations they couldn't have and feelings they couldn't share.

Of living with a stranger.

As she had predicted it was dark by the time he returned. She had sliced Rose's leftover turkey for sandwiches and set out two plates with tiny portions of half a dozen salads. Without a word she handed him one when he came into the kitchen.

"Would you like something to drink?" he asked.

"Lemonade would be nice."

He poured them both a glass and brought it to the kitchen table. It was large enough to seat a substantial family. Once they had sat beside each other. Now he chose a chair across from her. "It's cooling off."

"About time."

They ate in silence. Sam finished first and stood to clear her place.

"You didn't eat much," he said.

"I guess I had too much earlier. I'm not really hungry."

"Would you like to go out tonight? There's a couple of good movies on."

She was surprised at the offer. For a moment she felt like a dog who had just been patted on the head. Joe had noticed her, noticed the fact that she wanted to spend the evening with him, noticed it was their wedding anniversary. She started to say yes, but she found herself saying something else.

"Is that the best you can do?"

His expression didn't change, and he didn't answer.

"I asked you a question." She fought to control her tone, but her anger was obvious.

"No, you made a statement." He stood and shoved his plate across the table at her. Then he turned to leave.

She knew she couldn't let him go without finishing this. "All right, I did. It's our wedding anniversary. I want to spend it with you. I want to talk, make love, pretend we have a marriage that still works. I don't want to sit beside you in a movie theater. I can do that by myself."

"Maybe we don't!"

"Don't what?" She shoved the plate back at him. It slid off the edge and shattered against the floor.

"Don't have a marriage that works! Maybe I have a wife who nags until I'm sick of it! Maybe I don't want to spend the night listening to more of the same thing!"

"You don't want to spend the night listening to me because you're so caught up in your own self-pity you can't listen to anybody but yourself!"

For a moment she was frightened she had gone too far. His face contorted. She had never seen him so angry. Then as she watched he slowly mastered it. But his eyes were as cold as his words when he spoke. "You don't have to stay, Sam. You want to leave, leave."

He left, and she sank back into her chair. She put her head in her hands and shut her eyes, but nothing could wipe away the image of Joe's face.

The contrast with other anniversaries was so radical that visions of them danced in front of her eyes. Joe with the deed to the store and the world's biggest sheepish grin. Joe with theater tickets for a weekend in New York and a bottle of the best champagne Foxcove had to offer. Joe at a mountain cabin in front of a roaring fire.

The last memory was the most painful, but it was the

one she couldn't push aside now. In a way it was that night that had led them to this one.

THEY HAD BEEN married a year, one passionate, desperately poor, learning-to-accommodate year. They had married immediately after the afternoon in the room above the grocery store. Neither of them had had the presence of mind to think about birth control, and Joe had used potential pregnancy as an excuse to rush the wedding.

But they hadn't really needed excuses. When her period had started two days after their five private minutes with the justice of the peace, neither of them had felt cheated. They had married because they couldn't keep their hands off each other, because they both knew that there would never be anyone else they loved as much and because they could no longer bear even the shortest separation.

They had spent the remainder of the summer patching up their relationship with Sam's parents and forging relationships with Joe's family in North Carolina. At first Sam had been overwhelmed by the Giovanellis. They had no mercy and no restraint. They poured over her like marinara sauce on spaghetti, poking and prodding and making her theirs in the process. But before long she had fallen in love with them. She saw Joe in all his brothers and sisters, and that was all she needed.

In the fall Sam transferred for her final credits to a small college near the site of Joe's temporary teaching job in a North Carolina mill town. Since her parents refused to spend even one further dime on her education, she worked in the county library to pay her own tuition. But despite poverty, classes and homework, housework and the arguments of the newly married, she and Joe were blissfully happy. In May, after an internship at a local elementary school, Sam graduated with honors and a certificate to teach in the state of North Carolina.

On the afternoon of their first wedding anniversary, Joe packed everything they owned into suitcases as Sam watched, perplexed. Then he loaded her along with the cases into their car. Three hours later the secondhand Mazda climbed its first mountain. An hour after that, in the midst of a spectacular sunset, he stopped in front of an old log cabin.

"It's beautiful!" Sam threw herself into Joe's arms as soon as she could make her way around the side of the car. "But how can we afford it?"

"It's free for the summer in exchange for doing some fixing up."

"But your summer job! You told me you were going to find another job waiting tables so we could save some money."

"I lied."

She couldn't believe it. As far as she could see there were only trees, mountain laurel and wild azaleas. There were no other houses in sight. "But what about a job for me? I'm no handyman, Joe. I can't fix a thing."

"You get the summer off."

"What?"

"We both do. I'll enjoy puttering around here fixing plumbing and putting shingles on the roof. But most of the days will be free." He cut off her protests. "Look, Sam, we deserve this. We've both worked too hard this year. We'll have next to no expenses here, and with my job all sewed up for next year—"

"What?" She pushed him away so she could see

his face better. His last contract had been for only one year, a substitute for a junior high school social studies teacher who had been on sabbatical. The job had been his third one-year stint. Permanent jobs were hard to come by these days. Joe had assured her repeatedly that he would find another job, but to her knowledge the search had been fruitless. "The guy you replaced isn't coming back, after all?"

"No, he's coming back. We're moving. To a place called Foxcove. It's about two hours from the coast and an hour from most of my family. I'm the new assistant principal at the high school there."

She stared at him. "Assistant principal?"

"Francis does some contracting for the school board. When he heard the job had come up he thought of me. They were looking for somebody outside their own system who could be tough and still relate to the kids, and since I've had a variety of experiences and I'm twelve hours into my Ph.D. I had all the right academic credentials."

"But you've only had three years' experience in the classroom."

"I charmed their socks off."

She threw herself into his arms. "You did all this without telling me?" She beat on his chest.

"I flew to Foxcove while you were visiting your parents in the spring. I didn't want to disappoint you. It was such a long shot."

She could only think that they had a real home now. They no longer had to live from job to job, wishing and hoping that Joe would find something permanent. Not only did he have a real job, the pay would surely be high enough to live on.

"What about me?" She leaned back and searched his face. "What about a job for me?" They had agreed from the beginning that Joe would find a job first, then she would start her search in the same geographical area.

"There's all kinds of potential there. But I have another idea."

"What?"

"Let's go in, and I'll tell you."

They carried a load of suitcases inside. The cabin was two-room-tiny, with a loft for sleeping and a fieldstone fireplace that spread halfway across one wall of substantial chestnut logs.

Joe started toward the loft. "The owner said he'd leave some food to hold us over. I'll unpack if you'll rustle up something for dinner."

Her curiosity piqued, Sam searched the kitchen alcove cabinets and refrigerator. As she worked she watched Joe moving back and forth from outside, first with luggage, then with logs. By the time she finished, a fire roared in the fireplace to take the chill off the air, and Joe lay on the rag rug in front of it, propped against an old sofa.

She joined him carrying a platter of cheese and smoked oysters, crackers and fruit. He took it and set it on the stone hearth. He patted the floor between his legs, and she sank against him. "This is heaven. How did you find it?"

"I just answered an ad. God helps those…"

"You're a remarkable man."

"Tell me about it."

She fed him oysters and cheese heaped on a cracker while she considered. "You're energetic and committed." She laughed when he sucked on her fingertip. "And sexy as hell."

"You can forget the rest."

"I still can't believe you found such a terrific job." She stopped and frowned, turning a little so she could see his face. "What's the catch?"

"Oh, ye of little faith."

"Joe?"

His smile died. "It's a small town, and not terribly progressive. It's a pretty area, rural and unpolluted, but we'll have to drive a good distance for any kind of culture."

"Mayberry?"

"A good facsimile."

"I'll love it."

She thought she saw relief. "Really?"

"But why didn't you consult me?"

"It's my job to support you, and this was the best way."

She had heard different renditions of this speech in the year of their marriage. Sometimes Joe was an old-fashioned man masquerading in a modern man's body. He washed dishes and clothes and made a mean ravioli, and she knew when they had children he would share the responsibility. But underneath his genuine belief that they were equals was a niggling corollary that he had to be just a little more so.

"It is not your job to support me," she said gently. "It's your job to love me."

"I adore you." He took her into his arms. "And if you hate Foxcove I'll quit the job immediately. You know I will."

She did know it, just as she knew that she wouldn't

hate Foxcove. She would be there with him, and that was all that mattered. "What was that idea you had about my plans for the next year?"

He turned her in his arms until she was lying on top of him looking into his eyes. "It's too late to find a teaching job for this fall. Why don't you have a baby instead?"

Her eyes widened. "Joe..."

"We've been married a year. I'm twenty-six. I can support a family now. We'll have insurance, and we can find a house cheap in Foxcove. If you get pregnant right away—and why shouldn't you?—you'll be due sometime in late winter. The baby would be nearly six months old when you started teaching...if you did."

"If?"

"You might want to stay home and have another."

"Joe..."

"Would that be so awful? I know you want to teach, and I want you to. But we need to start our family, too."

More and more often her thoughts had drifted in the same direction, although she hadn't discussed that with him. Some urge as old as time had taken hold of her in the past year.

"A baby..."

"Our baby." He framed her face with his hands. "I love you. We've got everything anyone could ask for except that. Our child, Sam. A symbol of our love."

She thought of Joe's child growing inside her. A part of Joe to nurture and cherish. A little boy with Joe's dark eyes, or a little girl with his devastating smile.

"You know that diaphragm of yours?"

She smiled dreamily and said nothing.

"I didn't pack it," he finished.

"You can't make these decisions by yourself."

"Hey, I know that. We can drive back for it. Or we can forget about making love this summer."

"Now there's an idea." She stretched up to kiss him. "Will you stay with me while I'm in labor?"

"No one could tear me away."

"And in the delivery room?"

"I'll be right there rooting for you."

"Do you want a boy or a girl?"

"Right now I just want you."

She put her arms around his neck and brought his lips to hers. She imagined that the glow in his eyes was fierce enough, passionately male enough, to impregnate her.

"I'm yours, Joe. I'll have a million babies if you promise you'll always look at me this way."

"One will do for now." She felt his hand on her breast. And when she was undressed and his lips had replaced his hand, she imagined Joe's child suckling there.

MIDNIGHT HAD COME and gone before Joe returned home. Sam heard Killer's muffled roar, then only the chirping of crickets. She lay stiff and silent in the bed, wondering if he would come upstairs or choose to sleep on the couch.

Minutes later the bedroom door creaked open, and closed with a muffled click. She heard Joe undressing, heard him go into the bathroom, then heard him return. The bed sagged beside her. She lay very still and very alone, but when she had almost given up hope she felt the length of his legs against hers and his arm draped possessively over her breasts.

She said nothing, and neither did he. She moved a little closer; he pulled her a little closer. Finally, cocooned in his warmth, she shut her eyes and went to sleep.

CHAPTER FIVE

COREY HASKINS STOPPED only twice on the long hike down Old Scoggins. The first time she jumped to one side and watched as a pack of cars raced down the road. Dust settled over her as they disappeared, fine red dust that tickled her nose and made it hard to breathe.

The second time she stopped to rest under a tree shading the wide ditch that ran beside the road. She found a cool spot for the milk carton that she had cradled in her arms on the long trudge from town, then she lay on the grass and shut her eyes.

She knew that the bird nestling inside the carton didn't look so good. 'Course, he hadn't looked too good when she'd put him in the carton, either. Even though she'd put grass and stuff on the bottom.

And a worm, in case he got hungry.

Mr. Red—that's what she called him now—might need water. When she got back up maybe she could get him some from the ditch.

She was thirsty herself. She guessed she hadn't had anything to drink all morning. There'd been cereal for breakfast, but there hadn't been milk to go with it. And her mama had yelled at her and made her go outside before she could stick her head under the faucet for a drink. They didn't have more than a glass or two, and

Mama kept those high because a while ago Corey had dropped one.

She wished there was a fountain here like the one at school. Once Miss Sam had lifted her up so that she could get a drink from the grown-ups' fountain because the little kids' fountain wasn't working. She remembered the way that had felt, Miss Sam's arms around her and all. She'd felt like a little baby, but it had felt good, too. Miss Sam always smelled nice, and her hands were soft.

She would never hit anybody with those hands.

Corey hoped she could find Miss Sam's house. She knew it was on this road somewhere. She dug stuff out of trash cans when nobody was looking. She'd found a letter to Miss Sam once in the classroom trash can, and it had said Old Scoggins on it. She was just glad she could read. There were lots of things she could find out now that she could.

She hoped Miss Sam was home. Miss Sam might give her a drink. And she might be able to help Mr. Red.

Miss Sam could do just about anything.

IMPOSSIBLE WAS THE word. Impossible that one seven-year-old girl could be so filthy, so sweaty and smelly, so completely lacking in childish appeal.

A barefooted Corey Haskins, with all the style and tact of a street urchin, stood defiantly in front of Sam clutching half a plastic milk carton in her thin arms. "I walked all this way, Miss Sam. And it's a long way. You got anything birds like to eat?"

"Corey, how on earth did you find me?"

Corey glared at her. The noon sun might have sparkled in her white-blond hair if it had been clean, but as it was, the sun only pointed out suspicious specks in the chopped-up locks.

"Don't matter," she said sullenly.

"*Doesn't* matter, and of course it does. You must have walked five miles or more if you came straight from town. How did you find me?"

Corey shrugged.

Sam stepped closer. "And what did you bring me?"

Corey held out the milk carton, but not too far. Sam could see that she was ready to snatch it back if she didn't like Sam's reaction. "Just an old bird."

The bird in question was a male cardinal with an obviously broken wing. The last rites were in order. "Oh, poor thing," Sam murmured.

"I give him some water, but he didn't want it."

"That was the right thing to do," Sam assured her. "He's very lucky you found him, but I'm afraid it's too late to be much help. I think the best we can do is make him comfortable in the shade."

"He's gonna be fine. You can fix him, like you fixed my face that time."

Sam saw genuine distress in Corey's eyes. "How did his wing get like that, Corey?"

The little girl shrugged again, but the expression in her eyes grew bleaker. Something suspiciously like tears began to form.

Sam made an educated guess. "Did you maybe throw a stone at him and hit him by mistake?"

"I was just swinging a stick. That's all."

Sam squatted in front of her. "You can't hit a bird, Corey. Not if you try for a million years. He must have been sick to start with. It's not your fault, honey."

"I kilt him."

"Not on purpose. Besides, he would have died, anyway. And look what good care you've taken of him." Sam looked at the bird and saw that the discussion about his death was now academic. She held out her hands and Corey set the milk carton in them. "I know just the place for him. It's a good place to be buried."

Corey began to cry. Sam was immediately impressed with how foreign the whole process seemed to her. The tears made tracks down her dirty cheeks, and she didn't even seem to know to brush them away.

Sam set the carton beside her and gathered Corey in her arms. This, too, was obviously foreign. The little girl held herself stiffly, as if she didn't know what was expected of her. But she didn't try to move away.

Sam put her head against Corey's, despite the fact that it might mean a trip to the drugstore for medicated shampoo. "Poor sweetheart," she murmured. "Go ahead and cry."

"I ain't crying."

"Sure you are. It's okay."

"I *ain't* crying."

Samantha held her while Corey finished not crying. Then, when Corey's shoulders had stopped shaking, Sam brushed her hair back from her face. "You must be hot and hungry. Come on inside and I'll call your mother. She's got to be worried about you. Then I'll fix you something for lunch. How does that sound?"

"We gotta bury him first." Corey pointed at the bird. "Gotta."

"He'll be fine out here while we eat."

"I ain't going nowhere till we bury him."

"You're not going anywhere," Sam corrected.

"That's what I said."

"Okay. Wait while I get a shovel." Sam left Corey standing under the tree, tears still dripping down her cheeks. She wondered what Joe would say if he came home now and saw the ragged little girl one step from the impatiens he had planted in early May.

Now that it was mid-July the summer was shorter by half, and the night of their anniversary was a month and a half behind them. They had patched up their fight the same way they communicated about everything now. She hadn't commented on it again, and neither had he. Anyone watching would think that nothing was wrong between them, but anyone watching would have been wrong.

Things were terribly wrong, and Joe's absence today was proof of it. He had left the house early, just as he did most mornings, but today he hadn't even bothered to tell her where he was going. He was probably at the school, but she didn't need to know because she wouldn't need to call him. They seemed to have nothing to say to each other.

She found the shovel right beside all of Joe's neatly organized garden tools. Organizing the tools had been just one of his summer projects. Most of them had been outdoor activities. The message in that was not lost on her. She assumed that if she found things to do outside he would suddenly decide to finish the wiring and install the air conditioners.

When she returned she saw that Corey hadn't moved. Joe's impatiens were perfectly safe. "Let's go down to the pond," Sam said. "I'll bring the carton."

"No. Mr. Red's *my* bird."

"Mr. Red?"

"Yeah. That's his name."

"And a fine one." Sam led the way, checking occasionally to be sure Corey was behind her. She stopped near the water's edge at a soft clump of earth where Joe had removed a tree stump. "I think this will be perfect."

"You own a lake?"

Sam wondered if Joe just might like Corey, after all. "A pond."

"You got kids?"

Sam saw that Corey's gaze was fastened on the log cabin. "No kids."

"How come you got a playhouse?"

"We've got lots of nieces and nephews."

"They live here?"

"No." Sam began to dig. One foot down she stopped. "What do you think, Corey? Is this deep enough?"

Corey peered into the hole. "Deeper."

Sam was already damp with perspiration from the walk and work, but gamely she dug on. Two feet down she stopped. "Now?"

"I guess." Corey knelt beside the hole and lowered the bird, carton and all, into it. "'Bye, Mr. Red."

Sam wondered if she should say something. Corey looked up expectantly. Sam bowed her head. "We commend the spirit of this bird into his heavenly Father's hands." The image of a great red bird in the sky filled her mind, and for a moment she was afraid she was going to laugh.

Then she looked down at Corey and saw that the little girl's hands were folded and her eyes closed. Sam would bet that Corey had never been inside a church in her life, but somehow she had learned what was expected of her. It was another sign of the child's intelligence.

"Amen," Sam said.

"Amen." Corey opened her eyes. "Can I fill the hole?"

"Sure." Sam handed her the shovel, which was longer than Corey was. Gamely she struggled with the dirt, finally figuring that scraping it into the hole was the simplest way to accomplish her mission. When she had finished she patted the dirt with her bare foot.

"What if he's not really dead?"

Sam had visions of being required to dig the bird up again as proof. "He was very, very dead. I'm absolutely sure."

"I was hoping he could be my pet."

"I think you'll need to find something else." Sam held out her hand. "Let's go back to the house. I really do have to call your mother. She must be worried sick."

"Oh, she won't care."

Sam was terribly afraid that the little girl was right, but she knew her duty. Inside the house she made Corey wash her hands and face, then she settled her at the kitchen table with a peanut butter sandwich and a giant glass of lemonade while she looked up Verna Haskins's phone number. Corey, with an IQ near genius level, swore that she couldn't remember it herself.

The phone rang half a dozen times before there was an answer. By the time Sam hung up, she was shaking.

"Your mother was glad I called," she told Corey.

The real conversation echoed in her head as she smiled and lied.

Corey? She's 'round here someplace. What? She's at your house? Hell, I didn't know she was gone. No, don't bring her home. Make her walk. It'll wear her out, so's she won't be so much trouble tonight.

Corey didn't answer. She was chewing so fast Sam

was afraid she was going to choke. "Slow down, honey. If you eat too fast you'll be sick."

Corey chewed faster, as if she was afraid that Sam was going to snatch the sandwich out of her hand.

"What else would you like to have with it?" Sam asked, trying another tack. "Potato chips? An apple? I think I've got some cookies."

"All!"

Sam was shaking harder by the time Corey had finished her lunch. She had never seen a child eat this way. Even in school Corey hadn't eaten as if she were starving. But in school she had gotten a free breakfast and lunch—after the principal had threatened Verna if she didn't fill out the necessary forms. What did she eat in the summers? The answer was only too clear.

Corey scratched her head, and Sam closed her eyes. "Corey, you need a bath and a shampoo."

"Don't!"

"Yes, you do. And you know what? I've got something I think you might like to wear."

Corey looked suspicious, but Sam led her into the guest bedroom and opened a drawer. There was a pile of children's clothes inside, clothes left by various Giovanelli offspring who had stayed overnight in the first years they had moved to Foxcove.

"Look." Sam held up a blue T-shirt and striped shorts. "I think these'll fit. And the color will be pretty with your hair. You've got beautiful hair."

"I don't." Corey ran her hands through it until it stood on end. "Ma cut it all off when I got pine sap in it."

Sam remembered that day. As bad as the shorter cut was, it was an improvement. Corey had had a full yard of tangles before her mother had gone after her with scissors.

"Would you like me to wash it and trim it a little? I could even it out so it would look better. I don't think your mother would mind." She doubted that Verna would even notice.

Corey shrugged, but she looked interested, despite herself.

An hour later she hardly looked like the same child. She was clean from head to toe—and to Sam's delight she had found nothing on Corey's scalp except dirt. Now Corey's hair was almost as short as a boy's, but at least it was all one length, and as it grew out it wouldn't look ragged. She was much too thin, all eyes and legs like a newborn colt, but she looked presentable.

Samantha stood her in front of the bathroom mirror. "What do you think?"

"How come I'm not pretty?"

Sam didn't know what to say. Corey might very well be pretty someday. But now, despite Sam's efforts, she still looked underfed and awkward. "You're pretty to me."

"Not to me."

"Your hair's a wonderful color, honey, and your eyes are such a dark brown your hair looks even lighter. It's a very nice combination."

"I wish I looked like you."

"If I had a little girl I'd be happy if she was as pretty as you are." She heard herself say the words, then she heard them echoing through the room when she looked up and saw that Joe was standing in the doorway.

"Joe." She didn't know what else to say.

Corey whirled. "Who the hell's that?"

"Corey!" Sam couldn't imagine a worse introduction.

Corey glared at Joe. Joe stared at Corey. His face was a blank mask.

"Joe, this is Corey Haskins. She was my student last year. Corey, this is Mr. Joe, my husband."

"Why is Corey here?" Joe asked. He continued to stare at the little girl.

"It's a long story. I was just about to take her home."

"That sounds like a good idea." He disappeared.

"How come he don't smile?" Corey asked.

"How come you didn't?" Sam got to her feet. She suddenly felt very tired.

"Don't have to."

"I wish you'd wanted to. You'd like Mr. Joe if you got to know him."

"Don't think so."

Joe was in the living room when they walked through. "Why don't you come with us, Joe?" Sam asked.

"Sorry, but I've got things to do."

She was sure he did. Anything he could find. "Well, I'll be back in a little while."

He nodded at Corey. "Goodbye, Corey."

She stared at him, narrowing her eyes. "Miss Sam's a good teacher. Are you a good teacher?"

"I'm a principal."

"Same thing. 'Cept you spank kids and stuff."

"I don't spank anybody." He lifted a brow. "At least, I haven't spanked anybody yet."

"Look like you would."

Sam put her hand on Corey's shoulder. "We're going right now." She glanced once at Joe as she left the room. He was staring at the wall.

She measured the miles to Corey's house. The little girl had walked nearly six miles to bring her Mr. Red. Six miles on a July afternoon along country roads with no sidewalks. By the time she reached the dismal old house that had been sectioned off for three separate families, Sam was steaming. But there was no one home at Corey's to vent her anger on. The door was locked and Verna wasn't there.

"It's okay," Corey assured her. "She don't need to be home. I can get in through the window."

Sam turned back to the car. "We'll wait."

After dark, after three walking tours of Foxcove's small downtown, a hamburger, fries and a giant milk shake, one trip to the grocery store and another to the park to swing, Sam passed by Corey's house for the fourth time and saw a light in the Haskins's portion. "I think your mother's home," she said.

"Looks like it."

Sam walked Corey up to the door. The woman who opened it was overweight, prematurely aged and only slightly better groomed than her daughter had been before her bath. Verna snatched Corey inside and began to scream at her. Sam stuck her foot in the door so that Verna couldn't close it.

"Now listen and listen good," she said quietly. "I'm reporting your behavior to the authorities. And when they come to check on Corey tomorrow, I'm going to tell them to look her over carefully to be sure you haven't beaten her tonight. Do I make myself clear?"

"Who the hell do you think you are?" Verna screeched.

"I'm the mother she should have had."

Sam took one last look at Corey, who didn't seem

nearly as upset by her mother's behavior as Sam was, then she turned and walked down the front steps.

IF I HAD a little girl.

Joe poured rye over ice and swallowed it without a pause. It was hours since Sam had left but he still heard her words as if she had just said them. *If I had a little girl.*

But, of course, she would never have a little girl. She would never have a child of either sex. He had cheated her out of the opportunity.

When the door closed he poured himself another drink. The room was nearly dark, but the liquor was easy to find.

"Joe?" Sam came in and turned on the lights. "Did you start dinner? I called to tell you I was going to be late, but you must have been out. Did you get my message?"

"No."

"I hope you weren't worried. Next time check the machine."

"Where in the hell have you been?"

"Corey's mother wasn't home, and I couldn't just leave her there, although that's obviously what they both thought I should have done. I waited until she got home."

"She's not your problem."

"What?" Sam's voice was soft. It was usually soft when she was ready to explode.

"I know you couldn't just leave her. I understand that. But she's not your problem. You've got to let go. You shouldn't have brought her here today."

"I didn't bring her. She came on her two little feet carrying a dying bird she wanted me to fix."

He swallowed another drink. Three burning gulps, and somehow, the pain was welcome.

"Next time should I just turn her away?" Sam asked. "Is that what you would do? Tell her to walk the seven miles back home, never mind that she's only a baby and she could get killed by some joyriding teenager?"

"No."

"Then what should I do?"

"You should call child protective services and report her mother. Then let them handle it."

"What a great idea. So great, by the way, that I've already done it. I called the abuse hotline and told them the whole story. They'll investigate and they'll find out that Verna's just inside the law. They'll check for a while, maybe even do a little counseling, then they'll close the case."

"Your faith in the system is admirable."

"I have no faith!" Sam threw her purse on the chair. "What kind of faith am I supposed to have? Verna doesn't deserve that child! She's never going to be a good mother to her, no kind of mother at all! And then there's people like you and me—" She stopped.

"Go on, Sam." He faced her. "What about people like you and me?"

She lifted her chin. "Then there's people like you and me who would be wonderful parents, but we can't have children."

"But that's not quite it, is it?" He tossed down the rest of his drink. "You can have children. You're certifiably equipped to conceive and bear them. I'm the one who's deficient."

"You're the one who's infertile," she said. "There's nothing deficient about you, Joe."

"Except that I have no good sperm. A small deficiency."

She started toward him, but he turned away.

"Joe, if it had been me, how would you have felt?"

He didn't want to answer her; he didn't know how the conversation had started in the first place.

"Joe?"

"Leave it alone, Sam."

"No. It's a legitimate question. What if I had been the one who couldn't conceive? Would you have loved me less? Would you have thought I was less of a woman?"

"It's not the same thing."

"It very nearly is."

He felt her hand on his shoulder. It was all he could do not to shake it off. "I don't want to talk about this. We've been over it. Life goes on."

"But it isn't going on. You're so tied up with our infertility, so angry and hurt that you've completely shut me out. I love you. I need you."

"You need children!" He faced her. "Damn it, don't you think I can see that? You were born to be a mother. And I can't give you kids! Don't you know how that eats me up?"

"You can give me kids."

"No!"

"Joe, we can adopt. We both love other people's kids. That's why we do what we do for a living. We can raise other people's kids, too, and make them ours. Do they really have to have our genes?"

"Yes!" He turned away again. "I don't want somebody else's children." *I want my own,* hung unspoken in the air between them.

"This isn't about adoption or having kids at all." Her hand tightened on his shoulder. He could feel the sharp bite of her nails. "It's about Joseph Giovanelli and the way he feels about himself. It's about your pride."

He faced her again, and her hand fell to her side. "I don't need your psychological assessment, damn it! If you're not happy with things as they are, then you're married to the wrong man. I can't give you kids any way at all. If you can't accept that, then we have nothing to say to each other."

"So how would that be different? When was the last time we had anything to say to each other?" She moved closer. "I can't keep fighting this demon that's come between us, Joe. Not by myself. Give me something to hang on to. I can live without kids, but I can't live like this. I need you, but I'm not going to go on saying it over and over. I've got pride, too."

He wanted to grab her and hold her forever, but he couldn't reach out. He couldn't reach out.

She stood there for a long moment, then she turned and walked away. He watched her go, and he knew that one day she would leave and close the door behind her.

He wondered why she hadn't closed the door the day the doctor had told them that they would never be parents.

CHAPTER SIX

JOHNNY AND TEDDY lived in Goldsboro, where Johnny was a sales representative for a North Carolina furniture manufacturer. At the age of thirty-three, just after her husband's untimely death, Rose had pulled up stakes in Brooklyn and moved her young family to Goldsboro, where she had a brother to find her work and help with the raising of her brood.

Over the years all the Giovanelli children had drifted—but not far—to settle permanently in the state they'd grown to think of as home. Johnny was the only one to stay right in Goldsboro. When Rose complained that Johnny had stayed to watch over her, Johnny grinned the famous Giovanelli grin and refused to reply.

On the morning after the fight with Sam, Joe pulled in to Johnny's driveway. His brother's house was a comfortable brick ranch that was set apart from its neighbors by exquisitely perfect landscaping. Teddy was slowly pursuing a degree in landscape architecture, and their yard was an ongoing laboratory.

Johnny was in the garage working on his car when Joe got out. He looked up from under the hood, then went back to work without saying a word.

"What's the problem?" Joe asked.

"If I knew that, I'd be fixing it, not looking for it."

"Want some help?"

"From you? Since when did you know anything about cars that I didn't?"

"Forever." Joe took off his wristwatch and pocketed it before he ducked in beside his brother.

Johnny didn't look at him. "What are you doing here, anyway?"

"I was just out for a drive."

"That's a pretty long drive. Where's Sam?"

"At home."

"Too bad. She and Teddy could have gabbed."

"She's not in a gabbing mood."

"Neither are you most of the time."

Joe ignored what was an obvious opening. "What's this old wreck doing that it shouldn't?"

"Running rough."

"When? Low speed? High speed?"

"High, mostly. When I've been on the road too long."

"Could be a lot of things."

"You think I don't know that?"

"Did you reset the choke?"

"Not yet."

"Check the plugs?"

"I just got here! Check them yourself."

Joe dove in to do just that. Johnny attacked the air cleaner cover and both men were silent for a while. Finally Joe straightened. "Look at this." He came out from under the hood and stood by the door holding two spark plugs in his hand. "See the spots on the insulators?" He held them out to Johnny. "They're overheating. Maybe you got a vacuum leak, or maybe they were just put in wrong. You do them yourself?"

"Yeah, I did them and did them right. But they're a

different brand than I used to use. Maybe I should try colder plugs again."

"That could be it."

"Help me check the choke plate." Johnny fumbled in his pocket for keys and threw them to Joe. "Floor it."

Joe got behind the wheel and pushed the gas pedal to the floor. Then he stuck his head out the window. "See anything?"

"Looks fine. Start the engine."

The engine roared to life and Joe got out to poke his head under the hood with his brother. "Open just a crack, like it's supposed to be. Looks good so far."

"I'll let it run awhile. Want to come in and have some coffee?"

Joe thought about the friendly, family atmosphere of Johnny's house. Once he would have liked nothing better. "Not yet."

"Then what do you want to do?"

"Close the damned garage door and stick my head under the hood."

"Are you going to talk about this sometime?"

Joe didn't want to talk about his feelings ever, but he owed his brother an apology. He owed the whole world an apology. He was a walking apology, and he couldn't seem to get two words past the permanent barricade in his throat.

"Coffee on the patio, and I'll threaten the life of anybody who bothers us." Johnny disappeared before Joe could refuse.

The patio was another example of Teddy's genius. Planters of sculpted miniature pines were set at angles along the edge, with smaller planters of cascading annuals to soften the stark effect. The table backed against a stone barbecue that Johnny had built himself. Before their confrontation at the housewarming, they had planned to build one down by the lake at Joe's house.

"So, what is it?" Johnny asked. He set a tray of coffee and ham biscuits beside Joe. Joe saw Teddy's handiwork in the biscuits, the colorful pottery and linen napkins. He knew she would keep the children from bothering them as they talked. She was a lot like Sam.

He still didn't want to talk about his problems. "Did you check the choke again?"

"Yeah. It's open all the way. I'll try cooler plugs and see if that does it. No sense in checking everything else if that's the problem."

Joe sipped his coffee and stared at the backyard built around the needs of Johnny's children. There was a swing set, a tree house and a sandbox large enough for the entire Giovanelli younger generation when they visited.

Johnny spoke. "Are you and Sammy having troubles? I know I had too much to drink. I was out of line at the housewarming, but I didn't know I was stepping on toes. You've always been so happy together."

"We can't have kids, Johnny." Five words. Joe hadn't been sure he'd ever be able to say them. But he didn't feel better; he just felt exposed.

"What do you mean, you can't have them?" Johnny was incredulous.

Joe didn't laugh; he didn't even feel angry. Johnny's reaction was so much like his own that he understood it completely. He remembered the day the doctor had told him.

WHEN SAM HADN'T gotten pregnant during their summer in the mountains, neither Joe nor Sam had been particularly concerned. They made the move to Foxcove and settled in a small apartment while they looked for a house to rent or buy. Just a week before the school year started, one of the first-grade teachers at Foxcove Elementary fell ill and tendered her resignation. Sam was the only qualified teacher waiting anxiously in the wings, and she was given the job.

Since the school district had a generous maternity-leave policy, Sam and Joe decided to continue trying to have a baby. Even if she got pregnant immediately she could still finish most of the year. A more likely scenario was that the baby would be born in the summer. But even that scenario didn't come to pass.

A year after they had begun trying, Sam made her first trip to the office of a fertility specialist in Raleigh. The doctor did some simple preliminary tests, then told her to go home and return in six months if she still wasn't pregnant. Six months stretched to twelve before she made another appointment. Joe was opposed to Sam consulting a specialist at all. He told her stories of other couples who had taken time to conceive. Medical intervention seemed like an invasion of privacy.

When Sam finally returned to the specialist, she returned alone. Joe refused to participate, and Sam underwent the next round of tests without his support. But finally, when almost every avenue was exhausted and there seemed to be no medical reason that Sam couldn't conceive, Joe reluctantly returned with her.

He hated the tests every bit as much as he'd expected. But he hated the results most of all.

The morning they went in for the verdict had been cold and dreary. Sam had repeated some tests, too, and she was nervous. The drive to Raleigh was a long one.

He snapped at her for choosing a doctor so far away; she snapped at him for not cooperating earlier.

But by the time they arrived at the office they were a team again.

"It's going to be all right," Joe said, squeezing her arm. "We're going to get through this okay. If we've got a problem, they'll be able to help us. At least we'll know."

She was pale, clearly apprehensive. Her mother had been able to conceive only one child before a tumor had forced a hysterectomy. Despite the doctor's reassurances, Sam was convinced that her problems were going to be similar.

The waiting room was lavender, with expensive watercolors on the walls. Joe had seen the bills Sam had submitted to their insurance company. He had a good idea who was paying for the watercolors.

A nurse dressed in a soft print that matched the walls ushered them into the doctor's office. The doctor stood to greet them. Then he turned to Joe.

"IT'S ME WITH the problem, not Sam," Joe told Johnny. "I'm allergic to my own sperm. How do you like it? Couldn't have been dogs or dust, it had to be my sperm."

"What are you talking about?"

"A doctor in Raleigh did some tests. My sperm count is low to start with. The ones I manage to produce are attacked by antibodies before they can go anywhere. I've got as much chance of getting Sam pregnant as flying to Mars."

Johnny was silent. Then, "God, Joey, and what I said at the party..."

"You were just being your usual obnoxious self."

"But can't they do anything?"

"We tried a round of steroids. I reacted badly. It's not much of a help, anyway, even if the sperm count's high. A real long shot. Now there's nothing left to do."

"I don't know what to say."

"That makes two of us."

"How long have you known?"

"I found out late in the winter."

"And you didn't tell me?"

"No."

"What kind of brother keeps this to himself?"

"My kind." Staring straight ahead, Joe finished his coffee.

"You're ashamed of yourself, aren't you?"

Joe didn't answer.

"Like you had something to do with it. That's stupid. You know that, don't you?"

"And how would you feel?" Joe faced him. "What if it was you who couldn't get your wife pregnant? What if your backyard was full of nothing but Teddy's flowers and shrubs? What if you didn't have that tree house or sandbox or those kids watching television in there? How would you feel?"

Johnny's shoulders slumped. It was answer enough.

Joe set his cup down carefully, even though he wanted to send it crashing against the barbecue. "I wanted you to know. I don't want to blow up again at anybody in the family over this. And I don't want Mama to be sitting around waiting for us to reproduce. Because we aren't going to. Not ever."

"You want me to pass on the word?"

Joe felt the barrier in his throat again. He nodded.

"You've considered the alternatives? Other ways of making a family?"

"I've considered them, yeah."

"No go?"

"No go."

Johnny didn't argue, just as Joe had known he wouldn't. Johnny was brash and outspoken, but there was nobody living who would understand Joe's feelings better.

"You're no less of a man, Joey."

Joe didn't answer. He couldn't call his brother a liar to his face.

COREY STOPPED TO rest under the same tree that had sheltered her on her first trip down Old Scoggins. She was getting used to the walk. It was quiet here, not like around her house. The people next door fought a lot, and Corey could hear them late at night, yelling and throwing things.

She didn't know why they had to throw things. She guessed it made them feel better. Her mama had thrown a pot at her once, but she couldn't throw too good, and she'd missed. Still, it had scared Corey, because she knew that if her mama's aim had been better, that pot would have hurt pretty bad. Most of the time Mama just left her alone, but sometimes she got so mad Corey had to sneak around and hide until Mama went off somewheres.

She was off somewheres today. The house had been empty when Corey woke up. It was quiet, nice for a while. She'd eaten some peanut butter out of the jar and drunk all she liked from the faucet. She had even stayed inside and watched cartoons on television all morning, but after a while she'd gotten bored.

And then she'd thought about Miss Sam.

Her mama had told her not to go to Miss Sam's house again. Her mama had yelled a lot about Miss Sam making trouble and stuff. Corey didn't believe it. Miss Sam fixed trouble.

But if Mama found out that she'd gone to see Miss Sam again, she would be real mad. She might throw things at Corey, or she might do worse. When she hit, she hit hard.

So Corey hadn't visited Miss Sam again. Not exactly, anyway. She had been to Miss Sam's house. She had hidden in the trees beside her driveway and watched cars come and go. Once she had seen Miss Sam in the yard, planting something. She had been wearing yellow, the same color as her hair. She had looked all fresh and cool, like a drink of water after a long walk.

Corey had wanted to call her name, but she had been afraid. Her mama wasn't the only reason. Part of it was Mr. Joe. He was the biggest man Corey had ever seen. And he had the meanest eyes. He looked like he was mad at everything. She knew he didn't like little girls, not the way Miss Sam did. He didn't even look like he liked Miss Sam very much.

So Corey hadn't called Miss Sam's name that day, and she wouldn't call it today, either, even if Miss Sam was outside. She didn't want Miss Sam to see her. She just wanted to see Miss Sam. She didn't know why exactly.

She just did.

JOE STAYED AT Johnny's for lunch, braved the assaults of his nieces and nephew and gave them beloved uncle piggyback rides. But by the time he was on his way home, he felt as if he had been to hell and back.

He still had to face Sam. They hadn't spoken after their argument. Their days had become an endless progression of frostbitten conversation marked only by eruptions of rage. He didn't know how to change the pattern, or even if he wanted to. When Sam was angry or distant he wasn't forced to relate to her—something he no longer knew how to do.

A storm had come and gone, but the sky was still light when he pulled on to Old Scoggins Road. Several miles closer to home he realized he was driving faster than he should. Killer had become an outlet for his frustration. He had given dozens of lectures to juniors and seniors at Sadler High about the dangers of doing exactly what he was doing now, using his car to express his feelings. When he saw he was going sixty he lifted his foot from the accelerator.

But not soon enough.

A child darted across the road ahead of him. If he had been going thirty-five, as he should have been, he would have had plenty of time to slow, swerve clear and remain on the road. As it was, he hit the brake and fishtailed on the slick tarmac into a wide ditch. The car came to an abrupt halt against the root of a giant oak. He was thrown forward, but his seat belt and the airbag kept him from smacking the steering wheel. Killer shuddered twice, then died.

He didn't move for a moment. He was confused, because everything had happened so quickly. Then he was furious.

The door screeched ominously when he opened it and stepped into the ditch. It took only a glance to see that Johnny's car had needed an aspirin compared to the high-tech surgery Killer would need to recover from this.

Three steps and he was out of the ditch. Ten yards across the road and he had his hand on the back of Corey Haskins's neck.

"What in the blazes are you doing here?" He looked around. There were no houses in sight, nothing but pasture land and acres of tobacco.

She kicked at him, but he held her firmly. He was furious, but not so angry that he couldn't see she was scared to death. "I asked you a question," he said.

"Ain't none of your business!" She kicked at him again.

"Were you going to see Miss Sam?"

"What if I was?"

He could have been killed. Worse—much, much worse—*she* could have been. She was seven, a pitiful, scruffy, unloved child, and he wanted to shake her into submission.

"I'm going to let go of you," he said through clenched teeth, "but when I do, you'd better not go anywhere until we're done talking. Understand?"

"Don't have to do like you say!"

"It would be…in your best interests."

She seemed to consider, then she went limp, and he removed his hand. She moved away, but not very far. She lifted her hands to her hips and stuck out her chin. "So?"

"I just crashed my car because of you."

"It made a lot of noise."

"I'm glad you were entertained."

Her eyes narrowed. "It was better than TV."

Obviously sarcasm was not lost on her, although it would have been on most children her age. Joe realized she was probably every bit as intelligent as Sam claimed. "Were you going to see Miss Sam?"

"I go there sometimes."

He only knew of one time. He wondered if Sam had purposely failed to mention the others. "Often?"

"Maybe, but I don't bother her," she said proudly. "Just go to look."

"It's way too far for a little girl to walk. And it's dangerous. You could have been killed running across the road like that."

"Wasn't."

"Because I crashed my car!"

"You drive too fast!"

He couldn't argue with that, but he disliked her even more for reminding him. "Does your mother know where you are?"

"Don't matter." Her face grew more sullen. "She don't care if I go off."

From everything Sam had told him, Joe suspected Corey was right. "Come on, we're walking to my house so I can call a tow truck. Then I'll take you home in Miss Sam's car."

"Don't want to walk with you. Don't like you."

"You don't have to like me."

"Good, 'cause I don't!"

His hand itched, and he suspected the only cure was to apply it rapidly to the seat of Corey's filthy shorts. But he started to walk, and before long she fell in step beside him. He forced himself to walk more slowly to accommodate her short legs.

"How often do you come out here?" he asked at last.

He figured they had at least half a mile to trudge together.

"Don't know."

"Once a week? Twice? Every day?"

"When my mama goes away."

"And how often is that?"

"Whenever she can."

He suspected he was being baited by a seven-year-old, and he didn't like it. "How many times? One? Ten? Twenty?"

"Six, maybe."

"And Miss Sam doesn't know?"

"Told you."

Reluctantly he had to give the child credit. She hadn't uttered as much as one complaint. Time slogged right along with their footsteps. The road had begun to curve into the final stretch when she spoke again. "How come you got a playhouse and no kids?"

"Because we do."

"Miss Sam likes kids, but I guess you don't."

"I like kids who know how to behave."

"Like Alice Lambert."

"Who's Alice Lambert?"

"She's got shiny black hair like yours, and she can do cursive."

"Cursive?"

"You don't know what cursive is?"

"I know." He wished they were already home. "What's handwriting got to do with anything?"

"We're not s'posed to do cursive yet, but Miss Sam likes it. She says Alice's smart. Alice gets stickers on everything."

"How about you? Do you get stickers?"

"Not on my writing."

He told himself that one little girl's struggle with her handwriting was not his concern. The words that emerged were somewhat different. "I couldn't get the hang of writing until I was almost in fourth grade. I printed everything."

"Must have been pretty dumb."

"Dumb, but not dumb enough to insult somebody almost four feet taller than me."

"Why do you live out here? S'nothing to do."

Fortunately for Corey, Joe saw his mailbox in the distance. "Because we like privacy. That means that we don't want people coming out here who haven't been invited."

"Miss Sam likes me."

"That doesn't mean you can keep coming. When I take you home I'm going to tell your mother she has to keep a better eye on you. And I don't want you coming here again. Do you understand?"

She turned away. He couldn't see her face. "*I'm* not dumb."

"But you sure are rude."

"At least I don't scare little girls to death!"

"You don't act as if you're scared to death."

"Miss Sam's nice. How come she married you?"

He turned into his driveway. He was walking faster by now, and she was dragging behind. "So I could scare away everybody who doesn't belong here."

Her answer, whatever it was, was swallowed by the ferocious barking of a large Border collie who came streaking through the field beside the house. Joe recognized the dog as it closed the distance between them. Laddie belonged to Turner Insley, the man who had sold

Joe his land. But Corey didn't know that the dog's only earthly pleasure was to round up everything in sight. When Laddie, yapping excitedly, darted toward her, she began to shriek.

Joe heard Sam's shouts from the driveway behind him, but he didn't even turn. He leaped toward Corey and swung her away from the dog and into his arms.

She smelled the way she looked—which was terrible—and she weighed nothing in his arms. He held her tightly and kicked at Laddie to warn him away.

When the dog slunk off to find a cow or a butterfly to herd, Joe tipped Corey back so he could see her face.

"That's one of the reasons why you shouldn't be so far away from home by yourself," he said.

"Not by myself. I'm with you."

As Sam came up to join them, he set Corey firmly on the ground. "She's all yours," he said.

"What on earth is going on?"

"Your little friend will tell you." He glanced at Corey. She stuck her chin out defiantly. "Don't you forget," he told her. "I meant what I said. I don't want to see you out this way again."

"Don't know why I'd want to come out, with you here and all."

She stood like a soldier, as straight and defiant as a Prussian general. She was filthy—he'd never seen a child so dirty—homely and obviously undernourished. And still something amazing sparkled in her eyes. Under the defiance Corey yearned for more, for something she could see just out of reach. Joe couldn't give it to her; he had nothing to give anybody. But still, he could see her need.

He turned away, but not before he'd memorized that look. He knew it would haunt him.

Of all men, didn't he know what it was like to want something that he could never, never have?

CHAPTER SEVEN

FOR THREE FULL weeks Killer was the favorite topic of discussion at the Foxcove body shop. Parts drifted in slowly; opinions ranged on how best to complete the transformation. If Killer had been built in Japan or Germany instead of Detroit, the car would have been an antique by the time Joe was able to reclaim it. As it was, he had to reacquaint himself with the gearshift and clutch on the trip home. He drove slowly on Old Scoggins. If a turtle had ventured into the road, it would have had plenty of time to cross.

The pines lining the driveway rustled in a warm evening breeze. Joe parked next to Sam's sensible sedan. He had been away most of the day. He was back at work full-time now, preparing for the school year that would begin in a few short weeks. He wasn't sure how Sam was spending her time. The house sparkled, and there was always a wonderful hot meal at night, prepared with fresh vegetables from the garden she had dug and planted herself. But he doubted that the house and garden kept her so busy that she forgot about all the things that were missing from her life.

He opened the front door, expecting the scent of dinner. The house was dark and smelled only of lemon potpourri and freshly cut roses. He called Sam's name, but there was no answer.

He told himself Sam's car was in the driveway. She hadn't left. She hadn't left *him*. He called louder and began a search.

Ten minutes later he found her down at the lake, feeding the ducks, who were so tame she had to shoo them back into the water every time she went back to the house. She was wearing a strapless sundress that was the warm gold of her hair, and in the glow of a perfect sunset her skin was palest ivory. He sucked in a deep breath at the sight of her. His body responded in the most primal of ways.

She turned and only then did she seem to realize he was there. "Oh, Joe. I didn't know you were home."

He tried to sound natural. "I've been looking for you."

"Have you?" She sounded as if she doubted it.

"I'm later than I thought I'd be. I'm sorry."

"I'm never sure when you'll be home. I thought I'd wait and start dinner when you got here."

"Let's go out." He walked toward her. An arm's length away he forced himself to stop. "It's Friday. There's a fish fry at the Plantation House. Or we could drive over toward the coast and look for something there. We haven't been out together in a long time."

"Sit and talk over drinks and dinner?" She smiled sadly. "I think I've forgotten how."

He pulled her into his arms before he could think better of it. "I'm a bastard, Sam." She was stiff, but she yielded a little at his words. His blood heated and rushed swiftly to every distant appendage of his body. His arms tightened around her.

"Not a bastard. A stranger." She gazed up at him. "What happened to the man I married?"

He didn't know. But at the moment he felt exactly like that man. Desire and contrition crowded out all his anger at the fates and at his traitorous masculinity. He thought of Sam, of all the things she had been denied. Of how much he had denied her because of his own absorption in himself.

"I love you," he whispered. "That's never, never changed."

"No? Show me."

Desire was a freight train roaring through his head and blocking all his other feelings. He hadn't made love to her in a long time, so long he couldn't remember when. He had wanted to; God knows he had thought of little else. But each time he had tried to approach her, he had remembered...

The freight train picked up speed, and memory evaporated. Sam smelled like honeysuckle, like hot summer nights and a woman aroused. He ran his hands over her bare shoulders, down her arms, along the fabric-clad curve of her breasts. His breath caught in his throat; his hand touched the tab of her zipper.

"What do you wear under a dress like this?" he asked.

"Very little." She threw her head back. Her eyes were drowsy and passion glazed. No matter what was wrong between them, this was right. She wanted him as much as he wanted her.

"Then that's what you're going to be wearing." He inched the zipper down. He found her hair with his other hand. It was fine and as soft as dandelion down. He lifted it off her shoulders and bent to run his lips along her throat. She shivered against his lips. As the dress fell away, she shivered again.

"Don't tell me you're cold," he said.

"I won't." She wound her arms around his neck. "I'll tell you anything you want to hear."

"That you need me?"

"Desperately."

"And want me?"

"More than I can say."

"And you're going to do unspeakable things with me right here in the open?"

"Unspeakable, devastatingly intimate things."

He touched one breast, a feather-light caress as teasing as the warm breeze. She sighed, and he took advantage of her parted lips, plunging between them to taste her secrets.

She stroked her nails over the back of his neck, kneaded and stroked and drove him wild with her fingers and lips. He was breathing hard when the kiss ended, and she was smiling a woman's secretive smile.

She undressed him, but he couldn't stand quietly as she did. He filled his hands with her breasts, his lips with her sweetly scented hair. His mind was filled with nothing except thoughts of her, of the way she moved her hips when he made love to her, of her soft cries and murmured words. Of the way he filled her completely.

He filled her completely when they were both naked and stretched out together on a fragrant bed of clover and pine needles. She wrapped herself around him and drew him into her before he could even kiss her again. He lay surrounded by her, by her warmth, her scent, her love, and for a moment he forgot that he was giving her nothing but passion.

Then, in the throes of their mutual release, he remembered.

He held her afterward. Held her because it was expected, and he no more wanted to hurt her than he wanted to remember that the seed he had spilled inside her was devoid of life.

She drew a finger down his chest. "Are you all right?"

He closed his eyes. "Sure. That was terrific."

She turned so that she was facing him, her body strung languorously along the side of his. "You're a wonderful lover. You'll be wonderful when you're eighty. Nothing will ever change that."

He smiled, because it was expected, too. "You're every fantasy I ever had."

"Had?"

"Have. Have." He stroked her hair, although he wanted nothing so much as to be alone for a while.

"Shall I shower and change for dinner?"

"Is the dress ruined?"

"I doubt it. It landed on the grass. Would you like me to wear it?"

"If it's wearable."

"Then I will." She moved away from him and stood, a wood nymph moving gracefully against the darkening sky. He watched her find her dress and underclothing and slip them on for the trip back up to the house. Then she was gone.

He lay with his hands under his head, a man who should have been blissfully happy. Somewhere far in the distance he heard the lonesome whistle of a freight train.

WRAPPED IN HER robe, Sam dried her hair. It was growing late, and she was hungry, but she didn't want to hurry Joe. He didn't have to tell her that near the moment of his release he had realized that he couldn't make her pregnant. She had felt it in his sudden tension, seen it in the bleakness of his eyes. Until then he had been the sensual, confidently virile man she had married. His emotional withdrawal had stolen much of the pleasure of their encounter.

But he had made love to her. For minutes he had been the Joe she adored. Perhaps tonight was a new start. She could be patient if they were moving toward a better marriage together. If they could repeat tonight again and again, perhaps one night it would turn out completely right. He would hold her, look into her eyes and see that it didn't matter that he couldn't sire her children. He would finally realize that he was first in her life and always would be.

Her hair was nearly dry when he appeared in the doorway. "Go ahead and get in the shower," she said. "I'll just be another minute."

"I can wait."

"No, go ahead. I'm starving."

It was an opening for an appropriately sexy remark, but he passed over it. She watched in the mirror as he stripped off his clothes. In the years of their marriage he hadn't gained a pound, despite the fact that she fed him as well as his mother ever had. He would be a gorgeous older man, silver haired and olive skinned, a man who turned the silver heads of every passing older woman.

She listened to the water run as she dressed in the bedroom. Once upon a time Joe had sung in the shower, snatches of Mozart's *Magic Flute* and Mick Jagger's greatest hits. He had a terrible voice, gruff and tuneless. She yearned to hear it again.

She was nearly ready when he emerged. She watched him dress from the corner of her eye. He always threw on whatever shirt he came to first. She always made sure that the clothes in the front of the closet were co-ordinated.

She was just sliding on an earring post when the telephone rang. "I'll get it," she volunteered.

"Catch it downstairs. I unhooked this jack yesterday while I was working on the wiring."

She scurried down and grabbed the phone in the kitchen. The voice on the other end was unfamiliar.

"Mrs. Samantha Giovanelli?"

"That's right."

There was static on the line, possibly due to Joe's work on the wiring. Sam missed the next several sentences. The voice sounded far away. "…your niece."

"I'm sorry. Can you repeat that?"

"There's been an accident. Your niece has been injured."

Sam sank into the nearest chair. She swallowed. Joe had nieces on top of nieces. She loved them all. Fear closed her throat. She was terrified to ask who had been hurt.

"I'm calling from South Carolina."

"South Carolina?" She gripped the telephone. "I'm sorry. I'm having trouble hearing you. Did you say South Carolina?"

"Yes. Spartanburg."

No one in the family was vacationing out of the state. Sam was sure of it. The Giovanellis practically lived in each other's pockets. Rose would have told her if any of them had gone on vacation. But it was possible that one of Joe's brothers or sisters had sent a daughter to camp. Maybe they had given Sam and Joe's number for emergencies. "How badly is she hurt? And I'm sorry, but which niece is it?"

The line crackled again, and Sam missed another sentence. The line cleared. "But she's going to be fine. She has multiple bruises and a broken arm. She was thrown out of the car when it crashed."

"Oh, my God!"

"Now, don't worry. She's been checked over thoroughly and treated. You can visit next week." There was a pause. "I'm afraid her mother wasn't so lucky, Mrs. Giovanelli. I'm sorry I have to be the one to tell you this, but Mrs. Haskins was killed instantly."

Sorrow washed over Sam. She didn't know how she was going to tell Joe. No man loved his family as much as he did. His sisters and brothers were his closest friends. She didn't know how he would get through this. Then, as the woman on the other end remained respectfully silent, she gripped the telephone harder.

Sam's voice was only a shade louder than a whisper. "Excuse me, did you say Mrs. Haskins?"

Sometime later she heard Joe's footsteps on the stairs.

"I decided I ought to get dressed up, since you were." He came into the kitchen in dark slacks and a gray silk jacket. "What do you think?"

"Joe…" She was still sitting down.

He frowned. "What's wrong?"

"Corey's been in an accident. In South Carolina."

"South Carolina?"

"Yes. A car accident." She saw concern on his face. Joe wouldn't wish anyone, not even the brattiest child, so much as a splinter. "She's pretty battered, but apparently she's going to be fine."

"Poor little kid." He sounded genuinely distressed.

"Her mother was killed instantly."

"No one should die like that…"

She finished his sentence. "Not even Verna Haskins."

"No. Not even Verna." He touched her cheek. She covered his hand and held it there. "I'm sorry, sweetheart. I know you care about Corey."

"It must be so hard on her."

"Yeah. Even the worst mother is still a mother." He squatted in front of her. "Do you still feel like going out?"

"Sure. I'm fine. It's so late, though. Let's go somewhere nearby."

"The Plantation House?"

"Perfect. I'll get a jacket."

As they drove into town he told her about his day at school. She listened with half an ear, responding with all the enthusiasm she could muster. It had been so long since he had talked to her about anything. They parked on the street that passed for Foxcove's major shopping area and window-shopped its length before they headed a block east to the restaurant.

The Plantation House had never been that; it was six years old, built of wafer board and Sheetrock. But the architect-proprietor had been smitten with self-importance. Elaborate Corinthian columns graced an otherwise unassuming two-story building. The food was always good, traditionally Southern and high in calories. Inside, at a table in the center of the room, they ordered the fish fry.

"They hate to see you coming on Fridays," Sam said. "They lose money on an all-you-can-eat when you're here."

"But they gain it back with you."

"We've always been a balancing act."

They chatted casually—interrupted frequently by people who wanted to say hello—until it was time to tackle a plate of cole slaw and the first round of fish.

"Don't look now, but Bobby Ferguson's the busboy," Joe said. "Remember my stories about him the first year we moved here?"

Joe had stories about almost all the kids at the high school. And they had stories about him. He was the youngest principal in the history of Sadler County, chosen for the job after only a record two years as assistant principal, but it wasn't youth that had made him such a success with the students. Joe simply understood how to relate to teenagers. He possessed the magical combination of respect, suspicion and forgiveness.

Sam looked up from her plate. "You wanted to bring him home."

"Just for a week or two."

"I can't remember why."

"He had a problem with alcohol. I wanted to sober him up."

"And why didn't you?"

"His parents finally admitted he needed help. They sent him to a treatment program. This year he'll be going into his third year at Duke. Premed."

She heard something like pride in his voice. "You're a hands-on kind of guy, Joe."

"Sometimes that's the only way to get things done."

"I wouldn't have minded if Bobby had come to stay with us. I like helping kids turn around."

"That's why you're such a good teacher."

"Let's not forget how kind and full of love I am."

He looked up.

"And nurturing." She put her fork down. "Let's not

forget how nurturing both of us are. How concerned about kids. How caring."

He put his fork down, too. Carefully. "We're not talking about Bobby anymore, are we?"

"Close."

"What have you done, Sam?"

She stared at him and prayed he would forgive her. "I've told the social worker in Spartanburg that we'll be there Wednesday morning to pick up Corey and bring her here to stay with us."

"I CAN'T BELIEVE you!" Joe threw his sports coat on the hallway table and stalked toward the kitchen.

"Then you don't know me very well." Sam followed at a slower pace. She was in no hurry to continue the fight that had flamed since the moment they'd buckled up for the drive back home. Until that moment she had explained her position calmly and rationally, fully aware that even Joe, with his hair-trigger temper, wouldn't start a fight in front of half the town of Foxcove.

"Oh, I know you," he said. "Or I used to. But maybe I don't know the woman who would make a decision like this without consulting me!"

"And if I had consulted you, what would you have said?"

"No!"

"Somehow I knew that."

He slammed the refrigerator door in response. She watched him toss half a gallon of iced tea on the counter, and she was glad the container was plastic.

"I know you feel sorry for Corey." He slammed cupboard doors until he found the glass he wanted. "I don't blame you for that. But volunteering to take her is an-other thing!"

"I'll go over this one more time, Joe," she said qui-etly. "Shut up and listen and see if it penetrates. Corey told them I was her aunt. That's why they called me."

"So among other things she's a liar."

"Don't you realize what that means? I'm the only per-son in the world that one little girl could think of who might, just might, be willing to take care of her. She lied about our relationship so they'd take her seriously. She has no one else. The social worker said Verna took Corey to Spartanburg to look for Corey's father. Appar-ently she wanted to dump her with him, even though Corey's never met him. And you know why? I think Verna was tired of having the child welfare people on her case. It was easier to dump Corey on someone else than to try to become a better mother."

"And how do they know all this? The part you're not guessing about, I mean?"

She ignored his sarcasm. "Corey told them. Verna told Corey she was sick of taking care of her and it was time for her father to take her."

"She could be lying. She lied about you being her aunt."

"You've heard a lot about Verna. Does it sound like a lie?"

He poured a glass of tea and drank it between glares.

"So what?" he asked at last. "She's free of Verna now. There are certified foster-care homes in South Carolina. You've explained that we aren't related to her, and somewhere out there she has a father who may be searching for her."

"Not likely. Corey claims her mother said that her father probably wouldn't want her, either."

"If Corey's never met him, she wouldn't know."

"She's lived in Foxcove all her life. Can you really believe it would be better for her to wait in a strange state with strange foster parents until they find her father—if they do? Can you really believe that?"

"You know what I can't believe? I can't believe they're going to let you take her. Just like that. They've got laws."

"And we've got credentials up the wazoo. They'll investigate, sure, but we'll come out looking like God's gift to the system. I gave them the name of a psychologist who knows us, little Jeff Hartley's mother. They're going to call her, as well as Father Watkins. And the people at the agency here know how concerned we've been about Corey. They've been as helpful as the law would allow. They're not going to interfere if we're willing to keep her."

"*We* are not willing."

"You had better get willing, and quick." She heard the threat come out of her mouth, and she was astounded. But she couldn't take it back, because she had meant every single word.

He set his glass on the counter. "Just what does that mean?"

"It means that if you say no to me on this, I don't know if I'll ever be able to forgive you."

His dark eyes smoldered, but he didn't say a word.

"I've put up with hell for half of this past year, Joe. I've watched you withdraw until I've almost given up hope we can still have a marriage. I've watched you shut me out, little by little, and deny it the whole time.

I've watched you cut off all the options that could have helped us deal with our infertility. You won't consider marriage counseling. You won't consider artificial insemination. You won't consider adoption. You. You. You."

She touched her chest. "Well, this time I want something to help me ease my pain. I want to take a child I already love and help her through a terrible time. I want to keep her here until the state of North Carolina can make arrangements for her, good arrangements, not something shoddy and temporary. I'm Corey's one link with the good things inside her. No one else is as qualified to help her as I am. If I can do this, if I can be allowed to do this, then maybe it won't matter so much that I'll never get to raise a child from start to finish."

She stopped. She had said too much; she had said too little. And no matter how much or how little she'd said, she wasn't sure he had heard any of it.

"You've boxed me in, Sam."

"If that's possible, I'm glad I have."

"She's a smart kid. She's going to know I don't want her. She's already decided she doesn't like me."

"The two of you are peas in a pod." Sam's knees shook. She leaned against the stove. "Give her a chance, Joe. Nobody's better with kids than you are. You don't have to love her. You just have to get along with her for a little while."

"I don't like ultimatums."

"Neither do I. But you've given me one right after another this year. I suppose my turn's been coming."

She could see he wanted to deny what she'd said, but he didn't. "One condition," he said at last.

"What?"

"You don't even think about keeping her."

Her gaze didn't waver. "She has a father."

"Who may not want her. Promise me if he doesn't, or if for some reason he's not acceptable to the state, you won't bring up adoption."

"I promise. Her stay will be temporary."

"Very temporary. It wouldn't be fair to Corey to give her false hope."

"I don't want this to come between us." She moved toward him. Slowly. Apprehensively. "We were just making a new start tonight."

"Were we?"

"We made love. And it felt new."

He didn't open his arms.

"This means the world to me, Joe."

"It must."

She stopped right in front of him. "I love you."

"You love me because I'm doing what you want."

"I love you because even though you're still wading around in your own pain, you're willing to help me with mine."

He opened his arms and enclosed her inside them. But even though they stood that way for a long time, when they climbed the stairs to bed, neither of them could think of another thing to say.

CHAPTER EIGHT

THE HOSPITAL WHERE Corey had been taken could have been plopped down unnoticed in any state of the union. The building was medium sized and nondescript, complete with the frog-pond cacophony of intercom, beepers and smiling personnel determined to give out as little information as possible.

Joe and Sam waited for the county social worker on imitation leather chairs in the lobby. After fifteen minutes Sam found a coffee machine and returned with a cup for each of them, only to find Joe immersed in conversation with a young brunette.

For a moment Sam wanted to throw herself between her husband and the dark-haired woman. Joe had been quiet on the long drive. Yes, he had agreed to take Corey, but only under protest. Perhaps even at this late date he had decided to renege.

Then she realized how little credit she was giving him. Joe never went back on his word.

She handed him one of the cups and extended her hand to the woman. "Miss Davis?"

The woman, cuter than she was pretty and young enough to be Corey's sister, stood to shake hands. "You must be Samantha. I was just telling Joe that Corey's been a terror. You're not going to have an easy time of it."

"Corey's always been a terror." Samantha didn't look at Joe. "We're prepared. Has she been told that she's coming home with us?"

"I told her last night. I'm sorry we had to wait so long, but I wanted to be sure all the paperwork was cleared up. I didn't want to disappoint her if we ran into any snags."

"How did she take the news?"

Miss Davis hesitated. "I don't think she believed me. She thought we were just trying to get her to behave."

"She's had a hard life. She doesn't have much reason to trust anything an adult says to her."

"But she seems to trust you." Miss Davis turned to Joe. "I'm wondering, though. Have you had much contact with Corey?"

"Enough to be fully aware what we're getting into."

"She, um, said that you don't like her very well."

"She's not the kind of kid you necessarily like on sight."

That seemed to satisfy Miss Davis. Sam appreciated Joe's tact. She owed him one. "Look, we know she's had a hard time, not just since the accident, but since she was born. But she responds to love. She's extremely bright, and she wants to please if she thinks it's possible."

"Well, I can't tell you how glad I am that somebody wanted her. I think we might have had some real problems finding a foster home. Very few marriages can withstand the testing of a troubled child."

Sam couldn't look at Joe. For the first time she had doubts about this decision. Their marriage was shaky. Was Corey going to be the final blow? "Can we see her now?"

"Your timing's good. She's just had her bath, and the doctor's discharged her. She should be ready to go home with you."

But she wasn't ready. When they entered the room at the far end of the pediatric wing, one nurse was holding Corey down as a second tried to comb her hair. Somewhere there was a karate studio willing to give a scholarship on the basis of Corey's perfectly aimed kicks.

"Corey!" Sam crossed the room and waved away the nurse with the comb. "What on earth do you think you're doing?"

Corey took one look at Sam and started to wail. Sam fell to the bed beside the little girl and put her arms around her. "It's okay, honey, you're going to go home with Joe and me."

"My mama's dead, Miss Sam. I ain't got nobody."

Sam held her tighter and rested her head against Corey's hair. Corey looked past Sam to Joe.

Sam couldn't see Corey's expression, but Joe could. Mixed with genuine misery was challenge. Her thoughts were visible to him. *I've got her now. See if you can top this, buster.* Joe told himself she was just a little girl. He told himself that she was a little girl whose life had been tough and sad.

He told himself that he and Sam were making a big mistake.

Sam put her hands on Corey's shoulders and gazed into her eyes. "I mean it, Corey. You're coming home with Mr. Joe and me until Miss Davis can find your father or somebody else in your family."

"I ain't got nobody. My daddy was s'posed to be living here, but my mama couldn't find him."

"Well, Miss Davis knows just how to look for him. She's going to do the best she can."

"I'm going to sleep at your house and stuff?"

"You certainly are."

"With him?" She hunched one shoulder at Joe.

"I'm not moving out for the occasion," Joe said dryly.

"We've fixed up a room down the hall from ours," Sam said.

"Do I have to go to school?"

"I don't know how long you'll be with us. But if you're still there when the school year starts you'll have to go to school, just like all the other children." Sam stood. "First you've got to let me comb your hair, though, or they aren't going to let you out of here."

"I got a bruise on my head. It hurts!"

"I'll be careful." Sam held out her hand to the nurse who gratefully presented her with the comb.

Joe watched as Sam lovingly combed the child's stubby locks. Corey sat absolutely still. Beside him Miss Davis murmured something.

"I'm sorry. What'd you say?" he asked.

She turned. He thought he saw commiseration in her eyes. "I wouldn't want to be the one who comes between those two," she said softly. "When I find Corey's father I'll let *you* be the one to tell your wife. And Corey."

COREY WALKED WITH a limp—an ankle was sprained and appropriately bandaged—but it didn't keep her from thoroughly exploring her new home.

"What's that?" she asked in Joe's study.

He stood in the doorway just waiting for her to destroy something. "Encyclopedias."

"What're they for?"

"To learn things."

"Anything you want?"

"Just about."

She pointed at the wall behind his desk. "What's that?"

"A mandolin."

"What's a mandolin?"

"It's an instrument, a little like a guitar. Do you know what a guitar is?"

"I'm not dumb."

"So you've told me before." He stepped into the room to keep a better eye on her as she wandered.

"Why's it up high like that?"

"I don't play it well, but I like to look at it. It belonged to my grandfather."

"Ain't nothing much. 'S all beat up."

"So was my grandfather."

To his amazement she giggled. It was a normal little-girl sound. "That's not very nice," she said.

"If my grandfather was still alive he would have been the first to say it. He was ninety when he died, and he could really play."

"Play it."

"I told you, I don't play very well."

"Let me play it."

"No." He crossed the room and reached for the mandolin, which hung beside a window. He leaned against the desk and strummed a few chords.

"'S that all you can do?"

"Afraid so."

"You ain't very good."

He put the mandolin back. "I think you've seen everything. From now on this room's off-limits. There's nothing to play with in here, but I have papers I don't want messed up. You'll need to stay out."

She frowned. "What kind of papers?"

"Boring ones. But Miss Sam's put drawing paper in your room, and if you need more we'll get you more. You won't need to take anything from in here."

"My room's awful big." She looked unsure of herself for a moment.

Sam had spent the weekend clearing out the sewing room upstairs for Corey. Once the room had been intended as a nursery, but those days were past. Since then Sam had taken it over for sewing and school work, but she hadn't seemed to mind turning it over to Corey. Against Joe's better judgment she had bought curtains and sheets covered with pastel kittens. She'd also bought a hundred dollars' worth of toys and supplies. He knew that tomorrow she intended to take Corey shopping for clothes. The hospital had provided the little girl with only the clothes she'd walked out in, and they were a size too large.

Joe felt a nudge of sympathy. He wondered what kind of sleeping arrangements she was used to. "Your room's not that big. And you can keep your door open at night."

"Don't need no door open. Ain't afraid."

"Good." He shooed her out of his study and toward the kitchen where Sam was just putting dinner on the table.

"I hope you like chicken," Sam said with a smile.

"Can we dig up Mr. Red tomorrow and see if he's all bones and stuff?"

Sam dropped the chicken on the table. "Whoops."

"Yeah, Sam, can we?" Joe asked.

She laughed. "Let's not talk about birds until after dinner."

"I want a drumstick." Corey reached across the table with her left hand. Her right was firmly held to her side in a sling.

"I'll get it for you," Joe said, moving the platter out of her reach. "You ask, and I'll serve you."

"I can get it by myself!"

"No, you can't. Because I won't let you." Joe ignored the plea in Sam's eyes. "This is the way we serve dinner here."

"Want a drumstick." She pulled her hand back, but her eyes were mutinous.

"May I have a drumstick, please?" he coached.

She narrowed her eyes and refused to speak. He ignored her and turned to Sam. "What would you like?"

"May I have the platter?" She narrowed her eyes. "Please?"

"Why, certainly. A pleasure to wait on such a well-mannered and spectacularly beautiful woman." He passed her the platter. "Would you please pass the mashed potatoes?"

"I…would…be…thrilled." She passed them.

"Corey, would you like some?" he asked.

She wove her uninjured hand into her sling and stared at him, her lip jutting a record two inches.

"More for me, I guess," he said. "That's good because I love Sam's mashed potatoes."

"I'll have some," Corey said. "Now!"

"May I have some, please?" he coached again.

"You already got some! The whole damn bowl!"

Sam sputtered. Joe couldn't risk even a glance at her. "You'll have to leave the table and eat by yourself if you talk like that while you're here, Corey. Use some manners and ask politely."

"I'm hungry! I ain't had hardly nothing to eat today."

He was not impressed. He had seen Corey eat the equivalent of half a cow at a fast-food restaurant that afternoon. He leaned forward. "May I have a drumstick, please?"

"Miss Sam, he's being mean to me!"

"Joe…"

He turned to Sam and lifted one eyebrow.

"Thank you for trying to teach Corey some manners," she said.

"You're very welcome." He turned back to Corey. "Chicken's getting cold, kid."

A lesser man might have been felled by the expression in her eyes. "May I have some chicken and some mashed potatoes and what all else that I got to say please about?"

"You certainly may." He helped her dish up her dinner. Then he sat back to eat his own. The three of them chewed in a silent truce.

COREY OPENED HER eyes. The room was dark, even though Miss Sam had left two night-lights burning. It smelled funny, too, like lemons and stuff. She liked the smell, but it sure didn't smell like home.

The bed was softer than any bed she'd ever slept in. She had wanted to keep her eyes open all night, so Miss Sam would stay. But she'd kept sinking down in the bed. Then she'd closed her eyes a little. Then next thing she knew, Miss Sam was gone.

Now Corey closed her eyes again, this time because she was frightened to leave them open. There were funny shadows in the room, like long bony fingers pointing right at her. Sometimes they moved. Miss Sam said they were just the shadows of tree branches, but Corey wasn't too sure. One of the shadows looked like the head of a monster, and she'd sure never seen no tree branch that looked like that.

Miss Sam had given her a teddy bear to keep in bed. It was brown, like a real grizzly bear. Miss Sam had given her a book last year about a grizzly bear, a book to take home and keep. She had said that Corey could have it because Corey read so well. Her mama had put the book somewheres and Corey had never found it again. But now her mama was gone. She couldn't take the bear the way she had taken the book.

Corey clutched the bear tighter. She had thought about her mama's death a lot. Mama had been so still when the men had gotten her out of the car. But she hadn't looked sad. Just kind of surprised.

Mama had been driving too fast; Corey remembered that. The car had sailed through the air and Corey's door had come open and she had fallen out before the car crashed. One of the policemen said she would have died, too, if she hadn't landed where it was swampy and all. She had heard him say it, and somebody had told him to be quiet 'cause she was listening.

She didn't miss her mama, and that probably meant she was bad. She was sorry Mama had died, but she didn't miss her. Mama had never been around much, and she hadn't wanted Corey, anyway.

She tried not to think about the things Mama had said that night, about how her father probably wouldn't want her, either, and how nobody would ever want her. Maybe her mama was wrong. Mr. Joe didn't want her.

He practiced looking scary on her, just like tonight at the table. But Miss Sam was glad she was here.

Corey opened her eyes. The shadows were still there. She closed them again. The bed was soft. Softer than anything.

"She's asleep."

"So am I." Joe rolled over and stared at the moonlight pouring in through a bedroom window. It was well past midnight.

"No, you're not. You don't talk in your sleep."

He felt the bed sink. The provocative woman scent that always set his body on fire drifted over him. A long, smooth leg settled against the length of his. He felt the softness of breasts sinking against his chest. He put his arm around Sam before he could think better of it.

"It's a gorgeous night," she said. "The air's as soft as butter, and the flowers in the yard smell like the end of summer. I can smell the roses on the breeze."

"You'd know about the night. You've been up for most of it."

"I know, but Corey was scared. She's not used to a room by herself. She says she always slept on a couch in the living room in front of the television."

"While her mother entertained in the bedroom."

"What?"

"That's the rumor."

"Well, I never heard it."

"If it's true, it makes it unlikely that Corey's father is going to be genuinely pleased to have her dropped on his doorstep."

"We'll see what happens. I just hope it's something good. Can you see now what a special little girl she is?"

"What's called for here, the truth or a husbandly lie?"

"You must see how smart she is, and funny and…"

"I'm waiting."

"And endearing."

"I see three hundred teenagers every day during the school year. Three hundred kids with bad attitudes and learning problems and adult-hating smirks on their faces. I'd trade her for any one of them."

"Joe!"

He gathered her a little closer. "Actually, not for either of the Symonds girls. One of them comes on to every male teacher in the school and the other one makes a Saturday run over to Raleigh every weekend for a new supply of drugs."

"What are you trying to say? Corey places an easy third?"

"I wouldn't trade her for most of the wrestling team, either. One of these days they're going to gang up and get me in a headlock in the hallway. That'll be that."

"Do you know what she told me?"

"I can guess. She told you I was picking on her to-night."

"She said looking at you is scary because you're so big."

"I hope I stay big while she's here, then. A little fear can go a long way."

"You don't really want her to be afraid of you."

"I want her to know that one of us isn't going to be a pushover." He felt her stiffen. He continued to hold her until she relaxed.

"Okay," she said after a while. "I guess I deserved that."

"She's a manipulator, Sam. She'll come between us in a heartbeat if we let her."

"She's a sad little girl who's never been loved."

"And she knows it." He caressed her arm. "But that's not entirely bad. She's a survivor. She uses what little she has to try to make a place for herself in the world. If she didn't, she'd be even sadder."

"You just said something nice about her."

"No, I didn't."

"I heard you!"

He felt her hair against his lips. He inched his lips to her cheek and felt the warm, smooth curve of her flesh. "There's nothing nice to say."

"Joe, I love you for this."

"For what? Holding my own? Holding you?"

"For being the man I married."

That man lived somewhere else, somewhere in a fantasy land peopled by small children with cocky Giovanelli grins. He didn't respond, but she didn't seem to notice.

"I need your love and patience now." She kissed the curve of his throat. Her hair drifted over his cheek. "If I didn't have it, then I wouldn't have any love or patience to give Corey. You know that's the real test of a man, don't you? The way he supports his woman when she really needs him?"

He knew the real test of a man.

She continued. "The way he comforts her. The way he makes her feel like a woman. The way he shares his life with her. I wonder why fathers don't teach that to their sons? This world's full of children put here by men who think the only way they have to prove their masculinity is to shoot a few sperm in the right direction."

She wasn't pulling any punches. She had danced around Joe's fertility problem for most of the year; now she was moving in for the kill. "I get your point, Sam." He didn't like the obvious tension in his voice. He didn't like the way she could see into his very soul.

"Not well enough. Let me show you what kind of man you really are."

Her hands were cool against his skin. He wanted to push them away, but he couldn't seem to move. Impotence was not his problem. She had only to look at him to arouse him. It seemed like a terrible joke.

"You're the kind of man who knows how to make a woman feel like she's beautiful," she said. Her lips trailed kisses along his jaw.

"You *are* beautiful."

"Not really. Pretty, maybe. I'll be an elegant old woman because my bones are good. But I lack the spark for beauty."

"Ridiculous." He found himself turning toward her.

"No. And it doesn't matter. You've always made me feel beautiful. When you hold me and make love to me, I feel like some combination of a supermodel and Hollywood star."

"Supermodel?" He laughed, and the sound drifted seductively on the warm summer air.

"Sure. You make me feel sexy. Hey, I could pose in the nude, too, if it was you behind the camera. But the pictures would be too hot to print."

"It had better be me behind that camera if you're posing nude."

"And you're the kind of man who knows just what to do when the going gets rough." She stroked her hand over his chest. Lightly and thoroughly. Again, then again. "Remember when I told my parents we were getting married, and my father said he'd cut me off if I married you? And you said that was great because you wanted the pleasure of supporting me all to yourself? Well, he's still mulling that one over. It's the only time in his life that he couldn't think of an appropriately quelling response."

"Fischer's not so bad."

"And you're the kind of man who forgives." She stroked her hand over his hip, circling, circling the part of him that was ready to sink into the very core of her.

"I would have walked out of their house in Chevy Chase and never looked back," she said, "but it might have ruined my life. You knew just how to handle my parents so that they had an open door when they needed one. And when they walked through that door you never said an unkind word to them. They're still trying to figure out why they can't seem to dislike you. God knows, they've tried hard enough."

"You're trying to drive me crazy." His voice was thick, charged with desire.

"*I'm* crazy. Crazy about you, Joe. You're the only man I'll ever want. You're too much man for me sometimes. I don't know what to do with you."

"I think you've got it figured out." He took her lips, tasted and silenced them. She was the flavor of the warm night, the rose-scented breeze, the moisture-laden air. Her flesh was as soft as the rich North Carolina earth. He pulled her on top of him to feel her closer, to stretch her lithe body along the length of his and relearn its familiar secrets.

"No! No!"

For a minute he couldn't imagine who was screaming. Then Sam stiffened. "Corey!"

"No." He couldn't believe it. He had been ready for anything except this.

Sam rolled to the bed beside him and swung her legs over the side. "She sounds scared to death!"

"Her timing is impeccable."

"You don't think she's making this up, do you?"

He didn't. He wanted to, but he didn't. Joe knew terror and what it sounded like. He had suffered nightmares after the death of his father, and his mother had always been there, despite her own sadness, to comfort him.

"I've got to go to her." Sam had already thrown on her robe. The words stayed in the room longer than she did.

Joe stared at the ceiling, at the way the moonlight softened the swirls of plaster and cast shadows that looked like the heads of gargoyles. Then with a harsh sigh he got out of bed and found his robe, too.

"I was looking in my mama's grave." In the doorway Joe saw that Corey was sitting up in the lonely twin bed, her face wet with tears and the bear Sam had bought her clutched tightly in her arms. Sam was on the bed beside her, with her arm around Corey's shoulders. "I was looking, and I saw Mr. Red, 'cept he was all bones and stuff. And my mama was turning into bones, too."

Sam pulled her closer. "When people die they don't feel anything anymore. Same thing for birds or anything that dies. The Bible says we came from dust and turn to dust. That's the way it's supposed to be. But the real part of us, the part that makes us what we are, goes on to another, better place. And that's where your mother is."

Joe had real doubts about that, but he sure wasn't going to tell Corey. As the years passed she would come to terms with her memories of Verna, in her own way and in her own time. Now Sam was right to offer her comfort.

"She died real quick. Maybe it was a mistake. Maybe I was the one s'posed to die."

"No. Things happen the way they're supposed to. You're supposed to grow up to be a wonderful woman and live a good and happy life."

"Like you?"

"I don't know about that. I just know you're supposed to be happy. Your mother would want you to go on and be happy."

Corey looked doubtful. She looked up and saw Joe standing in the doorway. Her expression seemed to say that she thought Sam was probably wrong about Verna, but Corey wasn't going to tell her so.

Something inside Joe did a funny little lurch. Corey obviously didn't want Sam to feel any worse than she already did. She was protecting Sam. Corey would keep her secrets about her mother to herself, even if it might feel pretty good to share them.

"Why don't you pack up your pillow and blanket and come sleep in our room for tonight?" he said. He didn't know where the words had come from, but they continued. "We'll make you a bed on the floor next to ours."

She narrowed her eyes. "You'll step on me!"

"If I do, I'll try not to put all my weight on you."

Sam laughed. The look she sent him was laced with gratitude. "Would you like that, Corey? It might not be so lonely."

"If I can sleep on your side, Miss Sam."

Sam laughed again. "I'm sure Mr. Joe won't mind. Will you, Mr. Joe?"

He was going to mind terribly. He had other things he'd rather do in his bedroom than babysit tonight. But it seemed that one small child was already taking over his life…and his wife.

"I sure hope you don't snore," he said.

"I don't!"

"I'll be sure to tell you if you do." He started for the bedroom to set up Sam's exercise mat and a pile of sleeping bags as a base for Corey's new bed.

In the hallway he felt a hand on his shoulder. He turned his head.

"You're the kind of man who does what's necessary, even if it's not the least bit fun," Sam said. She stretched up to kiss him, a soft, lingering kiss that was filled with promise.

"I'm the kind of man who can't say no when he ought to."

"I hope that's the case, because tomorrow night I want to hear a resounding yes to every suggestion I make."

His heart beat faster as he went to fix Corey's bed.

CHAPTER NINE

JOE WAS GONE the next morning by the time the county social worker arrived. Since he had early meetings he had promised to stop by her office in the afternoon to introduce himself and answer any questions she might have. Now Sam and Corey braved examination alone.

Dinah Ryan was a no-nonsense woman, in sensible shoes and a conservative suit, who drove a spiffy red sports car that made Killer look sedate.

"So, Corey, how do you like it here?" She looked over the top of her bifocals.

"I like it fine."

"Settled in all right?"

Sam answered for her. "Would you like to see Corey's room?"

"You mean the room where Corey is staying?"

Sam heard the difference and was properly chastised. "Yes." She led the way with Corey right behind her.

"Very nice." Miss Ryan ran her hand over Corey's new comforter, then picked up the teddy bear. "A new friend, I see."

Corey grabbed the bear out of her hands. "Mine."

"I'm sorry, sugar, I should have asked your permission."

Sam relaxed a little. At least Miss Ryan understood children.

"This is a very comfortable room," Miss Ryan said. "Did you sleep all right last night?"

"I slept with Miss Sam."

Miss Ryan lifted an eyebrow. "Oh?"

Sam answered. "She was frightened. We made her a bed on the floor beside ours."

"A good idea. For a little while."

Sam relaxed a little more. "Would you like to see the rest of the house? We'd like to take you to the duck pond if you have time."

"It ain't no pond," Corey said. "It's a lake!"

Sam smiled and smoothed Corey's hair back from her forehead. "Tell that to Mr. Joe sometime."

They toured the house slowly. After a few minutes it was clear that Dinah Ryan was more interested in the antiques that Sam and Joe had refinished and the history of the building than whether the house was suitable for Corey.

Outside, Corey, despite her limp, outdistanced them on the path down to the pond.

"I'd give my car and my mother's diamonds for more homes like this for our children." Dinah—formality had lapsed by the time they had reached the kitchen—spread her arms wide. "All this space. Everything's clean and tidy and open. You have room for half a dozen Coreys here."

"One Corey is plenty."

"I've followed her case for years. I can't tell you how many complaints we had about Verna Haskins. I shouldn't even tell you that much."

"Then why wasn't anything done?" Sam realized how belligerent she sounded. "I'm sorry. I'm sure you tried."

"And tried hard. It would have been easier if she beat

the child, but she didn't, or at least not often or brutally enough to qualify as abuse. But neglect is much more difficult to pin down. We can't take one set of standards and apply them to all families. Parents have different ways of raising their children. Sometimes the differences are cultural, sometimes it's just personality or ignorance. I can tell you that Verna was an abused child, herself. She didn't have much left inside her by the time she had Corey."

"My husband and I can't have children." Sam didn't know where that little piece of information had come from. It had just seemed the right thing to say.

"And you look at people like Verna Haskins and wonder about fate?"

"Sometimes."

"I didn't have children, because I never met a man I wanted to marry. Over the years I watched the way other people ruined the lives of the kids they'd had, and I got so angry."

"But not anymore?"

"I figure I've had half a dozen children by now, if you add up all the kids I've worked with and loved and let go of."

"That's a nice way to think of it."

"There is always more than one way to skin a cat."

Or make a family. Sam heard an open invitation. Dinah approved of her. Heartily. And she would probably approve of Joe. If Sam and Joe were interested in becoming foster parents, or in adoption…

"Do you have many children who need homes?" Sam couldn't resist the question.

"Not babies. Most of the children we get are like Corey. Placing a newborn is almost unheard of these days. But we have children with physical or emotional problems who need families. Sometimes we have siblings. We work hard to place them, but sometimes we have to resort to looking outside the county. And we'd much prefer to keep our children here if we can."

"What will happen to Corey if her father can't be found?"

"I'm not sure. What will?" Dinah inclined her gray head.

Sam couldn't answer. She knew what she was supposed to say, what she had promised Joe she would say, but somehow, the words just wouldn't come.

SADLERS WAS THE closest thing to a department store in Foxcove. There were several strip malls out on the highway with nationally known chains. But Sadlers, with its two stories of odds and ends packed into nooks and crannies, was much more fun to shop in.

Sam determined Corey's size with one agonizing fitting. The little girl's hips and back were black-and-blue, and between her sprained ankle and broken arm, trying on clothes was a miserable experience. But once Sam had a pretty good idea what would fit, the fun began. Corey, wide-eyed and—for the moment, at least—enraptured, sat on a bench while Sam brought her things to look at.

Corey liked bright colors, and they looked surprisingly good against her tanned skin. She liked pants and jeans, but there was also a wistfully feminine little girl deep inside her who responded with enthusiasm to a red plaid dress and a fuchsia skirt and blouse.

Sam discovered that she couldn't say no to anything Corey really wanted. She remembered shopping for clothes with her own mother. Kathryn had disapproved of most of her choices, and only rarely had Sam come home with anything that excited her.

Between that memory and the realization that Corey had never shopped for clothes at all, Sam knew she lost all perspective. Corey had grown up in hand-me-downs, and the expression on her face when she was allowed to choose what she wanted blotted out the sensible voice inside Sam that told her she was setting Corey up for a fall.

There was almost no chance that Corey's father would indulge her this way. And if she went to live in permanent foster care, it was doubtful that the state of North Carolina would spend money so lavishly.

But Sam couldn't resist.

Sam had an armful of bundles by the time they left Sadlers. In addition to everything else they had bought shoes and socks for school and play, a backpack for school—and notebooks and a pencil box to go in it—a sweater, in case it turned cold early, a hat to go with the sweater and half a dozen T-shirts and cotton shorts to last for the rest of the summer. Then there had been underwear, a new brush and comb, female fripperies for the youthful set.... The bill had been enormous.

Sam dumped the bags in the trunk of her car and slammed it just in time to see Polly and her youngest daughter, Mary Nell, who was just two years older than Corey, waving from across the street.

Sam crossed with Corey's hand in hers and greeted Polly and Mary Nell on the opposite sidewalk.

"Well, hello, Miss Corey," Polly said cheerfully. "My, don't you look fine in that cast. Looks to me like it needs some decoration. Don't you think, Sammy?"

"I think Miss Polly wants you to ask her to sign it," Sam explained to Corey.

"Me, too!" Mary Nell said. "I could draw a picture on it."

Corey seemed to like that idea. The four of them descended on the drugstore, which, despite bright, wide aisles and a thoroughly modern pharmacy, had left its old-fashioned soda fountain intact during remodeling.

They settled at a table and ordered root-beer floats. "Come on, let's go look at the toys while they're getting it." Mary Nell, a wiry bundle of energy, was up and out of the booth before Corey could respond. Corey hesitated and looked at Sam.

"Go on, honey. I'll be waiting right here."

Polly watched Corey follow Mary Nell's path. "I can't believe you've got her."

"You'd believe it if you saw what I just spent."

"Overdoin' it a bit?"

"A bit."

"What's Joe think about all this?"

Polly knew all about the problems between Joe and Sam. She was the only person to whom Sam had been able to pour out her heart after the final visit to the fertility specialist.

"He's tolerating her," Sam said. "He's been wonderful, actually, considering that I forced her down his throat."

"It's not so bad to force a good thing down a man's throat now and then."

"You think this is a good thing?"

"Could be."

"He was fantastic last night. Corey was scared, and

he made a bed on the floor beside ours so that she wouldn't be afraid."

"Sounds like our Joe."

"Then this morning he left with hardly a word to either one of us." Sam thought about the silent man who had shaved, dressed and grabbed a cup of coffee on his way out the door. Last night she'd thought they were making wonderful progress. This morning had been like old times—or new times. The tension between them had been going on for so long she wasn't sure what to call it now.

"You've never really understood what he's feelin', have you?"

Sam waited until the floats had been placed in front of them before she answered. The girls still hadn't returned. "I understand. I'm just tired of it. I have feelings, too."

"Sure you do. Difference is, you're supposed to. He's not."

"That's not fair."

"No? Don't you think you married Joe 'cause he's strong and sure of himself? He likes to take care of you and everybody else. Nothing stops him, least nothing did till now."

"I married him because I love him."

"But what was it you loved?"

All the things Polly had just named. The answer was so clear that Polly might as well have said that, too. Sam looked down at her float. "Darn you."

"Oh, you can do better'n that, Sammy. I deserve at least a damn or two."

"But I don't expect him to be strong all the time," Sam said. "I really don't."

"Then give him some more time. Joe's used to bein' strong. Now he doesn't see himself that way anymore. And if you start naggin' at him to be stronger, it's going to make him feel weaker. Do you see what I'm gettin' at?"

"You ought to go into counseling and put Dr. Ray out of business."

"Now wouldn't that be a kick in the head?"

THE DRUGSTORE'S TOY shelves were full of wonderful things. "Look at that." Corey pointed to a jigsaw puzzle with a picture of a teddy bear much like the one that Sam had given her. "And that!" She pointed to another.

"You ever been out to the toy store on the highway? They got lots of stuff there. Better puzzles than these. I've got a bunch, but I don't play with them much."

Corey liked puzzles a lot. It was like magic to take all those little, no-count pieces and put them together to make something big and pretty. At school, every time she put that last piece in she felt better about lots of things. She wasn't sure why.

"You can have them," Mary Nell offered. "Mine, I mean."

"Really?"

"Sure. I've done them all already. You'll have fun."

Corey couldn't imagine anyone just giving away toys like that. Mary Nell, with her long brown ponytail and rosy cheeks, looked so much like the little girls who had tormented her in school that Corey fully expected her to say she'd been lying. But Mary Nell moved down to the books. "Do you read yet?"

"Sure!"

Mary Nell looked doubtful. Corey chose a book, one

with a picture of a horse on its shiny cover, and started to read out loud. "When the little colt E-E-bony was born, he couldn't stand on his wobbly legs."

"Eb-ony." Mary Nell pronounced it correctly for Corey. "But that's very good. I couldn't read that good in first grade."

"I'm in second grade now."

Mary Nell sighed. "Yeah. School starts pretty soon. I don't want to go back."

Corey reluctantly put the book back on the shelf. She wanted to find out what happened to Ebony. "I like school."

"Really?"

"Miss Sam's nice to me."

"My mom says your mom died and now you're staying with Miss Sam. That's sad." Mary Nell brightened. "I know, let's get some markers to decorate your cast." She took off down the aisle before Corey could answer. Corey started after her at a fast limp.

By the time she reached the school supplies Mary Nell had chosen a big, fat box of markers. "We can pay for 'em on the way out. I need some for school, anyway." She took out a bright red marker and tested it on Corey's cast by drawing a big heart. "Look, they work good."

Corey took out a yellow one. She couldn't draw too well with her left hand—it wasn't good for much at all—but she managed to uncap the marker and start a yellow flower next to Mary Nell's heart.

"What are you girls doing?"

The two girls had been so absorbed in their artwork that they hadn't heard anyone approach. Now Corey looked up and saw a tall woman frowning down at them. Before either girl could answer, the woman took them by their arms. "Are you here with anybody?"

"My mom's at the fountain," Mary Nell managed to say as the woman began to drag them in that direction. "We were going to buy the markers. We were just trying 'em out."

"You certainly *are* going to buy them!"

Corey saw the look on Sam's face as she and Mary Nell were dragged toward the wrong table. Then she saw the look on the woman's face as Mary Nell pointed toward Miss Polly. "That's my mom," she said. "And that's Miss Sam. She's taking care of Corey now."

The woman dropped their arms. Mary Nell sprinted across the short distance and fell into the booth next to her mother. Corey didn't know what to do. Miss Sam stood and beckoned. Corey had never been so glad to be wanted in her life. She threw herself into Miss Sam's arms and buried her head against her.

"They were using markers on her cast." The woman said the last word as if it were somehow distasteful and pointed to Corey. "They didn't pay for them."

"We were going to pay for 'em on the way out," Mary Nell told her mother. "I needed some for school. Remember?"

"I certainly do remember." Polly looked the woman up and down. "Next time, why don't you check with me before you scare my daughter half to death?" she asked in her best first-grade-teacher voice.

"I'm sorry. I really am. I just saw her—" she pointed to Corey again "—and I thought there was some trouble."

"Well, the next time, why don't you check with *me,*" Sam said, "before you scare my...little friend here?

She's staying with me now, and I'll expect her to be treated like any other little girl in town."

"Well, she's stolen things before," the woman said.

"Just a candy bar." Corey still had her head against Sam's side. "Once. Just one time." She wanted to add that she'd been pretty hungry that day waiting for her mother to come back home, but she didn't think it would make any difference.

Sam reached into her purse and fumbled for a dollar bill. Her hand was trembling. She held it out to the woman. "Consider it paid for."

"I don't want your money, Mrs. Giovanelli. I just didn't know the—"

"Take it," Sam said through clenched teeth. "And then we can both forget this ever happened. But I expect you to give Corey a fresh start."

The woman looked helplessly at Polly. Polly nodded. The woman stepped forward and took the bill. "This really isn't necessary."

"I think it is. Corey's part of my family now, and the Giovanellis take care of their own."

Corey didn't understand exactly what Miss Sam was saying, but she knew that from that moment on she wasn't going to have to be afraid of anybody in town again. She felt the way she always did when she fit that last jigsaw-puzzle piece into place. She didn't know why. She just did.

JOE WATCHED COREY limp into the kitchen in one of the new outfits that Sam had bought for her. One of the many new outfits.

"It looks wonderful," Sam said enthusiastically. "You look wonderful."

"Don't," Corey said.

"You look very pretty," Joe said. "Did you get your hair cut, too?"

Corey looked away, obviously embarrassed at the attention.

"I took her in to my stylist to have her bangs trimmed and the rest of it shaped up just a little. She wants to let it grow long."

Like Sam's. Joe knew that as surely as if Corey had told him herself. If the child hadn't already worshiped Sam before today, now she would probably be willing to lie down on a holy altar as a human sacrifice to the goddess Samantha Giovanelli.

"How did you fit in all those appointments?" Joe had heard about trips to the pediatrician—Corey was basically healthy, although definitely undernourished; the dentist—Corey would definitely need more trips there; and now, the hairdresser. Not to mention a buying spree that would go down in Foxcove economic history.

"Well, we worked hard," Sam answered. "That's why we're having pizza from town. Besides, it's one of Corey's favorites."

"What don't you eat?" Joe asked Corey.

The little girl seemed perplexed, and he felt immediately ashamed of himself for putting her on the spot. "How do you feel about spinach?"

"Don't know."

He wondered if she had ever eaten vegetables at home.

Sam seemed to read his mind. "Corey's going to help me in the vegetable garden tomorrow. Then we're going to cook whatever we pick for dinner."

Corey wasn't as big as the row of withering cornstalks in the back of the garden or the hoe that Sam would probably give her to wield. She would be nothing but a threat to all vegetable life and a huge distraction. But Sam seemed hardly able to wait for the experience.

Joe could feel something simmering inside him. It had simmered since the morning and heated up since he'd come back home to find Sam and Corey trooping inside with half a ton of shopping bags. He didn't begrudge the money. His feelings had nothing to do with money.

"Corey, run on upstairs and wash your face and hands," Sam said. "Then why don't you unpack the puzzles Mary Nell gave you and start one on your desk? I'll call you when the pizza's ready."

Corey looked rebellious at the first suggestion, but the second seemed to intrigue her. She left the kitchen, and Joe could hear her clattering up the stairs in her new shoes.

"That was another stop I didn't tell you about," Sam said. "Mary Nell insisted we follow Polly home so she could give Corey about two dozen puzzles and a bagful of books, besides. You should have seen Corey's face."

"Thunderstruck, I'd imagine," Joe said.

"At least that. Anyway, this will keep her busy for a while so you and I can chat in peace. How was your day?"

"Calm by comparison."

"Oh, come on, things at the high school are never calm. Even when the kids aren't there yet."

He described his day in as few words as possible. She didn't seem to notice his brevity.

"Well, it sounds as if the year's getting off to a good start," she said.

He watched as she bent over to slide the pizza, cardboard box and all, into the oven. When she straightened her cheeks were flushed with heat. "I feel like I accomplished about a bazillion things today. And I'm still brimming with energy." She smiled, a seductive Samantha smile. "I hope you are, too, because I seem to remember we have plans for later."

He saw the sparkle in her eyes, the flush that wasn't fading in the cooler air, and he knew why she felt so alive. Not because of him and a promised night of lovemaking, but because today she had lived out her fantasies of motherhood, fantasies that his sterility had made impossible.

"Playing fairy godmother must be energizing," he said.

"Is that what I was doing?" she asked, still smiling.

"Yes. To Corey's Cinderella."

The smile faded slowly. "You're angry, aren't you?"

"No. I'm not angry. I just see the handwriting on the wall."

"What do you mean?"

"Do you know what it's going to be like for that child when she has to leave? Anybody ever give you a Christmas package and then snatch it away at the last minute?"

She looked away. "I thought about that. I really did."

"Not hard enough."

She drummed her fingers on the stove. "What was I supposed to do, Joe? Was I supposed to treat her like a secondhand piece of merchandise so she won't get used to feeling special? Should I have done all her shopping at the Goodwill store? Bought her only a couple of things and washed them every night?"

"You overdid it, big time."

"All right, I did. Like I said, I knew it. But I couldn't seem to stop myself. I remember what it was like to be that age. I can't tell you what I would have given to have someone focus on me and what I wanted."

"You? You had everything! What did you ever want that you couldn't have?" The words were out of his mouth before he could take them back. And it took only a second to realize how wrong and how cruel they were.

"I was given everything my parents thought I should have and not one thing more. And nobody ever looked me in the eye or paid attention to who I really was. Not until you came along."

He felt lower than an earthworm. He stood and took her in his arms. "I'm sorry."

She pulled away. "You know what I think? I think you're right. In the short term caring so much for Corey might make it harder for her when she has to leave. But I'm willing to take the chance that in the long run she'll remember that somebody did care, somebody paid attention, and it'll make her a happier, more secure person."

"No. You're setting her up."

Sam kept her voice low. "You're setting *me* up. You didn't want Corey here and you still don't. And now it's eating you up because it means so much to me. Today was wonderful, and now you're trying to make it a lot less so. You've forgotten how to look me in the eye and see what I really need. You've forgotten how to pay attention to anybody but yourself!"

"I'm not talking about you or me. I'm talking about that little girl and what's best for her." But even as he proclaimed his innocence, Joe knew she was right.

"Do you even care?" she asked. "Can you remember

how to care about a kid, Joe? Or did you stop caring the day you found out that you were never going to father one of your own?"

COREY WASHED HER hands and face, even though she didn't see why she should. Miss Sam had funny ideas about how clean a little girl should be. Sometimes she was afraid her skin was going to peel right off the way Miss Sam scrubbed. Washing the hand in the cast was hard, and using one hand to wash her face was harder. But she managed.

In her room she peered around warily. There were no shadows now. It was still early, and the room looked pretty nice. There were kittens on the curtains just like the ones on the bed. They looked alive, and almost as pretty as Tinkerbelle's kittens. Miss Sam had let Corey hold Tink's kittens in the summer, when she had brought Mr. Red here for her to fix. Corey was sorry the kittens were all grown up now and gone.

She hugged her bear, then stuck it down between her cast and her body. The cast was a lot prettier now. Mary Nell could draw real good. She thought maybe Mary Nell was going to be her friend.

She put the puzzles on the shelf that Miss Sam had said to use for her toys. Having toys of her own felt kind of strange. She'd had a few from time to time, but never so many and all at once. Besides the puzzles and books there was the bear, and all kinds of things to draw and color on and with. And there was a doll that sat in the corner and stared at her. Miss Sam said it was mostly a looking doll because it was very old, but she said that tomorrow she and Corey would shop for a playing doll.

Corey wondered if they really would.

She saved the best puzzle to dump out on the desk. It was a big one, with lots of bitty little pieces. The picture on the front of the box was a farm, with cows and horses and a little girl—blond like her and Miss Sam—feeding a rooster and a whole flock of hens. She was just about to start it when she heard voices downstairs.

They weren't loud voices, but they weren't talking voices, either. Frowning, she went to the door and poked her head into the hallway.

She couldn't hear what Mr. Joe was saying, but he sounded angry. When Miss Sam answered, she sounded angry, too, almost as angry as she had sounded at the drugstore.

Corey remembered the way Miss Sam had talked to the lady at the store. She hadn't even asked Corey why she had stolen the candy bar that time. She had stuck up for Corey then, and Corey thought maybe she was sticking up for her again with Mr. Joe.

The thought pleased her. She liked Miss Sam a lot, but Mr. Joe was another thing. He didn't like her. She could tell. She guessed he would do just about anything to make her leave. But maybe if he and Miss Sam were mad at each other, he would leave instead.

That thought gave her real pleasure. If Mr. Joe left, then Miss Sam might just keep Corey there. She would need company, wouldn't she? And Corey could help out and stuff. She could do lots of things.

The voices stopped. When Miss Sam finally called her to dinner, Mr. Joe wasn't there anymore. Miss Sam said that he'd had to go out for a while. Sitting next to Miss Sam at the table, Corey hoped that he wouldn't ever find his way back home.

CHAPTER TEN

SAM KISSED HER mother's cool cheek and inhaled a faint drift of the specially blended scent that was as much a part of Kathryn Whitehurst as her perfectly groomed blond hair. Kathryn was dressed in clothes only she would consider perfect for a Labor Day family barbecue: white linen slacks with a knife-edged crease that pointed the way to powder blue sandals, a short-sleeved blue silk sweater and understated platinum jewelry. Never mind that a drop of barbecue sauce would ruin the slacks, a walk to the pond would ruin the sandals. This was Kathryn at her most casual. Sam was learning to be tolerant.

"I wish you could have come to see us, Samantha," Kathryn said after she had pulled away. "This was too much of a trip after all the traveling we did this summer."

"I know, but it would have been Thanksgiving before Joe and I could have gotten out of town. School starts tomorrow. I'm glad you decided to come."

"Your father decided." Her tone implied that she had been against it, but Sam suspected that Kathryn found some sort of pleasure in getting together with Joe's family, even if it was just perverse fascination that her only child had married into such a rowdy crew.

"Well, I fixed your favorite picnic food, just to make it worth the trip," Sam said.

"It was worth the trip just to see you," Kathryn said, unbending just a trifle. "And to catch a glimpse of this child we've heard so much about."

"You'll probably only catch a glimpse. Corey's off playing somewhere with the nieces and nephews." Sam turned to greet her father, who had been on the other side of the car talking to Joe. Joe was always unfailingly polite to both of her parents. He found them every bit as fascinating as they found the Giovanellis.

She said all the appropriate things to her father and listened politely to his responses, but her eyes flicked over and over again to Joe. His polo shirt was a blinding white against his tanned skin, and his shorts were just tight enough to hint at delicious secrets.

Unfortunately everything about Joe was secret these days. In the weeks since Corey had come to live with them he had thrown himself into his work with a fervor that, even for Joe, was obsessive. Sometimes she found herself longing for the days before Corey had come, days when there had been the occasional, if rare, shared moment. Since the day she and Corey had come home from their marathon shopping trip, Joe had been a total stranger.

Sometimes she wasn't even sure she was still a married woman.

Joe caught her gaze and held it as her father made one more comment about the house. Something simmered behind Joe's dark stare. She didn't know what; she would probably be the last to know. She wanted to take him by the arm, lead him into a sheltering bough of pine trees and demand that he talk to her. But she knew where that would lead. Nowhere. And she wasn't Kathryn and Fischer Whitehurst's daughter for nothing. She knew the duties of a hostess.

She settled her parents on the front porch with drinks and Rose. Rose adored Kathryn because she listened raptly to Rose's stories about her grandchildren. Sam suspected that her mother was in the market for a couple of grandchildren of her own, even though she had never mentioned the subject to Sam. Sam hadn't yet told her that there would be no children with Whitehurst-Giovanelli blood running through their veins.

Back in the empty kitchen she stood at the counter for a moment, resting before the next onslaught of guests. All Joe's family had been invited, along with Polly and her husband and Mary Nell, who to Sam's surprise seemed to genuinely enjoy spending time with Corey. Johnny and Teddy were already down at the pond with their children, who were having the last swim of the season. Francis and his brood were there, too, along with one of Joe's sisters and her family. The others would probably arrive later because they had farther to come.

She felt warm hands on her shoulders before she even knew that Joe was there. "Do you need any help in here?" he asked.

She experienced the rumble of his deep voice in parts of her body that had nothing to do with her hearing. She leaned against him, and his arms came around her. For a moment she was frightened to breathe, frightened that anything would scare him away.

"I could make another gallon of lemonade, boil water for tea, make more hamburger patties," he offered.

"Just do what you're doing."

He nuzzled an ear. "I'll add a thing or two."

"Oh, by all means."

"Mama's showing your mother my baby pictures."

"She's sure my mother loves you like a son."

"She can't imagine anyone who doesn't adore me."

"Neither can I." Sam turned in his arms and threaded hers around his neck. "I adore you."

He didn't smile, but his gaze remained fixed on hers. "I don't know why. But I'm damned grateful."

"Joe—"

He put his finger on her lips. "Shh... This isn't the time or place for confessions. But I'm sorry. I've made the past few weeks harder for you than they needed to be."

She kissed his finger; then she kissed him. He tasted like hickory smoke and sunshine, the end of warm summer days. "It's an adjustment having Corey around. I know it's hard sometimes."

"She's not your garden variety seven-year-old."

"That she's not."

"You're wonderful with her."

She glowed from the compliment. "Really? Do you think I'm doing all right?"

"I think you're spoiling her rotten, but along the way you're teaching her patience and manners. Even self-discipline."

"I'm still spoiling her?"

"The last part of the critique was the most important."

"Maybe I just need your level head to guide me."

He didn't answer, and she didn't push. "Let me finish up in here and I'll meet you down at the pond. You can take the cooler with the meat in it," she said.

"You don't need any help?"

"Everything's all done. All we need now are extra arms to carry things down to the picnic tables."

"I'll send likely candidates your way." He kissed her once more before he left the kitchen. The day took on a decidedly rosier glow.

She was packing a jug of lemonade and containers of salad into a box for someone to carry down to the pond when Corey ran inside through the kitchen.

"Corey!" Sam called her back.

"What?"

"What on earth have you been doing?" Sam had helped Corey choose her clothes that morning. Not one of the Giovanellis would care if Corey spent the day in rags, but Sam's mother would.

Sam wanted her parents to like Corey. She wanted them to see her for what she really was, a wonderful little girl with a facade that just needed an alteration or two. Her manners were improving, and so was her grammar. She laughed occasionally now, and the nightmares were disappearing. But none of those improvements were visible at first glance, and the visible improvements, the fading bruises, the weight she had already gained, were hopelessly obscured now by a layer of dirt.

"Corey?" Sam asked when the little girl didn't answer.

"I was digging for treasure!"

"Treasure?"

"Yeah. Patrick said there was treasure in the woods. Me and him and Mary Nell were digging for it."

"Find anything?"

"A whole lot more dirt!"

"Looks that way."

Corey took off.

"Corey!" Sam went after her. "Where are you going?"

"I'm gonna swim."

"You're going to wade," Sam said.

Corey narrowed her eyes. It had been a terrible temptation all summer to have the pond so close. But with the cast on her arm, she hadn't been able to do more than sink her toes in the soft mud of the pond bottom. And that wasn't much fun.

"You're going to have to jump in the bathtub first before you put on your suit," Sam said.

"But I'm gonna be in the water! I'll get clean."

"You have to take a bath."

"Why?"

Why, indeed. Because Sam didn't want her mother and father to pass judgment on the grubby little urchin standing in front of her. First impressions were important. But she didn't want to admit that out loud.

"Because you'll get dirt all over your bathing suit. And only your legs will get clean in the pond," Sam said. "Now scoot. You don't have to stay in long."

Corey looked rebellious, but she didn't argue. A few minutes later Sam heard the sound of water running.

"I wish you'd let me get you some household help," Kathryn said from the doorway, when everything was packed and ready for the trip to the pond. "Just someone to come in a couple of times a week to clean and cook."

"I don't need help. I like doing it myself."

"Do you?" Kathryn seemed genuinely interested.

"I like taking care of my family."

"Family? You and Joe and that little girl?"

"Corey."

"I'm still surprised that you and Joe took in some-one else's child."

Sam heard all the things her mother didn't say. "It's temporary, Mother. Just until they can find her father."

"They haven't found him yet?"

"No. Apparently he moves frequently." Sam didn't add how unhappy that piece of news—delivered the previous week by Dinah Ryan—had made her. Apparently Corey's father hadn't lived in Spartanburg for more than five years, and Verna Haskins hadn't even been aware that he had moved. They had traced him to two more towns, but the trail had since grown cold. If Corey's father was ever located and he wanted his daughter, Corey would live the life of a vagabond.

"Well, it's kind of you to take her...."

"She's a wonderful little girl." Sam heard the water stop. "She'll be down in a minute."

"Isn't this rather an odd way to start a family?" Kathryn asked.

"I told you. It's temporary."

"You always wanted to take in strays."

Sam faced her mother. "Corey is not a stray. She's a child. And if you'll give her a chance, you'll see just how wonderful she is. But if you look at her like some mangy hound dog who followed me home from school one day, then you'll be missing something pretty special."

"About that mangy hound dog..."

Sam realized that what she had meant as merely a figure of speech had really been more. Now she re-membered that there had been such a dog. Once, when she wasn't much older than Corey. The dog had been whisked away at the Whitehurst front door on Kathryn's command, and Sam's heart had been broken.

"I'd forgotten," Sam said, turning away. "There was a stray once, wasn't there? And you disapproved."

"No, actually, I took him to the vet, or rather, I had someone on staff do it. Melwin, I think."

"Melwin never told me."

"We didn't want you to know. The dog was sick, too sick to help, as it turned out. He died after a week of treatment. We thought it would be better for you to think that we had just chased him away."

"What?" Sam sneaked a peek at her mother. "Mother, you have a soft heart."

"Absolutely not." But Kathryn looked pleased with herself.

They talked about the Whitehursts' trip to Europe and friends that Sam knew until their fund of small talk ran out. Corey chose that moment to arrive. She had put on her suit backward, and her hair stood in wet spikes all over her head. Sam could see that she had tried to wash herself, but with one arm that had to be held out of the water, she hadn't succeeded very well.

"Come here, honey," she said. Sam took a clean dish-cloth from a drawer. "You missed a spot or two."

"I want to go to the lake!"

"I'll bet. And you can go just as soon as you put your bathing suit on right and let me wash your face and neck."

"I don't want to!"

"I don't blame you. It's hot, and you want to get in the water. But you have to let me wash your face."

Corey's eyes were slits in her face, and her bottom

lip hung nearly to her chin. Sam turned away to wet the washcloth. And when she turned back, Corey was gone.

Sam saw the look of consternation on her mother's face. She chalked one up for Corey.

"Guess who that was?" Sam said with a nonchalance she didn't feel. She had wanted Kathryn to approve of Corey. It had been important to her, although she wasn't sure why.

"Samantha, what have you gotten yourself into?"

Corey came streaking back through the kitchen. Joe walked through the door a few moments later. "Upstairs," he told her in his best high-school-principal voice. "Turn the bathing suit around, wash your face and comb your hair."

Sam stared at him.

"I gather she was escaping," he said.

"How did you know?"

"She knocked down a Giovanelli and a Carter on her flight out of the house. Not to mention that she kept looking over her shoulder."

Sam had never been more grateful to him. "Thanks. I was going to come after her."

"Looks like you're busy. I'll just station myself at the bottom of the stairs and do a little inspection when she comes back down. Did I miss anything?"

"That'll do."

"So you've met Corey?" Joe asked Kathryn.

"Not exactly." Kathryn shook her head. "Samantha was just trying to explain why you've taken her in. Something about a wonderful little girl."

"She's not a bad little monster," Joe said. "Give her a chance. You might grow to like her."

Joe went to stand at the bottom of the stairs as Sam stared at his retreating back.

THE AFTERNOON WAS cloudless, the sky as blue as Samantha's eyes. But even if the weather had cooperated fully for a perfect Labor Day party, one small girl had not.

Joe watched Corey skipping stones over the surface of the lake. She missed one of his nephews, Magdalena's son, by inches.

Sam missed the entire breathtaking event, but Joe saw that Kathryn and Fischer had not. They exchanged looks that said what they thought of this child from the nether regions. He imagined that Sam, on the very worst day of her childhood, had never behaved half so outrageously.

Joe strolled to the edge of the pond and squatted beside Corey. She tried to move away, so he put his arm around her. Firmly. "You're about to go inside for the rest of the day."

"Let go!"

"Be smart and don't struggle. I'm bigger than you."

"Can't make me do nothin'," she said bravely. But she stopped trying to get away from him.

"Now, here's the deal. I know it's hot, and you want to swim. And I know you feel strange because everybody knows everybody else and you're new—"

"Don't care."

"And I know Miss Sam's too busy to hang all over you today."

"You're mean!"

"You're not the first kid who's thought so. But if you can behave a little better, even just a little, like stop throwing stones at people and stop spitting in the water, things like that, then I'll take you swimming. All the way in."

She was as stiff as her cast, but Joe could feel her yearning to believe him. He knew kids, and despite all his efforts, he was beginning to know this one in particular.

"Miss Sam says I can't go in the water," she said.

He felt a moment of real admiration. Despite her desperate longing to get in the water with the other children, her loyalty to Sam was more important.

"I'll clear it with Miss Sam. We'll wrap your cast in plastic bags, and I'll carry you out, so you can hold it out of the water."

"You won't drown me, or nothing?"

"With all these people watching?"

That seemed to impress her. He released her and stood. "But remember what I said. I've got to see some better behavior from you, or the deal's off."

"How long?"

"How long what?"

"How long I gotta be good?"

"As long as it takes to show everybody you're not really a devil child."

Clearly she thought that was a long, long time. On that one thing at least, they agreed.

He went back to his table, where Rose was rhapsodizing about something that Corey had said to her. Rose was used to bratty little kids. She'd given birth to a full measure herself. Joe supposed that Johnny had told her that Joe wouldn't be making her a grandmother again. She'd never said a word to him about it, but she seemed to have fully accepted Corey as a surrogate, despite the fact that Corey's days in their home were numbered.

"Then she says, she says, 'Well, how come, if you're Mr. Joe's mama, you don't make him come and live with you?'"

Joe grinned, despite himself. He caught Sam's eye, and she was smiling, too. "She'd like nothing better," he said. "Then she'd have Miss Sam here all to herself."

"Don't you think the child needs more…help than the two of you can give her?" Kathryn asked. "I mean, she's…" Her voice trailed off, as if there was no word strong enough that a woman of breeding could use.

"She's what, Mother?" Sam asked, a decided edge to her voice. "Lively? Spirited? Normal, considering what she's just been through? I think Joe and I can handle that."

Joe was always captivated when Sam stood up to her parents. Through the years of their marriage Sam had always chosen her battles well, ignoring the small skirmishes to save strength for those that were needed to win the war. Until now the war had been her self-esteem and independence. It seemed a new war had just been declared.

"Don't dance around it, Samantha," Fischer said, always the businessman cutting straight to the point. "The child's got problems. I don't understand why you're putting yourself through such a difficult time when she's going to be leaving, anyway. You've got enough to handle, don't you? And surely you're planning to have children of your own to lavish some of this attention on."

"No, sir," Joe said. "We won't be having children of our own." He waited until Fischer looked at him. "We can't and won't be able to conceive."

There was shocked silence. Kathryn was the first to breach it. "But surely there are doctors who can help."

She turned to her daughter. "They're doing so much now. A friend of mine is married to one of the best fertility specialists in Maryland. I can get you an appointment—"

"I'm the one with the problem," Joe said. "Not Sam. And there's nothing to be done."

"The problem is both of ours," Sam said. "No matter who got the wrong end of the diagnosis. Joe and I can't have children, and that's that."

"So now you're taking in other people's problems? I don't understand the point," Fischer said. "What do you have to gain? That child is obviously not from a good family, and from the looks of her there's not much you'll be able to accomplish. She's rude and hostile and probably not very bright. She's not even pretty."

Joe saw the horror on Sam's face. He saw Kathryn's eyes widen in dismay. He didn't even chance a glance at his mother, who was probably gasping for breath.

He didn't know he was standing until he felt the ground firmly under his feet. "That *child*," he said slowly and distinctly, "is a member of my family. She may not be a permanent member, but as long as she's living here, she's mine. I hope you'll reconsider your opinion, Fischer, but if you don't, Sam and I don't want to listen to it again."

Now Fischer looked as shocked as everyone else at the table. Sam stood, too. "I think it's time to bring out the desserts. Joe, will you help?"

She marched off. He joined her on the path back to the house, waiting as Francis's children passed before he spoke. "I'm sorry," he said.

"For what? For putting old Fischer in his place? It was masterful. I wish I could have done it as well."

He stopped her with a hand on her shoulder. Her eyes were glowing, but not with anger. "Just be sure you understand," he said.

"Understand what?"

"That I was reacting to your father's attitudes, Sam. What would life have been like for you if you hadn't met his standards? What if you hadn't been intelligent enough? Or, God forbid, pretty?"

"I guess I'll never know."

He saw that she did know, that all her life she'd fought for approval from both her parents when they hadn't had it in their hearts to give. He pulled her close for a rib-crushing hug.

"You stood up for Corey," she said against his chest.

"I'm a sucker for lost causes. That's all."

"What's life going to be like for Corey if nobody ever approves of her?"

"Corey's going to make it. She's a survivor, a tough little bird."

"You're standing up for her again."

"Not a chance."

She kissed him. He felt warmth flowing through him that had nothing to do with North Carolina sunshine. Then he felt something—or someone—tugging at his shirt.

"I been good a long time," Corey said.

He moved away from Sam to gaze down at the intruder. She was dirty again, and her cheeks were flushed from the heat. Her eyes were narrowed into slits. Most of the time he couldn't see enough of her eyes to tell what color they were.

"Not long enough," he said.

He watched her droop, a black-eyed Susan wilting in the sun.

"But I'll take you swimming anyway," he added.

She didn't smile or say thank-you, but he knew her well enough now to see that she was grateful. After all, she didn't kick him or spit on his shoe.

IT HAD FELT funny to have Mr. Joe hold her in the water. His hands didn't feel like Miss Sam's, all soft and smooth. They were giant, wide hands that could crush her if he wanted. But he didn't. He held her just tight enough so she wouldn't sink.

At first she was scared. She didn't know how to swim, and if Mr. Joe dropped her where it was deep, she figured she'd drown real quick. But after a while she knew he wasn't going to drop her. Miss Sam liked her and all. It would be pretty hard to explain to Miss Sam that Corey was lying on the bottom of the lake somewheres.

It was a lake, too, not a pond like Miss Sam always said. Mr. Joe told her how it used to be nothing but a spring at the bottom of a hill, and how his brother Francis had come in with bulldozers and giant machines to make a lake. She couldn't imagine such a thing. She wished she had lived here then, just to see it.

She had been sorry when it was time to get out. Mr. Joe brought her up to the grass and wrapped her in a towel. Then she felt just like all the other kids. They were wet, too, shivering while the sun dried them off. Mary Nell had asked her if she wanted to play hide-and-go-seek, and she'd said sure. Mr. Joe had told her not to get too dirty again, or he'd have to throw her in the lake and leave her this time.

But he'd smiled when he said it. Then he'd gone off to help Miss Sam. She wondered if they were kissing again. If Mr. Joe and Miss Sam did a lot of kissing, it meant that Miss Sam wasn't going to need her to stay around and all, 'cause Mr. Joe wasn't going to leave.

By the time the sun went down, most of the other kids were gone. Only Erin, Patrick and Shannon were still around. Miss Sam's parents and Grandma Rose were gone, too. She'd wanted to like Miss Sam's parents, but she hadn't. Miss Sam's father didn't know how to smile, and her mother kind of looked like she smelled something bad all the time. Grandma Rose was different, though. She laughed a lot, and sitting on her lap just seemed like the right thing to do.

"Hey, Corey, want to go down to the fort?"

Next to Mary Nell, Corey liked Patrick the best of all the kids who had been at the party. He was seven, too, and he had red hair that stuck out all over his head, just like hers did sometimes. He was bigger than her, but he didn't act like it mattered.

She wanted to go. The grown-ups were just sitting inside the house now, talking and drinking coffee. The kids weren't supposed to leave the yard. With the lake and all, Miss Sam got worried if they went off where nobody could see them.

But Patrick didn't want to go in the lake. He wanted to play in the fort—she let him call it that, instead of playhouse. Forts were fun, too.

She looked around. Erin and Shannon were up on the porch, playing with Tinkerbelle. They weren't old enough to go anywhere in the dark. But she and Patrick could find their way along the path. Maybe they could just go for a little while.

Somebody came to the window and looked out. It was Miss Teddy. Corey stood where she could be seen, then as soon as Miss Teddy left she motioned to Patrick. In a minute they were running toward the fort.

She stopped just before the entrance. "What do you want to do?"

"Let's go inside and see if there's any ghosts."

"Ghosts?" She didn't like that idea.

"Yeah, Indian ghosts. Used to be Indians around here. My daddy said so."

Corey let Patrick go inside first. The fort was real dark now without sunshine coming through the windows. It didn't look friendly. "Don't like it here," she said.

"Ghost gonna get you."

"Ain't no ghosts in here."

"Just can't see 'em."

She didn't want to believe him, but there was a sound outside now, like somebody moaning. Sometimes when her mama had left her alone at night she'd been afraid of ghosts, so she'd turned on all the lights. But there weren't any lights in the fort.

"I'm going back."

"Scaredy-cat," Patrick said.

He was right, and that made her doubly furious. "Am not!"

"Want to see if there's really ghosts?"

She stopped in the doorway. "How?"

"Light a fire."

"How're we gonna do that?"

"I'll show you." Patrick led the way outside to the stone ring that Mr. Joe and Mr. Johnny had built close to the water. There were coals glowing inside it, left from the wood Mr. Joe had used to cook with. And the metal grates were stored away now, so the coals were easy to reach. "We can take some of those inside the fort and build a fire. Then we can see everything."

Corey was doubtful. She didn't even know how they were going to get the coals. But before she could tell him, Patrick went down to the water's edge and came back with a metal pail that some of the kids had used to make castles with. Icky mud castles.

"We can put 'em in here." Patrick scooped the coals into the bucket with a stick. "Get some wood."

Corey was excited now. It would be their own campfire. Like they lived in the fort all the time, or something. Beside the stone ring she found branches and a small log that hadn't been burned. Then she followed Patrick inside the fort. The wood was dry and the coals were still hot. There was wind blowing through the door and windows of the fort. Pretty soon the camp fire was burning.

"See," she said. "No ghosts. Told you."

Patrick looked disappointed. The light from the fire was so bright she could tell he wasn't happy. "I'm going to get more wood. There's ghosts here. I know it."

The night air was cool and the fire was warm. She was glad to be sitting beside it. When Patrick returned he threw a stick nearly as big as he was on the fire. The flames leaped higher.

"Still ain't no ghosts," Corey said. She watched the flames climb nearly to the roof. Patrick knew how to make a real good fire.

"I guess there's not," Patrick said.

"Miss Sam's gonna be wondering where we are."

"Yeah." Patrick stood, and Corey stood with him.

"Gotta put this out first before we go back." The floor was covered with pine needles. He kicked pile after pile into the fire. The fire burned brighter and higher. He frowned. In the firelight Corey could see he was worried.

"We could throw some water on it," Corey said, remembering the pail.

They ran out the door together to go down to the lake. At the water's edge Corey swung the pail down deep, then turned. Smoke was pouring out of the fort now, through the windows and door. As she stared, the roof burst into flames. From the direction of the house she heard Miss Sam calling her name.

"At least neither of them were hurt," Sam said. "And it didn't spread to the woods. We were lucky they didn't start a forest fire."

"Why'd they do it?" Joe looked over the smoldering heap of ashes that had been the fort he'd built for the children he would never have.

"Corey says they were looking for ghosts."

There had been ghosts in the fort, but none Corey could see. Joe jammed his hands into his pockets.

"Patrick insists it was his idea," Sam said. "He was very gallant."

"Well, he's going to be very sore tomorrow. Johnny's raising his kids like we were raised. Swat, forgive, forget."

"Joe, I'm sorry. You worked so hard, and the fort was wonderful. All the kids are going to miss it when they come over."

"She has to be punished."

Sam moved away. He could feel the space. "Why?

She knows she did something wrong. And she was scared to death when the fire started. Isn't that enough?"

"She knew she was supposed to stay close to the house. She knew she wasn't supposed to go down to the water without an adult. That's been the rule since the first day she came to live with us."

"I think she's been punished enough. Please. Let's just let it go."

"Earlier you said you needed my level head where Corey's concerned. Well, here it is. If she thinks she can get away with anything she does, she'll just keep doing more and more." Joe folded his arms. "You feel so sorry for her, Sam, you're not thinking clearly."

"And you dislike having her here so much, you aren't, either."

He was hurt. Then he was angry. "You're letting her come between us."

"No. Corey isn't coming between us. You are."

"You want her to stay with us, but you don't want me to have any say in what she does or what we do about it? Are those the rules?"

"I know her better than you do."

"She destroyed something that meant a lot to me. I have the right to be sure she understands that our rules have to be obeyed so she doesn't destroy anything else."

"You'll scare her to death."

He faced her. "You don't even trust me to be fair?"

She didn't answer.

"What's happening to us?"

Again, she didn't or couldn't answer.

He left her standing beside the ashes of his dreams. Inside, the house was silent. He took the steps upstairs to Corey's room two at a time. He paused at her door, but decided not to knock. He pushed it open. Her head turned toward the door. In the glow of two night-lights he could see that her eyes were wide open.

"You and I are going to talk," he said.

"Are you gonna hit me?"

"No. I don't hit little girls."

Her eyes glistened suspiciously. He told himself not to be swayed. "You really blew it tonight, Corey. You went down by the water without permission. You started a fire in the fort. You burned it down. Do you realize how serious all of that is?"

"Mama said I was just born bad."

He moved a little closer. "Well, she was wrong. No one's born bad. Sometimes people just do bad things."

"Well, I do 'em a lot." She moved to the other side of the bed as he got closer, as if she didn't believe that he wasn't going to hit her.

He stopped when he realized what she was doing. "I said I wasn't going to hit you, and I mean it."

"You look mean at me all the time, like you wanna hit me."

"I don't want to hit you." He thought that one over and decided that wasn't quite the truth, but close enough. "But you do make me angry. I built that fort, and now it's gone. And you could have been hurt, or worse, just because you disobeyed us. We're responsible for you. You have to do what we say."

"Miss Sam's not mad. She says I didn't mean it."

"You meant to go down to the water, didn't you? And you meant to start a fire."

She didn't answer.

"Besides, it's what we do, not what we mean, that's important." He felt impotent. It would be so much better to give Corey consequences, to let her work off her guilt. But Sam had decreed otherwise. Now all he could do was talk, and talk without action was nearly useless.

"I'd like you to help me tomorrow after school. I'm going to have to start cleaning up that mess down there."

"I don't wanna help you. I wanna stay up at the house with Miss Sam."

Joe turned and saw Sam standing in the doorway. He waited for her to support him, but she said nothing. He turned back to Corey. "Go to sleep now."

Sam started toward her. Joe put his hand on her arm. "Haven't you already said good-night?"

Sam's eyes were wide and angry, but she didn't protest. She turned and preceded him out the door.

CHAPTER ELEVEN

THERE WERE ONLY two words written on the card. *I'm sorry.*

Joe put the tiny card back in its tiny envelope and examined the Boston fern that had come with it. The card hadn't been signed; it hadn't needed to be. The graceful, feminine penmanship had been acquired at a prestigious New Hampshire residential academy, along with the social savvy to send a gift along with an apology.

"I really am," said a familiar voice from the doorway.

He looked up. "This wasn't necessary."

"Maybe not, but it was fun. Besides, it's always bothered me that you have this terrific eastern exposure and nothing to take advantage of it. I came prepared to hang." Sam held up a hook and a drill. "Have hardware, will travel."

"How did you know I'd still be here?"

"I know what the first day of school is like. In fact, this is a little earlier than I intended to get here. Are all your meetings finished?"

"They'd better be, because I'm not staying another minute."

"Not even to drill a hole for the plant?"

"Not a minute past that."

She smiled, and he smiled, too. She looked good enough to eat in a candy-cane-striped dress that she'd bought especially for this day. Her hair was loose, held back from her face with a narrow pink ribbon, and her shoes had low heels, to bring her closer to the twenty-five first graders who would be a large part of her world for the next nine months.

"How'd it go?" she asked.

"Chaos, pure and simple. I had people in here all day complaining, an even mix of teachers and kids. I thought about stowing them all in a locked room together and keeping them there until June."

"Well, that would solve some of your problems."

"But it might give me others when the school board found out about it."

"True." Sam moved a little closer. "You look tired."

"So do you. How'd it go?"

"Good. Three kids cried for a solid hour, another three cried on and off all day. One mother called twice and came by once, just to see how her little darling was doing."

"Problems separating."

"Just her. Her son looked relieved when she left him this morning. He whistled all day."

"Is it going to be a good year?"

"Different from last, I think."

"How so?"

She smiled sheepishly. "An easy class. No Corey."

"Except at home."

"At least there I can tackle her one to one." She moved a little closer.

Joe liked the way she edged toward him, the way she put the hook and drill on his desk to free her hands. Anticipation built. "Speaking of whom, where is she?"

"At home with a babysitter."

"What?"

"I got one of the Insley girls to come down and sit with her. I thought we could have a quiet dinner alone."

He realized that Sam had made this sacrifice for him. He had no doubts that she had been looking forward to sharing stories of Corey's first day back at school— and probably had shared a fair number already. But instead of a family dinner, she had left Corey at home and sought him out. She was telling him that he was more important than her own needs, that patching up their fight was more important.

She put her hand on his arm, slid it slowly to his shoulder. "Unless you don't want to go out with me."

"I want to go out with you." He moved a little closer until she was in his arms. She smelled like honeysuckle, like the last roses of summer. She felt like paradise with all its lavish sensory delights and tempting, forbidden fruit.

"Actually, I want to take you home, straight up to our bed, and make love to you," he said. He heard her breath catch. He smiled against her hair. "You, too, huh?"

"Joe, it's so good to hear you say that."

He gathered her closer. "I've forgotten to say it for a long, long time now."

"Maybe we could rent a motel room."

"Foxcove's notoriously short on the kind that rent by the hour."

"Maybe we could improvise. Aren't there beds in the clinic?"

"I think we'll just spend the evening in anticipation." He lifted her face to his, taking his time to woo her gently with a long, slow kiss. Her lips were soft and vulnerable. He felt her doubts, her fears, and he cursed himself for his failings.

When he finally pulled away her eyes were sparkling suspiciously. "It's a new school year, Joe. A new start."

He stroked her hair. "Yeah. I think we should celebrate."

"Where?"

"Somewhere that has fried chicken on the menu."

She cocked her head in question.

"If I had to make a guess, I'd say chicken's Corey's favorite food, wouldn't you?" he asked.

"Corey?"

"It's her first day of school, too. We're going home to get her. Then we'll drive somewhere out of town, where nobody we know will have to watch her eat—"

Sam laughed, low and throaty and suspiciously tear choked.

"And we'll feed her so much she falls asleep in the car on the way home so we can say seductive—"

"Provocative—"

"Passionate—"

"Erotic—"

"Lustful things." He dropped his hands. They weren't quite steady.

"Things like what we plan to do to each other tonight?"

"A good start."

"You're the best, Joe. You always will be."

"I won't ask you what I'm best at." He put his arm around her and started toward the door.

"We forgot to hang the plant."

"Come back tomorrow and we'll do this scene all over again."

She tucked her arm around his waist. "It turned out well enough to repeat, didn't it?"

COREY BOUNCED ON Killer's narrow back seat as they drove down the highway.

"Tighten your seat belt," Joe said, glancing over his shoulder. "If it's loose enough so you can bounce, it's loose enough to be dangerous."

Sam noted that Corey sat back and stopped bouncing, but that she did nothing about her belt. Sam reached around and pulled the strap tighter herself. "There. Now, that's how it's done."

"Can't breathe!"

"You're talking, aren't you?" Joe asked. "You must be breathing."

"You'd like it if I didn't!"

"Didn't what? Breathe or talk?"

"Miss Sam!"

"*I'd* like it if you'd stop yelling," Sam said. "And Mr. Joe's right. It's not too tight. You're fine, and now you're safe."

"My mama didn't make me wear no belt!"

Silence greeted that pronouncement. Sam looked at Joe and he shrugged. Neither of them had the heart to point out the obvious.

"My mama didn't make me do nothing," Corey said.

"Saint Verna," Joe said under his breath.

"Why don't you tell Mr. Joe about your new teacher?" Sam said, hoping to turn the tide of Corey's hostility.

"Yeah, is she an old witch like that teacher you had last year?" Joe teased. "With a wart on her nose and no teeth? Does she ride a broom to school?"

There was silence from the back seat.

"Guess not," Joe said.

"She's not pretty like Miss Sam!"

"Nobody's as pretty as Miss Sam," Joe agreed.

"And she yelled at me."

"Did she, now?" Joe could understand that. He'd done it himself a time or two.

"And she said I couldn't read good enough to be in the apple group. I'm a banana!"

"Well, I've always been a banana fan, myself."

"But I can read better'n she thinks. Just didn't want to."

"How come?" Joe asked.

"'Cause the book's dumb. I read it already."

Despite himself, Joe was becoming interested. Sam could see it happening before her eyes. "Did you? When?" he asked.

"This morning. When everybody was adding and subtracting."

"Well, why weren't you adding and subtracting?"

"Already done it. Went on to the next page and got in trouble, too. She yelled at me again."

"Corey, I've never heard Miss Simpson yell at anyone. You're exaggerating," Sam said.

"She don't like me."

"Is that possible?" Joe asked Sam. He looked at her for an answer. She gave the tiniest shrug. It was answer enough. He frowned.

"Did you go outside for recess today?" Sam asked, changing the subject to something that hopefully would be more positive. "I didn't see your class."

"We was there."

"Did you have fun?" Sam remembered last year, when Corey had often been forced to play alone because the other children hadn't wanted anything to do with her.

"A little. Mary Nell came over and played with me."

Sam said a prayer of gratitude to Mary Nell. She was well liked by everyone, children and teachers alike. Her friendship would do more to help Corey become accepted than anything an adult could do.

"And then Jennifer Hansen came over and said she liked my new dress."

Sam added Jennifer to her prayers.

They stopped just off the highway at a restaurant with cheery yellow walls and polished pine floors. The menu was varied, with barbecue the specialty. The smell of smoking pork and tangy sauce permeated the room.

Corey's eyes widened. Sam wondered if she had ever been in a real restaurant before. They had eaten fast food together, but this might be an entirely new experience.

Joe seemed to sense Corey's awe. "We'd like a table near a window," he told the hostess, a girl who probably hadn't yet graduated from high school. "I think this might be a first for one of us, and she'll want to see everything."

"Aren't you a cutie?" the hostess said, bending over to gaze at Corey. "You've got your daddy's brown eyes and your mommy's blond hair. What a combination. Some people are just plain lucky."

Sam didn't know what to say. Corey stared at the young woman, clearly puzzled. Joe cleared his throat. "A table by the window, please, if you have one."

"Sure thing."

At the table Sam and Joe sipped iced tea from Mason jars while Corey worked on a lemonade. Sam didn't look at Joe. The hostess's comment still rang in her ears. She could imagine what he was thinking.

"How'd she know what color my daddy's eyes are?" Corey asked, long after Sam thought the subject had died. "And my mama didn't have no blond hair."

"She meant us, Corey," Sam said. "Joe and me."

"I thought maybe she knew my daddy." Corey didn't seem unhappy that she had misunderstood. "I never seen him. My mama never told me nothing about him. I don't know what he looks like."

"Do you see anything on the menu that you'd like?" Sam asked. "They've got fried chicken, ribs, hamburgers."

"She thought you were my mama and Mr. Joe was my daddy." Corey looked sideways at Joe. "You do got eyes like mine."

He narrowed his eyes. "Mean eyes?"

She giggled. "Go on!"

"I'm not going anywhere. I'm staying to eat. I'm getting spareribs and corn on the cob and potato salad."

Corey didn't look at her child-sized menu. "Me, too."

"Me, too," Sam said, closing hers. "And lemon pudding cake for dessert."

"Me, too," Corey said.

"Me, too," Joe said.

They were all smiling. Sam watched the way Corey's eyes widened and crinkled at the corners when she was happy. Like…Joe's. She looked down at the checkered tablecloth, too full of emotion to risk smiling for even a second longer at the two people she loved best.

"She's dead to the world," Sam said, tiptoeing down the stairs to the living room. She closed the double wooden doors behind her, just in case, so that they would be guaranteed privacy. "She's exhausted and full of more food than she's probably used to eating in a week."

"I hope she's not too full. I had doubts about that second helping of lemon pudding cake."

"She seems okay, but I'll get up with her if there's trouble. I'm the one who said yes."

"A word that comes easily to your lips."

She smiled seductively. "Well, shall I work on no, Mr. Joe? Is this the time?"

"Not a chance." He'd made a fire in the old brick fireplace, even though the night had only the faintest chill. As he opened his arms to Sam he had a fleeting vision of last night's fire. But suddenly last night seemed years away.

She joined him on the rug and settled herself against him. "This is heavenly. But both of us should be working. I've got lesson plans to finish. And if I know you…"

"I probably won't have to do a thing this year. I've worked so hard for the past six months or more that I'm caught up through the next century."

Since the day he had learned he would never be a father. Sam understood, and she was touched that he had admitted it. "In that case, maybe I'll just use last year's lesson plans and forget about working."

"Oh, I have some work in mind for you."

"Something I have some talent for, I hope."

"Something you were born for."

She softened against him, as if desire were melting her bones. "I was born for you, Joe."

He nuzzled her neck, inhaling the sweet fragrance of her hair. "Sometimes I think you were. Sometimes I think that destiny brought us together. That you knew

I'd be waiting for you at La Scala that night. If you think about all the things that might have been different…"

She didn't want to think about any of them. "I wouldn't trade a moment of our life together."

"I can think of a moment or two I'd like to trade."

"Why? Because some of them have been hard? But there might be harder ones in store. What matters is that we come through them together."

"Are we coming through them? Together?"

She knew he wasn't really ready to talk about their infertility. But he was asking for reassurance. Something he had never done before. She loved him more because of it.

"We have to come through them together. You're the center of my days and nights, Joe. I could go on without you and I would if I had to, but I'd be hollow inside. The part of me you fill would be empty."

"There would be a dozen men in line if I walked out of your life."

She turned in his arms and put her fingertips against his cheeks. "None of them would be you."

"But all of them could give you children."

She gazed into his eyes and saw the flicker of despair. She shook her head slowly. "None of them would be you."

"There must have been times in the past months when you wished I was anybody else."

"There've been times in the past months when I wished *I* was anybody else, anybody who knew what to say or do to make everything all right."

"None of this has been your fault."

"But I should have been able to help."

"You helped more than you know." He didn't elaborate. He stroked her back, and let his hands apologize and comfort.

She caressed his bottom lip with her thumb. She loved Joe's face, the high, wide cheekbones, the square chin, the winged black brows and brooding eyes that made him look dangerously sexy, even when he was laughing. She had fallen in love with the face, then with the body, the long legs and lean torso, the wide shoulders and muscular arms. Last, but so rapidly she wouldn't have thought it possible, she had fallen in love with the man.

"I'd like to help some more," she murmured. She leaned forward to kiss him, brushing her lips where her thumb had been. "Suddenly I can think of a way."

His eyes glowed. "But who would be helping whom?"

"I'm fairly secure it's mutual."

"Are you?" His arms tightened. "What makes you think so?"

Her hands drifted down his shirt, slowly, with tantalizing pressure. They settled temporarily at his waist, then he felt his belt sliding open. "Going straight for the evidence," he said. "Is that fair?"

"All's fair in love."

"What happened to the rest of the saying?"

"There is no war here," she whispered. "Only love, Joe. Only love."

COREY CAME AWAKE suddenly. At first she didn't know where she was, then she remembered that she was living at Miss Sam's now. She squinted at the ceiling and watched the shadows play across it. She had made her peace with the shadows. Most of the time now they seemed more like friends who came every night to dance for her when Miss Sam thought she was sleeping.

She heard a noise in the hall outside her room. It was Miss Sam laughing softly. Corey recognized the sound. When Miss Sam laughed it sounded like music. Mr. Joe didn't laugh much, but when he did it was different, like drums in a parade. Now she heard the rumble of his laughter, and she knew that he was passing her room, too.

She squinted into the darkness, directly at the crack where her door opened into the hallway, and saw them as they passed. She thought Mr. Joe had his arm around Miss Sam. They sounded happy.

She didn't feel happy.

She didn't feel good.

She got up and went to the window. She couldn't see another house from her window. Just trees and sometimes, when the moon was just right, water sparkling in the lake. It was a lonely view, and it made her feel even lonelier now.

She wondered if her daddy ever felt lonely. She didn't guess he did. Her mama had told her he didn't have any feelings. Mama had said he left her before Corey was even born, and when the judge said he had to pay money for Corey anyway, he still didn't. Mama used to tell her that a lot. It was just about all she ever said about him. Except for the day that they'd driven to South Carolina to find him. Then Mama had said he was a snake, and Corey could just go live with him, since Corey wasn't worth much, either.

Her stomach hurt. It had hurt sometimes at Mama's, but not like this. Then she'd known that if she could find something to eat, she would feel better. Now she didn't think eating would help much. She didn't like to think about eating at all.

She found her bear sitting at the table Miss Sam had put in the corner. Miss Sam had bought her a doll, too, a doll with blond hair like hers and a silly smile. Corey didn't know what that doll had to smile about. She liked the bear best, but she liked the books almost as much. She chose one now and took it to the window where she could see the pages in the moonlight.

It was a story about a little deer who'd lost his mama. She wished she'd picked a different book to read. This one made her sad. She turned the pages to the part where the little deer, Bambi, was born. His mama looked real happy, even though she had to have a baby in the woods and all. She turned more pages to the part where his mama taught Bambi how to do things. Then there was the sad part where the hunter shot the mama.

Corey was sad that Mama had died, too, but not the way Miss Sam seemed to think. She was sad because she couldn't be sad enough. That was hard to explain. It was funny. She thought maybe Mr. Joe, as mean as he was, might just understand. But if Corey told Miss Sam, she'd just feel bad. Corey didn't want Miss Sam to feel bad. Not ever.

Her stomach hurt worse. She put the book away and took the bear back to bed. Even when she held him close, resting him on her stomach, she felt worse and worse. Everything was all mixed up inside her. Miss Sam laughing in the hall, and Mr. Joe laughing, too. Bambi's mama being so happy, then dying. Mama being so angry at Corey and her daddy, then dying. Miss Sam maybe not needing her 'cause Mr. Joe made her laugh now.

She shut her eyes, and the shadows danced anyway.

JOE HEARD THE bathroom door creaking before he heard the moans. He came awake immediately. In a split second he knew exactly what was happening. He turned to Sam, but she slept on, a replete, satisfied woman.

He didn't have the heart to wake her. He sat up and felt for his pants, pulling them on and snapping them as he started for the bedroom door.

In the hallway he turned to the bathroom. An extraordinarily pale little girl knelt on the tile floor with her head over the toilet. He smoothed her hair back from her face and murmured comforting words as she lost the rest of her dinner. He was sorry for a number of reasons, one being that she needed more weight on her thin little frame, and the dinner would easily have added a pound.

"I don't feel so good," she said, between heaves.

"Shh…" He smoothed her hair some more.

"I can't help it!"

"Of course you can't." He patted her back. He remembered holding Magdalena's head once as a teenager, when she'd had too much to drink at a party, and he had tried to keep the noise from waking Mama. Magda had owed him one after that, and she had quietly ironed his shirts for the rest of the month.

"Don't tell Miss Sam!" Corey could hardly raise her head.

Joe suspected she was finished. He stood and searched for a clean washcloth, then held it under the faucet. "Why not?"

"She'll get all worried and stuff."

The child was a smart little bugger, obviously aware of all the dynamics around her. For the first time he wondered how much of his own hostility she was picking up. He felt ashamed. "It's all right if she worries a little," he said. "She worries because she likes you so much."

"I don't want to make her sad."

He thought there was probably more to that sentence. *Because I know what it feels like.* He approached the toilet and flushed it, noting how careful she'd been to hit her target exactly. "Do you think you're all done?"

She nodded.

"Then let's see if you can stand up now."

He helped her to her feet, then he sat on the edge of the bathtub and pulled her to stand between his legs so he could wash her face. He felt her trembling against him. Before he knew what he was doing, he lifted her to sit sideways on his lap. "Here, this is better."

She scowled at him, but he ignored her. She was still shaking hard. He brushed the cloth across her forehead, then over her cheeks. She was as white as the thin cotton nightgown Sam had bought her. "Does that feel good?"

She nodded. Reluctantly, he was sure.

"You know, this happens to everybody at one time or another. We shouldn't have let you have second helpings of dessert. You just had too much to eat."

"Can't eat too much."

"'Fraid you can. Especially if it's as good as dinner was tonight. I've done it myself."

"You?"

"Yeah. Someday you'll have to taste my mother's lasagna." He heard what he'd said, and his hand paused. He had no right or reason to talk about the future with this child.

"I like Grandma Rose. How come you got a nice mama and Miss Sam don't?"

"I was born lucky. It's too bad we don't always get to pick who our parents are going to be."

"I'da picked Miss Sam."

"I know." He set her on the floor. "Feel any better?"

"Sure." She lifted her chin. She was still as pale as her gown.

"Let's get you some water to rinse your mouth out with." He filled a cup with cold water and handed it to her. She did as he'd suggested.

"Come on, I'll tuck you back in," he said.

"You?" She made it absolutely clear that this was an inconceivable way to end the night.

"See anybody else who could do it?"

She stared at him, all big brown eyes and shaggy blond hair. For a moment he glimpsed the woman she would become if she was ever given the chance. Feisty, intelligent, inquisitive, pretty—possibly even more. "You know, Brown Eyes, you're a pretty neat little kid."

"Am not."

"Sure you are. Don't let anybody tell you differently." He thought about all the people who probably would, starting with the deadbeat father whom the state of North Carolina was trying so desperately to find. Anger filled him. He had an urge to hug her close for a moment, to somehow infuse her with the strength she would need to plow through the rest of her life.

Then he looked in her defiant dark eyes and saw that the strength was already there. He held out his hand. "Come on. Let's sneak back down the hall so we don't wake Miss Sam."

She looked doubtful that placing her hand in his was a good idea. He waited. The corners of her mouth turned down, but finally she stuck out her hand.

In her bedroom he pulled the sheet up to her chin before he perched on the edge of her bed. "Need anything?"

Her eyes were already drifting shut. "Bambi's mama died."

He couldn't imagine what that had to do with anything. "Yeah, I guess she did."

"But his daddy found him. In the forest."

Joe seemed to remember something like that. Bambi was a cartoon he'd avoided since childhood, Bambi and every cartoon and movie where an animal died. Life was already too sad.

"My daddy's no good," Corey said.

Joe suspected she was right. "You don't know that, Brown Eyes."

"My mama said."

"Maybe your mama was wrong about him."

"I'd like to have a dad…dy." The last word drifted into silence.

He stood and looked down at her. In the glow of her night-lights her face was wistfully angelic. "I'd like to have a little girl," he whispered.

Sam cuddled against Joe as he slid back into his own bed. He put his arms around her and closed his eyes. But sleep didn't come for a long, long time.

CHAPTER TWELVE

TURKEYS MADE FROM brown paper shopping bags hung from the classroom ceiling grid on green and gold ribbons, and costumed Native American chiefs hand in hand with Pilgrim men in wide-brimmed black hats smiled from crayon drawings that lined the walls. Sam tidied tabletops so that she could place the children's chairs on top of them for the night. The school janitor always appreciated the help.

"Corey, help me gather up these workbooks, would you?"

Corey started on the other side of the room, piling books against her chest. The cast had been gone for weeks now, and her arm had healed perfectly.

The missing cast wasn't the only difference in the little girl. She weighed more, noticeably so. The extra weight particularly showed in her cheeks and torso. Corey would never be plump; she seemed to burn off most of what she ate. But she looked decidedly healthier, no longer pale and undernourished. Her hair had grown a bit longer and Sam tied it back from her face with ribbons or barrettes every morning. The effect was charming.

This afternoon she was dressed in a deep violet shirt with matching pants and bright pink sneakers. She wore plastic rings on every finger, and she wanted to get her ears pierced, just like Mary Nell. Sam was going to let her do it as a Christmas present.

If Corey was still living with her at Christmas.

"I'm getting tired, Miss Sam," she said. "Can I go out and swing?"

"Promise you'll stay in the school yard? No chasing after kittens or blue jays?"

"Just did that once!"

"Once was enough. I thought I'd lost you for good." The words had a hollow ring. Sam *was* going to lose her for good. It was only a matter of time.

Corey slipped into her jacket. "I promise."

Sam watched Corey skip out the classroom door, then she went back to her work. Only somehow she never quite got to it. She stared out the window until a woman cleared her throat in the doorway.

"Penny for your thoughts? Heck, you're worth more than that. I'll give a dime apiece."

Sam turned to smile at Polly. "Sorry. Nothing I'm thinking is worth even a penny."

"I just saw Corey runnin' down the hall. Mary Nell's still here, too. She went after her."

"Good. She'll be sure Corey stays around. Sometimes she forgets she's got someone taking care of her now. She's used to being able to go off and do what she wants, when she wants."

"Yep. Her life's different, all right. So's yours."

"That it is." Sam started clearing tables again.

"You going to the bonfire tonight?"

"Wouldn't miss it for the world."

"Well, we're headin' over that way, too. Thought, if you didn't mind, we'd take Corey home with us for the afternoon so she and Mary Nell can play. Then we'll feed her dinner and bring her to meet you at the high school."

"Mary Nell really enjoys being with her, doesn't she?"

"That's one smart little girl. Even keeps Mary Nell on her toes."

"I wish Carol saw it that way." Sam had already talked to Polly about the antagonism between Corey and her second grade teacher, Carol Simpson. Until Corey had become Carol's student, Sam hadn't realized how rigid Carol's standards were. But it had become increasingly clear as the months of school progressed that Carol disliked Corey as much for her high IQ as for her primitive manners and occasional grammar lapses.

"Have you tried to talk to her?"

"I don't know what to say. I don't want to make things worse for Corey, and I don't want to create a rift with Carol. I keep hoping she'll see what a great little girl Corey is and loosen up a bit. This can't be the first gifted child she's taught. She must have learned some strategies for coping."

"Yep. Shuttin' her eyes."

"Polly!" Sam couldn't help herself. She laughed.

"What's so funny?" Joe asked from the doorway.

"Polly's being outrageous." Sam went to greet him. She put her arms around his neck and gave him a light kiss on the lips. "That shirt should be illegal."

The junior clothing and fashion design class had made the shirt for Joe as a classroom project. Wide vertical stripes of red and gold traversed the width. The high school motto, Scholarship Is Its Own Reward, was embroidered on the pocket.

"Turn around, Joe," Polly ordered. "Let me see the back."

He complied. An appliquéd bulldog, sequined saliva dripping from three-inch fangs, covered the whole panel. Once upon a time the Sadler High mascot had been—quite naturally—a fox, since the school was located in Foxcove. But the first time it became clear that the new girls' varsity basketball team would have to be called the Sadler Foxes, the mascot had been changed. Jokes about being full of bulldog were easier to take.

"You can just stand next to that bonfire tonight and ignite it with that shirt," Polly said.

"He has to stand there to give a speech, anyway," Sam said.

Joe faced them again. "More like a pep talk. Rah-rah stuff. Why we're going to win the homecoming game tomorrow, even if we haven't won a game this season."

"Are we goin' to win?" Polly asked.

"Are you kidding? Half the team's in bed with the flu, the other half wishes it was. I might have to get out there and play myself."

"Now that's a game I'd watch with real interest. Real interest. You in those tight pants and all." Polly patted Joe on the cheeks as she squeezed past him. "Don't forget, I'm takin' Corey. See you tonight."

"She's taking Corey?" Joe's eyes sparkled.

Sam laughed. "You sound like a man in the market for an uninterrupted dinner."

"I wish." He put his arms around her, even though there were people passing in the hallway. "But there's a pep-squad hot-dog roast before the bonfire. Did you forget?"

"I guess I did."

"You're invited, you know."

"Maybe I'll come. I can fend off the cheerleaders for you."

"Oh, the pleasures of having a wife."

"Don't think I don't notice they're all crazy about you. I know what goes on in the hearts and minds of teenage girls."

"Really? What does?"

"Things no teenage boy would believe."

"What about elementary school teachers? What goes on in their hearts and minds?"

"Exactly the same things."

He laughed, a deep, seductive rumble that made her wish there was no hot-dog roast. "I've got to be back at school early, but there might be time to run home and...change," he said.

The invitation was clear. She smiled her answer. Their relationship had been filled with unfamiliar twists and turns for almost a year now, but she was beginning to have faith that the road would straighten out for them again. If Joe wasn't exactly the same man she had married, he also wasn't the man who had withdrawn completely at the diagnosis of his infertility. He was quieter and more self-contained than in the early years of their marriage, but with his personal pain had come a new maturity, a new patience with the faults of others.

She still yearned for their old intimacy, for sex unhampered by shadows of their failure, for evenings spent planning their future. There was no talk of the future now, as if it were still in jeopardy. And despite what appeared to be a truce on the subject of Corey, it was still clear that Joe had no intentions of permanently welcoming her into their home if her father couldn't be found.

But he was still the man she adored, the only man she ever wanted in her life. And now, faced with the blatantly sensual flicker in his eyes, her heart beat gratefully—and faster.

"Samantha? Joe? I'm glad I caught you both."

Sam recognized the voice before she saw the man standing behind Joe. She watched Joe close his eyes, as if saying a prayer for patience.

"Ray." She stepped back to give Joe space to compose himself. Dr. Ray Flynn, the sole purveyor of psychological services for all of Sadler County, was not Joe's favorite colleague. Nor hers. "What can we do for you?"

"I'd like to see you in my office, if you don't mind."

"I've got a busy schedule this afternoon, and so does Sam. Can it wait?" Joe asked, turning to face him.

"It could, I suppose. But the problem just keeps growing and growing...."

Sam knew immediately what, or rather whom, the problem must be.

Joe nodded. "All right, then. But let's be brief."

Sam admired Joe for asking the impossible. Ray had never been brief in his life. He was a man who could take a full minute to say excuse me, half an hour to tell about his drive to school, half a day to recap the other half. And in addition to being long-winded, he was narrow-minded and shortsighted.

They followed Ray into his office. Sam had known Ray would want to talk to them here, where he felt relatively safe and in charge. In the hallway, with Joe looking down at his balding dome, Ray would feel his authority was under challenge. Here he could sit behind his desk and tap a pencil in emphasis as he spoke.

"Have a seat. Have a seat."

Sam wondered if Ray was going to repeat everything because there were two people in front of him. It promised to be a long session.

"I won't beat around the bush," Ray said after long minutes of doing just that. Sam knew he believed that small talk would put them at ease. Instead Joe looked like a man on the edge of an explosion. "I've been talking to Carol Simpson about the child."

Sam felt her temperature rising. "What child?"

Ray frowned. "Why, Corey. Corey Haskins."

"There are a lot of children in the building," Sam said pleasantly. "It does help to identify them by name."

"She is living with you? Still living with you?"

"Yes." Sam bit her lip to stop herself from repeating it.

"And you plan to continue letting her live with you?" His distaste was clear. He might as well have asked if Sam and Joe planned to continue to dump their garbage in the school hallway every morning.

"We plan to keep her with us until her father is found," Sam said.

Ray sat back and made a tepee of his fingers. Sam thought Elmer Fudd would look much the same sitting that way—except noticeably cuter. "And when do you suppose that might be? Do you know? Can you guess?"

Sam started to speak, but Joe interrupted. "Neither Sam or I predicts the future very well. The authorities are still looking. What's your concern?"

Ray's eyes widened with distaste. "I'm just trying to help, Joe. That's what the school board hired me to do."

"Well, we'd like to help, too," Sam said. "But we can't until you tell us what the problem is."

"The child is the problem."

"Corey, you mean."

"Yes, of course. Who else would I be talking about?"

Sam gave up trying to make her point. "Exactly how is Corey a problem?"

"She was your student last year. Just last year."

"Yes." Sam waited.

"Samantha, you know how disruptive she can be in a classroom. How disobedient. Yet you insisted that we not send her to a special needs school. That was a very grave mistake. Very grave."

Sam remembered exactly how furious she had been last year at Ray's insistence that Corey be placed in a special school. Now she was twice as furious. Too furious to speak.

"Let me get this straight," Joe said, leaning forward. "You've done tests, and the results show that Corey's emotionally disturbed?"

For a moment Sam thought Joe was using Ray to prove his own misgivings about Corey. Then she saw that Joe's foot was tapping. It was a sign Ray should heed.

"Yes, of course I've done tests."

"Exactly what?"

"The standard tests for a situation like this one."

"Which are?"

"Well, I'd have to pull her records. I test a lot of children. I can't be expected to remember every test I've given."

"Yet you called us in to give vague opinions? Even though you don't have any data in front of you?"

"Carol Simpson has been talking to me. Every day. To me."

"I saw the workup that was done on Corey last year," Sam said. "There was nothing, nothing at all that indicated she was really disturbed. She was an incredibly intelligent child in an unfortunate home situation. Her behavior was a reflection of both, not of any problems that couldn't be dealt with in the classroom."

"Your bias is obvious."

"Our bias." Joe touched his chest. "Ours, as in both of us. If Miss Simpson is having problems with Corey, then she'll need to give some consideration to better ways of solving them. We can give her suggestions. Like allowing Corey to read ahead, to supplement her daily busy work with some creative projects, like not raising her voice at Corey when she makes a mistake."

Ray looked stunned. "I can't believe what I'm hearing. Here you sit, two teachers—and you a principal, Joe—and you're refusing to listen to another professional? She's not even your child. She's living with you. Just living there."

"And as long as she does, we'll keep her best interests uppermost in our minds," Joe said.

"You're making a mistake. A big mistake." Ray began to tap his pencil. "Not just in defending her now, in spite of the assessment of a respected teacher, but in keeping the child at your home at all. You have a special place in this community. This isn't a big city. Maybe you don't understand. This is a small town, and we look up to our teachers and administrators here. We look up to them. Having that child stay with you is only going to hurt your image in the community. Your standing. You have your standing in the community to consider."

He was getting more and more flustered. He tapped louder and harder.

Joe stared at him, narrowing his eyes like a certain blond hellion. "I want to understand, Ray, I really do. Let's both be absolutely clear about what you're saying. First, there's a young resident of Foxcove, a child born and raised here, who has no standing in this community herself?"

Ray swallowed audibly and tapped.

Joe went on. "And you're recommending that we dump this child somewhere else, somewhere out of this community, or at the very least in a program out of everybody's sight? Not because she's really disturbed, but because her family was poor, and her behavior isn't always exemplary? Am I clear about what you're saying?"

"She is disruptive. She is an angry, disruptive child."

"I have about a hundred kids at the high school who fit that description. Shall we send them all off, Ray? Shall we find homes for them outside Sadler County?"

"You're being unreasonable."

Joe stood. "Then I'll be reasonable. Here's what we're going to do. You're going to call a meeting with Sam and me and Carol Simpson. You're going to sit there and smile, and Sam and I are going to tell Carol exactly what she can do to make her job easier and more enjoyable. Luckily for her, we live with Corey, so we know what works and what doesn't. Luckily for everyone in Sadler County, see? Because now, Corey's got someone in her corner, and that should smooth over any problems that might come up."

"But—"

Joe waved away Ray's response. "And when we're all done, you'll enter our suggestions into Corey's permanent record. That way it'll be clear to personnel in any school she's transferred to that this is an extremely bright child who responds well to additional stimulation. Your notes will help one little girl find her place in this world, and you will have done your job. Admirably." Joe leaned farther forward. "Admirably, Ray."

"Well, that's not a bad idea, I—"

"You'll have to excuse us now. I hate to rush off, but Sam and I've got a busy afternoon ahead. Glad you cared enough to bring us in." Joe motioned to Sam and she leaped to her feet.

"'Bye, Ray," she said as Joe tugged her from the room.

"Tornado alert. Whoops, too late, it's already passed," she said in the hallway.

"I wonder how many kids have been pigeonholed and sent away by old Elmer Fudd in there," Joe said when they were halfway to their cars. "I'm going to start pulling records tomorrow."

"Joe…"

"No, I mean it. We're under obligation to provide the least restrictive environment for all the kids of this county. Tomorrow I'm going to find out if that's what we're doing."

He was a knight on a white horse, Corey's personal knight. No one, Carol Simpson or any other teacher Sam knew, would willingly take on Joe. Intimidating was a bland word for the expression on his face.

"You went to bat for Corey," she said in the parking lot.

"Of course I did. I live with the kid. I know what she's about, and she's not disturbed. She's coped better with poverty and rejection and sudden changes in her life than any kid could be expected to. They try to put her in a special school, they'll have me on their doorstep."

"I think you made that abundantly clear." She took his arm. "Now, relax. You've got to be all smiles tonight."

He looked at his watch. He turned, his eyes full of regrets. "Now I really don't have time to go home and still get back for the beginning of the hot-dog roast."

"You're dressed appropriately, but I'm not. I'm going home to change, then I'll come back and join you. Save me a hot dog?"

"If you're smart, you'll grab something to eat at home and pass on the dogs. I know what the pep squad spent. If there was ever any real meat in those things, it just wandered through on its way somewhere else."

She made a face. "Thanks for the warning."

"But I'll save you anything that looks good."

"You look good." She rose on tiptoe to kiss him. "I could have handled Ray alone if I'd had to. But it was a lot more fun watching you take him down a notch. Thanks for caring about Corey."

"I wouldn't do what I do for a living if I didn't care about kids."

"I know." She kissed him again, lingering over it this time. "But I think Corey's growing on you."

His eyes were opaque. "Don't get any ideas, Sam. Nothing's changed."

But it had. She didn't know exactly what or how, and she certainly had no insight into where it might lead. But something had changed. The man in Ray's office had been the Joe she'd married. She welcomed him back with a third kiss before she left him standing in the parking lot.

COREY HAD NEVER heard so much noise. She had been to football games with Miss Sam and Mr. Joe, so she was used to the band. But tonight they were louder than they'd ever been before. Some of the instruments were bigger than she was, and they rumbled and blared until her ears felt as if they were going to fall off her head. There was a lot of yelling, too. People jumping up and down, cheerleaders clapping their hands and doing cartwheels. She had yelled a time or two herself, and nobody had told her not to.

"Come on, let's go under the bleachers." Mary Nell motioned for Corey to follow her.

Corey looked around, to see if it was all right.

"Come on, my mom knows," Mary Nell said. "All the kids do it."

Corey wondered if she should tell Miss Sam, then she decided against it. Miss Sam hadn't paid her much attention since the bonfire began. She had been up front with Mr. Joe, laughing and shouting and clapping. She looked at Mr. Joe like he was the president or something, like he was a king. Corey knew what that look meant. It meant that Miss Sam didn't need a little girl to keep her happy. She just needed Mr. Joe.

The night was cold, but Corey's jacket was warm, warmer than anything she'd ever owned. She threaded her way across the seats, hopping from one row to another after Mary Nell until they were on the ground. The bonfire still burned brightly at the edge of the football field, but the cheerleaders had stopped dancing around it a while ago. Now some of the football players, dressed like cheerleaders in red-and-gold skirts, were out on the field pretending to do cheers while the crowd roared and clapped. One football player-cheerleader threw his pom-poms into the air and they landed on another one's head. They started a pretend fight.

Corey covered her ears as the noise grew louder. She saw Mary Nell beckoning her, and she ran along behind her. The noise was loud under the bleachers, too, because Corey could hear the feet stomping above her.

"Why'd you want to come here?" Corey shouted.

"Looking for friends."

"Oh." Corey looked around. She didn't see anybody else dumb enough to come down here. "I don't see nobody."

"You want to look for candy bar wrappers?"

"Yeah!" Corey and Mary Nell had started saving wrappers. One company, maker of several different brands, was giving away prizes for fifty or more wrappers. Corey had to save two thousand to get a bike, but she already had ten.

The noise receded. Corey began to pick over the trash under the bleachers. She wished there was more. The floodlights on the field shone in narrow strips between bleacher seats, and she couldn't see very well.

"Look! I found one!" Mary Nell held it up.

"Ain't... Isn't the right kind."

"I know, but it's a clue. There'll be more."

Corey went back to looking. At the back of the bleachers, where they had come in, she saw three little girls approaching. She turned to tell Mary Nell, but she was up at the front now, poking through the litter there with her foot.

Corey recognized all three girls. They were in Miss Simpson's class, too, and one of them, Ann Grady, was the teacher's pet. None of them liked Corey.

Ann reached her first. "What are you doing here?"

"Playing." Corey stood her ground.

"Playing what?"

"Looking for candy bar wrappers. You can save 'em and get prizes."

"Ick. That's dirty, going through other people's trash."

"I wash my hands."

"Corey's going through the trash," Ann told the other girls. "She likes trash."

Corey turned away. There was no use in trying to explain anything to these girls. They were never going to be her friends. She wanted to find Mary Nell and go back up where Miss Polly and Mr. Harlan were sitting. Or she wanted to find Miss Sam. Then she remembered that Miss Sam hadn't hardly looked at her that night.

"Corey likes trash," one of the other girls said. "My mama says Corey *is* trash, and so was her mama."

Corey turned back to her. "That's a mean thing!"

"I know Miss Simpson doesn't think you belong in her class. Maybe you belong in the trash can!" Ann danced with glee at her own joke.

"Stop it!" Corey said.

"Don't have to!"

Corey pushed her. Not hard, just hard enough to make her point. "Leave me alone!"

"Ooo… Your hands are dirty, trash girl. Don't touch me."

Corey pushed her again. Mary Nell appeared magically at her side. "Stop, Corey. What's wrong?"

"She called me trash girl!"

"Why'd you go and do that?" Mary Nell asked Ann.

"She's your friend, you're a trash girl, too." Ann didn't look quite so brave now that the odds were evening out. She had two friends with her, but Mary Nell was bigger than anyone there.

"Take it back," Mary Nell said. "Right now!"

"Not going to."

Corey pushed Ann again. "Take it back!"

"Not going to!" But now Ann's eyes were frightened.

"Oh, leave her alone, Corey," Mary Nell said. "She can't think of anything else to say 'cause she's got no brains and no manners. Come on, let's go."

Corey wanted to push Ann again. It felt good to scare her a little after she'd gone and said bad things about Mary Nell and all. She had started to follow Mary Nell out from under the bleachers when she heard Ann speak again. Quietly this time.

"My mama says Miss Sam's trash for letting you live with her."

Corey couldn't answer. Her voice wouldn't work, as if somebody had just reached in and shut it off. Her hands began to shake, then her knees. She had Ann on the ground under her before she even knew what she'd done.

"Corey!" Mary Nell tried to get her off Ann.

Ann began to scream, and the two other girls screamed with her. Mary Nell tugged at Corey again. "Stop, Corey." She managed to drag her off Ann. "You'll hurt her!"

"I wanna hurt her!"

Ann jumped to her feet, but instead of running, which is what Corey had expected, she ran at Corey with her head lowered and aimed right at Corey's chest. In a moment they were a tangle of arms and legs on the ground.

"Corey!" Mary Nell yelled once more.

"Take it back!" Corey said, punching Ann again and again. "Take back what you said!"

"Miss Sam's trash!" Ann yelled.

Mary Nell heard her that time. She joined in the fight, grabbing Ann's hair. One of the other little girls jumped on her. The other one took off running.

The rest passed in a blur. Corey thumped Ann's shoulders against the ground, but Ann got her hair and pulled it till Corey's head felt as if it was on fire. Beside her she could hear Mary Nell and the other little girl thrashing and banging on the ground.

Then strong hands pulled her off Ann and stood her on her feet. "Just what are you doing?" an angry voice demanded.

Corey looked up and saw a strange man, his eyes blazing and his face contorted in anger.

"She called me—"

"I don't care what she called you!" He bent to lift Ann to her feet. A crowd began to gather. First just one or two people, a man who separated Mary Nell and the other girl and a woman Corey had seen somewhere before.

Corey clung to Mary Nell, frightened for the first time. More grown-ups were coming. Somebody dragged her and Mary Nell out from under the bleachers. Somebody else separated them.

Corey saw Miss Polly at the edge of the crowd, trying to make her way through. Then she saw Miss Sam.

"What's goin' on?" Miss Polly asked. Corey tried to reach her, but there were too many people in the way.

"That girl there started a fight with my Ann," the man who had pulled her off Ann said. "Ann says she just jumped on her and started hitting her. That's what she was doing when I found them."

Miss Polly looked in Corey's direction. Her eyes said that this was a very serious matter.

Some people drifted away; the band was still playing and the pep squad was still shouting cheers.

Miss Sam reached her, but she didn't take Corey in her arms. She just stood beside her, several feet away.

"She hit me. I didn't do anything." Ann was crying now, her shoulders shaking. "She hates me. I didn't do anything."

"You called me names!" Corey started toward her. "That's not true, you called me and…" She didn't want to finish. She didn't want anybody to know what Ann had said about Miss Sam.

"Mary Nell? Who started the fight?" Miss Polly asked.

Mary Nell looked miserable. She hung her head.

"Did Corey start the fight?"

"Ann called her names," Mary Nell mumbled, loyal to the end.

"That's not enough of a reason to hit somebody," Miss Sam said. Corey could tell Miss Sam was angry, even though Miss Sam wasn't looking at her. Worse, Miss Sam was disappointed. Corey felt as if there was a hole inside her and all the good things were just draining out.

"We'll take care of this," Miss Sam said, still not looking at Corey. "In the meantime Corey will apologize."

Corey saw Mr. Joe approaching. She wondered if every single person at the football field knew about the fight. Her head was beginning to hurt, and she had a scratch on her knee. She looked down and saw that her pants, the nicest Miss Sam had bought her, were torn.

"What's going on?" he asked.

"There was a fight," Miss Sam said.

The woman, who had her arm around Ann, spoke. "Yes, that child you're taking care of attacked my daughter."

Corey realized Ann's mother was the lady from the drugstore. Corey glanced at Mary Nell, and Mary Nell rolled her eyes. Corey felt a little warmer inside.

"Corey attacked your daughter?" Mr. Joe turned to her. He had the same mixture of expressions on his face as Miss Sam. "Is that true?"

"I've already taken care of it, Joe," Miss Sam said. "Corey's going to apologize, then we'll straighten this out at home."

"Mary Nell will apologize, too," Miss Polly said. "Right now."

Mary Nell, looking at the ground, mumbled something that could have been the pledge of allegiance. Corey didn't know. But everyone seemed to think it was good enough. Then all eyes were on her.

"Not going to." She scuffed her toe in the dirt.

"Corey." Mr. Joe's voice was firm.

"Didn't do nothing wrong," Corey said, not looking at him. "It was her."

"Did you hit her?" Mr. Joe asked.

Corey nodded.

"Then apologize."

Corey looked up. She saw the expression on Ann's face, and she knew if she said she was sorry now that she would never be able to face her again. Ann and her friends would never leave her alone. "Not sorry," she said. "And it'd be a lie if I said so."

She turned her gaze to Mr. Joe because she was way too scared to look at Miss Sam. Something had changed in his expression. She couldn't be sure, but she thought maybe he'd liked her answer just a little, teeny bit.

"At least she's honest," he told Ann's parents. "We'll take this matter up at home."

"Mr. Giovanelli, from now on keep that child away from our daughter," Ann's father said. "Or I'll hold you responsible."

"Teach your daughter not to call Corey names, and I can guarantee that Corey won't have anything to do with her."

The man made a sound low in his throat, like a cough. Then he and his wife walked away with Ann between them.

Miss Polly marched Mary Nell up the bleachers, and the other little girl and her mother disappeared. Corey was left alone with Mr. Joe and Miss Sam. By now, everyone else had gone.

"I've got to get back out front," Mr. Joe said, kissing Miss Sam's cheek. "Are you going to take her home?" he asked, as if Corey wasn't even there.

"Right away."

"It's all right, sweetheart." He touched Miss Sam's arm. "These things happen."

"In front of the whole town?"

"Yeah, why embarrass us in private when it's much more fun in public?"

Corey hung her head. She realized that she had made a terrible mistake. She should have lied. She still couldn't even look at Miss Sam. Miss Sam started to walk away, and she realized she was supposed to follow. She wanted Miss Sam to put her arm around her. She wanted somebody to understand.

But Miss Sam just kept walking, and finally Corey followed.

CHAPTER THIRTEEN

JOE WATCHED COREY out of the corner of his eye. She picked at her dinner, as if food no longer interested her. Her appetite had dwindled since the night of the bonfire a week before. Sam thought that since Corey had gained some much-needed weight, her appetite was tapering off to a normal level. But Joe wasn't so sure that was it.

"Want some cranberry sauce to go on that?" he asked. "Or are you just getting tired of turkey?"

"I'm tired of it," Sam said when Corey shook her head and didn't speak. "We've had it four nights in a row since Thanksgiving. The rest of the leftovers go in the freezer."

"Tinkerbelle deserves a holiday treat," Joe said.

"Got you. The rest goes to Tink."

"It was nice of your mother to pack this up and send it home with us. I'll give her that."

"Wonderfully generous, even if she didn't have to cook it or pack it herself." Sam got up and began to carry dishes to the sink. "And the fact that roast turkey is to Mother like stewed roots and grass is to the rest of us doesn't detract a bit."

"Give her credit. When she found out we were coming she made sure we had the traditional dinner." He didn't add that Kathryn obviously had pulled out all the stops just for Corey's sake. Kathryn, for all her faults, had made an attempt to include Corey in all the festivities. Even Fischer had mended his ways and addressed occasional booming questions in the little girl's direction.

Only Corey had refused to enter into the spirit of the gathering.

"Next year we eat at Mama Rose's house with everybody else." Sam returned for more dishes. "If my parents want to spend the holiday with us, they can come, too."

"No leftovers that way. There's never anything left over after my family gets through."

"More reason to go there." Sam stacked Corey's plate on top of the others. "Corey, will you help me with the dishes?"

"I got homework."

"Not enough to get you out of doing the dishes. Come on, Mr. Joe put out the dinner, so we've got to clean up."

"Can I feed Tinkerbelle?"

"Sure."

Sam had answered just a little too fast. Joe knew that, even though she wasn't admitting it, she was worried about Corey, too. But then, he and Sam didn't talk about Corey. They could talk about almost anything else now, but not Corey.

He stood to help them clear off the table, but Sam waved him away. "You've got work, don't you?"

"Just some papers I've got to look over."

"Why don't you do that now?"

Then there'll be time tonight for other things. The words were as clear as if Sam had said them out loud. She was looking straight at him, her eyes a smoky blue.

He sent her half a grin and began to look forward to having Corey asleep.

In his study he sat back in the soft leather chair that had been last year's Christmas present and leafed through the papers he was supposed to review. He was tired, and the words blurred in front of his face. He set them on the desk and rose to lift his grandfather's mandolin off the wall. He strummed a chord, then another. He had never mastered trilling, the quavery, signature strum of the instrument. He remembered how the same mandolin had sounded under his grandfather's tender ministrations. Much, much better.

He played another chord and tried to pick out a tune before he set the mandolin beside his computer. He had sat at his grandfather's feet countless times while the old man played and sang for him. Grandpa Giuseppe had never been too busy for his grandchildren. He had loved them all, enjoyed every moment he spent with them. Joe sometimes thought that he had gotten his own love of kids from his grandfather.

Sometimes, like tonight, he wished he was back teaching in the classroom rather than sitting in the main office. He missed the interaction with impressionable students, the heady feeling that they were clay for him to gently mold. He hadn't done enough teaching to get burned out. Now his favorite days were those rare ones when he had to hold down a classroom while a substitute was on the way or a teacher had an emergency.

Sometimes it seemed as if he spent more time with spreadsheets, with forms and all the other endless documentation that was required of administrators, than with kids. But none of that had mattered as much since Corey had come to stay.

Joe wasn't sure where that last thought had come from. It was too momentous to ignore. The thought wasn't new; it had cropped up before. He examined it, waiting for the pain that should arrive, too.

There was no pain. Just a jolt of anger. What was he thinking? He was grateful to a snot-nosed little kid because she had brought childhood, all its anxieties and sorrows, into his home? And who was he kidding? He was thanking Corey, troublemaker *extraordinaire,* because nothing was the same as it used to be, and every time he looked at her he remembered that he would never father a child of his own?

Apparently he was.

"Mr. Joe?"

The troublemaker in question stood in his doorway, her eyes—what he could see of them—filled with hostility.

"What do you want, Corey?" His voice came out harsher than he had intended.

"Miss Sam says there's a leak under the sink."

He stood, rounding his desk to squeeze past her before she could say any more. Only when he was in the kitchen and heard the throb of strings and the unmistakable splintering of wood did he remember that he had forgotten to put his grandfather's mandolin back on the wall.

"SHE'S SCARED TO death, Joe." Sam came out of Corey's bedroom and closed the door behind her so that Corey couldn't hear them arguing.

"She should be."

Sam motioned him toward their bedroom. Her hand wasn't quite steady. He followed, but only reluctantly.

Corey had gone straight to her room after breaking the mandolin. He had wanted to storm right after her, but so far Sam had prevented him. That wasn't going to be the case much longer.

In the bedroom she shut the door before she turned. "Corey says she was just looking at the mandolin and it slipped out of her hands."

"Then Corey's lying."

"I know how awful this is, but please, don't make it worse."

"Worse?" He ran his hand through his hair, a sure sign he was furious.

"Yes, it's bad enough this happened, but maybe we can salvage something from it."

"Not the mandolin, that's for damned sure."

"We don't know that. There are repair shops that specialize—"

"She smashed it against the desk, Sam. She didn't drop it. The back is splintered, not cracked."

Sam wanted to argue. She didn't want to believe that Corey had been so willfully destructive, so calculated in her hatred of Joe. But Joe was right—the instrument was shattered. Even if someone was willing to reconstruct it, very little could be salvaged. It would never be more than a facsimile of the same beloved mandolin.

"She was making a statement," Joe said.

"We don't know that—"

"*I* know it. She was making a statement loud and clear."

"Let's just leave her alone for the night, until we're thinking clearly."

"No!" Joe had paced as they argued. Now he faced her. "What are you talking about, Sam? Is that what your parents did to you? You made a mistake and they let you lie awake all night and worry about what they were going to do to you in the morning?"

"Of course that's not what I'm saying. I've already talked to her. She knows we're unhappy about what she did."

"Unhappy? You think this is unhappy? I'm furious."

"Then you should give yourself time to calm down before we talk to her."

"*We're* not going to talk to her. I'm going to talk to her. You're going to stay in here."

"What?"

He moved closer. "I said I'm going to talk to her. Alone. This is between Corey and me."

"No. You can't!"

"What?"

"I said you can't. You don't even like her, Joe. You don't think she belongs here. You've made that point over and over again. And now you've got proof that she shouldn't be living with us. You'll be too harsh with her. You don't love her like I do!"

"Just who do you think you married?" He advanced on her. His fury was congealing into something as heavy as stone. "A monster? A man who doesn't understand kids? I grew up with kids! Half a dozen of them. I helped raise Johnny and my sisters. I'm a high school principal. I deal with kids every day, and I've never beaten one yet, and I've never ruined anyone's life or even his self-esteem."

"I know that, but this is—"

"Different? How? Because she lives here? Because you love her? How does that make it different? Suddenly you don't trust me? Suddenly you think that I've turned into some vendetta-seeking maniac?"

"But it was your mandolin—"

"Yes, it was." He let his words settle between them for a moment. "It was my mandolin, and that makes this my situation to settle. And if you can't trust me to do it fairly and compassionately, then you're obviously married to the wrong man."

"I love her...."

"Yes. Apparently you love her so much that your head's not screwed on straight anymore. You've forgotten everything you ever knew about kids. You don't leave them hanging, Sam. And you don't pretend they haven't done anything wrong when they have. You talk to them, then you tell them the consequences. There are always consequences, whether we set them or not, and I'm not going to let one of them be a wider rift between Corey and me."

"But—"

He ignored her. "She was testing me. She wants to know my limits. She wants to know if we'll keep her after this kind of behavior. She wants to know if this will come between you and me so she can squeeze into the gap and fill it herself."

Sam stared at him. "Come between us?"

"You bet. And it's working."

Sam felt suddenly sick. The truth was so apparent that she couldn't believe she hadn't seen it. Worse, much worse, she hadn't trusted Joe enough.

She fell to the bed. "Oh, Joe..."

"You wouldn't let me deal with her when she burned down the fort. This time I'm going to deal with her no matter what you say. If you can't live with it, then Corey's won and we've both lost."

"I'm sorry." She looked up at him. "So, so sorry. Of course you'll be fair. My God, what's wrong with me?"

"About one year of doubts and fears."

"I—"

He waved her comment away. "We'll finish this later." He reached the door in two strides and opened it. He paused, but she didn't say anything else. Satisfied, he went out into the hall and shut the door behind him.

He knocked on Corey's door, but there was no answer. He knocked again louder and called her name. There was still no answer. He was glad there was no lock.

He pushed open the door and stepped inside. The room was lit by the soft glow of night-lights. There was a mound under Corey's covers, a little-girl-sized mound.

He crossed the room without a word and sat on the edge of the bed. Then he tugged down the covers.

"Go 'way," she said.

"Yeah, I bet you'd love that."

"I told Miss Sam I was sorry."

"Do you really think that's good enough?"

"Don't know what you mean."

Joe saw that she was clutching the bear Sam had given her. She never carried it out of the room; she was much too old and tough to be caught with a fuzzy teddy bear. But he had never seen her in this room when she hadn't been holding on to her teddy for dear life.

He was touched—he didn't want to be and fought it hard. But she was scared to death, and the bear was the only thing she had to comfort her. He was a hard man to impress. He loved kids, but with a professional's distance. Sentiment had little place in his job; it blurred the distinction between what was good for a kid in the long run, and what was the easiest or most comfortable response.

Now the easy, comfortable response was to walk out of this room. But it wasn't emotional distance that made him sit tight. Something else kept him there, something he had no time to examine.

"Let me tell you about that mandolin," he said. "It belonged to my grandfather."

"You told me!"

"I know. But I didn't tell you enough. He was a wonderful old man. His name was Giuseppe. That's Joe in Italian. I was named for him."

"So?" Her eyes were shining with tears, and despite all her obvious resolve her bottom lip trembled.

"Grandpa Giuseppe could really play that mandolin. I wish you could have heard him. And he had a wonderful voice. He'd sing, always in Italian, because he'd been born in Italy and that's the language he knew best. I can't sing at all, but when I hold that mandolin and strum a few chords, I can always see him."

He was silent for a while, and she said nothing.

"The best way to make somebody angry is to hurt them," he said at last. "If I really wanted to make you angry I would find something you really love, like your teddy bear, and rip it to shreds."

"No!" She clutched the bear harder.

"Yeah. That's exactly what I'd do if I was trying to hurt you and make you angry. But that's not what I'm trying to do. I'm trying to explain that I understand why you broke the mandolin."

"I dropped it! On accident!"

"No. You smashed it against the desk to make me mad. And you did. I'm mad, and I'm hurt because now I may never be able to play it again. I'll remember my grandfather, but not in that special way. Do you understand?"

"No!"

"You know what? I think you're smarter than that. I think you understand perfectly."

Her bottom lip trembled harder, and she didn't answer.

He stood and walked to the window. "What do you think we should do about this?"

"'Bout what?"

"About what you did."

Again she didn't answer.

"We have to do something," he said. "I think you should have some say in what happens to you. We don't spank little girls in this house, but we have to do something."

"Don't care."

"I think you care a lot. I think you want a chance to make this better. I'm giving you that chance." He turned and faced her. "What would be fair, Corey? I think kids always understand what's fair."

She sat up, still clutching her bear.

"Can you think of some jobs you could do for a while to help me?" he prompted. "Since I'm the one you hurt?"

She shook her head.

He nodded. "Okay. Can you think of something you might be able to do that would make me feel better, like bringing me the paper at night?"

She shook her head again.

He felt frustration build. He hadn't expected this to be easy, but he'd learned from experience that all but the most intractable kids usually came around in a discussion like this one. And usually the punishment they assigned themselves was twice as harsh as he would have given them.

"There are still some leaves that need raking," he said. "And that's a job I always do." He tried not to picture Corey with a rake twice as tall as she was. "Let's see. My car also needs washing."

She shook her head, but she didn't look at him. She looked down at the bear in her arms, then she held it toward him. "Here."

For a moment he didn't understand. "What?"

"Take Bear."

He moved closer. "You want me to take your bear?"

"Rip him up." The tears were flowing down her cheeks now, and she didn't try to wipe them.

"Not a chance. I'd never do that."

"Take him."

He reached for the bear. "You really want me to have him?"

She released it, and the bear was in his possession.

For a moment he couldn't speak. Then he pulled the words from somewhere. "Okay, this is what we'll do. I'll take the mandolin into town and have it sent off for repairs. When it's all fixed, I'll give you back the bear. Is that fair?"

"You're not gonna rip him up?"

"I told you, I'd never, never do that. I don't want to hurt you."

"But I hurt you."

"Yeah, but you're a little girl and I'm a grown-up."

He sat on the edge of the bed, but not within touching distance. They definitely still needed space between them. "I don't want to hurt you, and I'm sorry I have to take your bear. I just want you to understand and re-member that we have rules, and you have to obey them. The rules keep everybody from getting hurt, you, me and Miss Sam."

"Miss Sam hates me now."

"Nobody here hates you."

"You hate me!"

"Nope. I don't." He couldn't trust himself to add an-other word. He wasn't sure what would come out of his mouth. He was a roiling, seething mass of emotions, none of which were easy to understand.

"Bear's scared of the dark."

"Is he?" Joe looked down at the bear. "Then I'll be sure to put him by the window, where he can see the moon."

"He gets cold."

"Tell you what." He stood. "I think you'll need to come into my room before bedtime at night and tuck blankets around him to make him comfortable. None of this is his fault, after all."

"I can visit him?"

"Any time you want. And if you think of something you'd rather do than lend me the bear, just tell me."

"No. Bear'll make you feel better."

She was dead wrong. He was going to feel much, much worse. He wanted to stuff the bear back into her thin little arms. He wanted to tuck her in tightly and tell her she was forgiven. He wanted to kiss her wet little cheek and tell her how proud he was of her. He did none of those things, because he knew what was really needed.

He had to take the damned bear.

"I don't hate you at all," he said. "And neither does Miss Sam. We think you're somebody pretty special."

"Not." She burrowed back under the covers.

He was at her side before he knew it. He tucked the covers around her. He could feel her shoulders shaking, but she didn't make a sound.

"Everybody makes mistakes," he whispered. "Someday I'll tell you about all the ones I've made."

She didn't answer. He touched her hair. Just one quick, forgiving swipe of his hand. "Sleep tight, Brown Eyes."

Back in his bedroom he found Sam sitting on the edge of the bed where he'd left her. He held up the bear. "An exchange," he said. "I'm going to ship off that damned mandolin tomorrow morning and ask for a rush job. I don't care if they repair it with sheet metal. I can't give this back to Corey until I have the mandolin again."

"Joe…" Sam began to cry.

He set the bear on the windowsill, but he'd be damned if he was going to cover it with a blanket. "It was Corey's idea," he said, staring out the window. "She was the one who thought of it. I made the mistake of trying to explain that destroying the mandolin was the same as if somebody ripped her bear to shreds." His voice sounded funny, even to him.

"She wanted to make you feel better."

"Yeah. That's what she said." He felt Sam's arms sneak around his waist. "I feel like hell."

"She's so confused and unhappy, Joe."

"You don't have to tell me." He turned and gathered

her into his arms. He pulled her hard against him and buried his face in her hair.

Sam's cheeks were damp against his shirt. "She doesn't know how to make people love her."

"She's done a pretty darned good job of making you love her."

"But you're right. I love her too much. I can't see clearly enough. I want to take care of her and protect her so much I can't see what's really good for her."

"That's where I come in." He held her tighter and realized what he'd said. But it was true. He balanced Sam's intensity with his own levelheaded good sense. His years of experience in a big family, his years of training, of teaching and beyond, had given him valuable insights. As painful as tonight had been for everyone, he had done what was right.

"You have so much to give her," Sam said. "And I've stood in the way. But not anymore. I promise, not anymore."

She lifted her face to his. He knew he should remind her that no real harm had been done, that the situation was temporary, anyway. But that seemed irrelevant. There was a more important message in her words, and he heard it.

You have so much to give.

"No, *I've* stood in the way," he said. "I'm the one who's been out of touch with what I have to offer. I've been so tied up with my sperm count. I've only remembered what I can't give you, not what I can."

"It doesn't matter."

"Yeah, it does." He buried his hands in her hair. "Somehow I let making you pregnant become the cornerstone of my whole existence. I've been brooding like a spoiled child."

"Never that."

"Too much like that. I haven't been the husband you needed. I haven't been the man you married."

"Don't you think I know how hard this has been for you?"

"So what? It's been hard for you, too. I'm sorry, sorrier than I can tell you. I've failed you miserably."

"Never, never failed. But we've both been wrong not to face this squarely. You wouldn't talk, and I tried to cope by taking Corey—"

He put a finger over her lips. "Don't start on that. Having Corey hasn't been a bad thing."

"Really?"

"Really." It was all he could say; he didn't know what else he could add right now. He still had miles of unexplored territory inside him.

"Thank you."

He kissed her, promised her with his hands and lips that they would make a new start.

Later, asleep with Sam cuddled close beside him, he realized that for the first time in many months he had made love to her without remembering that he would never make her pregnant.

Tonight it just hadn't mattered.

CHAPTER FOURTEEN

FROM THE CORNER of her eye Sam watched Corey plodding away at her homework on the kitchen table. Her teacher, at Joe's prompting, had begun to assign more creative challenges for the little girl. The reports from school were encouraging. Corey was more manageable in class and less disruptive. At home, though, she was simply listless. Sam had tried to compensate by lavishing more attention on her, but Corey's response had been erratic. Sometimes she clung, but most of the time she withdrew.

Sam didn't need a child psychologist to explain the problem. Corey was suffering the fate of many foster children. She knew her life with Sam and Joe was temporary. As time dragged on and her father couldn't be found, her situation grew more unstable. Sam never talked to her about the future, because she didn't know what to say. Until Corey's father was located, the future was, at best, a question mark.

"Did you finish your math?" Sam asked when Corey closed the book.

"It's dumb."

Sam sensed a rebellion brewing. "You won't think so someday when you have to balance your bank account. Bring it here and let me see what you've done."

Corey slowly slid her chair back from the table, but

the telephone interrupted her snail's-pace progress to the stove where Sam was stirring homemade vegetable soup.

"Stay right there," Sam told her when Corey looked longingly at the stairs. "I'll be back." She squeezed past the little girl on the way to the phone. The voice on the other end of the line was familiar.

"Samantha?"

Sam had talked to Dinah Ryan so often in the past months that now they were collaborators, never adversaries. "Hi, Dinah. Any news?"

"Are you going to be home for a while?"

Sam's heart beat faster. Usually Dinah's answer was no, nothing important to report. "Sure. Joe's going to be late. Corey and I are making soup. Would you like to stay for dinner?"

"Not tonight."

Sam's heart beat a little faster still. She lowered herself into a chair. "Are you coming right over?"

"Just as soon as I can get away."

"Fine. I'll be waiting."

"Find something for Corey to do while we talk."

"I will." Sam hung up. She pasted a smile on her face. "That was Miss Ryan."

"Are you gonna look at my math?"

"You bet." Sam got up and told herself to be calm. She took Corey's paper and stared at it, but the numbers blurred in front of her eyes. "Looks good."

"I'm not finished."

"Thanks for telling me. I didn't notice."

"Why'd Miss Ryan call?"

"You know how she is. She likes to come over and see us whenever she can. She's on her way over now."

If Corey knew Sam was lying she didn't contradict her. Sam imagined she didn't want to hear the truth. "Mr. Joe called earlier. He's going to be home late, but he said he has something good to tell you."

"What?"

"If I told you, it wouldn't be a surprise."

Corey didn't even pout. She seemed miles away.

Sam knew Joe's news. The local music store had found a man in the Smokies who made dulcimers, banjos and mandolins. For a sizable bribe he had been willing to make the repair of Joe's mandolin his first priority. According to the music store, the man was a superb craftsman. Best of all, the mandolin was now on its way back to Foxcove. If it wasn't the same instrument, it was probably nearly as good.

Joe was most pleased that soon he could give Bear back to Corey. More than once he had complained about the way Bear stared at him in the darkness.

Corey went back to the table to finish her math and Sam poured too much salt into the soup. By the time she heard Dinah's car in the driveway she was about to explode.

"Did you clean your room when you got home?" Sam asked Corey as Dinah parked.

"No."

"Well, after you say hi to Miss Ryan I want you to pick up your toys like we talked about. Then you can finish your homework up there, while Miss Ryan and I chat."

"Don't have any more."

"Aren't you supposed to read a book and tell about it in class next week?"

Corey mumbled something. By then Sam was on her

way to answer the front door. She passed through the living room, decorated with the biggest pine tree that Joe had been able to get through the front door. They hadn't talked about reasons, but this year the Christmas tree had gone up earlier than usual. There were still almost two weeks before the holiday, but the house was in full regalia.

She and Joe had both wanted Corey to have some part of Christmas with them, even if she was gone by Christmas Day.

Dinah's expression was always as no-nonsense as her clothes. But today there was something different and impossible to read on her face. She greeted Corey with affection and listened to her report about school. She took a tour of the tree and the fireplace mantel with its collection of antique, hand-carved toys nestled among spruce boughs and sprigs of holly. She exclaimed over the candles that Corey and Sam had made the previous weekend and the gingerbread house that was suspiciously less ornate than before Corey had decided to eat the licorice fence. But when Corey finally went upstairs to clean her room, Dinah grew solemn.

"Let's talk in the kitchen," Sam said. "I made a fresh pot of tea."

Dinah settled herself at the table as Sam poured. When her cup was in front of her she just stared at it.

"Go ahead," Sam said. "I'm braced."

"I don't know if the news is good or bad," Dinah said. "I won't know until you tell me."

"We found Corey's father, or at least the man that Verna Haskins always claimed was Corey's father."

"You mean he's not?" Because of confidentiality Dinah had never told Sam or Joe the name of the man they had been looking for, and Corey had never mentioned it. Sam had never wanted to know.

"I mean he says there's no proof. And he refuses to take a blood test, which by law we might be able to insist on but only after an expensive legal battle."

Sam stared at her tea, too. "That sounds as if he's afraid of the results."

"There seems to be no real question he's our man. But it's almost beside the point. He's completely unsuitable whether he's Corey's father or not. Apparently he's fathered a string of kids from here to Savannah, and no court's ever been able to get him to be responsible. He has no income. He lives off women, then he moves on when they boot him out. He's been in and out of jail for the past ten years and seems to have no intention of improving his situation."

Sam looked up. "That bastard."

"Probably too kind a word." Dinah played with her spoon. "The point here is that we're willing to let him off the hook. Going after this guy for support would be an exercise in futility. And he says if we don't prosecute him he'll sign a statement admitting he's Corey's father and relinquish all his rights to her."

Sam could hardly breathe. "And he calls himself a man."

"Some men measure their manhood in very peculiar ways."

Sam knew Dinah wanted to say more, but years of good North Carolina breeding prohibited it. "How do I tell Corey?"

"I think the real question is *what* do you tell Corey?"

Sam looked away.

"I won't beat around the bush. Corey's going to be

eligible for adoption very soon, Samantha," Dinah said. "We're going to accept her father's offer and terminate all his rights as soon as possible. And our thrust at the agency is to place children in permanent families. We're not going to let Corey linger in foster care. If we can't place her here in Sadler County, we'll send her away, to another state if we must."

"Who would be eligible to take her?"

"You would," Dinah said. "But only if you and Joe both want her. And if you decide you really do, there's absolutely nothing to stand in your way."

THERE'S ABSOLUTELY NOTHING to stand in your way.

The words echoed in Sam's head as she, Joe and Corey ate salty vegetable soup and biscuits for dinner. They echoed in her head as Corey fed Tinkerbelle and she and Joe cleaned up the kitchen. They echoed as she helped Corey pick out clothes for the morning, as she read her a story and tucked her into bed.

There was absolutely nothing to stand in their way.

Nothing but Joe.

Sam lingered upstairs after she tucked Corey in. She knew that she had to go downstairs and face Joe with the news. She also knew what she couldn't add. She couldn't ask Joe to reconsider keeping Corey. She had promised she would put that possibility out of her mind. These months had been tolerable for him only because he had known that they would come to an end. She had no right to ask that they strike a new bargain. The old one still stood.

Corey would have to go away.

She dropped to the bed and put her face in her hands. She had always known this would be hard; she had always believed she would find the strength to deal with it. But she had no strength. She couldn't love Corey more if the little girl were her own child, if she had come from her body as a tiny baby.

Corey was the child of her heart. She understood how a mother giving up her newborn must feel. Sam would never know where Corey had gone, or to whom. She would never know if she was happy, or fully accepted. She would never have the pleasures of watching Corey graduate from high school and college, of watching her marry and raise her own children. Corey would be dead to her.

Tears streamed down her cheeks. She wondered how she could tell Joe. They had made a bargain, and she had no right to burden him with guilt about his part in it. From the beginning she had known his feelings on adoption. She couldn't ask more than he could give. She couldn't destroy her marriage with resentments. She had to be calm when she told him, and she had to be reasonable. Most of all she had to let him know that she didn't blame him. Because if she didn't let him know, all the good things that had slowly come back into their marriage in the past months would disappear again.

She hadn't heard the door open, then softly close. She hadn't heard footsteps. The first she knew that Joe was in the room was when she felt the bed sag beside her and his arm slip around her shoulder.

"Are you going to tell me what's wrong?" he asked.

She didn't want to tell him now. She wanted to be strong. She searched wildly for any explanation except the real one, but nothing occurred to her.

"Did you talk to Dinah Ryan today, by any chance?" he asked.

She nodded.

"They found Corey's father?"

She burrowed her face against his chest. "Yes."

"And he's going to come and get her?"

She knew Joe would immediately think that, because he was an honorable man. He would assume, despite constant evidence to the contrary, that other men would be as honorable. She shook her head.

"No?"

"He doesn't want her." She fought her tears. This was exactly what could not happen. She had no right to put Joe through this.

"What happened, exactly?"

His voice sounded strained. Hers sounded worse. She heard herself saying exactly the wrong things. "Oh, he's a real man, Joe. A real stud. He's fathered a bunch of kids. He doesn't have any problem getting women pregnant. Of course, he skips out on them and leaves them to raise their babies alone. But he's done his job, right? He's shared his fabulous gene pool. That's enough. He knows he's got what it takes."

"What are you trying to say?" He moved away from her.

She sat up straight and tried to wipe her face with her fingertips. "I'm telling it like it is. Apparently Corey's father has prided himself on populating the southeast U.S. He doesn't support the kids he fathers, and when push comes to shove he doesn't even acknowledge them. He's happy just to do his manly thing and send a part of himself into the future."

"He won't admit he's Corey's father?"

"He's not her father!" She stood. "Oh, he'll say he is if the state promises not to require anything from him.

And he'll gladly relinquish all rights to her. But he's not her father! Maybe he's the man who got her mother pregnant, but he's no more her father than Verna was her mother. Even less so, because Verna at least tried to be a parent. She was a miserable failure, but at least she gave it a shot."

"Is that why you're crying?"

"Yes."

"You're furious."

"Yes. At him!" She faced him. She was still trying to control her voice, her thoughts.

"And those comments about real men, about sending gene pools into the future, they had nothing to do with me?"

She swallowed. "No."

"You're a damned lousy liar."

She saw anger in his eyes. She knew that she had said too much already, and that there was still so much more to say.

"I'm upset. I'm not thinking very clearly," she said. "We can talk about this later."

"We'll talk about it now." He stood and took her by the shoulders. "Make your point. Say what you really want to say."

"No."

"Do it, Sam."

She knew they had come too far, but not quite far enough. Worse, she knew that it was too late to turn back. "He has what you want, doesn't he, Joe? Corey's father? He can impregnate any woman he takes to bed. And does that make him a man?"

He dropped his hands. "It makes him an animal!"

"Joe…"

"Don't you think I can see the difference?"

"I don't know."

He turned away from her. He was silent for a long time. It was a silence she knew she couldn't break.

"I always thought I'd grow up and make a houseful of babies." He didn't turn around. Instead he went to the window. He touched Corey's bear, stroking it lightly as he talked. "I thought I'd be the kind of father my old man was. I was only ten when he died, but I remember him as if he was here today. He was never too busy to throw a baseball or go to one of Teresa's tea parties. Every Sunday he stood us in the hallway, tallest to smallest, and checked us over to be sure we'd do him proud at Mass. We were Giovanellis, and that was something special."

"It still is."

"You know what? Maybe it isn't. Or maybe somewhere along the way I got screwed up about what that meant. We weren't the kind of family you hardly see anymore just because he and Mama had one baby after another. We weren't happy just because we could trace our family tree back to a village in northern Italy. We were happy, we were special because he cared and Mama cared, and they let us know. They gave us strength. They gave us the desire to make something out of our lives. My old man was a real man. And he would have been a real man even if he'd never been able to make a single baby. He was a real man because he was a good man. It's that simple."

She wanted to cheer; she wanted to cry harder. "You're a real man," she managed. "You've never been anything else."

"No, that's where you're wrong. I haven't been a real

man since the moment I found out I was the one with the fertility problem. You asked me once what I would have done if I'd discovered the problem was yours. You know what?" He faced her. "I would have accepted it, Sam. I would have been sad. I would have felt as if we'd lost something. Then I would have accepted it. And I would have gone out and studied all the options that were left to us."

"Adoption?"

"Especially that."

"But it wasn't my problem."

"No. And I couldn't face myself. I was unhappy I'd failed you, but I was more unhappy that somebody up there had failed me. Somebody snatched my manhood away the day I found out the problem was mine. You know who that somebody was?" He put his fist to his chest. "Me. Only me."

"Oh, Joe." She wiped her cheeks.

"And now I see the difference, and where the problem really lies. I'm the problem. Not because of a screwed-up sperm count, but because of a screwed-up attitude. And you know what? Maybe I can't do anything about one thing, but I can damned sure do something about the other."

"What are you saying?"

"What's the state going to do about Corey?"

"She's going to be put up for adoption."

"Are you willing?"

She started toward him. "We can't make a decision this way. We can't take her just because you want to make me happy."

"You?" He hit his chest again. "Since when are we talking about you?"

She stood absolutely still. "What are you saying?"

"I'm saying what you think I'm saying. We're the closest things to real parents that kid's ever had. I think we should get one step closer."

"Keep her?"

"Things happen for a reason. There's a world of kids out there who need what you and I can give, and one of them is living under our roof. She needs us. And we need children. Nothing could be simpler."

"Oh, God, it's not simple!"

He took two steps and gathered her close. "It's as simple as a call to Dinah."

"I told Dinah you'd never consider adoption! I told her today."

"Did you? I'll tell her differently tomorrow. She'll understand."

"I don't know what to say. I don't know what to think."

"I'll tell you what to think. I love you. And there's a wretched, bratty little hellion down the hall…"

She lifted her face to his. "What?"

"I guess I want her to be my daughter."

She looked in his eyes and saw it was true. "You really do?"

"Yeah. I want to be her father. Her real father. So, you see, it's simple, after all."

"Joe…"

She felt his lips on hers, his hands flowing over her body. She wrapped her arms around him and held him close. She was dizzy with love. Through all Joe's torment she had never stopped loving him, but she loved this man who had emerged from the torment more.

"You're sure?" she whispered.

"I've never been surer of anything."

His hands were warm on her skin, strong, sure hands that skimmed over her as if he were relearning the contours and textures of her body. He was a man restaking a claim, a man who had just discovered that treasure, not the treasure first sought but one as cherished, as valuable, had always waited just under the surface.

He inched her shirt over her head and removed the rest of her clothes with the same unhurried exploration. Her breath caught as he lifted her and carried her to the bed. She lay quietly when he moved away to undress. Silvery moonlight lapped at the contours of his body. He was every woman's most dangerously exciting dream, the male to her female, the god to her goddess.

When he stood before her proudly, undeniably aroused, she opened her arms to him. He came to her without flourish or hesitation. The bed sagged and he was beside her, the muscled length of one leg stretched over hers, the breadth of his hard chest pressing against the soft curves of hers.

He smiled the smile that had never failed to excite her, and she saw the confidence of old in his dark eyes. "We're going to conceive our first child tonight, Sam."

Tears rose in her eyes. Tears of gratitude. She was filled with more love than she had ever known, love for this man who had come through so much and emerged stronger and somehow better.

"And I don't think she'll be our last," he whispered.

"Ours," she said. "In every way."

"In every way that matters." He touched his lips to hers, as if to seal his words. She trembled with pleasure and embraced him. The kiss deepened and became another until she could feel only desire. His hands wandered, stroking the most sensitive places of her body. He had always been a considerate lover; now there was no give-and-take, only mutual need and answering passion, pleasure that scorched them both.

She gasped when he entered and filled her completely. She was united with him in a way that she had never been before. In that moment Joe was part of her, and she could feel his strength and resolve. He began to move, sealing the commitment they had made so long ago. She looked into his eyes and this time she saw only love. She knew then that this love they shared, the love they were expressing so perfectly, would guide them safely down the path of parenthood and into the future.

As they found joy in each other's arms, she knew that a child had truly been conceived that night. A child of their hearts and of their love for each other.

There had never been a sweeter moment in her life.

Corey saw shadows dancing on the ceiling. Not the ones she had grown accustomed to. These were ghostly fingers, the very first things she saw when she opened her eyes after the nightmare. For a moment she wasn't even sure she was still in her room at Miss Sam's. Then, with a spurt of courage, she looked around and saw that she was, but the room was darker than usual.

She managed to sit up, even though she was scared to death that the shadow fingers would grab her. She saw that only one of her night-lights was burning, and most of the light was blocked by a chair.

She wanted to stand, to move the chair so that the light would shine brighter, but she was too scared. Tears welled as she thought about the dream. She had been chasing her father, a tall man with black hair, just like

Mr. Joe. She had just about reached him when he disappeared. And then, when she had looked around to find Miss Sam and Mr. Joe, she saw that they weren't there. They hadn't been in her dream at all. She was alone.

Tears flowed down her cheeks. Miss Sam didn't think Corey had heard her talking to Miss Ryan, but she had. She hadn't heard it all, but she had heard Miss Ryan say that her father didn't want her. Then Miss Sam had said that Mr. Joe would never adopt. She didn't understand exactly what all that meant, but she was more afraid than she had ever been.

She had known Mr. Joe didn't want her. She had wrecked his car, burned down his fort. Then, because she didn't want to wait any longer to find out if he was going to send her away, she had broken his mandolin. At least, she thought that's why she had done it. It was all a confusion inside her. Sometimes she did things she didn't understand.

She did know that she'd tried real hard to make Miss Sam love her best. When Miss Sam and Mr. Joe fought, she had even thought that maybe it had worked. But they hadn't fought in a long time now. Not since the night she had broken the mandolin. They kissed sometimes when they thought she wasn't looking. And Mr. Joe held Miss Sam's hand in a way that made Corey's own hand feel real empty.

Sometimes she didn't think Miss Sam loved her at all. Not anymore. And now she was sure she wouldn't be staying with Miss Sam. She just didn't know where she would be going.

She wondered if Miss Ryan was wrong. Maybe her father would want her if he just met her. Maybe he'd love her right away and keep her with him.

She remembered his name. Her mama had said it over and over, like it was something bad. And he had to live somewheres in South Carolina, because that's where her mama had died.

The shadows moved again, and terror washed over her. All at once she was too terrified to think about anything except getting out of the room. She managed to get to the door and open it. Miss Sam's door was closed, but Corey thought she heard noises. She crept along the hallway until she stood just outside their room.

She heard Mr. Joe laugh, and Miss Sam laugh, too. She could hear the low murmur of their voices, although she couldn't understand what they were saying. They sounded happy, like people always sounded when they were telling jokes or secrets. They knew Corey was leaving, but they were still happy.

She wanted to knock on the door, to let Miss Sam hug her, maybe even to sleep on the floor beside their bed. But she heard Miss Sam laugh again. It was the loneliest sound she had ever heard.

She crept back down the hallway. Inside her room the shadows didn't look as scary anymore. There were some things scarier than shadows. She slid between her covers and pulled them to her chin. Then she lay in the darkness and said her father's name over and over again.

CHAPTER FIFTEEN

"THIS BACKPACK WEIGHS a ton." Joe hefted Corey's school pack and pretended to wince.

"Gimme."

He relinquished it. "Hey, don't be such a grouch. Miss Sam tells me you've only got half a day of school, then you're going on a field trip to the candy-cane factory."

She looked away. As she'd gotten ready for school that morning she had hardly said a word.

Joe was surprised, but he didn't have time to explore her bad mood. He and Sam had decided to place their call to Dinah Ryan before they talked to Corey. They wanted to be sure that nothing was going to go wrong with their plans to adopt her before they told the little girl that she was going to be their daughter. He didn't know how she would react to the news—an edited version—about her father, but he thought that when she'd had time to adjust, she would be happy she was staying with them.

"Hey, Brown Eyes," he said. "It's going to be a good day. Let's have a smile."

"Don't you have to be off to school, Joe?" Sam asked as she came into the hallway.

"Yes, Mommy," he said, with a very private wink. She blushed. "Then get going."

"Okay, but I'm planning to be home early tonight."

"I'll make something special for dinner."

"Do that. Fried chicken's good."

"Would you like that, Corey?" Sam asked.

Corey shrugged.

Joe shrugged, too, then he leaned over to kiss Sam. He ruffled Corey's hair, but she moved away before he could do any affectionate damage.

"We'll be waiting for you," Sam said meaningfully.

"I'm looking forward to coming home."

Joe disappeared out the door and Sam went upstairs to get her purse. When she came back down Corey wasn't in the hallway anymore. "Corey?"

"Coming."

She wondered what Corey had been doing in the kitchen, but she didn't give it much thought. The second graders had been instructed to bring a lunch to school, since there was going to be an afternoon field trip. The children were going to eat on the bus. She imagined that Corey was just adding an apple or banana to her bag.

"All ready?" she asked when Corey joined her.

Corey looked around, staring for a moment at the tree. "Guess so."

"Good, I'm afraid we're running late." Sam shepherded her to the car, and once at the school, she sent her off to her classroom.

The morning passed swiftly, despite the fact that Sam watched the clock continually. Joe had wanted to make the call to Dinah Ryan himself. She imagined their conversation a hundred times, until by noon, when she heard the clatter of second grade feet in the hallway, she could hardly wait to talk to him.

Through the windows of her classroom she glimpsed

the second graders boarding their bus. She wished she was going with them. She would have loved to share the field trip with Corey, but she could content herself with hearing an account of it that evening.

It promised to be a very special evening.

As soon as her own students made their way into the lunchroom she slipped into the office to call Joe, but his news was disappointing. Dinah was in meetings all day. He had left a message requesting she return his call, but so far she hadn't.

The rest of the day dragged. By the time the bus with the second graders returned, Sam felt as if she had lived two lifetimes. When the final bell rang she assisted the last of her students into their bulky coats and mittens and sent them on their way. While she waited for Corey to join her she straightened up her classroom, placing items in drawers and turning chairs over on tables.

She began to get concerned when there was nothing left to do. By this time Corey had usually arrived. She wondered if the little girl had gotten into trouble and been kept after class. She slipped on her own coat and gloves and turned off the light. Then she walked down the hall to Carol Simpson's classroom.

The room was dark and Carol was gone.

She checked with the teacher in the room next door to Carol's. Carol had left earlier than usual because she was having company for dinner.

No one in the main office had seen Corey that afternoon. Sam began to systematically check all the classrooms. Polly was just turning off her light when Sam got to her room.

"I can't find Corey," Sam said. "She's not with Mary Nell, is she?"

"No, Mary Nell's at home with the flu. Remember?"

Sam had forgotten. "I don't understand. She always comes to my room after school and we go home together. She's not in her own classroom. Where could she be?"

"I'll help you look. Have you checked the west wing?"

Sam shook her head. Polly started in that direction as Sam finished the east wing and the playground. They met in the hallway where one wing joined the other. "No sign of her," Polly said. "Did she go on the field trip?"

"Sure. I mean, I think so. She had her lunch and her permission slip. Why wouldn't she have gone? You don't suppose they left her there, do you?"

"Anything's possible."

"I'm going to check with the office again."

"I think you oughta call Joe."

"I'll call from the office. Thanks for your help, but I know you want to go home, Polly. You need to check on Mary Nell."

"Harlan's there. I'll just give him a call. I'm not leavin' till that little girl's been found."

"I appreciate it, but—"

"You think I'm goin' home and tell Mary Nell we went and lost her best friend?"

Sam squeezed Polly's hand. She was beginning to feel the first flutters of panic.

The office had no list of who had gone on the field trip or who had returned. But they began to make calls. Sam phoned Joe as she waited. "I can't get through to Dinah," he said when he answered. "I've tried three times."

"Corey's missing."

She hung up after he assured her that he'd be right over.

"Samantha?" The school secretary, a motherly woman who was usually unflappable, motioned her to the counter. There was no reassuring smile on her face. "I talked to one of the field trip chaperones. She doesn't remember seeing Corey after they got off the bus at the factory. There were a lot of kids. It's not time to panic yet...."

The principal arrived, fresh from a meeting at the administration building. By the time Joe got there, the office was filled with people trying to put together the events of the day.

Sam went into Joe's arms in front of everyone. She didn't care about image. She needed him. He stroked her hair and murmured encouragement.

Carol Simpson walked in the door. She was a pale woman, thin and high-strung. Now she looked on the edge of a breakdown. "This is my fault." She began to cry. "I didn't take roll on the bus. It's unforgivable. I just didn't do it. All the mothers had children assigned to be with them. I thought that would be enough."

Sam felt Joe's tension, but to his credit he didn't criticize Carol. "Did you see Corey?"

Carol shook her head. "I don't remember seeing her at all. I'm sorry. That doesn't mean she wasn't there."

"And you didn't notice that she wasn't at her seat when you got back to the classroom?"

"It was chaos. The kids were wound tight. I knew better than to try to get them to sit quietly. So in the short time we had left I let them do any activities they wanted. Some of them went to the reading corner, some to the computers—"

"Did you see Corey anywhere? Think."

"I just don't remember."

"Did you help her with her coat?" Sam asked. "Any time today?"

Carol appeared to be grasping at memory straws. "No. I just don't remember! I have twenty-six children in that class."

"Twenty-five," Joe said. "Because it looks as if you've lost one, Carol. Ours."

COREY KNEW BETTER than to walk by the side of the road. There were lots of cars going real fast. Some of them slid funny when they rounded the bend she had just passed. The woods were wet, slick with rain like the road, but there was a path she could follow if she was real careful.

She had been walking a long time. She didn't know how long, but she knew it was a lot more than an hour. It was starting to get dark. She had forgotten how it got dark so early now that it was almost Christmas. There hadn't been much sun when she'd left the bus at the factory because it was such a cloudy day, but now there was hardly any.

Getting away from her teacher had been easy. She had gotten off the bus at the factory and told the mother she was supposed to walk with that she was going to walk with another mother. Then, when no one was looking, she had hidden behind a car in the parking lot and waited until everyone had gone inside. From there it had been easy to get back out to the road that the bus had come on.

On the trip she had paid attention to which way to go. She knew which way the bus had turned, so she had gone the other way. If one way led to Foxcove, the other had to go to South Carolina. That part had been easy.

Now she knew it was time to start looking for a place to spend the night. Her legs were tired and sore, and she was cold, even though she had brought an extra sweatshirt to wear over her school clothes and under her jacket. She had known it would be cold. She had stuffed the sweatshirt in her backpack that morning, along with six cans of tuna fish from Miss Sam's cupboard.

But she hadn't brought a can opener, because that had felt like stealing. She was going to have to hit the can with a rock or something. Just as soon as she found a place to sleep.

She had brought something else. Bear. She hoped Mr. Joe wouldn't be too mad that she'd taken him. But Mr. Joe had told her that the mandolin was all fixed. She thought that maybe he wouldn't care because she wasn't going to be living there anymore, anyway. She had Bear, the cans, what was left of her lunch and her sweatshirt. She had even brought a can of root beer, but she had already drunk that.

She was thirsty again, and hungry. She remembered that Miss Sam had said she was going to make fried chicken for dinner. The thought made her sad. She had left Miss Sam a note in the kitchen, right before she went to school that morning. She didn't want her to worry.

She heard dogs barking somewhere in the distance, and she wondered if there was a farm with a barn nearby. Once Miss Sam had read her a book about children who lived in an old boxcar. They didn't have any parents, but they had been so smart they had known just what to do. They had never gotten hungry or cold. She was going to be just the same. She was going to find a warm place to stay and make a little home for the night. Then she and Bear could wait until morning and start walking again. The tuna fish would last a long time. If she needed more food she even had some money Miss Sam had given her to buy Christmas presents.

She wished she had bought Miss Sam a Christmas present and left it behind. She even wished she had bought something for Mr. Joe. She thought about the way he had messed up her hair that morning, and the funny way he called her Brown Eyes. Whenever she thought about her father, she thought maybe he looked like Mr. Joe. Maybe someday her father would call her Brown Eyes, too.

She stopped for a moment. Her cheeks felt wet, even though it wasn't raining anymore. She was tired, and it was getting darker every minute. She took off her backpack and unzipped it to take out Bear. Then, holding him tightly, she trudged on.

"DINAH, SHE WAS on the bus going there. We know that much. Nobody remembers seeing her after that." Joe gripped the telephone tighter. "Yeah. I've already called the police. They're organizing a search party to fan out from the factory." He listened. Sam watched the distracted way he brushed his hair back from his forehead. "Yeah, I've told them she's a foster child. They know to contact you when she's found."

He said a few parting words and hung up. Sam wanted to go to him to offer comfort, but she was fast growing numb.

"That wasn't the talk I'd planned to have with Dinah," he said.

She went to him then, and slipped her arms around his waist. They were alone for the moment. The principal had lent them her office to make the call to Dinah. "Where could she be?"

"I'm going out with the cops. Harlan's coming, too,

and somebody's calling my faculty to see if they'll volunteer. Dinah suggested you go home and wait. It's possible Corey will call there or even find her way home."

"I want to search, too." Sam moved away from him.

"I know. But you need to go home and wait."

"No!"

"Please go home first and check around really well. Then if you can find somebody to stay by the telephone, you can come. Please?"

He was making sense, even though she wanted nothing more than to start searching. "All right."

He clutched her to him again. "We're going to find her."

"It's cold out there, and wet. How is she going to manage? What if some maniac took her?"

"It's not likely somebody took her from the factory parking lot with all those people around. It looks as if she's run away."

"But why?"

"We'll find out when we find her."

"When?"

"I'm not coming home until she's found."

She could feel tears starting. She fought them. "I feel so helpless."

"See if you can get some people to come to the house to make sandwiches and coffee. Then you can bring them when you join us. The search team's going to need refueling."

She pulled away again. "What if she heard us talking last night? What if she doesn't want to live with us forever, and that's why she left?"

"You can't second-guess a child, Sam. You know that."

"I couldn't get through this if I didn't have you."

He touched her cheek. His voice was rough. "You've got me. And so does she. We'll find her. We'll get through this."

Chaos reigned outside the closed doors of the principal's office. Four teachers volunteered to go home with Sam to begin making sandwiches and jugs of coffee. Polly planned to come over as soon as one of her older children arrived home to stay with Mary Nell. A small search party had already formed in the hall. The police were working on another, and someone was organizing volunteers at the high school. In only a short time there were nearly fifty people ready to begin the search.

Sam watched Joe drive away, then she started for her car. The other women planned to follow after a stop at the grocery store for bread and lunch meat.

The house seemed unforgivably empty when she walked in. She called Corey's name, expecting no response. The sound echoed off the walls, but there was no answer. Even Tinkerbelle seemed to have gone into seclusion.

She checked upstairs first, going from room to room, checking closets and under beds in case Corey was hiding. Then she started downstairs. She almost missed the note. It was on the memo pad beside the telephone. She picked it up to turn over a fresh sheet so that she could keep track of any calls that might come in from Joe or the police. Printed neatly at the bottom was one sentence. "I gone to find my fahter and I took bear."

Sam held the note to her heart as hot tears spilled down her cheeks. Corey hadn't run away because of unkind words on the bus that morning, or because Miss Simpson still hadn't moved her to the apple reading group. She had run away to find her father. She had planned carefully enough to leave this note.

She was still crying when Joe called to see what she had found. And after she managed to tell him, she thought there were tears at the other end of the line, too.

THE SEARCH WAS called off at two in the morning. Fog had rolled in, and visibility was near zero. In the interest of safety, the men and women who had volunteered to comb the woods along the highway were sent home. A fresh shift of police continued to search the outbuildings of farms in the area, but no one expected to find anything until the sun came up the next morning.

"It's still in the high forties," Sam said, repeating the one fact that had given her hope throughout the long night.

"Her jacket's warm." Joe's response was just as familiar. He had tried not to picture the little girl huddled under the bulk of her jacket, shivering and crying. But the image had tormented him all night.

He opened the front door of their house and stepped back to let Sam pass. Most of Sam's co-workers had long since gone home. There were only so many sandwiches that could be made and eaten, so much coffee that could be drunk.

They found Polly asleep beside the telephone. Sam woke her gently and sent her on her way. School would open as usual in the morning, and Polly needed her sleep to cope with the questions of her students.

"We're going to bed," Joe told Sam after Polly had left.

"I'll never sleep."

"We're going to bed. Why don't you take a shower

and change into whatever you're planning to wear tomorrow? Then you can get up and get going right away
if we get a call or as soon as the sun comes up."

He made the suggestion because he knew it was the
only way he could get Sam to sleep. He had agreed to
come home for that reason alone. Pale and drawn, she
nodded. His heart broke when he looked at her. "We're
going to find her," he promised.

"I wanted to keep looking."

"There was no point." Roughly he pulled her to him,
clutching her tightly. Then he pushed her away. "Go get
in the shower. I'll be right behind you."

"I wish it was me out there."

"Sam, please..."

She started up the stairs. He wandered the house looking for—what? For clues? That was a joke. The letter had
been clue enough. Corey had gone to find her father. And
she had taken nothing with her. Sam thought there might
be some cans of tuna fish missing, but she wasn't sure.
Other than tuna and one missing bear, it was as if the little
girl hadn't wanted anything he and Sam had given her.

He heard the shower running. In the kitchen he
flopped down beside the telephone because he was too
tired to stand. He put his head back and closed his eyes.
The sound of the telephone edged him awake.

Groggily he lifted the receiver. "Yeah?" He tried to
make sense out of where he was and why. Somewhere
in the distance he could hear water running. Then he
came awake suddenly as the voice on the other end
began to speak.

Upstairs he was waiting for Sam when she emerged
from the shower. "They found her," he said with no ceremony. "She's fine."

"Oh, my God." Sam's legs buckled, but Joe had foreseen that possibility and he grabbed her.

"When it got dark she found a nice warm spot in some farmer's hayloft. Apparently she told the cop who found her all about some book you read her...."

Sam began to cry.

He hugged her. "It's all right. I'm going to go get her right now."

"You're going to go? *We're* going to go. I just have to get dressed."

She definitely wasn't dressed. She was also wet and shivering. He held on to her, but he didn't know if he was giving strength or seeking it. "I'm going," he said. "This is between me and her."

"What are you talking about?"

"That was Dinah on the phone. The sheriff called her first. She's with Corey at the emergency room."

"Emergency—"

"Standard procedure. Dinah says she seems to be fine but hungry. She's working on a bowl of soup."

"What did you mean when you said this was between you and Corey?" Sam grabbed a towel and began to wind it around her.

He watched her glowing skin disappear under the folds of the towel. Suddenly he had enough adrenaline pumping through his bloodstream to wish he had the time to unwind it again. "She told Dinah I didn't want her, Sam. She thought maybe she'd have better luck persuading her real father to take her."

"Oh, no."

"Between that and what you told Dinah yesterday, now Dinah's trying to decide what to do with her. She's afraid if she sends her back here, Corey will just run away again."

"No. Joe…"

"I'm going to persuade her otherwise."

"But we can do that together."

"No. This one's on me. I'm the reason Corey left. I have to be the reason she comes back. Trust me on this."

Sam stared at him. Then she nodded. "Yes. Go on. Do it."

He smiled, his battle half won. "Get her bed ready. I think she'll be one tired little girl."

"I will."

He hesitated. "Wish me luck."

"I don't think I need to. It's going to be all right."

He kissed her hard and made plans to unwrap the towel—or whatever was equivalent—as soon as Corey was safely at home asleep in her own bed. He left the bathroom, and quickly, the house.

The hospital where Corey had been taken was at the border of the next county. On the telephone Dinah had said that the deputy who found the little girl estimated that she had walked nearly ten miles.

Joe's little girl was a real trouper.

He made the trip as fast as he safely could in the fog, glad that he had succumbed to Killer's lure. At the first opportunity he planned to trade the sports car in for something larger, like a minivan, but in the meantime he appreciated the way Killer covered the miles. He parked in a doctor's private parking space and took the yards to the emergency room at a jog.

Inside, Dinah Ryan was waiting near the cubicle where a nurse told him an exhausted Corey lay sleeping. As he approached, Dinah stationed herself in front of the curtains that separated the little girl from the rest of the noisy room. "We have to talk first, Joe," she said.

He was impatient, but he understood paperwork and details.

"Shoot." He crossed his arms.

"She doesn't want to go home with you."

"Did she say why?"

"She says you don't want her."

"She's wrong."

Dinah's expression softened. "I understand what you've been through tonight. You've been out of your mind with worry. You're a good man. You like kids and you don't want to see one hurt. But that's not the same as wanting to keep her forever. Sam told me yesterday how you feel about adoption."

"Sam was wrong. And I called on and off most of the day to tell you so. Long before I knew Corey had disappeared."

"Be that as it may, you haven't convinced Corey you want her."

"We only found out yesterday that her father was out of the picture, Dinah! For Pete's sake, you couldn't expect us to tell Corey we were going to keep her last night, before we'd had a chance to discuss everything with you. We were afraid Sam had given you second thoughts about me. We didn't want to take any chances you'd say no."

"She heard me talking about her father yesterday."

Joe's anger drained away. "Poor little kid. Does she understand?"

"As well as any kid can. It's not like she ever knew him. I think I've convinced her that he's out of the picture for good."

"And what's in the picture?"

"I guess that will be up to you. And Corey."

Joe saw the curtains parting. An inch at a time. He saw a small hand with plastic rings on every finger peek out from between them. He wanted to grab that small hand, enclose it in his, but he didn't move. He was as still as he had ever been in his life. He pulled his gaze back to Dinah's face.

"I love Corey." He heard what he'd said and knew it was true. He was shaken by his own announcement. Yesterday he had realized he wanted Corey as his daughter, but he hadn't come this far. He and Sam had needed a child; Corey had needed parents. Sam already loved Corey. For the first time in almost a year everything had seemed simple and right. Now it wasn't simple at all.

He loved Corey and probably had for some time. If he couldn't convince her to come home with him, he was going to lose her forever.

He swallowed, but his voice still sounded suspiciously husky. "I love her because she likes bright colors and puzzles and bears better than dolls."

Dinah frowned.

He was picking up speed now and couldn't stop to reassure Dinah. "And because she has trouble with cursive, but her printing's great. And because she likes to read and she remembers everything that's on the pages." He spoke a little faster, determined to get it all in. "See, Dinah, I love Corey because she sneaks into my study sometimes when she's not supposed to, just so she can look at the pictures in my encyclopedia. I know she does it, because she doesn't always put them back in the right place."

"What are you talking about, Joe?" Dinah looked puzzled.

"And she's a kid who knows how to call a lake a lake, never a pond."

"A lake? Joe, are you all right?"

"And I love her because she eats fried chicken like a veteran. And because when she's sick, she doesn't want to bother anybody."

The curtains parted, and a little face squinted out at him. "Well, you woke up anyway that time I was sick!"

"That's because nobody should have to be sick alone." He squatted slowly so that they were eye to eye. But he didn't move toward her. At the periphery of his vision he saw Dinah step aside. "And I love Corey because she has brown eyes like mine and blond hair like Sam's. Of course, I'd love her if she came in shades of purple, too."

"Purple?" She stuck her finger in her mouth.

"And I love her because even when things get really bad, she's brave and she tries not to lie and she tries to think about how other people will feel. I love her for about a million other reasons." His voice caught. "But that's a start."

She dragged her foot on the ground in front of her. He didn't move, and neither did she.

"And because I wrecked your car and burned the fort and broke your mandolin?" she asked at last.

"Those wouldn't be my best reasons."

She frowned. "As much as you love Miss Sam?"

"Different."

She nodded. That seemed to make sense to her. "Like Mr. Harlan loves Mary Nell?"

"Exactly."

"And you want to take me home again?"

"I want to be your father. Your forever father. Will you let me?"

"Does Miss Sam know?"

"Yeah. She says it's okay if I'm your father as long as she gets to be your mother."

Corey looked up from the ground. There was a space between them that seemed like a million miles. "I heard your voice. You woke me up."

"I'm glad."

"And I hoped…maybe you liked me after all."

He opened his arms. She took one step and she was enveloped in a bear hug.

Joe wrapped his arms tightly around her. Corey's arms threatened to choke off his air supply, but he didn't care. He stood and looked straight at Dinah. "You ever heard the expression that possession is nine-tenths of the law?"

She was wiping her eyes. "Go ahead, take her home."

"You'll start the paperwork tomorrow?"

"First thing in the morning."

He turned before she could change her mind. Ten yards across the floor he saw Sam waiting in the doorway. He thought that when he was an old man he would remember her exactly that way. Blond hair loose on her shoulders, a brilliant smile and tears running unchecked down her cheeks. She crossed the room at a run and embraced both of them in a tearful hug.

Joe stood with Corey in his arms and Sam's warm arms around them. And he knew he was a man who lacked nothing.

He was a man who had it all.

EPILOGUE

SAM LISTENED FROM the dining room as Joe talked on the kitchen telephone.

"Sure, I understand you're having a problem with Corey. And I'm telling you what you can do about it. First of all, you've got to throw away all the busy work. Then you've got to find something challenging for her to do instead."

Sam chuckled softly. She could almost see Connie Antonio's face as Joe outlined his plan for keeping his fourth-grade daughter out of trouble. He had outlined it to Corey's third-grade teacher last year, at about this same time in the fall. She suspected that there would be a string of these conversations in the years to come.

A purple blur with flopping blond pigtails raced past. "Don't go too far," she called after Corey. "Dinner's early tonight. P.T.A. open house. Remember?"

Tennis shoes screeched against the old pine floors. "What're we having?"

"Chicken."

"Fried?"

"Yep."

"Josh!" Corey shouted.

Sam watched her daughter poised on the brink of flight. Corey had Joe's awesome energy, and she was just learning how to control it. Joe gave her frequent pointers.

Corey was two years taller and two years healthier than she had been when they adopted her. She smiled often, and her brown eyes sparkled. Her face was alive with intelligence and curiosity, and her petite body was tanned and fit. She was in Camp Fire with a talent for gymnastics and a passion for horseback riding, which she shared with Mary Nell, who was still her best friend. Corey didn't know it yet, but she was going to get her heart's desire for Christmas. A horse of her own.

"Josh!" Corey shouted again.

"You'll bring the house down," Sam scolded.

"Sure. Sure." She said the words just as Joe might have.

A dark-haired little boy came limping into the room. He was a head shorter than Corey, still pale from too many months in a hospital room. Sam's heart turned over at the sight of him, just as it had every day since Josh had come to stay.

"Come on, Josh," Corey said, hands on lavender hips. "You've got to learn to catch me. I'm going to beat you to the lake."

She took off and the door slammed behind her. From the window Sam could see just how slowly she was moving.

Joe came into the room, and Josh gave him a heart-breaking grin before he limped after his sister. Sam went to the door to watch his progress.

"He's moving faster," she said. "I've got to give Corey credit. Josh is definitely moving faster."

Joe came to her and put his arms around her waist. "You look tired."

"This mother stuff is hard work. I'm glad I'm on leave for a while."

"Josh isn't favoring his leg as much. He's looking stronger."

"Corey makes sure he does his exercises. She says that's what big sisters do."

"He's in danger of being mothered to death."

"He needed a mother. Now he's got two."

"And a dad."

"Who he adores."

"Dinah called right before Connie."

Sam leaned back. Joe's arms were warm and strong, arms that could hold a thousand burdens. She closed her eyes and luxuriated in the feel of his body against hers. She thought wicked thoughts. "Was she checking on Josh?"

"Not exactly."

When he didn't elaborate she opened her eyes. "Joe, don't tell me…"

"Okay."

"Another child?"

"You said not to tell you."

"You're right. Don't tell me now. Take me to bed tonight. Make perfect love to me. Then you can tell me."

She felt his hand in her hair. Stroking, soothing. He tucked one long, silky lock behind her ear. His lips were warm against her earlobe. "Twins," he whispered.

COREY THREW DOG food into the lake. Attila honked in protest, then started for the opposite shore. "See, Josh? The catfish are coming right up to the edge to eat it."

"How come you feed catfish dog food?"

"I don't know. Maybe it's made with worms and

stuff fish like." She stared out to the middle of the lake where her father had built a raft. She could swim all the way out and back by herself. Of course, a grown-up had to be watching.

"Did you always live here?" Josh asked.

Corey thought about his question. Josh asked a lot of questions. "I lived somewhere else once, but I don't remember much about it."

"I don't remember much about the hospital."

"I remember when I was in the hospital once, and Daddy came and got me."

"And he took you home?"

"When we went outside he kissed me and told me I was his little girl." She threw another handful of dog food in the water. "'Course, I wasn't big then."

"I like living here."

Corey thought about all the things she liked. Warm hugs and cold swims in the lake. The new fort sitting back among the trees. Mom teaching her to do cart-wheels and Daddy coaching her soccer team. The funny shadows dancing on her ceiling at night when the moon was full. The silly stuffed bear who slept on her pillow. Grandma Rose. Even Grandma Kathryn and Grandpa Fischer. She shrugged. "It's just home."

Josh shrugged, too. "Yeah, just home."

They stood watching the catfish feed. Then hand in hand they walked back home together.

* * * * *

Dear Reader,

I'm really excited that *Someone Like Her* is being reprinted. One of the big drawbacks to writing series romance is that the books don't stay on the shelves very long. A reprint gives a well-loved story a chance to revisit its glory days. But this reprint is even better, because Emilie Richards is an author whose books always go straight to my keeper shelf. Love to see our books together!

As I said in my original letter to readers, the plot of *Someone Like Her* came to me from a newspaper article that reported about an elderly homeless woman who had died in a small town, and how community members who had cared for her all contributed to pay for her funeral. The notion intrigued me. How did she end up there, and why did she stay? Did she really have no family? I imagined what family—a son, say—would think to learn that Mom had lived this kind of life, lost in one way, yet somehow having found a real home, too.

The timing of this reprint is bittersweet for me, as I am currently losing my mother to dementia. I hadn't yet had that experience with anyone I loved when I wrote *Someone Like Her,* and yet, upon reading it, I seemed to understand the emotions all too well. Mental illness is different, of course, but for the family has many parallels. Yes, this person is my mom, but some times more than other times. And yes, day by day, whatever quality made her Mom is being lost. How do you remind her of the woman she was? Hold on to your own memories once hers are gone?

I truly loved this story, and never more than now.

There's nothing I like more than hearing from readers! Look for my Facebook page and my website at www.janicekayjohnson.com.

Janice

SOMEONE LIKE HER

Janice Kay Johnson

For Mom, with all my love

CHAPTER ONE

"EVERY TABLE FULL except the reserved one, and it's a Tuesday." Carrying two glasses of iced tea, Mabel paused to grin at Lucy Peterson. "Those new soups are a hit."

She continued into the crowded dining room of the café. Lucy, who had just finished ringing up a customer, looked around with satisfaction. Mabel was right. Business kept getting better and better.

The bell over the door rang. Lucy's head turned as her guest slipped in, her carriage confident, her gaze shy. The hat lady.

Last time Lucy had seen her, the day before yesterday, she'd carried herself decorously and yet with regal authority. The pillbox hat had said it all. She was often Queen Elizabeth—the second, she always emphasized. She didn't actually look much like Queen Elizabeth II, being slender rather than matronly in build, with hair that had been blond when she first appeared in Middleton, perhaps ten years ago. Now her hair was primarily white, as wispy and flyaway as the woman whose head it crowned.

But today, she wore a flower-printed dress and a broad-brimmed hat festooned with flowers. Her face was softer, her carriage more youthful, her gaze vaguer.

This was always the awkward moment. Lucy had

to pretend she knew who Middleton's one and only homeless person was. Calling her by the wrong name seemed so insulting.

Talk in the café hadn't dimmed at all. Everyone knew the hat lady was a project of Lucy's. Lucy's Aunt Marian called, "Your majesty," and resumed her one-sided conversation with Uncle Sidney, who almost never said a word, and failed entirely to notice the hat lady's astonished stare.

Lucy went to her and said in a gentle voice, "I'm so glad you could come to lunch today. Your table's right here, by the window. Did you see the crocuses are blooming?"

The hat lady smiled at her, her face crinkling with pleasure. "God's gifts put man's best dreams to shame."

Okay. It was a clue. She still had a British accent, which was mostly a given, although not long ago she'd been Elizabeth Taylor, the accent wholly American. She had an astonishing gift for accents; a few months ago, she'd done a splendid Eliza Doolittle, starting with a nearly indecipherable Cockney accent skillfully revised over several weeks until she spoke with a pure, somewhat stilted upper-crust accent worthy of the most carefully tutored student.

Lucy had taken to rereading English literature and watching classic films so she wouldn't be completely lost every time the hat lady changed personas.

"Please. Sit down." Lucy gestured her to the tiny table for two in front of the bow window, which she'd reserved especially for the hat lady. Yellow and purple crocuses bloomed in the windowbox outside. Her shopping cart, neatly packed, was parked on the sidewalk where she could see it. That was why Lucy always saved the window seat for her. "Would you care for tea?"

"Please."

She gazed with seeming delight and no boredom out the window until Lucy returned with a teapot, loose tea steeping inside. One did not offer the hat lady tea improperly made.

From the menu she chose only soup and a scone. Lucy had tried persuading her to have a hearty meal when she was here, but had never succeeded.

"Won't you join me?" she did ask, with vague surprise as if unaware there was a busy restaurant around them, and that Lucy was in charge.

"I might sit down with you for a moment a little later," she promised. Her friend had aged noticeably these past few months, Lucy noted with dismay. Her spine was as straight as ever, her pinkie finger extended as she sipped tea, but she must have lost weight. She seemed frail today. If only she could be persuaded to settle into a rented room! Hiding her worry, Lucy asked, "How are you?"

She tilted her face up. Her blue eyes, fading like her hair, seemed unusually perceptive all of a sudden, as if she saw the doubts and unhappiness Lucy scarcely acknowledged even to herself. In a voice too low for anyone at neighboring tables to hear, she said, "I might ask you the same."

Lucy's mouth opened and closed.

After a moment, the cornflower-blue eyes softened, looked inward, and she murmured, "Did you know the sorrow comes with the years?"

"I…" Something seemed to clog Lucy's throat. "Yes. Yes, I did."

This smile seemed to forgive her. "Grief may be joy misunderstood."

Oh! That line she'd heard. Somewhere, sometime. It had to have been written, or said, by a Beth, or Liza, Lizbet, or Elizabeth… Yes! Lucy thought in triumph. Elizabeth Barrett Browning. Of course. The hat lady was very fond of her poetry. Only, the first couple of things she said had seemed so sensible, if also profound, Lucy hadn't recognized them as poetry.

"Miss Browning," she said, "I'm so glad you could join me today."

She meant to get back to the hat lady and sit with her, as promised. She did. But the kitchen ran out of spinach, and she had to race to Safeway for more, then Aunt Marian expressed her opinion at some length on the very peculiar soup—which was delicious, but she did miss the split pea Lucy used to offer. And then Samantha, Lucy's youngest and most compatible sister, who had recently opened a bed-and-breakfast inn, suggested they join together to put on a murder mystery weekend, with the guests staying at Doveport B and B and Lucy catering the meals. Samantha had scarcely left than Lucy's niece Bridget came in to apply to be a waitress, her air of defiance suggesting to Lucy that Bridget's mother hadn't liked the idea of her working. Bridget was resisting the idea of staying close to home after graduation and doing her first two years at the community college in Port Angeles rather than going away. Was she trying to earn enough to pay a significant part of her own expenses? If so, there was no doubt whose side Lucy was on.

Still, she wished every decision she made didn't have family repercussions. The tiniest stone spread ripples of gossip, hurt feelings, righteous indignation. That was the problem with having such a large family who all lived so close by. Making a face, Lucy thought wistfully, *Why can't one side or the other live in Minneapolis or Houston instead? Anywhere but here?*

Dad's family, by preference. His sister, her Aunt Lynn, was a particular trial. Come to think of it, Lucy didn't like most of her cousins on Dad's side, either.

The trouble was, Dad had a sister and a brother, who had kids, all of whom had already started families of their own. Mom had two sisters, and *they* had kids, and… Aagh! There was a reason Lucy had yearned to leave Middleton for most of her life.

She ran the cash register as the full restaurant gradually emptied, and by the time she thought to look at the small table in the bow window, it was empty. Erin, another employee, was starting to clear it, and Lucy was disappointed to see that the soup bowl was half-full, and Miss Browning hadn't even finished her scone.

Oh, dear, she thought. If only the hat lady would fill up when she was here. Or take leftovers in a doggie bag. She accepted invitations to dine, but wouldn't come more than a couple of times a week. Lucy knew that she did get food elsewhere. George, down at Safeway, saw to it that expired canned goods and slightly wilted produce got set outside the back door when the hat lady's route took her that way. And Winona Carlson, who ran the Pancake Haus out by the highway, fed her breakfast at least another couple of days a week. Still… When Lucy thought about the hat lady—gentle, whimsical, yet somehow sad—she worried.

Today, though, she was too busy to do more than shake her head and feel slightly guilty that she hadn't made time to sit down, if only for a minute or two. Then she went back to work in the kitchen, prepping for dinner.

Hands busy, she let her mind wander. That one achingly perceptive look from the hat lady set her to analyzing why she'd felt so down lately.

Of course, she knew in part: this wasn't the life she'd dreamed of having. Like her niece Bridget, she'd been sure she would leave Middleton behind and never be back except for visits. But after college she'd let herself get enveloped again by family. First a job at the café, the chance to be creative in the kitchen and the pleasure of seeing how her food was received. Wan lettuce and all-American comfort foods were gradually replaced by wraps, spinach and romaine salads and her signature soups. When the opportunity to buy the café came up, she'd still told herself this didn't have to be permanent. She'd improve business and make a profit when she sold the café in turn. Perhaps she could start a restaurant in Seattle or San Francisco, or get a job as an executive chef.

Her hands went still as her chest filled with something very like panic. All of a sudden she had a terrible urge to turn the sign on the door to Closed, scrap preparation for dinner and just…run away.

Lucy grimaced. She was far too responsible to do any such thing. Okay, then; why not put the café up for sale and use the proceeds to travel for a couple of years? Give in to all the yearnings that made her so restless. Spend a year traveling between hostels in…Romania. Or Swaziland. Or…

The hat lady's face popped into her mind, and a smile curved her mouth. *England. How silly of me! Of course it has to be the British Isles.* Images of thatched roofs and hedgerows, church spires and castle towers rose before her mind's eye. Perhaps she would bike between villages, staying as long as she chose in each. She'd have to start over financially when she came home, if she ever came home, but she was young. At least she'd have lived a little before she settled into being a small-town businesswoman.

Elizabeth Barrett Browning would certainly approve.

Only a pair of tourists sat in front eating pie in the late afternoon when the front door opened so precipitously, the bell rattled and banged against the glass. Startled, Lucy let the dough she'd been kneading drop and peered over the divider between the kitchen and dining room.

It was George who'd rushed in, expression distraught. George, fifty-five and counting the years until retirement, who Lucy had believed had only one speed: measured, deliberate. George, who now let the door slam behind him with a bang.

"Lucy! Did you hear?"

Hands covered with flour, she used her shoulder to push the swinging door open and go into the dining room. She was vaguely aware that both the tourists and gray-haired Mabel, who was wiping down tables, had turned to stare. "Hear? Hear what?"

"The hat lady was hit crossing the highway." His eyes were red-rimmed and he looked as if he might cry. "She was pushing her shopping cart, and apparently didn't look. God." He rubbed a hand over his face. "She's not dead, but it doesn't sound good."

"Did they take her to the hospital?"

He nodded.

"But…she doesn't have insurance."

A silly thing to say, since the hat lady also didn't have a name. Not a real name, one that was her own for sure.

"I didn't hear anybody quibbling." So he'd been to the hospital.

Lucy took a deep breath. "I'll get over there as soon as I can."

He nodded and left, perhaps to spread the word further.

Lucy called for Mabel to take over the dough, and remembered another line written by Elizabeth Barrett Browning, whose poetry she, too, had loved, back when she was romantic and firmly believed her path would take her far from too familiar Middleton.

Life, struck sharp on death,
Makes awful lightning.

ADRIAN RUTLEDGE WAS immersed in the notes his associates had made on legal precedents for a complex case that would be coming to trial next month when his phone rang. He glanced at it irritably; he'd asked Carol, his administrative assistant, not to interrupt him until his three o'clock appointment.

He reached for the phone immediately, however. She wouldn't have bothered him without good reason.

"Yes?"

She cleared her throat. "Mr. Rutledge, there's a woman here who doesn't have an appointment."

His eyebrows rose. People without appointments rarely bothered a partner in a rarified Seattle law firm. If they did, Carol was quite capable of sending them on their way.

"She says it's about your mother."

"My mother," he repeated. He felt as if he were sounding out a word in Farsi or Mandarin, a language utterly foreign to him. Yeah, he knew what a mother was; yeah, he'd had one, but at this moment he couldn't picture her face.

"Yes, sir." Carol's generally crisp tones were hesitant.

"What about my mother?" he asked.

She cleared her throat again. "This woman…ah, Ms. Peterson, says she's in the hospital and needs you."

In the hospital? That meant…she was *alive?* His heart did a peculiar stutter. Adrian had assumed she was dead. Maybe preferred thinking she was.

Oh, hell, he thought in disgust, this was probably some kind of hoax. Still, he didn't seem to have any choice but to hear her out. "Send her in," he ordered, and hung up.

The wait seemed long. When the door did open, he saw Carol first, elegant in a sleek black suit and heels that made the most of her legs. He quit noticing his administrative assistant the moment the other woman walked in. Nor was he aware of Carol quietly closing the door behind her. He couldn't take his eyes from this unexpected visitor.

He guessed her age as late twenties. Lacking the style of an average urban high schooler, she was as out of place as a girl from small-town Iowa wandering into the big city for the first time. Of middle height and slender, she wore a dress, something flowery that came nearly to her knees. Bare legs, flat shoes. Her hair, a soft, mousy brown, was parted in the middle and partially clipped back. He doubted she wore any makeup at all, which was too bad; she might be beautiful after a few hours at a good salon. It was her eyes that he reacted to, despite himself. Huge and blue, they devoured his face as she crossed the room, the intensity enough to make him shift in his seat.

Adrian had never seen her in his life, and couldn't imagine how she'd found him.

Showing no emotion, he held out a hand. "I'm Adrian Rutledge."

She shook with utter composure. "My name's Lucy Peterson."

"Ms. Peterson." He gestured at a chair. "Please. Have a seat."

"Thank you." She sat, smoothing her skirt over her knees.

She didn't look like his mother. He realized that had been his first fear; that he had an unknown half sister. Not that children always did look like their parents, he reminded himself. The possibility was still on the table.

"What can I do for you?"

"I assume you know nothing of your mother's whereabouts."

Dark anger rose in him at this blunt beginning. Who the hell was she to sit in judgment on him? And she was, he could tell, despite her careful tone.

"And you know this because…?"

"I live over on the peninsula. Your mother has been homeless in my town for the past ten years. I'm reasonably certain no family has visited her or offered any support."

What in hell?

Adrian sat back in his leather desk chair. After a moment, he said, "You're correct in thinking I have no contact with my mother. But tell me just why it is that you believe some homeless woman is my mother? Did she give you my name?"

This Lucy Peterson shook her head. "No. After she was in the accident, I searched her things. It wasn't easy." She seemed to assume he'd care. "She had a shopping cart, but she also had several stashes around town. She liked clothes. And hats. Especially hats. We called her the hat lady." She paused, as if embarrassed.

Between one blink and the next, Adrian saw a park, maybe—lots of lawn, flowering trees in the background. His mother barefoot and twirling, a cotton skirt swirling bell-like, her arms flung out in exuberance. She was laughing; he could almost hear the laugh, openly joyous. And see the hat, broad brimmed and encircled with flowers. The image seemed skewed, as if he'd been dizzy, and he suspected he might have been twirling, too.

He stamped down on the memory. Unclenching his jaw, he asked hoarsely, "What did you find?"

In answer, she bent to open the purse she'd set at her feet and removed a white envelope. "A very old driver's license," she said, and handed it to him.

In shock, he stared at his mother's face. She was so pretty. He'd forgotten. Department of Motor Vehicles photos were usually god-awful, the equivalent of mug shots, but hers was the exception. A soft smile curved her mouth, although her eyes looked sad. Honey-blond, wavy hair was cut, flapper style, at chin length. She'd had beautiful cheekbones, a small, straight nose and that mouth, a cupid's bow.

He forced himself to read the information: Elizabeth H. Rutledge, the expiration date—one year after she disappeared from his life—and the basic stats, hair blond, height five foot five, weight 118, eyes blue.

Not as blue as Lucy Peterson's, he thought involuntarily, looking up.

He had no idea what his face showed, but those eyes were filled with compassion as she handed him something else. As he accepted it involuntarily he looked down, and experienced a spasm of agony. The photograph had faded and cracked, but he remembered the moment. They had dressed for church, and his grandmother had snapped it. His father was tall and stern, but his arm wrapped his wife protectively. She wore a pretty, navy-blue dress with a wide red belt, and on her head was a hat, this one a small red cloche with only a feather decorating it. And he…he stood beside her, his arm about her waist, her hand resting on his shoulder. He remembered feeling proud and mature and yet filled with some anxiety, as though there had been a family quarrel earlier. He might have been seven or eight, his dark hair slicked firmly into place, the suit and white shirt and tie a near match to his father's. He could just make out the house behind them, the one in Edmonds where they'd lived, painted sunny yellow with white trim, the yard brimming with flowers.

He was speechless. His mother had left him, and never once in all the intervening years made contact, yet she'd kept and treasured this photo?

Not just the photo—Lucy was handing over yet one more memento, this one made of red construction paper. On the front was a drawing, the next best thing to stick figures, an adult and a child seemingly holding hands. A woman, because she wore a skirt. His mother, because she also wore a hat festooned with…God. Those had to be flowers. And beneath, in big, uneven letters that suggested he might have been in kindergarten or first grade, it said "Mom and me."

As if through a time warp, he heard his own voice say, "Mom and me are going to the park." *And don't try to stop us,* the defiance in the words suggested. As if he had an eye pressed to a kaleidoscope that spun dizzily, he saw scene after scene, all accompanied by his voice, younger, older, in between, saying, "Mom and me are gonna…" She was his playmate, his best friend, his charge. He stayed close to her. He took care of her.

Until she disappeared, the summer he wasn't home to take care of her.

"God," he whispered, and let the card fall to the desk. He bowed his head and pinched the bridge of his nose.

Lucy Peterson sat silent, letting him process all of this.

He felt as if he'd just been in a car accident. No warning; another vehicle running a red light, maybe, slamming into his. This was the moment of silence afterward, when he sat stunned, trying to decide if he was injured, knowing he'd start hurting any minute.

He lifted his head and said fiercely, "And you know this…homeless person is her? Elizabeth Rutledge."

Lucy bit her lip and nodded. "I had no idea, until I found the driver's license. I guessed her name was Elizabeth. She always went by some variant of it. But that's all any of us knew."

"She didn't tell you her *name?*"

"She…took on different names. All famous people, or fictional ones. I think she believed she was them, for a while. I never saw the moment of transition. One day she'd be Elizabeth Bennett, from *Pride and Prejudice,* you know, and then Queen Elizabeth. Not the first," she added hastily. "She said Queen Bess was bloodthirsty. Elizabeth the second."

"I'm surprised she wasn't the Queen Mother," he said involuntarily.

"Because of the hats? But she wasn't an Elizabeth, and your mother didn't take on any persona that wasn't."

Abruptly he heard the verb tense she was using. *Took on. She believed.* Not *takes on,* or *believes.*

"I thought you said she was in the hospital."

She looked startled. "I did."

"You're talking about her as if she's dead."

"Oh." Once again she worried the lip, as if she often did. "I'm sorry. It's just...the prognosis isn't very good, I'm afraid. She's in a coma."

When he asked, she told him what had happened. That she'd been pushing her shopping cart across the highway, probably on her way to the Safeway store on the other side. The car that hit her had been going too fast, the police had determined, but she had likely been in her own world and hadn't looked before starting across, either.

"She was sent flying twenty feet. The cart..." She swallowed. "It was flattened. Her things strewn everywhere. That was over a week ago. She hasn't stirred since. There was swelling in her brain at first, of course, but they drilled into her skull to relieve it. Which sounds gruesome, but..."

He nodded jerkily. "I understand."

"The thing is, until now it never occurred to any of us to try to find her family. I'm ashamed that it didn't. We tried to take care of her, as much as she'd let us, but… She was just a fixture. You know? Now I wonder, if I'd pushed her—"

"If she didn't know who she was, how could she tell you?"

"But she must have remembered something, or she wouldn't have held on to those. Oh, and these rings." She took them from the envelope and dropped them into his outstretched hand.

A delicate gold wedding band, and an engagement ring with a sizeable diamond. Undoubtedly his father's choice. Adrian remembered it digging into his palm when he grabbed at his mother's hand.

He wanted to feel numb. "She could have sold these."

"It wasn't just the rings she was holding on to," Lucy said softly, her gaze on them. "She was holding on to who she was. On to *you*."

"I haven't heard from her in twenty-three years." He felt sick and angry, and the words were harsh.

"Do you think she didn't love you?"

He hated seeing the pity in her eyes. Jaw tightening, he said, "Let's get back to facts. Where is she?"

"Middleton Community Hospital. Middleton's not far off Highway 101, over the Hood Canal Bridge."

He nodded, already calculating what he had to cancel. Of course, he'd want to transfer her to a Seattle hospital rather than leave her in the hands of a small-town doctor, but first he had to get over there and assess the situation.

"I was hoping you might come," Lucy said.

Glancing at the clock, he said, "I'll be there by evening. I have to clear my schedule and pack a few things."

He saw the relief on her face, and knew she hadn't been sure how he'd react. He might not be willing to drop everything and come running, had his mother walked out on her family for another man, say, or for mercenary reasons. As it was, he might never know why she'd gone, but it was clear she was mentally ill. His childish self had known she wasn't quite like other mothers. Even then, she'd battled depression and a tendency to hear voices and see people no one else saw.

Schizophrenia, he'd guessed coldly as an adult, and still guessed. Her reasons for whatever she'd done were unlikely to make sense to anyone but her. There might be nothing he could do for her now, but she was his obligation and no one else's.

He rose to his feet. "You can tell her doctor to expect me."

She nodded, thanked him rather gravely, and left, apparently satisfied by the success of her errand.

He called Carol and told her to cancel everything on his book for the rest of the week. Then, with practiced efficiency, he began to pack his briefcase. Hospital visiting hours would be limited. Once he'd seen the doctor, he could get plenty done in his hotel room.

CHAPTER TWO

ADRIAN HAD NEVER taken a journey during which he'd been less eager to reach his destination.

Instead of turning on his laptop to work while he waited in line for the ferry, he brooded about what awaited him in Middleton.

He knew one thing: other people besides Lucy Peterson would be looking at him with silent condemnation as they wondered how a man misplaced his mother.

Yeah, Dad, how did *you lose her?*

Or had he discarded her? In retrospect, Adrian had often wondered. He loved his grandparents, but he hadn't wanted to spend an entire summer in Nova Scotia without his mother. Some part of him had known she needed him. Years later, as he grew older, he'd realized that his father had arranged the lengthy visit so that no fiercely protective little boy would be around to object or ask questions when Elizabeth was sent away.

Supposedly she'd gone to a mental hospital. His father had never taken Adrian to visit, probably never visited himself. Perhaps a year later he'd told Adrian that she had checked herself out of the hospital.

With a shrug, he said, "Clearly, she didn't want to get well and come home. I doubt we'll ever hear from her again."

Subject dismissed. That was the last said between

them. The last that ever would be said; his father had died two years ago in a small plane crash.

Adrian moved his shoulders to release tension. Let the good citizens of Middleton stare; he didn't care what they thought. He was there to claim his mother, that was all.

What if he didn't recognize her? If he gazed at the face of this unconscious woman and couldn't find even a trace of the mother he remembered in her?

Ask for DNA testing, of course, but was that really what worried him? Or did his unease come from a fear that he wouldn't recognize her on a more primitive level? Shouldn't he *know* his mother? What if he saw her and felt nothing?

He grunted and started the car as the line in front of him began to move. God knows he hadn't felt much for his mother. Why would he expect to, for a woman he hadn't seen in twenty-three years?

Usually, he would have stayed in his car during the crossing and worked. But his mood was strange today, and he knew he wouldn't be able to concentrate. Instead, he followed most of the passengers to the upper deck, then went outside at the prow.

This early in the spring, the wind on the sound had a bite. He hadn't bothered to change clothes at home, had stopped at his Belltown condominium only long enough to throw what he thought he'd need into a suitcase. He buttoned his suit jacket to keep his tie from whipping over his shoulders, leaned against the railing and watched the gulls swoop over the ferry and the late-afternoon sunlight dance in shards off the choppy waves.

Why would his mother have chosen Middleton? Adrian wondered. How had she even found it? It was barely a dot on the map, likely a logging town once upon a time. Logging had been the major industry over here on the Olympic Peninsula until the forests had been devastated and hard times had come. Tourism had replaced logging on much of the peninsula, but what tourist would seek out Middleton, for God's sake? It wasn't on Hood Canal or the Strait of Juan de Fuca to the north. It was out in the middle of goddamn nowhere.

Why, Mom? Why?

He drove off the ferry at Winslow, on the tip of Bainbridge Island, then followed the two-lane highway that was a near straight-shot the length of the island, across the bridge and past the quaint town of Poulsbo. From then on, civilization pretty much disappeared but for a few gas stations and houses. Traffic was heavy, with this a Friday, so he couldn't eat up the miles the way he'd have liked to. No chance to pass, no advantage if he'd been able to. He crossed the Hood Canal Bridge, the water glittering in the setting sunlight. Summer homes clung like barnacles along the shore. Then forest closed in, second-growth and empty of any evidence of human habitation.

Reluctance swelled in him and clotted in his chest. A couple of times he rubbed his breastbone as if he'd relieve heartburn. The light was fading by the time he spotted the sign: Middleton, 5 Miles.

He was the only one in the line of traffic to make the turn. And why would anyone? Along with distaste for what lay ahead came increasing bafflement at his mother's choice. How had she even gotten here? Did the town boast a Greyhound station? Had she gone as far as her money held out? Stabbed her finger at a map? Or had some vagary of fate washed her up here?

So close to Seattle, and yet she'd never tried to get in touch with him.

So weirdly far from Seattle in every way that counted.

The speed limit dropped to thirty-five and he obediently slowed as the highway—if you could dignify it with that name—entered the outskirts. He saw the Safeway store almost immediately, and his foot lifted involuntarily from the gas pedal. Here. She was hit here. Flung to one of these narrow paved shoulders. With dark encroaching, he couldn't see where, or if any evidence remained.

Ahead, he saw the blue hospital sign, but some impulse made him turn the other direction, toward downtown. The Burger King on the left seemed the only outpost of the modern world. Otherwise, the town he saw under streetlights probably hadn't changed since the 1950s. There was an old-fashioned department store, churches—he saw three church spires without looking hard—pharmacy, hardware store. Some of the buildings had false fronts. All of the town's meager commerce seemed to lie along the one main street, except for the Safeway.

A memory stirred in his head. Wasn't there a Middleton in Nova Scotia? Or a Middleburg, or Middle*something?* Had this town *sounded* like home to his mother? Had she stayed, then, because it felt like home, or because people here were good to her? Lucy Peterson had expressed guilt that they hadn't done more, but she'd obviously cared.

More than Elizabeth Rutledge's own family had.

His jaw muscles spasmed. If this woman was his mother, he'd have to tell his grandmother, who was frail but at eighty-two was still living in her house in the town of Brookfield in Nova Scotia. Would she be glad? Or grieve terribly to know what her daughter's life had been like?

He ran out of excuses not to go to the hospital after a half dozen city blocks. There wasn't much to this town.

The hospital was about what he'd expected: two-story in the central block, with wings to each side. He parked and walked in the front entrance. The white-haired woman behind the desk looked puzzled when he asked for Elizabeth Rutledge. Then her face abruptly cleared.

"Oh! The hat lady! That's what Lucy said her name is. You must be the son." She scrutinized him with interest and finally disappointment. "You don't look like her, do you?"

With thinning patience, he repeated, "Her room number?"

She beamed, oblivious to his strained civility. "Two sixty-eight." She waved. "Just go right up the elevators there and then turn to your left."

Despite a headache, he forced himself to nod. "Thank you."

The elevator door opened as soon as he pushed the button. Not much business at—he glanced at his watch—7:13 in the evening. The doors opened again almost immediately, and he had no choice but to step out. He turned left, as ordered. A white-capped woman at the nurses' station was writing in a chart and didn't notice him when he passed.

Most of the doors to patient rooms stood ajar. TVs were on. Voices murmured. Laughter came from one room. From another, an ominous gurgling. In 264 a woman in a hospital gown was shuffling to the bathroom, her IV pole going with her, someone who might be a daughter hovering at her side. 266 was dark.

The door to 268 was wide open and the first bed was unoccupied. The curtain around the second bed was pulled, blocking his view. He heard a voice beyond the curtain; a nurse, maybe? Adrian stopped and took a deep breath. He couldn't understand why this was bothering him so much. Whether she was his mother or not, this woman was a stranger to him. An obligation. No more, no less.

He walked in.

Hooked to an IV and to monitors that softly beeped, a woman lay in the hospital bed.

One look, and he knew. Still as death, she was his mother. For a moment, he quit breathing.

Beside the bed, Lucy Peterson sat in a chair reading aloud.

Poetry, of all things.

She had a beautiful voice, surprisingly rich and expressive for a woman as subdued in appearance as she was. For a moment, he just listened, wondering if his mother heard at all. Was the voice a beacon, a golden glow, that led her back toward life? A puzzle that no longer made sense? Or was she no longer capable of understanding or caring?

However quiet his footfall, Lucy heard him and looked up, with a flash of those expressive blue eyes. She immediately closed the book without marking any place and set it on the table. "You're here."

She sounded ambivalent; pleased, maybe, in one way, less so in another. Glad he'd lived up to his word, but not sure she liked him?

He didn't care, although he was equally ambivalent

about her presence. He wanted to focus on this woman in the bed—his mother—with no witnesses to his emotional turbulence. And yet he felt obscurely grateful that Lucy was here, a buffer. For once in his life, he needed her brand of simple kindness.

In response to her words, but ignoring her tone, he said, "Why so surprised? You beat me here."

"I didn't have to stop to pack."

He nodded. And made himself look fully at his mother's face.

After a long moment, he said, almost conversationally, "Do you know she's only fifty-six?"

"When I saw her driver's license."

"She looks…" He couldn't finish.

Very softly, Lucy said, "I thought she might be seventy."

His mother's face was weathered and lined far beyond her years, although the bone structure was the same. The slightly pointed chin, too, that had given her an elfin appearance. He'd noticed it most when her mood was fey, although it was nearly sharp now, whittled by hardship. Her hair was white, and thin. Her hands, still atop the coverlet, were knobbed with arthritis.

This was what a lifetime without adequate nutrition or medical care or beauty products did. Elizabeth Rutledge had been a beautiful woman. Now she was an old one.

Still, he devoured the sight of her face, the slightness of the body beneath the covers, the tired hands, with a hunger that felt bottomless. Inside, he was still the child who needed his mom and knew she needed him.

He stepped forward, gripping the round metal railing on this side of the bed. The pain in his chest seared him.

"Mom." The word came out guttural, shocking him. He swallowed and tried again. "Mom. It's me. Adrian."

Of course, she didn't stir; no flicker of response twitched even an eyelid. She breathed. In and out, unaided, the only sign of life beyond the numbers on the monitor.

"I wish I'd known where you were. I would have come to get you a long time ago."

If he'd come two weeks ago, before the accident, would she have known him? She had changed, but at least in his memory she was an adult. How much did he resemble his ten-year-old self? Even his voice would still have been a child's. What were his chances now of getting through to her?

After a minute, in self-defense, he raised his gaze to Lucy Peterson, who watched him. "What was that you were reading?"

She glanced at the book. "Elizabeth Barrett Browning. I think I told you—" she bit her lip "—how much your mother liked her poetry."

So much, she'd believed she *was* Elizabeth Barrett Browning. And a host of other Elizabeths, real and imaginary. Just never herself, Elizabeth Hamlin Rutledge, once daughter of Burt and Lana Hamlin, then wife of Maxwell Rutledge and mother of Adrian.

Perhaps when he went away that summer and let go of his grip on her hand, she'd forgotten who she was. Had she lost herself that long ago?

"I wish I knew…" he murmured, unsure what he wished. For the true story of that summer, and the year that followed? To find out what happened after, how she'd washed up here, how she had come to grasp for identities that had only a given name in common with her true self? All of the above?

"Ah," said a voice behind him. "You must be the son."

Adrian let go of the railing and turned. The doctor who'd entered was an elderly man, short and cherubic, head bald but for a white tonsure. He wore a lab coat open over a plaid golf shirt. Smiling, he held out his hand and they shook.

Then he looked past Adrian and shook his head in disapproval. "Lucy, you're back. You know, she won't float away if you go home and watch a sitcom, take a long bath, get to bed early."

Adrian supposed that was a good way to describe his childish fears about his mother: that she might float away if he let go. There had always been something insubstantial about her, not quite anchored to the here and now.

Lucy smiled, but said, "I didn't want Mr. Rutledge to feel abandoned."

Adrian knew vaguely that women like this did exist—caretakers, nurturers. Or perhaps he was jumping to a conclusion where she was concerned. Maybe it was only his mother who inspired this fierce need to protect.

"It sounds as if Ms. Peterson went to a lot of effort to locate me," he said.

"And thank God she succeeded. Ah…I'm Ben Slater."

"I appreciate your taking care of her, Doctor. I'm hoping you can tell me more about what's going on with my mother so that I can make decisions about her care."

"I haven't been able to do much. The truth is, with

brain injuries we're most often left waiting. However much we learn, there's more we don't know. Someone who got a minor knock on the head dies, someone who falls ten stories to the sidewalk barely has a headache. I wish I could tell you how much damage she sustained, but I can't. She has a broken hip and ribs as well as some internal bleeding from the impact of the car, but the real problem is that she was lifted in the air and flung a fair distance onto the pavement. She struck her head hard. We did relieve some swelling in the brain, but it's subsided satisfactorily. She may yet simply open her eyes and ask where she is."

And she may not. Adrian had no trouble hearing what Slater didn't say.

On the other hand, how many head injuries had this small-town doc actually seen? What was he? Their trauma specialist? They did have an E.R., so they must have a specialist.

"Has she been seen by a neurologist?" Adrian asked, knowing the answer.

"Oh, I'm a neurosurgeon," Dr. Slater said cheerily. "Retired, of course. My wife was from Middleton, and we always intended to retire here. But I still do some consulting."

This fat little guy in the plaid shirt was a *neurosurgeon?* Was that possible?

Barely managing to suppress his you've-got-to-be-kidding reaction, Adrian asked, "Where did you work?"

"Ended up at Harborview in Seattle. I was on the University of Washington faculty."

Adrian's preconceptions didn't quite vanish—it was more like watching a piece of paper slowly burn until only grey, weightless ash hung insubstantially in the air.

His mother wasn't being cared for by some small-town practitioner who'd probably been in the bottom quarter of his class. By bizarre chance, her doctor might be one of the most highly qualified specialists in the country.

"My mother is fortunate you happened to be here."

"She would have been if I could fix her. I can't."

"And you don't think anyone can."

He shook his head, his gaze resting on his patient's face. "It's up to her now. Or to God, if you believe. Lucy—" he smiled at the young woman "—may do more good by sitting here talking and reading to your mother than I can with all the technology at my disposal."

Neurosurgeons were not known for their humility or fatalism. Adrian still had trouble believing in this one. But perhaps a lifetime of trying to salvage brain-damaged people made a man both fatalistic and humble.

Dr. Slater talked some more, about reflexes and brainwaves, but Adrian had begun to feel numb. The guy noticed, and abruptly stopped. "We should talk about this tomorrow. I understand you haven't seen your mother in years. You must be in shock."

"You could say that," Adrian admitted.

"Lucy," the doctor said briskly, "did you make arrangements for him for the night?"

Rebellion stirred, but honestly Adrian hoped she had a better suggestion than the crummy motel with kitchenettes he'd seen half a mile back.

"Yes, Sam's holding a room for him," she said. "If that's all right," she added, looking at him.

"Sam?"

"My sister Samantha. She owns a bed-and-breakfast. It's very nice."

He nodded. "Then thank you."

"And unless you had dinner on the way…" Seeing his expression, she said firmly, "We'll stop at the café on the way. It's late, but we'll come up with something."

"Good." The doctor patted her hand, shook Adrian's, said "I'll see you tomorrow," then departed.

Lucy picked up her book and started toward the door in turn. "I'll leave you alone with your mother for a few minutes. Just come on out when you're ready."

He was ready now, but in the face of her faith that he wanted to commune with this unconscious woman, he once again stepped to the bedside and looked down at her face. The resemblance to the mother he remembered was undeniably there, but in a way that made him uncomfortable. Age aside, it was like the difference between a living, breathing person and an eerily real cast of that person at a wax museum. He might as well have been standing here looking at his mother's body at the morgue.

But he knew why Lucy had been reading aloud. The silence had to be filled. "It's Adrian," he said tentatively. "I missed you. I didn't know what happened. Why you went away. I still don't know. I'd like to hear about it, when you wake up."

He couldn't quite bring himself to touch her. Not surprising, given that he wasn't much for hugs and handholding. Maybe he was afraid he'd find her hands to be icy cold.

"Well. Ah. I'll be back in the morning. I'll probably make arrangements to move you to Seattle, where you can be close to me."

An uneasy sense that she might, in fact, not like his plan stirred in him, but what the hell else was he supposed to do? Leave her here and drive back and forth for obligatory visits? Did they even have a long-term nursing facility here, assuming that's what she required?

He cleared his throat, said, "Good night," and escaped.

LUCY WAS PRETTY sure she didn't like Adrian Rutledge, but she was prepared to feel sorry for him when he walked out of his mother's hospital room. This had to be hard for him.

However, his expression was utterly composed when he appeared. "You needn't feel you have to feed me. If you just want to tell me the options and directions to the bed-and-breakfast."

"I have to stop by the café and see how they're doing without me," she explained. "I own it. Friday evening is one of our busiest times. I'm usually there. I may not have time to sit down with you."

He didn't look thrilled to be going anywhere with her, but finally nodded. "Fine. Should I follow you?"

"My car's right out front. Yours, too, I assume?"

He nodded again, the motion a little jerky. Maybe he wasn't as cold as he seemed. Lucy tried to imagine how disoriented he must feel by now.

Be charitable, she reminded herself. *For the hat lady's sake, if not his.*

Lisa Enger, the night nurse, greeted them. "I'll keep a good eye on her," she promised.

They rode down in the elevator silently, both staring straight ahead like two strangers pretending the other wasn't there. Lucy was usually able to chat with just about anybody, but she was pretty sure he wouldn't welcome conversation right now. Not until they were out in the parking lot did she speak.

"There's my car."

He nodded and pointed out his, a gray Mercedes sedan.

"I'll come down your row."

"All right."

Her small Ford Escort felt shabbier when the Mercedes fell in behind it, and she sympathized. She felt plain and uninteresting in his presence, too. She and her car had a lot in common.

He parked beyond her on Olympic Avenue half a block from the café, then joined her on the sidewalk.

"I'm sorry you had to take the day off to drive all the way to Seattle."

"Would you have believed a word I said if I'd just called?"

He was silent until they reached the door. "I don't know."

Well, at least he was honest.

He held open the door for her. Slipping past him, Lucy was more aware of him than she'd let herself be to this point. She'd known he was handsome, of course, and physically imposing. That his thick, dark hair was expensively cut, his charcoal suit probably cost more than she spent on clothes in a year and that his eyes were a chilly shade of gray. She refused to be intimidated by him. But just for a second, looking at his big, capable hand gripping the door and feeling the heat of his body as she brushed him, she felt her heart skip a beat.

He'd definitely be sexy if only he were more likeable. If he didn't look at her as if she were the janitor who'd quit scrubbing the floor long enough to try to tell him his business.

She grimaced. Okay, that might be her own self-esteem issues talking. He probably looked down on everyone. It was probably an advantage in corporate law, turning every potential litigant into a stuttering idiot.

Following her into the restaurant, he glanced around, apparently unimpressed by the casual interior and the half dozen remaining diners.

"Your mother ate here a couple of times a week," she told him.

His eyebrows rose. "She had money…?"

Lucy shook her head. "She was my guest."

A muscle ticked in his cheek. "Oh."

For a moment Lucy thought he would feel compelled to thank her. A surprisingly fierce sense of repugnance filled her. Who was he to speak for the mother he didn't even know?

She hastily grabbed a menu and led him to the same table where his mother always sat, right in front of the window. "I'll be back to take your order as soon as I check in the kitchen."

It was easy to pretend she was immersed in some crisis and send Melody out to take his order instead. Once his food was delivered, Lucy stole surreptitious looks as he ate. She was pleased to see that he actually looked startled after the first spoonful of curried lentil soup, one of her specialties and personal favorites. He'd probably expected something out of a can.

Melody was prepared to close up for her, so once she saw him decline dessert, Lucy went back out to reclaim him. Without comment she took his money, then said, "I'm ready to go if you'd like to follow me again."

A hint of acerbity crept into his tone. "Do you think I'd get lost?"

"I pass Sam's place on my way home. I won't stop."

He nodded. "Then thank you."

It was getting harder for him to squeeze those *thank-yous* out, Lucy judged. Clearly, he wasn't in the habit of being in anyone's debt.

Once again he held open the door for her, the courtesy automatic. At least he was polite.

Outside, she said, "It's called Doveport Bed and Breakfast. You'll see it on the right, about half a mile from here. There's a sign out front."

He nodded, pausing on the sidewalk while she opened her car door and got in. More good manners, Lucy realized; in Seattle, a woman might be in danger if she were alone even momentarily on a dark street. Maybe his mother had instilled some good qualities in him, before she disappeared from his life.

However *that* happened.

Her forehead crinkled. How old had he been when his parents divorced, or his mother went away? Twenty-three years ago, he'd said. Surely he wasn't more than in his mid-thirties now. So he probably wasn't even a teenager when he lost her.

Was he bitter at what he saw as abandonment? Lucy hadn't been able to tell. Since she'd handed him the driver's license and photo in his office, he'd seemed more stunned than anything. She'd almost had the sense he was sleepwalking, that he hadn't yet figured out how to react. At least, she hoped that's what he was doing, and that he wasn't always so unemotional. Because if he was, she hated to think of the hat lady consigned to his care.

Lucy made sure the lights of his car were right behind her until she reached Sam's B and B. His headlights swept the sign, and his turn signal went on. She accelerated and left him behind, wondering if she'd arrive at the hospital tomorrow and find he had already made plans to have his mother moved to Seattle.

She shuddered to think of the gentle, confused hat lady waking to the stern face of this son she didn't remember, her bewildered gaze searching for other, familiar faces.

Unhappily she wondered if finding him had been the right thing to do after all.

CHAPTER THREE

STRANGELY, WHEN Adrian lay in bed that night, he kept thinking about Lucy Peterson instead of his mother. Maybe he was practicing avoidance. He didn't know, but he was bothered by the fact that he didn't understand her. He prided himself on being able to read people. The ability to anticipate reactions made him good at his job.

He'd long since learned that self-interest was paramount in most people. But if a single thing Lucy had done for his mother—and now for him—helped her in any way, he couldn't see it. So what motivated her? Why had she noticed his mother in the first place? Downtown Seattle was rife with homeless people, sleeping in doorways, curled on park benches, begging on corners, huddling from the rain in bus shelters. To most people, they fell somewhere between annoying and invisible. When had Lucy first stopped to talk to his mother? Offered her a meal?

Why had she cared so much that she'd been determined to find the confused old lady's family?

He kept puzzling it out and not arriving at any answers. That bugged him. Yeah, she might just be the nurturing kind. But even people like that didn't usually nurture a homeless person. Anyway, she wasn't a completely soft touch, ready to expect the best of everyone. She'd certainly made a judgment about him before she even met him. She was doing her best for him because of his mother, but she didn't like having to do it.

That stung, which bothered him, too. Why in hell would he care what a small-town café owner thought of him?

He shifted restlessly in bed, picturing the way she looked at him, her eyes seeming to dissect him.

Adrian fell asleep eventually, but his dreams were uneasy and he jerked awake several times. The damn bed was too soft. The down pillows kept wadding into lumps beneath his head. Even the scent of potpourri in the room was unfamiliar and too sweet, slipping into his dreams.

He got up in the morning feeling jittery yet exhausted. The room was nice enough if you liked such things, he'd noted last night, and was decorated with obligatory old-fashioned floral wallpaper and antiques. He didn't much care, but was relieved to have his own bathroom. This morning, though, he walked into it and stopped dead, staring at the enormous, claw-footed tub.

"What the hell…?" His incredulous gaze searched the wall above, and returned to the faucet that didn't even have a handheld showerhead. He hated taking baths. All he wanted was a hard spray of hot water to bring him to his senses.

Given no choice, however, he took a hasty bath, got dressed and went downstairs to sample the breakfast.

If he had to sit at a common table, he'd head to town instead. Chatting over breakfast with complete strangers held no appeal. He'd find a diner if he had to drive to Sequim. Fortunately, the dining room held several tables. A family sat at one, a couple at another. He took a place as far from the others as he could get.

He hadn't paid much attention to his hostess last night, but this morning he studied her in search of a resemblance to her sister. They did both have blue eyes. Samantha Peterson was less striking but prettier. She wore her curly blond hair cut short and had a curvy figure. *She* didn't look at him as if he'd crawled out from a sewer drain. Instead, she chatted in a sunny way as she served thick slabs of French toast covered with huckleberries and powdered sugar, oatmeal and bacon that made his mouth water. It was the best breakfast he'd had in years; creativity in the kitchen obviously ran in the family.

Funny thing was, he knew he wouldn't remember her face two days from now. Her sister's would stick in his mind.

When Samantha paused to refill his coffee after everyone else had left the dining room, he asked, "Did you know my mother?"

"The hat lady? Sure, but not as well as Lucy. I'm not on her route, you know."

Puzzled, he asked, "Her route?"

"Um." As casually as if he'd invited her, she filled a second cup with coffee for herself and sat across from him. "Your mom had a routine. On a given day, you knew she'd have certain stops. The library on Mondays—they let her check out books even though she didn't have an address—the thrift shop Tuesdays, because they're closed Sunday and Monday and they always had new stuff then—"

"But she didn't have money."

She shrugged, the gesture both careless and generous. "It's run by the Faith Lutheran Church. They let her take whatever she wanted."

"Like hats," he reflected.

"Right. Another of her stops was Yvonne's Needle and Thread. Yvonne let her pick out trims, silk flowers, whatever, that she used to decorate the hats. The senior center has a pancake breakfast on Wednesday and a spaghetti dinner on Friday, and she was always at those. Lucy's twice a week, the Pancake Haus once a week, and so on."

What was with this town? Was every single citizen willing to give away whatever she'd wanted? Would any needy soul qualify, or just his mother? As a child he'd loved his mother, but he couldn't imagine that one vague old lady was that special.

"She loved garage sales," Samantha continued. "Oh, and rummage sales, like at one of the churches. During the season, she'd deviate from her usual route to take in any sales. She was always the first one there."

"She must have picked up the newspaper then, to read the classifieds."

"Probably," she said cheerfully.

Had his mother read the front page news? What did a woman who believed she was a nineteenth-century poet make of the presidential election or Mideast politics? Or did she skip anything that perplexed her?

Frowning, he asked, "Where did she sleep?"

"We're not quite sure. I offered her a room over the winter, but she wouldn't accept. I'm a little too far out from the center of town for her, I think. Father Joseph at Saint Mary's left a basement door unlocked for her when the weather was cold, and he says she did sleep there on a cot sometimes. And Marie at Olympic Motel says she'd occasionally stay there, too."

Adrian continued to grapple with the concept of an

entire town full of do-gooders. "In other words, every-body knew her."

"Oh, sure." She smiled at him. "We did our best."

"I'm...grateful." The words were hard to say for a man who'd never in his life taken charity. Depending entirely on the kindness of strangers...he couldn't imagine.

No—maybe not strangers. She'd stayed here in Middleton long enough that she'd been theirs, in a sense. Lucy Peterson clearly felt proprietary.

Adrian discovered he didn't like the idea that every shopkeeper in this miserable town knew his mother, and he didn't.

Samantha waved off his gratitude. "Oh, heavens! We loved her."

There it was again, that past tense. Nobody expected her to survive. Or perhaps they assumed he'd take care of her now, as, of course, he intended to do.

He drained his coffee and made his excuses. Back in his room, he sat at the small desk and took out his cell phone. It was early enough he got through to an old friend.

Tom Groendyk and he had shared an old house in the U district through grad school. Tom was an orthopedic surgeon now at Swedish Medical Center, having left the area for his internship and residency but coming home two years ago.

"Hey. I have a favor to ask of you," Adrian said, after brief greetings. "You heard of a neurosurgeon named Ben Slater?"

"Are you kidding?" Tom laughed. "The guy looks like Santa Claus and grades like Scrooge."

"Is he any good?"

"Only the best. Hell of a teacher, and hell of a surgeon from what I hear." His voice sharpened. "Why? Is there something you haven't told me?"

Adrian and Tom played racquetball once a week, had dinner or met for drinks every couple of weeks. Tom hadn't married, either, although he was seeing a woman pretty seriously right now.

Adrian wouldn't have told many other people, but Tom did know some of his history. "I'm over on the peninsula," he said. "My mother has showed up."

There was a momentary silence. "Showed up?"

"She's apparently mentally ill. She's been homeless. Nobody knew who she was until she got hit by a car. When they searched her stuff, they found an old driver's license and tracked me down."

He didn't mention the photograph of his father, mother and him, or that Mother's Day card. He still wasn't ready to face the memories they had conjured up.

"If you're looking for the best to treat her, Slater's it," Tom said, adding, "But the guy's retired. I guess I could ask around and find out where he is, but I can give you some other names instead."

"He's here, believe it or not. Evidently his wife grew up here in Middleton, and they came back when he retired. He must have gotten bored. He's consulting now."

Tom let out a low whistle. "You got lucky then."

"He says there's nothing he can do for her. Either she comes out of the coma or she doesn't."

"So what are you asking me? Whether a different guy would tell you something else?"

Adrian squeezed the bridge of his nose. "Yeah. I guess that is what I'm asking. Should I get a second opinion?"

"If it were my mother," his friend said, "I wouldn't bother." However blunt the answer, his voice had softened. "Man, I'm sorry."

"Yeah. Thanks."

"So what are you going to do?"

"I don't know," Adrian admitted. "Go on over to the hospital, I guess. See how it goes over the next day or two. Then I suppose I'd better find someplace to move her to. I had Carol cancel my appointments through Tuesday. Fortunately, I didn't have anything earthshaking in the works."

"Yeah, listen, if there's anything I can do…"

"Thanks." He had to clear his throat. "I'll call." He hit End and sat there for a minute, his chest tight. What a bizarre conclusion to his childhood fantasies of finding his mom.

He felt no great eagerness to go sit at her bedside, but finally stood. He looked at his laptop and decided not to take it. Maybe this afternoon, if he went back to the hospital. He locked his room and left without seeing his hostess.

The hospital appeared even smaller and less prepossessing in daylight. He doubted it had sixty beds. It probably existed primarily as an emergency facility, given the recreational opportunities nearby in the Olympic National Park and on the water. Mountain climbers, hikers and boaters had plenty of accidents, and Highway 101, crowded with tourists, undoubtedly produced its share. Once stabilized, patients could be moved to a larger facility in Port Angeles or Bremerton if not across the sound to Seattle.

He knew his way today, and didn't pause at the information desk. This time a nurse intercepted him upstairs and said firmly, "May I help you?"

"I'm Elizabeth Rutledge's son."

"Oh! The hat lady." She flushed. "That is…"

He shook his head. "Don't worry about it."

"Dr. Slater stopped in briefly this morning. He said to tell you he'd be back this afternoon."

He nodded. "I thought I'd just sit with her for a while."

"We're so glad you're here. We're all very fond of her, you know."

Adrian studied the woman, graying and sturdy. "You knew her, too?"

"Not well, but my sister owns the Hair Do. Cindy washed and styled her hair regularly. Gave her perms every few months, too."

"Why?" Adrian asked bluntly.

She blinked. "Why?"

"Your sister is a businesswoman. Why would she give away her services to a homeless woman?"

She raised her eyebrows, her friendliness evaporating. "Lucy didn't say what you do for a living."

"I'm an attorney."

"Don't you do pro bono work?"

Everyone in the firm was required to handle the occasional pro bono case on a rotating schedule. "Yes," he admitted.

"What's the difference? Cindy likes your mom. Whenever I walked in, they'd be laughing like they were having the best time ever."

That was the payback? Laughter? And what the hell did a woman who couldn't remember who she was and who lived on the streets have to laugh about?

He went on to his mother's room, feeling the nurse's stare following him.

Somehow, he wasn't surprised to hear Lucy's voice when he walked in the open door.

She wasn't reading this morning, just talking.

"Yesterday, I saw some early daffodils opening. I know you'd have been as excited as I was. Well, they might have been narcissus or some species daffodil. Is there such a thing? These had orange centers and were small. But they were beautiful and bright." She paused, as if listening to an answer. When she went on, Lucy sounded regretful. "I wish I had time to garden. Every time I lug out the mower and tackle the lawn, I think about where I'd put flower beds. You know how much I'd like to grow old roses. I love to get out my books and think, too bad the China roses couldn't stand the cold here, but I'll definitely grow some of the really old ones. Rosamunde and Cardinal de Richelieu and Autumn Damask. Oh, and Celestial. And a moss rose. Have you ever seen one, with the fuzz all over the bud? I think they look fascinating. Even the names of the roses are beautiful. Fantin-Latour." She made every syllable sensuous. "Comte Chambord. Ispahan." She laughed. "Of course, I'm undoubtedly butchering them, since I don't speak French."

So she was sentimental. Why wasn't he surprised?

Adrian continued in, brushing the curtain as he rounded it. "Good morning."

She looked up, startled. "I didn't hear you coming."

Irrelevantly, he noticed what beautiful skin she had, almost translucent. Tiny freckles scattered from the bridge of her nose to her cheekbones. They hadn't been noticeable until now, with sunlight falling across her.

"I heard you talking about gardening."

Her cheeks pinkened, but Lucy only nodded. "Your mother told me spring was her favorite season. She loved to walk around town and look at everyone's gardens. Sometimes we dreamed together."

What a way to put it. Had he ever in his life dreamed together with anyone?

He knew the answer: with his mother.

Almost against his will, his gaze was drawn to her, looking like a marble effigy lying in that hospital bed. It was hard to believe this was the vivacious woman of his memory.

"We had a garden when I was growing up," he said abruptly. "In Edmonds. We didn't have a big yard, but it was beautiful. She spent hours out there every day on her knees digging in flower beds. I remember the hollyhocks, a row of them in front of the dining-room windows. Delphinium and foxgloves and climbing roses. Mom said she liked flowers that grew toward the sky instead of hugging the ground."

"Oh," Lucy breathed. "What a lovely thing to say."

"She talked like that a lot. My father would grunt and ignore her." Damn it, why had he said that? Adrian wondered, disconcerted. Reminiscing about his mother was one thing, about the tensions in his family another thing altogether.

"I'm sorry," Lucy said softly. Perhaps she saw his face tighten, because instead of asking more about his father or when his mother had disappeared from his life, she said, "I thought about starting a small flower bed under my front windows this spring." Almost apologetically, she told him, "I don't have very much time to work in my yard. I wanted to take Elizabeth with me to the nursery to pick out the plants. She has such a good eye." Her hand crept onto the coverlet and squeezed the inert, gnarled hand of his mother. "I wish she'd wake up and say, 'When shall we go?'"

She sounded so unhappy, he thought with faint shock, *she loves Mom.* How did that happen?

"I'm surprised to see you here again this morning."

She wrinkled her nose. "Because Dr. Slater tried to bully me into staying away?"

His mouth twitched. He doubted Ben Slater knew how to bully anyone. Although… "I have a friend who took a class from him in med school. Tom says he's a tough grader."

"You checked up on him."

"Wouldn't you have?" he countered.

The pause was long enough to tell him how reluctant she was when she conceded, "I suppose so. Did he get a satisfactory rating?"

"A gold star. He's the best, Tom says."

"I could have told you that."

But he wouldn't have believed her. They both knew that.

When he didn't respond, she asked, "Have you made a plan yet?"

He looked back at his mother, watching as her chest rose and fell, the stirring of the covers so subtle he had to watch carefully to see it. "Move her to Seattle. What else can I do?"

As if he'd asked quite seriously, Lucy said, "Leave her here for now. Until Dr. Slater says she can go to a nursing home. And we even have one of those here in Middleton, you know."

God, he was tempted. Leave her to people who cared. Whose faces she'd recognized if she opened her eyes.

Abdicate.

He shook his head reluctantly. "I don't have time to be running over here constantly. And it sounds as if the chances are good she won't be waking up."

Lucy pinched her lips together. After a long time, she said, "I suppose that's true." She gazed at his mother, not him. "How soon will you be taking her?"

"I don't know. I'll get my assistant hunting for a place with an open bed."

Now she did turn a cool look on him. "Won't you want to check it out yourself?"

"Why do you dislike me?" he surprised himself by asking.

With a flash of alarm in her eyes, she drew back. "What would make you think—"

"Come on. It's obvious. You think I should have found her. Taken care of her."

Her chin rose fractionally. "I suppose I do."

Adrian shoved his hands in his pockets. "I did look for her some years back." He rotated his shoulders in discomfiture. "I suppose…not that hard. I thought she was dead."

Her brow crinkled. "Why?"

"Even as a kid, I knew there was something wrong with her. My father claimed she'd gone to a hospital to be treated. Then he told me she'd checked herself out because she didn't want to get well. I was young enough to believe that if she was alive, she wouldn't have left me."

She stared at him, and prompted, "Young enough to believe…? Does that mean, now that you're an adult, you don't have any trouble believing she'd ditch you without a second thought?"

God. He felt sick. That rich breakfast wasn't settling well in his stomach.

"Apparently she did," he said flatly.

He felt himself reddening as her extraordinary eyes studied him like a bug under a microscope.

She surprised him, though, by sounding gentle. "How old were you?"

His jaw tightened. "Ten."

"And you never saw her or heard from her again?"

He shook his head.

"How awful," she murmured, as if to herself. "Your father doesn't sound like a, um…"

"Warm man?" Irony in his voice, Adrian finished her thought. "No. You could say that."

"Have you told him…" She nodded toward the bed.

"He's dead."

"Oh." Compassion and an array of other emotions crossed her face, as if the sunlight coming through the window were suddenly dappled with small, fluttering shadows. "Do you have other family? I didn't think to ask if you had sisters or brothers."

Adrian shook his head. "Just me. Dad remarried, but as far as I know he and my stepmother never considered having kids."

She nodded, her gaze softer now, less piercing.

Without knowing why, he kept talking. "His parents are still alive. I'm not close to them." He hesitated. "My maternal grandmother is alive, too. I haven't told her yet."

"Oh! But won't she be thrilled?"

"I'm not so sure. She might have preferred to think

her child was dead. To find out she didn't care enough to ever call home…" He shrugged.

"That's not fair! She forgot who she was!"

"But then *Maman* may feel she failed her in some way."

"Oh," Lucy said again. "*Maman?* Is that what you call her? Is she French?"

"French Canadian. She lives in Nova Scotia. That's where I was, with my grandparents, the summer my mother went away."

"What a sad story."

Oh, good. He'd gone from being a monster in her eyes to being pitiable. Adrian wasn't sure he welcomed the change.

When he said nothing, she flushed and rose to her feet. "I really had better go. I don't do breakfast, but it's time for me to start lunch." She hesitated. "If you'd like…"

What was she going to suggest? That she could feed him free of charge like she had his mother?

"Like?" he prodded, when she didn't finish.

"I was going to say that, after lunch, I could take an hour or two and introduce you to some of the people who knew your mother. They could tell you something about her life."

"Your sister started to."

He felt weirdly uncomfortable with the idea. But if his mother died without ever coming out of the coma, this might be the only way he'd ever find out who she'd become. Perhaps she'd even given someone a clue as to where she'd been in the years before she came to Middleton. He thought his grandmother, at least, would want to know as much as he could find out.

After a minute he nodded and said formally, "Thank you. I'd appreciate that."

Lucy smiled, lighting her pale, serious face, making her suddenly, startlingly beautiful in a way unfamiliar to him. Adrian's chest constricted.

He thought he took a step toward her, searching her eyes the way she often did his. Her pupils dilated as she stared back at him, her smile dying. He felt cruel when wariness replaced it.

She inched around him as if afraid to take her gaze from him, then backed toward the door. "I'll, um, see you later then? Say, two o'clock?"

"I'll come and eat lunch first." He paused. "Your soup was amazing."

The tiniest of smiles curved her lips again. "Wait until you taste my basil mushroom tomato soup."

His own mouth crooked up. "I'll look forward to it."

"Well, then…" She backed into the door frame and gave an involuntarily "umph" before she flushed in embarrassment, cast him one more alarmed look and fled.

He stood there by the curtain, the soft beep of the machines that monitored his mother's life signs in his ears, and wondered what in hell had just happened.

CHAPTER FOUR

THE CAFÉ WAS BUSY, which made it even more ridiculous that Lucy's heart insisted on skipping a beat every time the door opened and a customer entered. Was she excited at the prospect of spending more time with Adrian? Nervous about it? She didn't even know, but she didn't like reacting so strongly for no good reason at all.

For goodness' sake, he was going to eat lunch in the café! He'd eaten here last night. She planned to introduce him to a few people. He'd probably freeze her out in between stops. He was good at that.

Reason didn't seem to be helping. Something had changed between them this morning. He'd let her see the cracks in his facade of invulnerability. Well, he might not have *chosen* to show them, but they were there. He did hurt. This wasn't easy for him.

And he'd looked at her. Really looked, and maybe even liked what he'd seen. For just a moment, she'd seen something on his face that had stolen her breath and panicked her.

Common sense and reason did work to stifle any sense of expectation that he was suddenly, madly attracted to her. Okay, there might have been a brief flicker. But Lucy hated to think how she compared to the women he usually dated.

Her hands froze in the act of tossing salad in a huge bowl.

Dated? He could conceivably be married. When she researched him on the Internet before going over to Seattle that day, she didn't see anything to make her think he was, and he certainly hadn't mentioned a wife, as in, *My wife will visit any nursing homes my assistant finds,* which you'd think would be natural. But he was closemouthed enough that it was still possible.

And what difference did it make if he was? she asked herself with unaccountable depression. He was here in Middleton until Tuesday. Today was Saturday. Once he was gone, she'd probably get a nice note thanking her for taking care of his mother and that was it. Oh, and the chances were his assistant would've written the note. Wasn't that what assistants did?

Mabel stuck her head in the kitchen. "Erin just called in sick. She has a cold."

Lucy groaned. "Oh, no. Is it bad? Or an I-need-a-personal-day bug?"

"I didn't recognize her voice. It sounded like she has a doozy of a cold."

"Which we'd better not catch." Lucy frowned. "Okay. Why don't you call Bridget? I was going to hire her anyway. See if she can start tonight. She's spent enough time here she ought to be able to jump right in."

Mabel knew Lucy's aunt as well as Lucy did. "Beth doesn't want her to work."

"Yeah, I kinda suspected that. That's between them. I can't imagine she'd mind Bridget filling in."

"Probably not," Mabel conceded. She flapped a hand and retreated.

The bell on the door tinkled and Lucy's head snapped around. For the hundredth time.

It was him. He looked more human today, wearing

running shoes, jeans and a V-neck blue jersey. Sexier, she realized, her pulse tap-dancing. Even his hair was a little disheveled.

Unlike last night, when his single glance around the café had been distant and even dismissive, today his gaze moved slowly and comprehensively from the old-fashioned, gilt-trimmed cash register and the jar of free mints to the artwork hanging on the walls, the windows with their red-checked curtains below lacy valances, the townsfolk and tourists nearly filling the tables and row of booths along the back wall and finally the cut-out that allowed her to see him.

Their eyes met, and he nodded.

Lucy nodded, too, hastily, and ducked out of sight, her cheeks hot. He'd caught her gaping.

No, he hadn't. She'd glanced up because a patron had entered the café. She always kept half an eye on the front of the house even while she was cooking. Of course she did; it was her restaurant.

He had no reason to suspect he made her heart flutter, and she wouldn't give him any reason to.

What the heck. He'd probably be rude this afternoon to someone she really liked, and her heart would quit fluttering anyway.

When she looked out at the restaurant again, Mabel had seated him and he was studying a menu. Other people were covertly watching him. Lucy's cousin Jen was murmuring behind her hand to her best friend, Rhonda, who owned the Clip and Curl, the competition to the Hair Do. Rhonda had been heard saying disdainfully, "*I* wouldn't have washed some homeless woman's hair. Imagine how disgusting it must be." Lucy didn't like Rhonda, and Jen wasn't her favorite relative, either. Jen, who liked feeling important, would be telling all she knew about the rich lawyer who was the homeless woman's son. The two were probably both thrilled that he'd be ridding Middleton of the scourge of homelessness.

Jen had come by her tendency to gossip naturally. Her mom was Lucy's Aunt Lynn. The one who was a trial.

Lucy had worked herself up to being annoyed enough that she took off her apron and marched out, ignoring Jen and Rhonda, straight to Adrian.

Maybe, if she were lucky, she'd start the whole family talking. Hadn't she wished for years that she'd done something exciting enough to scandalize them?

"I'm glad you made it," she said.

He looked up from the menu. "You thought I was afraid to show up?" Before she could answer, he said, "How's the grilled-chicken sandwich with red-pepper aioli?"

"Fabulous," Lucy assured him. "Sam bakes the focaccia bread for us."

"Ah." That apparently decided him, because he set down the menu. "This is a family enterprise, huh?"

"No, it's mine, except that I've been buying baked goods from Sam. And now we're talking about me catering dinners for some special events she's thinking of holding at the B and B. Like a mystery weekend. You know." She paused. "Well, and I just added one of my cousins to the waitstaff. Although her mom won't be happy." Oh, brilliant. Like he'd care. "Are you ready for me to take your order?"

His eyes held a glint. "*Did* you think I wasn't going to show?"

"No. I doubt you ever back away from whatever you've decided is the best course."

Did that sound as rude to him as it had to her own ears?

His mouth twisted. "Oh, I have my cowardly impulses." Then his expression closed and he said, "I'd like the grilled-chicken sandwich and a cup of your soup."

"Anything to drink?"

"Just coffee."

"It'll be right out," she said, and went back to the kitchen.

Mabel was dishing up soup. Voice dry, she said, "Bridget squealed and said, 'I can start tonight? Awesome!'"

"She's young."

"She'll do fine," Mabel said comfortably. "If she's floundering, I'll stay late."

Lucy smiled at her. "Thank you. You're a lifesaver."

"What'd Mr. Attorney order?"

"Adrian." Lucy moderated a voice that had come out sharper than she'd intended. "His name is Adrian Rutledge."

Mabel's carefully plucked eyebrows rose. "Didn't mean to be insulting."

"It *sounded* insulting." Lucy sighed. "Forget it. Rhonda and Jen are out there whispering, and that got my back up."

"They get my back up every time they come in here. Don't worry." She nodded toward the front. "Are you getting his order?"

"Yes, and I'm going to take a couple of hours after the rush is over to introduce him to people who knew his mom. He wants to find out what he can about her."

"Uh-huh." Mabel's skepticism was plain, but she grabbed two salads and whisked out of the kitchen before Lucy could demand to know why she was hostile to Adrian.

Lucy did deliver his food, but she didn't have time

to sit with him any more than she had with the hat lady the last time she'd come here. The better business was, the less time Lucy had to do anything but hustle. Between cooking and doing the ordering, she had precious few hours away from the café, and in some of those she kept the books, made deposits and created new recipes.

She *liked* cooking. She liked experimenting, and chatting with customers, and showing everyone she could succeed. But the responsibility of owning the place and having half a dozen other people's livelihoods depend on her was so overwhelming, she had no chance to even imagine what else she could do with her life. She hadn't been on a date in… Lucy had to count back. Four and a half months, and that was playing tennis at the club in Port Angeles and lunch afterward with Owen Marshall. And that hadn't been what you'd call a success. After watching him throw a temper tantrum when he lost a set to her, she hadn't hesitated to say no the next time he called.

Lately, no one else was asking, and it didn't appear likely anyone would in the near future. She knew every single guy in Middleton entirely too well to be interested, and anyway, when would she go out with a guy? Friday and Saturday were the busiest nights of the week at the café. She had to be here.

What's more, she knew she wasn't any more than pretty. Lucy wasn't alone in considering herself to be the plain one in her family. Put her next to her sisters Samantha and Melissa, and she faded into the background. Disconcerting but true. *They* had regular dates.

Which was undoubtedly why her heart had bounced just because Adrian Rutledge had looked intrigued by her for one brief moment. How often did that happen?

Never?

You're pathetic, she told herself, before stealing another look out to see how he liked his lunch.

Hard to tell, when a man was chewing then swallowing.

It was two o'clock before she could escape, and then not without guilt. But Shea, her assistant cook, had shown up, and Bridget was to come at four to help set the tables for dinner. Lucy could spare a couple of hours.

Adrian had waited with apparent patience, sipping coffee and reading the weekly *Middleton Courier.*

"My mother's accident is in here," he said, closing the newspaper and folding it when Lucy walked up.

"Well, of course it is. I told you, everyone knows her. And we don't have that many accidents right here in town."

The editor had referred to her as "the kind woman known affectionately as 'the hat lady,'" which Lucy had thought was particularly tactful. She was glad he hadn't mentioned that the hat lady was homeless. From his write-up, it sounded as if she might have been a respectable senior citizen who was borrowing a Safeway shopping cart to get her groceries home, rather than an indigent whose shopping cart was the next thing *to* a home. Adrian wouldn't have to be embarrassed after reading the article in the *Courier.*

"Where do we start?" he asked.

"The library." Lucy had already decided. "I know Wendy is working this afternoon. She was really fond of your mother."

He held open the door for her. "She's the librarian?"

Lucy nodded, and after suggesting they walk since the library was only three blocks away, she said, "Yes.

Wendy's from Yakima, but she married Glenn Monsey who was working for a builder over there. Our old librarian was ready to retire when Glenn decided to come home to work with his dad, who's a contractor."

"I hadn't noticed any new building."

Was he bored? Or sneering at her town? Just because she sometimes thought Middleton was dull didn't mean she'd put up with an outsider saying so. Eyeing him suspiciously, she said, "They do more over in Sequim than here in town, but we have new houses, too. Plus, they do remodeling."

He nodded, but she wasn't sure he'd even paid attention to what she said. His steps had slowed. "You have an attorney in town."

The office that had caught his attention was narrow, sandwiched between a gift-and-card shop and Middleton's only real estate office. On the window, gold letters announced in an elegant script, Elton Weatherby, Attorney-At-Law.

She waved through the window at Mr. Weatherby, who she happened to know was seventy-four years old. He and her grandfather had been in the same grade in school. He was thin and stooped, with a white shock of hair and a luxuriant mustache that actually curled up on the ends. He waved back.

"I suppose he doesn't do much but write wills," Adrian said thoughtfully.

"Why would you think that? Middleton's a normal town with all the usual lawsuits and squabbles. He does quite a bit of criminal defense, although most of it might be small potatoes by your standards."

"Tavern brawls?"

Lucy was pleased to find that she was starting once

again to dislike Adrian Rutledge. His condescension annoyed her.

"We have murder and rape and domestic disturbances, just like everyone else," she said shortly, then nodded at a business on the next corner. "We'll stop at the Hair Do later and talk to Cindy."

"Your sister mentioned her. She said Cindy cut my mother's hair."

He always said *my mother* in the same, stilted way. On impulse Lucy asked, "You must have called her *Mom* when you were a kid."

Adrian glanced at her. "That was a long time ago."

"You just always sound so…uncomfortable. As if you don't want to acknowledge her."

Out of the corner of her eye she saw his jaw muscles knot. After a minute he said, "But I have, haven't I? I'm here."

Immediately ashamed, Lucy said, "You're right. I'm sorry."

They walked in silence then, Lucy nodding at passersby whom she knew. She was very conscious that everyone was noticing them, wondering where they were going and why.

It was lowering to know that nobody would speculate, even for a minute, that Lucy Peterson had snagged herself a handsome new man. If she'd been Samantha, that's exactly what they would be thinking. But she knew all too well what they thought about her. *Poor Lucy would certainly get married someday, she was such a nice young woman and a good cook, too, but of course her husband would be a local boy, not anyone truly exciting. Because* she *wasn't exciting.*

No, today they were staring because they'd heard

Adrian had come to town. People were obviously dying
to know why an obviously wealthy attorney's mother
had been homeless. As far as Lucy knew, she was the
only person he'd talked to at all about his family history,
and despite her mixed feelings about him, she would
keep to herself everything he'd told her. At least until
he and the hat lady were gone, and there was no reason
that townspeople couldn't gossip to their hearts' content.

The library was a block off the main street, built just
four years back. When Lucy was growing up, the library
had been on the second story of an aging granite-block
municipal building, which meant it wasn't accessible to
anyone who couldn't climb the stairs. The room, cold in
winter and hot in the summer, had only been about six
hundred square feet. Since the new building opened,
the collection had tripled and the library even had a
meeting room for public use. The land it stood on was
donated, and every cent spent on raising the building
had been donated. Middleton was proud of its library.
If Adrian sneered, Lucy was prepared to turn around
and head right back to the café. She wouldn't waste another second on him.

But when they walked in he actually looked mildly
impressed. "Wouldn't have thought you had the popu-
lation to support a library this size."

Before she could answer, Wendy spotted them from
the information desk. She rose to her feet as they approached. "Lucy! I never see you on Saturdays!"

"I brought the hat lady's son to meet you. I was hoping you'd have a few minutes to talk about her. Wendy
Monsey, this is Adrian Rutledge."

They shook hands, Wendy looking him over with
interest, and she suggested they go to her office. The

fact that she *had* an office was one of the things she appreciated most about the new library.

Wendy was about Lucy's age, beanpole tall and skinny, with curly dark hair that tended to frizz during the incessantly rainy winter. They'd become friends right away when Glenn brought her home to Middleton. Wendy had a master's degree from the University of Washington and had been working in the Yakima public library system before coming here. She was energetic, and enthusiastic, and full of ideas.

Her office wasn't very big, and she had to lift bags of books—"Donations," she explained—from one of the chairs before they could sit.

Lucy wished the limited space didn't force her to sit quite so close to Adrian. Their shoulders brushed as they faced Wendy across her desk.

"I understand you let my mother check out books even though she didn't have an address," Adrian said.

"She was probably my favorite patron," Wendy explained. "I set aside books for her, and when she brought them back we'd talk about them. Not that many people have the time or interest in doing that. I mean, half the patrons only come in here when they need a book on writing résumés, or an automobile repair manual. Or they read nothing but mysteries, or check out only gardening books, or…"

Lucy's cheeks warmed just a little. She had a couple of gardening books checked out most of the time. She especially enjoyed the ones with lots of gorgeous photographs.

"What did she read?" Adrian asked, leaning forward slightly. "I've tried to imagine how a woman who thought she was an impoverished young lady of good breeding and small fortune in Regency England coped with modern life all around her."

Lucy looked at him sharply. Had he actually *read* Jane Austen? She wouldn't have expected that.

"She had all these supposed identities, but she was still herself, too. I don't know how to explain."

Lucy agreed, "It's as if the identity of the day was only on the surface. She'd choose different hats, and her accent would change, and even her mannerisms, but... she was always the hat lady. I could talk about gardens with her no matter whether she was Queen Elizabeth or Elizabeth Taylor. Queen Elizabeth never missed a garage sale any more than Eliza Doolittle would. Something essential stayed the same."

Wendy nodded. "And she actually lived in the here and now. But only sort of. She didn't read, oh, about politics or terrorism or anything really current. I'm not even sure how much she understood local politics or the school bond issues. She liked to read fiction and poetry and biographies. Anything Arthurian, although she always said *The Once and Future King* was the best. She did love mysteries, mostly the old ones. Josephine Tey, and Dorothy Sayers's Lord Peter Wimsey series, especially after he met Harriet Vane. *Gaudy Night* and *Busman's Honeymoon*."

They could both see his bewilderment.

"I hooked her on some modern authors, too, though. Elizabeth George—"

"That figures," he muttered.

Wendy laughed. "She probably was more willing to try the books because of the author's name. But she liked Martha Grimes and P. D. James, too. Oh, and Ellis Peters's Brother Cadfael mysteries, although I guess we can't exactly call Ellis Peters modern." She talked about how gifted his mother was at finding the tiniest of plot flaws, and how when she really loved a book she'd bring it back with passages marked. "She'd read them aloud. She did it so beautifully, as if she were on stage. I could see how much pleasure she took in language."

Adrian stirred. "She read aloud to me when I was little." His voice was strange, as though the memories weren't entirely welcome. "Even later, when I was reading myself. At first, books just a little beyond me, like *The Wind in the Willows.* Once I was eight or nine, I'd have died before I told anyone else, but she still read a chapter to me most nights. By then, it was stuff that was way beyond my reading level. Those books by Mary Renault about Theseus."

"The King Must Die," the librarian murmured.

"Yeah. I loved those. When she left—" he cleared his throat. "We finished *The Hobbit* the night before I left to visit my grandparents. She said we'd start *The Fellowship of the Ring* when I got home."

Heart jumping into her throat, Lucy swung to face him. "She had it! Just that one! I thought it was strange, because I didn't find the other two. It's only a paperback, and the pages are yellowing, the way older paperbacks always are. But...she must have kept it."

"She'd...already bought it. I remember thinking how fat it was and wondering how long it would take us to read it. But I really liked *The Hobbit,* so I was okay with the idea."

"Did you ever read *The Lord of the Rings?*" Lucy asked softly.

"No." His voice was harsh. "Skipped the movies, too."

"She never did, either." Wendy sounded extraordinarily sad. "I suggested them once. She said no, she was waiting."

His hands tightened on the arms of the chair. Lucy saw his knuckles go white. "Waiting? Did she say for what?"

Wendy shook her head. "Her voice trailed off and she looked so bewildered and unhappy I started talking about something else as if I hadn't noticed."

They sat silent for a moment.

Lucy and Adrian left shortly thereafter. They had reached the sidewalk when he stopped suddenly. "Can you give me a minute?"

A wrought-iron bench had been placed there for library patrons waiting for a ride. He sank onto it as if his knees had given out.

"Of course." Watching him worriedly, she sat, too.

He rested his elbows on his knees and hung his head. He'd obviously been more shaken by talking about his mother than she'd realized.

A little shocked that he was letting her see him so agitated, Lucy waited.

After a minute, Adrian sighed and straightened. "I've forgotten so much."

"Most of us put away things from our childhood."

"I'd come pretty close to putting it all away." He didn't look at her. "Dad didn't talk about her. He didn't like it when I tried. Without a sister or brother…"

"You had no one to…to help you keep her alive."

"My grandparents, of course. But after that summer I only flew up there a couple of times for shorter visits. I think Dad would have cut *Maman* and *Grandpère* off all together if they hadn't been insistent."

Her heart wrung, Lucy said, "But you do remember. You just…haven't let yourself."

"Yeah. I suppose that's it." He turned his head at last, his attempt at a smile wry and far from happy. "You're dunking me in the deep end."

"If you'd rather not—"

"No, you're right. I'm here. Later, I'll regret it if I don't talk to people who knew her. Especially if—"

His mother died without ever opening her eyes and knowing him.

"She knew she had a son," Lucy told him. "She mentioned you several times. As if you were so wound into a memory she *couldn't* forget you. And then she'd get this look on her face." She fell silent for a moment. "I thought… I assumed her little boy had died. So I never pressed her."

"You thought her grief was what derailed her."

"Um…something like that."

His eyes narrowed. "And that made you even madder, when you discovered I was alive and well."

She couldn't seem to look away from him. "I don't know," she said honestly. "Maybe."

Once again his mouth twisted and Adrian turned his head abruptly to stare across the street again. "I can't even blame you."

"I'm sorry," she whispered.

"About?"

"Misjudging you."

He met her gaze again, his face unreadable. "Are you so sure yet that you did?"

Lucy nodded, the movement jerky. "Pretty sure."

After a moment of searching her face, he said, "Thank you for that, then." He stood and held out a hand. "I know you don't have all afternoon. Shall we move on?"

Lucy stared at his hand, absurdly afraid that, if she laid hers in it, she would be sorry. Touching him might be dangerous to her peace of mind.

But of course she had no choice, unless she wanted to insult him, so she took his hand and let him pull her to her feet.

His grip was firm and warm and strong, his hand big enough to entirely engulf hers. Once she was standing, facing him, he seemed reluctant to release her. When he did, her fingers curled into a fist and she tucked her hand behind her back.

"I am running out of time," she said, trying to sound unaffected. "I was thinking, why don't I introduce you to Cindy and leave you to talk to her? And then you might go up to Safeway and ask for the manager. George did more for your mother than anyone. You haven't run into him at the hospital, have you? I know he'd be glad to talk to you."

A couple of vertical lines appeared between Adrian's dark eyebrows. "When will I see you again?"

He sounded…perturbed. As though he would *miss* her.

I'm in trouble, she thought dizzily, and knew she wasn't smart enough to keep herself out of it.

Before she could think better of it, Lucy heard herself say, "We could go to church tomorrow. Was your mother Catholic? She seemed drawn to Saint Mary's."

"She was raised in the Catholic church." His face tightened. "I have a vague memory of going to church with her sometimes when I was little. My father didn't approve."

Of course he wouldn't have, Lucy thought uncharitably. For the first time in her life, she was *glad* someone was dead.

Adrian studied her. "Do you mind going to a service at Saint Mary's?"

Lucy shook her head.

"What time?"

"Let's go to the second service at nine. That way Father Joseph might have time afterward to talk to us."

At some point they had started walking without her realizing.

When Adrian said nothing, she stole a look at him. "I have your mother's things at home. Maybe after church you can come and get them." In a rush she finished, "I can make us lunch."

"Is the café not open tomorrow?"

"No. It's closed on Sunday and Monday. For my sanity."

They'd reached the main street and had to pause while cars passed before crossing. Once there was a break, he put a hand on her back as if the protective gesture was as natural to him as breathing.

"That sounds good," he said, stopping on the sidewalk in front of the Hair Do to meet her eyes. "Thank you, Lucy Peterson. For everything."

Flustered, she argued, "It's…not so much."

"Yes. It is." He held open the door to the hair salon. "After you."

Hoping she wasn't blushing furiously, Lucy went in.

CHAPTER FIVE

ADRIAN DID NOT GO to the café for dinner. He dined on a surprisingly good filet mignon and baked potato at the Steak House, where not a soul evinced any sign of knowing who he was. He had bought a newspaper earlier in the day and not had a chance to read beyond the front page headlines; now he read while he ate, discovering that the Mariners had lost to Texas, that the Seattle city council had another ludicrous idea for replacing the Alaska Way Viaduct, and that the ferry he had ridden over on had been dry-docked for repairs and replaced temporarily with a smaller one, meaning long lines at the terminals during school spring breaks.

By the time he folded up the newspaper and paid, he couldn't remember much of what he'd read. He hadn't been concentrating. He'd been thinking about his afternoon and what the librarian, the hairdresser and the Safeway manager had told him about his mother.

He wished Lucy had gone with him to the latter two meetings. Neither Cindy nor George had relaxed with him as readily as they would have if Lucy had been there. He'd always believed he was skilled with people, but this context was different. He was an outsider. They looked at him like everyone in this damn town did, certain his mother wouldn't have been homeless if he'd done his duty as her son.

He'd buried his guilt years ago, but now it was as if everyone in Middleton were scrabbling at the dirt with their bare hands, flinging it aside to bare the coffin enclosing all his suppressed emotions. They were doing it willfully, and, God help him, he was encouraging them.

"Crap," he muttered, then grimaced when the passing waitress turned, startled. "Sorry."

"We all have days like that," she said with a comforting smile, and continued on with a tray laden with dirty dishes. The restaurant was emptying out. Apparently Middleton shut down early, even on Saturday nights.

They all had days like this? He seriously doubted it.

He went to the hospital, exchanging greetings with the same nurse that had been on last night, and went into his mother's room, where nothing had changed.

This was the first time, Adrian realized, that he'd walked in when Lucy wasn't here, talking or reading to his mother. Tonight, the chair—her chair—was empty. The only sound was the soft *beep beep* of the monitors. He wished he'd brought something to read to the woman who lay in this bed. That was pure genius on Lucy's part. It filled the silence without requiring any real effort. He had no idea what he would have read to her, though. He hadn't brought anything from home but work. Nothing in the *Times* seemed suitable, and he'd left it behind anyway.

He walked around the bed and sat in the chair. "Hi, Mom. It's Adrian. I'm back." *Yeah, brilliant.* "I had dinner at the Steak House. I'm told you ate there sometimes." More charity, but he hadn't asked for the manager to find out what about his mother had awakened the kind impulse. He felt battered enough by what the other people had told him.

"I wonder why you picked Middleton. Did it remind you of Brookfield? It sounds like people here were pretty nice to you, so I can see why you stayed. I wish I'd known where you were, though. That you'd given me a chance."

To do what? he wondered. Commit her to a mental hospital? What *would* he have done with his mother if he'd come upon her down on First Avenue in Seattle ten years ago and recognized her in the dirty, hopeless street person looking up at him from a doorway?

He had an uncomfortable feeling he would have been embarrassed. He'd have wanted to whisk her out of sight. Get her on meds and insist they be regularized until she was a normal, functioning human being.

Except that she'd never been quite normal and he'd loved her anyway. Not for the first time Adrian tried to imagine how two people as disparate as his parents had ever imagined themselves in love. Perhaps the answer was that they'd been drawn to the qualities in each other that they themselves lacked. His father had seemed solid, the very embodiment of stability and sanity, while his mother…she had been whimsical, creative and mysterious. Maybe they'd each thought they could soak up some of the other's best qualities. If so, they'd failed. It was as if the marriage had accentuated their differences; Adrian's father had become increasingly stern, while his mother had drifted further from the here and now and from her husband.

Adrian sat looking at her face, which seemed to have more color tonight. She could have simply been asleep. Her eyelids were traced with the pale blue lines of veins beneath the skin. As he stared, her lids quivered.

Was she trying to open her eyes? He tensed, watching, scarcely breathing for fear of missing some tiny movement. None came, and gradually he relaxed. He'd seen some reflex, no more. Or perhaps she was still capable of dreaming. If so, did her unconscious brain weave the voices she heard into those dreams?

He cleared his throat. "Today I was remembering how you read to me every night. *The King Must Die* and *The Bull from the Sea*. I went to Greece a couple of years ago. Not to Crete, but to Athens and one of the other islands. Everything I saw was colored by those books. When you get better, maybe we could go together. I'd like to see Knossos."

He rambled some more, about other books they'd read, about the jokes she'd taken such childlike delight in and still did, according to Cindy. He'd gone through a phase of thinking knock-knock jokes were the funniest thing ever. His father had refused to participate in them. His mother's face would invariably brighten and she'd say happily, "Who's there?" She had made *him* feel incredibly witty.

Adrian couldn't remember the last time he'd told a joke. He laughed at the occasional off-color ones told in the locker room at his health club, but he hadn't had a good belly laugh in…God. Years. Humor had never been uncomplicated for him again, after his mother went away.

He kept wishing Lucy would walk in, while knowing she wouldn't. She'd told him that Saturday night was her busiest of the week. The café closed at ten, but she was probably busy cleaning the kitchen and closing out the cash register until midnight or later. Visiting hours would be long over. He'd felt half-trapped by her presence before, both grateful and resentful that she insisted on being here.

Now…damn it, he wanted to tell her what Cindy and George had said. He wanted her to talk about the perplexing woman who lay in the hospital bed and who, even in her mental illness, had been a chameleon, someone different to each person who knew her. He had a suspicion that if anyone had known her through and through, it was Lucy.

"She made me laugh like no one else," the middle-aged hairdresser with cheap-looking red curls had told him.

"I know she took the food I put out back for her," the balding grocer said, "but sometimes even when I saw her come down the alley I had trouble seeing her. You know? It was like she was a ghost. Not quite there. As though she *wanted* to be invisible."

Was it Lucy who'd said she was a chameleon? But why the protective coloration around the kind, portly grocer when she was so capable of letting loose peals of laughter around Cindy of the crimson curls? Was it because George was a man, and she was afraid of men?

Adrian tried to remember how his mother had related to men back when he was a child, but in those memories it seemed he and Mom were always alone. She'd gone to some parent-teacher meetings, but his elementary school teachers had all been women. His parents hadn't entertained, that he remembered. Even then he'd known Dad was ashamed of her. There had been…not fights. Just scenes, when his father, wearing a dark suit or even a tuxedo, had left the house in the evening and his mother had looked unbearably sad when the front door shut in her face.

Had she actually been afraid of Dad? he wondered. He'd never seen his father raise his hand to her, but he'd been very good at freezing her with one look or a few scathing words. At best he wasn't a warm man, and Adrian could recall no scrap of tenderness between them. They'd had separate bedrooms, something he'd been too young then to think twice about. Likely, to Adrian's father she'd been more like a flighty, untrustworthy child than a wife, and a child who would never grow up at that.

"Were you frightened of him?" Adrian asked, his voice low in case someone walked into the room behind the concealing curtain. "Did you have any idea what he was thinking of doing to you? When I left that day, did you have any clue what was happening?"

Thinking back, he knew she'd been odd that morning; even odder than usual. A dervish of activity, anxious he hadn't forgotten anything, checking, rechecking, hovering with the quivering intensity of a hummingbird. And yet he'd seen the sheen of tears in her eyes, which had upset him and made him exclaim, "I shouldn't go! Why do I have to go without you? I want *you* to come, Mom! Why can't you?"

She didn't quite answer. His father, who had already loaded his stuff in the car, came back brimming with impatience and tore him away.

"Mom, can't you come to the airport?" Adrian had begged, but she had shaken her head frantically, tears sliding down her cheeks, as she stood on the front porch and watched his father drag him to the car and bundle him in.

"For God's sake!" his father snapped, backing out of the driveway as Adrian pressed his hands and face to the window and breathed in ragged gasps.

He shuddered now at the memory and thought, *You did know. Not everything, but something.*

Enough to fear she might never see him again.

"Did he promise you'd get better and be able to come home if you went?" Adrian asked the silent, unresponsive woman in the bed. "Did he use me somehow?"

Again her eyelids quivered. Was he upsetting her? He couldn't imagine she understood anything he was saying. Perhaps his voice, rough with long-suppressed anger, alarmed her.

He pushed back the chair and stood. "I'm sorry. I'm not very good company tonight, am I, Mom? I should have brought something to read. Maybe tomorrow I'll go back to the library." No, he realized, tomorrow was Sunday. He'd noticed it wasn't open on Sundays. Probably nothing in town would be but the churches.

"I'll just, ah, let you sleep." If that's what she was doing. He hesitated, feeling awkward. He hadn't touched her yet. He couldn't imagine kissing her cheek. Adrian wasn't much for touching, although he had liked the feel of Lucy's back. For a ridiculous instant, he'd even imagined letting his hand slide lower.

He said good-night and left, realizing he hadn't seen Slater today. Had he been by? Did it matter? All they could do was wait, he'd said.

Adrian wasn't a patient man.

ADRIAN ALSO WASN'T a churchgoer. As he'd told Lucy, his mother had taken him to Sunday school and then services when he was really young. But either his father must have forbidden it at some point or his mother had become too uncomfortable around so many people, because they'd quit going by the time Adrian was seven years old or so.

He had no trouble finding Lucy's house, which appeared to date from the 1930s, as much of the town did. Wood-frame, modest porch, it lacked any distinguishing architectural features but had a plain, farmhouse-style charm. The lot was good-size, and most of the houses on the block were identical. Put up by the logging company that had probably once employed nearly every man in Middleton? All had large lawns that ran together with no fences in front. Hers boasted a big fruit tree in the front that was in bloom right now.

After some hesitation that morning, Adrian had worn a suit, and was glad when Lucy came out the moment his car stopped at the curb. She wore a pretty, flowery dress and pearls in her earlobes, which he could see because she'd taken a wing of hair from each side of her face and clipped it in back. When she hopped in on the passenger side and smiled at him, his body tightened. She was pretty this morning, with high cheekbones and a pixie shape to her face, a wide mouth that smiled more naturally than it pursed when she was irritated, and creamy skin that had to feel like satin to the touch. Her neck was long and slender and pale in a world where most women tanned. Her breasts and belly would be just as pale, unbisected by the lines left by a bikini. And he knew already she had long, gorgeous legs; the filmy fabric of her dress had settled, baring the shape of her thighs and hips.

They were on their way to church, and he was getting aroused by a woman wearing a dress conservative enough not to stand out in the 1950s. What was wrong with him?

"Good morning," she said. "Do you know how to find Saint Mary's?"

"Morning." Adrian put the car into gear. "It would be hard to get lost in Middleton."

In the silence that followed, he realized how rude that had sounded. Then, worse yet, he thought, *My mother was lost here.*

Her sunniness dimmed, Lucy said stiffly, "I didn't know if you'd paid any attention to the churches."

"I drove around yesterday, after I talked to George McKenzie. I looked for it and the Lutheran Church. Someone mentioned that it runs the thrift store where she…shopped." He couldn't bring himself to say "accepted charity."

"She worked there, too. Did I tell you that?"

Startled, he looked at her. "No. Worked?"

"Sorting donations, hanging up the clothes, even putting things out for display. The thrift store is run entirely by volunteers. Your mother earned what she took."

He'd been that obvious?

"Your sister said she stopped by on… Some day of the week. Tuesday," he stated. "Because they were closed on Sunday and Monday." What had Samantha said? That they let her take what she wanted? "I assumed…"

"She helped in the day care at church, too. She didn't usually attend services, although she liked being able to hear the hymns."

"She was crazy! People trusted her with their kids?"

Her look made him feel as if he were a grease spot she'd just noticed on her dress.

"The hat lady was gentle and sweet. She was wonderful with children, especially the little ones. They'd beam at her when they saw her. And no, she wasn't alone with the children. Mothers take turns supervising the day care."

Adrian shook his head. "I don't get it."

"What don't you get? You'd better park," she added. "This is as close as we'll find."

They had to be four blocks from the redbrick church with the gilt Jesus nailed to the cross on the spire. He took her word for it, though, and pulled in to the first spot he saw that was big enough for his Mercedes. A family in front of them was getting out of their car, everyone scrubbed and in their Sunday best, the little boy's hair slicked down, the girl's in pigtails. Adrian remembered his mother ruthlessly taming his thick hair, using spit if they neared the church and his cowlick rebelled. He'd felt as uncomfortable in a suit as that poor kid did, holding his mother's hand and dragging his feet.

He and Lucy got out, too. Adrian locked the car with the remote before dropping it in his pocket and joining her on the sidewalk. A regular parade of townspeople was streaming toward the church, and even the teenagers dressed up, not a one sullen. Wasn't there a sixteen-year-old in town who sported a nose ring?

"What don't you get?" Lucy repeated.

He liked her height. She'd be perfect to dance with. A tall man, he'd never liked looking down at the top of a woman's head. She had an easy, comfortable stride, too, when they fell into step together.

"Why she was so easily accepted," he said. "Get offended if you want, but the truth is, she was nuts. The homeless make people uneasy. Except, apparently, in Middleton."

She was silent for a moment. "Maybe," she said at last, "that's because she was our only homeless person. And also… Well, it's not true that she was easily accepted, or even that everyone was nice to her. There are people who'd cross the street so they didn't have to get too close to her. She just…well, found refuges. Places she *was* accepted and even welcome." Sadness infused Lucy's voice. "She knew there were places she wasn't."

A jolt of anger surprised him. "Like?"

She shook her head, and he realized they'd reached the crowded front steps of the church.

He let Lucy lead the way inside and choose a pew toward the back. A few curious glances turned toward them, but she only smiled and nodded at people she apparently knew.

Father Joseph in robes and surplice proved to be elderly, his hair scant and white, his face so thin Adrian wondered if he were ill. But he had that air of certainty that clergy so often had, a kind of inner peace that comforted his flock. He spoke of forgiveness of sins small and large.

Adrian suppressed a snort. Too much forgiveness would put his law firm out of business. Somehow, he didn't think there was any danger of that happening.

A choir of children in white robes sang, their voices astonishingly pure and high and beautiful. The entire congregation sat transfixed. Lucy's face shone as she listened. Adrian could easily imagine his mother as captivated. He had trouble turning his gaze to the front. He would rather have watched Lucy.

When parishioners stood to take communion, Lucy poked him with her elbow and they slipped out. Once they were in the lobby, she said, "I thought we could visit the day care until Father Joseph is free."

Sitting there watching a ritual being repeated a hundred times or more hadn't held much appeal, but neither did checking out the toddlers. Adrian had no close friends with young children, and until these past couple

of days had had only rare memories of being one himself. Still, he nodded and followed her down the steps
into the basement.

The room was bright, with white paint and high windows and cheerful pictures on the walls. Several cribs
stood along one wall, while kids up to maybe four or
five finger-painted at a long table in the middle. A baby
slept in one crib, and another sat up and shook the bars
of the crib, working from a grumble to a scream. There
were only two adults in the room, one a teenager and the
other likely a mother. She was changing a kid's diaper
at a table designed and stocked for the purpose, while
the teenage girl supervised the painting.

Lucy headed right for the screamer and lifted her as
naturally as if she had a brood of her own. Adrian hovered in the doorway.

"My goodness!" she told the baby, a girl—no, probably a boy despite the golden curls, given the blue striped
T-shirt. "Is nobody paying any attention to you at all?"

The mother laughed. "Lucy. Here, I'll trade you. Unless you want to change his diaper?"

A boy then.

"I don't mind," Lucy said, expertly laying him out
on the table vacated by a little girl now being set on the
carpeted floor.

"Cruising for a new church?" the mother asked.

"No, we just wanted to talk to Father Joseph. But
he'll be awhile. I have to get my baby fix." She nuzzled
the little boy, whose legs kicked wildly.

The woman gave Adrian an idle glance that became
more interested. "Come on in," she said cordially.

"I'm, uh, fine." He eyed a couple of toddlers squealing and running straight toward him. Thank God, they veered at the last second.

Adrian continued to hover while Lucy chatted companionably with the other woman and even the teenager, helping out with an ease that told him she'd spent plenty of time with children. All those cousins once-removed? Or maybe she'd babysat her way through her teenage years.

Did she dream of having her own children? Of course she did; she obviously adored these little ones. Lucy Peterson was made to be a mother. She hadn't mentioned a boyfriend or fiancé, but then why would she? Adrian frowned, disliking the idea of her confiding in this unknown man, maybe telling him all about the hat lady and her arrogant lawyer son.

Or did he just dislike the idea of her with a man at all?

Ridiculous. He was simply avoiding thinking about his mother and her sad life. Impatient with himself, Adrian looked away from Lucy and watched the older kids finger-painting instead.

His mother had *chosen* to spend her mornings changing soggy diapers and wiping snotty noses? If she liked children so much, why didn't he have a host of brothers and sisters?

He knew the answer, of course: his father. Adrian couldn't imagine him changing a diaper or enjoying a two-year-old. And once he realized his wife was unstable, that would have been a further deterrent. Assuming he'd ever wanted children at all. Certainly he hadn't chosen to have more when he remarried.

Adrian was surprised by a peculiar emotion that was something like jealousy. The kid in him who'd lost his mom didn't like the idea of her snuggling giggling toddlers, of her laughing with them or telling the older ones knock-knock jokes. *His* knock-knock jokes. She'd loved her Sunday mornings here, but she didn't remember him.

Annoyed to feel something so irrational, he frowned. Finding out what his mother's life had been like was one thing; regressing into childhood himself was another. So his mentally ill mother had disappeared from his life when he was ten. What if she hadn't? The average thirteen-year-old boy was embarrassed by his parents anyway. Imagine how hurt she'd have been if he'd rejected her, when Mom and me ceased to be a unit and became a lonely woman and a teenage boy who didn't want to be seen with her.

Footsteps and voices and laughter on the stairs heralded the arrival of parents to pick up their youngsters. Some ignored Adrian; a few stared covertly. Lucy chatted with nearly everyone while they claimed their offspring.

Only a few were left when Father Joseph appeared, beaming. "Lucy! I knew I'd find you down here."

She laughed. "Where else? I wouldn't need to lurk in random day-care centers if I could just persuade Samantha to get married and start a family...."

Adrian's eyes narrowed. Why did she seem to assume her sister would get married first?

"Or choose a good man and start one yourself," the good father suggested.

Lucy's gaze strayed to Adrian, waiting to one side. Immediately, color ran over her cheeks. "Um, Father Joseph, I'd like you to meet Adrian Rutledge, the hat lady's son."

"Ah." Father Joseph held out a hand, his generous

smile holding no hint of the accusation Adrian had felt from nearly everyone else. "What a blessing that Lucy found you."

Adrian accepted the handshake. "And that all of you took such good care of her."

"I think those of us lucky enough to become her friends received more than we gave. Lucy told you how much she loved the children?"

Adrian nodded, that uncomfortable feeling swelling in his chest again. "Yes."

Father Joseph's smile didn't waver, but his hazel eyes seemed to read everything Adrian felt. His tone became especially gentle. "She brought joy to them, and they brought joy to her."

Adrian swallowed. "I'm glad." He was a little surprised to realize he meant it. "I understand you let her sleep here at the church sometimes."

"Yes, we have a room with a cot. Occasionally a parishioner needs a temporary refuge from troubles at home, or feels poorly during a service and must lie down. Your mother took advantage of it rarely." He shook his head sorrowfully. "She came only on the coldest or stormiest nights."

"It was good of you to offer the room."

"Does she show any improvement?" the father asked, looking from Adrian to Lucy and back. "I haven't visited since Thursday, but I pray every day for her."

Lucy shook her head. "Not yet. Unless…?" She, too, turned her gaze to Adrian.

"Not that I could see."

He waited while Father Joseph said goodbye to a family taking the golden-haired boy, then asked, "Did my mother ever talk about her past?"

"Remembering at all upset her. Once she told me she had a boy. 'He loved to watch the ferry leave the pier,' she said. I asked where she'd lived, but she couldn't or wouldn't tell me. I suggested that one day we take a drive and ride the ferry, thinking it might bring back good memories, but she looked so frightened I didn't press her."

"I worry about the years before she came here to Middleton," Adrian admitted. "I suppose it doesn't really matter, but—"

"Of course it matters. She's your mother." Father Joseph hesitated, his face creasing. "Once she told me about riding a train for days. To go home, she said, only she didn't have a ticket and they put her off. Wherever it was, it was cold and so flat the land went on forever. She couldn't remember who she should call and got confused about where she was going anyway. Some nice people bought her a ticket back to Seattle, where she'd come from. 'I am the queen,' she said, 'so I thought I ought to see the king.' I didn't know what she meant."

Throat thick, Adrian said, "The King Street Station. That's the train station in Seattle."

"Ah." Father Joseph's face cleared. "She did see signs in everything. Was she from Seattle originally?"

"Nova Scotia. But she and my father lived in Edmonds. She must have been trying to go to her parents." He imagined her, abandoned at some small train station in Saskatchewan, and felt rage at the conductor who hadn't been able to see how desperately she needed help.

He told the priest more about his mother and his regret that he had never pressed his father for answers.

Lucy stood silent as he spoke, listening, her eyes never leaving his face. The priest talked more about his mother, too, her ability to relate to every child at his or her level, to make them giggle, to heal any woe. "Most of the mothers here adored her."

"Most?"

"There are always doubters," Father Joseph said with unimpaired serenity, but Adrian had no trouble interpreting that. Some parents hadn't trusted their children to his mother. He couldn't even blame them.

Adrian realized the room was empty but for them. Voices upstairs suggested that other people were waiting to speak to Father Joseph. He thanked him and was told, "Bless you, my son."

Feeling numb, he followed Lucy upstairs and out into the sunshine.

My mother tried to go home. He imagined the devastation of her failure. Was that when she had sought the next best thing, a place that reminded her of home?

One phone call. So little, and *Maman* would have found a way to bring her home.

Two blocks from the church, he said aloud, "She did try."

"Are you going to call your grandmother then?"

He nodded. "Yeah. I'll have to persuade her not to come. She isn't well." She'd want to anyway. Adrian walled off the worry. He'd deal with it later.

After he went through his mother's pathetic cache of possessions and tried to be a halfway pleasant lunchtime companion, the least he owed Lucy.

CHAPTER SIX

IN LUCY'S GUEST bedroom, Adrian sat in an antique rocking chair, one of his mother's many hats in his hands. He didn't know what this style was called, but it looked like the ones upper-crust women wore to the Kentucky Derby. Lightweight, cream-colored and fashioned of some woven material, it had a broad, sweeping brim to shade a lady's complexion and a cluster of peach and white silk flowers sewn to the band. The silk flowers were just a little tattered, and a dirty spot marred the brim.

Something about this hat hit him. He could see her, real as day, smiling at him from beneath the shade of her hat. She was young, and happy, and beautiful, at least to him.

He turned it slowly in his hands, then flipped it over—he didn't know why. A hair clung inside, not blond like he remembered, but white. He touched it with one forefinger and had to swallow hard to suppress... he didn't know. Tears, maybe.

Why did his mother seem more alive to him here than she did breathing in that hospital bed?

With a guttural sound, he laid the hat on the bed, hung his head for a moment, then made himself open another box.

Lucy had packed his mother's possessions carefully,

the hats in plastic boxes with lids, the clothes and mis-
cellany in cardboard boxes.

This box held a few books, a plain wooden chest and
some oddities. Like a big conch shell. Why in hell would
a homeless woman want one? Yet he could imagine her
stroking its satiny pink interior or holding it up to her
ear to listen for the beat of the ocean.

A couple of the books were from the library. Adrian
guessed that Lucy had forgotten they were there. He
set them aside to be returned. His mother wouldn't be
reading them in the near future.

At the bottom was the single paperback, *The Fellowship of the Ring*. Hardly breathing, he picked it up. Lucy
was right; it looked unread, the spine unmarred, yet the
pages were yellowed with age. He started to open it to
the beginning, then hastily closed it. Stupid, maybe, but
he'd had a sort of superstition about the damn book, one
he'd never analyzed. Tolkien made him think about his
mother, ergo he didn't think about Tolkien.

But now he realized, with a grunt of surprise, that his
feelings were more complicated than that. He *couldn't*
read it without her, not without abandoning hope. Apparently he clung to more sentiment than he'd believed.

It was in the wooden chest, Lucy had told him, that
she'd found the driver's license, the photo and the hand-
made Mother's Day card. When he opened the small
chest it contained a few more pictures—a couple of
school photos of him and an old black-and-white photograph, curling at the edges, of a little girl. His mother
as a child. Blond, thin, ethereal, yet something already
sad in her face.

He didn't understand the trinkets. A thin gold ring
with a single seed pearl, nice enough she could have

gotten some money for it. Had his father given it to her? Adrian fingered it. Maybe she'd had it longer than that. As pretty as she was, she'd have had boyfriends along the way. Was this a memento of one in particular, remembered with fondness?

There was other jewelry, mostly cheap, and a few items that must have held some meaning. He didn't recognize any. Or...wait. At the bottom was a shard of porcelain, waterworn but the blue-and-white glaze still visible on one side. The style was Asian.

In a flash, Adrian remembered himself walking along a beach, gazing intently at the streaks of pebbles among the miles of ocean sand. The Oregon coast? Near Kalaloch on the Washington coast? They'd vacationed at both. He was hoping for something wondrous. A sand dollar, maybe, unchipped. Or a glass float, like the man at the gift shop had talked about, or... He saw something poking from the sand that didn't belong and pounced. In his hand lay the shard.

"Mom! Mom! Look what I found!"

She hurried to him and gazed in delight at his find. "Why, I'll bet the ocean carried that all the way here from China. See the curve? It must have come from a pot or bowl. I think that's porcelain, which means it was probably valuable. How do you suppose it got broken?"

They'd speculated, bending together over the two-inch-long shard. Finally, his hand had closed tightly over it and he'd placed it ever so carefully in his pocket, determined not to lose it. It wasn't a glass float, but it had come all the way from China. That's what Mom had said, so it must be true.

"How are you doing?" Lucy asked from the doorway.

Adrian started, his hand closing around the shard of pottery just as it had then.

"Fine," he said, voice harsh, scratchy.

She hesitated. "Lunch is almost ready. But there's no hurry."

"I think I'm mostly done." His gaze swept the pitifully few boxes. "What a life."

"Did you find anything else you remembered?"

He hesitated, then opened his hand. "This."

Lucy stepped forward and peered at it with interest. "How pretty! I've seen jewelry made with antique shards of pottery like that. Where did it come from?"

"China."

"Really? Did you go?"

She looked so interested, and was so easy to talk to, he found himself telling her the story.

"I must have forgotten about it by the time I got home. Or maybe later I lost interest but it reminded her of the fun we had on that vacation. I wonder if you'd asked her, what she'd have said about it."

Lucy sat on the edge of the bed, still gazing pensively at the worthless piece of pottery in his hand. "I grew very fond of her, but she never showed me any of her treasures. I don't know why."

"Maybe because she didn't remember why she'd kept them."

She nodded slowly. "That would have bothered her terribly. Or perhaps she remembered snatches but not enough to put them into any kind of coherent narrative. That's what distressed her most, when some bit floated through her mind but she couldn't nail it down."

"Some bit, like the fact that she had a son?"

She frowned at him. "Do you think she forgot you because she didn't love you at all?"

Adrian hated the clutch at his throat that would have made speaking difficult. He liked to be in control. He knew underlings at the firm whispered about what a cold bastard he was, and he wouldn't have argued about the characterization. But something had happened to him since he arrived at this strange little town in the middle of nowhere.

Middle. Suddenly he wanted to laugh. Now he knew how it had received its name. It was in the middle of goddamn nowhere.

Depression swept over him. "No. I know she did." He dropped the shard into the box and closed it. "Lunch sounds good."

Lucy let him get away with the change of subject and led the way to her kitchen.

He liked her house. She'd filled it with antiques, but she hadn't gone over the top like her sister had at the bed-and-breakfast. No wallpaper, but the walls were painted with color. Moss-green in the living room, a softer shade of it down the hall above cream-colored wainscotting, rust and peach in the kitchen to set off white cabinets. He guessed they were the original ones. Old glass bottles lined the kitchen windowsill, the midday sun lighting them with soft hues. Every room had potted plants, too, all luxuriant and healthy. African violets lined the sill in the dining room, where the table was set for two with quilted place mats and a jug filled with daffodils.

The house was comfortable, Adrian decided, as well as…loved. He could see Lucy in it: nothing flashy, but the decor was serene and pretty. His mother had liked brighter colors and whimsical treasures found at garage sales and art fairs, all of which had disappeared from her house shortly after she had.

"Smells good," he said, meaning it.

"I should have asked if you liked Mexican. We're having black-bean burritos. At home I like to make different food than I serve at the café."

"No soup?"

She laughed. "Well…sometimes. And I do my experimenting at home, although not usually for company. The other day, I tried a coconut-potato soup that—"

A brisk rapping on the front door brought her around. Almost without pause, it apparently opened, and a woman called, "Yoo-hoo! Are you home, Lucy?"

"Crap," she muttered.

"Lucy, dear!" another voice chimed in.

Adrian thought he heard Lucy growl.

"In the kitchen," she said, unnecessarily, for two women appeared in the doorway.

Both studied him with interest. "Oh, dear," one of them said. "Are we interrupting?"

Lucy had gotten over her flash of irritation—or maybe just hidden it—and said resignedly, "Mom, Aunt Marian, meet Adrian Rutledge. He's—"

"The hat lady's son," the taller, more buxom of the two said. "Weren't you at the café the other day?"

"Well, of course he was," the other woman said. "You know Lucy's taking care of him."

He could see the resemblance between Helen Peterson and Lucy. Her hair was short and styled, her eyes brown rather than blue, but the bone structure and shape of the face was the same. She'd remained as slim as her daughter. Today she wore a light blue skirt and short jacket over a white blouse.

He shook hands and mused that although the two were sisters they didn't look much alike. Marian was shorter, plump, darker-haired.

"We missed you at church," Helen told Lucy, studying Adrian quite frankly. "We thought we'd stop by to be sure you were all right."

"I took Adrian to the service at Saint Mary's so he could meet Father Joseph."

"Are you Catholic?" her aunt asked.

Lucy's eyes rolled.

He shook his head. "Mom was raised Catholic, though. She grew up in Nova Scotia. My grandmother is French Canadian."

"Really." Lucy's mother actually sounded interested. "She sounded so very British."

"My grandfather was."

They all looked at him and waited. Apparently he was expected to elaborate.

"Ah...*Grandpère* emigrated when he was a teenager. He let my grandmother decide on the church, but he talked about home a lot. That's what he always called England. Home." Adrian pictured his grandfather, tall and white-haired and invariably dressed in rumpled tweeds like any country squire. He smoked a pipe, too, although he chewed thoughtfully on it more often than he actually lit it. "He graduated from Cambridge with a first in English literature and was...a gentleman, I guess you'd say. Mom loved his stories. I suppose those were what she reached for, when she got confused."

"That makes sense," Lucy mused. "Elizabeth Barrett Browning, and Beth from *Little Women*... And of course she'd have loved *My Fair Lady*."

"But Elizabeth Taylor?" her mother asked.

"My grandfather admired her," Adrian said, recalling his grandmother's pique when *Grandpère* had rented several Elizabeth Taylor movies to share with his grandson. *Cleopatra* and *The Taming of the Shrew*. "Wait. Wasn't she in *Little Women*, too?"

"All the pieces go together, don't they?" Lucy observed.

Did they? As far as he was concerned, the missing years gaped horrifically, and he sensed that those pieces would never be found.

Lucy invited her mother and aunt to lunch. What else could she do? "I've made burritos," she told them.

"Beans?" Aunt Marian said. "You know they give me..." She cleared her throat. "Indigestion."

"No, no," her mother said. "Everyone's coming to the house. I have a turkey roasting. It's Sunday." A cardinal sin, apparently. "How could you forget?"

"I didn't forget, Mom!" Lucy's cheeks colored. "I just...well, didn't call you. I'm sorry."

So, she'd ditched her family for him. It should bother him, how pleased he was to know that.

Her mother and aunt left at last. When Lucy came back from seeing them out, Adrian said wryly, "I can guess what everyone in the family will be talking about this afternoon."

Lucy made a face. "I'm afraid so. I'm sorry. I should have known if I didn't let her know in advance Mom would come by to find out why I wasn't at church."

"Close family?" The idea was foreign to him.

"You have no idea," she said in a tone of loathing.

Giving herself a little shake, she went to the refrigerator. "What can I get you to drink?"

As they poured drinks, he asked, "If you don't like having all your family nearby, why do you live here?"

She slipped by him into the dining room, enabling him to catch a scent he hadn't noticed outside. Lavender, maybe?

"I ask myself that at least every other day." Setting the drinks on the table, she sighed. "It just...happened."

"Happened?"

Dumb question; of all people, he knew how easily life just happened. Hell, hadn't most of his been in lockstep with his father's expectations?

Again, she whisked past him, not being obvious, but also clearly self-conscious about being too close to him. Adrian was glad, until he remembered how obvious her dislike had been earlier. Maybe he repulsed her.

When he offered belatedly to help, she handed him a bowl of salsa and a basket of chips, warm from the oven, then carried the casserole dish with the burritos to the table.

Once they'd sat, Lucy continued as if there'd been no interruption. "I came home from college thinking I'd work here for the summer, put away a little money for first and last month's rent when I moved to Seattle or Portland. Somewhere more exciting. I started cooking at the café, and then I had the chance to buy it, and..." She spread her hands.

They dished up, and he wasn't surprised to find her burritos were delicious. She admitted to making the salsa herself.

"What about you? I know your father was an attorney."

"Yeah, I think it was a given that I'd go in to law, too."

"Do you like it?"

Head cocked slightly, she asked as if she really wanted to know. Instead of the brusque, "Why else would I do it?" he might have returned to someone else, he found himself hesitating. Did he?

Adrian couldn't quite imagine doing anything else. It wasn't as if he'd been fixated on some other career, beyond the usual fancies any kid had. He remembered wanting to be an airline pilot at one point, a veterinarian at another. That dream withered, given that his father had never let him have a pet. Even earlier, he'd been determined to grow up to be a ferryboat captain. He supposed that had come from living in Edmonds, where they saw the ferry come and go all day long. One summer, he remembered begging to walk down to the beach beside the ferry dock almost every day.

"Mostly," he finally said, dishing up a second burrito and adding salsa and sour cream. "Although in law school—" He stopped.

"What?"

After a moment, he shrugged. "I thought I'd go into criminal law. Most law students go through a phase of imagining themselves saving the world, or at least some lives. I ended up wooed into corporate law."

"By money."

He studied her suspiciously, trying to decide whether she was disgusted or simply neutral.

"That's where the money is."

Lucy only nodded, applying herself to her plate.

"Do you dream of doing something else?"

She pursed her lips, as if giving serious thought to

the question. "I love to cook. I've always imagined I'd end up an executive chef at a chic restaurant in Seattle or some other city. Someplace people actually appreciate variety and unique flavor combinations. Where they don't grumble because you don't have that potato soup on the menu *every* day."

Adrian grinned. "Didn't you tell me it was one of your best?"

"Yes, but that's not the point." She sounded indignant. "If you want to eat the same thing every day, you might as well stay home. If you're going to eat out, shouldn't you want to try something new?"

"Not necessarily. I have favorites at some restaurants. Don't you?"

"No, but I'm an adventurer." She went very still, a couple of creases appearing in her forehead. In a much smaller voice, Lucy said, "About food. I guess not in any other way."

She sounded sad, as though she were disappointed in herself for not living more recklessly.

Adrian sought for a way to comfort her, an unusual impulse for him, and finally settled on distraction.

"Why my mother?" he asked.

Her gaze flew to his. "What do you mean?"

"You obviously felt sorry for her. You're kind, so why not offer her a meal now and then? But you did more than that. Something about her must have drawn you."

She hesitated, and he wondered if she was reconsidering some glib answer, as he'd done earlier.

"A lot of things," Lucy said finally. "I loved it when she talked about books, and gardens, and when she told stories. I'd swear she'd *known* Bonnie Prince Charlie. Although I have to say, she made me curious enough to read a biography about him, and she was way more sympathetic to him than he deserved." She sounded indignant, as though it were his fault his mother had been such a romantic.

"At least you didn't have to dress up as him," Adrian said involuntarily.

Her eyes widened. "You did?"

He couldn't remember ever telling anyone else about the dramas he and Mom had reenacted. With a grimace, he said, "I'm afraid I wore kneesocks and an old plaid skirt of hers. I endured it only because she let me stick a steak knife in the sock. Seems as if I had a plastic sword, too."

Lucy giggled. "Oh, dear. That's a picture."

"Not a pretty one." He should have been embarrassed. Why *had* he told her? Oddly enough, her laughter let him enjoy the memory.

"Who else did you act out?"

"Oh, King Richard the First. White cross cut out of an old pillowcase, pinned on…I don't know, a red vest of Mom's, maybe?" He was thinking less about the memories than about Lucy, who listened as if she imagined herself playing out the productions with him and his mother. Her mouth, he thought irrelevantly, was very kissable when it curved like that. Almost at random, he continued, "Let's see… I was supposed to be Winston Churchill once. I read a speech into a pretend microphone. Paper towel roll, I think. My dad had a hat that looked enough like Churchill's bowler hats, I guess, to satisfy Mom. I didn't get what he—I—was saying, except that it was supposed to be noble stuff that would make his countrymen strong in wartime.

Churchill wasn't anywhere near as much fun as Richard going to the Crusades."

Once again she chuckled. "History lessons wrapped in fun."

"I suppose they were. They seemed like games to me. And I'm not so sure Mom really thought she was teaching me anything. I think we acted out stories for her benefit."

"But you enjoyed them, too."

"When I was younger. By that last summer, I was starting to get embarrassed. Guys didn't dress up. I think—" He moved his shoulders uncomfortably.

Lucy finished for him. "Soon, you would have told her no."

He nodded. "I was thinking about that earlier. I felt so protective of her. But what would have happened when I got to be twelve, thirteen, and didn't want my friends to notice how weird she was?"

She looked at him with understanding. "So now you feel guilty about something that didn't happen."

"No." He scowled. "Oh, hell. Maybe. Because I was starting to have stirrings of dissatisfaction. They made me feel disloyal. Then she disappeared, and I never faced any of those decisions. Which made me wonder—" He let out a ragged breath, surprised at the force of long-ago emotions.

"You thought it might be your fault," Lucy said softly.

"Yeah. I suppose… Yeah." He rubbed a hand over his chin. "Stupid, huh?"

"Natural, don't you think? Kids are egocentric enough to believe somewhere inside that everything happens because of them. Did you think your mom had gone away because she sensed that you were ashamed of her? Or did you think your father had gotten rid of her because he didn't think she was good for you?"

"I don't know," Adrian said slowly. "I just felt guilty. Shocked and lonely and scared, but guilty, too."

"And I suppose your father—" she named him as if he were Attila the Hun "—didn't talk to you about her or what happened."

He gave a grunt that masqueraded as a laugh. "Our sole conversation about Mom took about five minutes. After that, he froze me out if I tried to ask about her."

"What a...a creep!" She pressed her lips together. "I suppose I shouldn't say that about your father, but honestly."

"She did embarrass him. I knew even then. As far as he was concerned, a problem was solved. Years later, he looked irritated when I mentioned something that happened when we were still a family. 'Old history,' he said, like that meant it wasn't worth acknowledgement."

He could tell Lucy wanted to burst out with another condemnation of his father and barely restrained herself. Watching her struggle amused him enough that he was able to relax.

"It's okay. You won't hurt my feelings," he told her.

"Honestly!" she exclaimed again. "It's a wonder you're not in psychotherapy." She flushed. "That is, maybe you are. I don't mean there's anything wrong—"

Adrian laughed. "No. I'm not."

Maybe he should be, but the truth was that he'd learned it was easier to cut off that part of his life. Two weeks ago, if someone had asked about his mother, he'd have likely shrugged and dismissed the question. *Old history.*

God, he thought. *I've become him.*

Not a welcome realization, nor the first time he'd had it.

He couldn't pretend to know who he'd become since coming to Middleton, though. All he seemed to do was talk about his feelings, at least around Lucy. And think about 'em. Some kind of floodgate had opened, and the past was rushing through. He'd tried surfing in Hawaii once, and hated the panic that had clawed at him when he fell from the board and the waves flung him over and over until he didn't know up from down.

A kernel of that same panic knotted in his gut, and he didn't like the sensation now any better. This was idiotic. He hadn't changed because his mother had unexpectedly turned up or because he'd spent a grand total of two days in this godforsaken town. All he was doing was a research job. He'd find out what he could about his mother, then file the memories where they belonged and do what he had to for her.

End of story.

He asked Lucy…something. He couldn't have said what, but it got her talking about Middleton with a fondness she didn't seem to realize she felt. And put the conversation back where he wanted it: superficial, pleasant, unmemorable.

CHAPTER SEVEN

AFTER ADRIAN LEFT without asking when he would see her again, Lucy resolved to stay away from the hospital on Monday. The hat lady had her son now and no longer needed Lucy. If Lucy kept showing up there, it might look as if she were seeking him out.

If only she weren't attracted to him, it wouldn't have occurred to her to worry about any such thing. Since she was, she'd become ridiculously self-conscious about everything she said and did. So…the best thing was to avoid him, unless he actually came looking for her.

Having loaded the dishwasher, she added soap, set the dial to Wash and gave a firm nod. She then stood there without the slightest idea how she'd spend the rest of the afternoon, never mind all day tomorrow with the café closed.

Talk about ridiculous. Of course she had things to do. On her days off, she always had a long list of household chores and errands, never mind plans for what she'd do if only she came up with a spare hour, which she rarely did.

The trouble was, she'd gotten up extra early this morning to clean house, since she was having company, and she didn't really need groceries. Most every business in town was closed on Sunday and she had no particular errands to run anyway.

She could be lazy and read. Pour some lemonade and take it and her book outside, since the day was so nice.

But despite the early-morning housecleaning and the cooking, Lucy still felt…restless. She wanted to think over everything she'd learned about the hat lady and her son, but she wanted to be doing something while she thought.

Maybe…why, maybe she'd dig out the flower bed under the front window that she'd dreamed about for so long. She hadn't decided what to put in it yet, but digging the sod out and amending the soil would be plenty of work for one—or even two—days. Think how much fun it would be then to go to the nursery and pick out the plants.

A pang struck her, because the hat lady wouldn't be with her to help decide. But this could be…well, a sort of tribute.

No, she decided hastily, having been struck by a deeper pang, not a tribute. That sounded like a memorial, and the hat lady could wake up anytime. Thinking about her as if she were dead was just wrong.

Still, if she did recover, she'd like knowing that Lucy had finally started the garden they'd so often talked about. And this single bed beneath the window was only the beginning; there'd be more the hat lady could help with.

If her son didn't sweep her away to a nursing home in Seattle.

Adrian wouldn't do that if she *really* recovered, would he? If so, Lucy decided she'd have her for visits. The hat lady could see all her friends and favorite haunts, and they could plan the garden.

A bed on the other side of the porch, Lucy was certain about that, and ones extending to each side of the walkway. She wanted an arch covered with roses and clematis, too, right there where her concrete walk turned in from the sidewalk. She'd always wished she had box-wood hedges, too, but they took so long to grow...

Well, it's past time you start, she told herself, and quit just imagining. She couldn't even think why she *had* hesitated so long. Had she become too used to plodding along day to day, not taking time to do anything just to please herself? Or was it the other way around, that she'd been secretly afraid starting a garden was an acknowledgement that she wasn't going anywhere after all?

She found both possibilities disquieting, but refused to examine them too closely. Today, she would make a beginning.

Leaving the dishwasher running, Lucy went to her bedroom and changed into her oldest jeans and a T-shirt with a tomato-sauce stain down the front she'd never managed to get out.

The gardening gloves she found in the garage out back were stiff from disuse and the shovel was rusting. The tire on the wheelbarrow looked a little low on air, but was still rolling. None of that was going to stop her. The gloves would become pliable, and she could take some steel wool to the shovel another day. And if she really started gardening seriously, she'd want a better wheelbarrow anyway. Maybe one of those garden carts, deep and stable.

She might as well do this right. Because—why not admit it?—she wasn't likely, daydreams aside, to sell the café and embark on some adventure. Honestly, she was beginning to wonder whether she was really disappointed in herself because she hadn't overcome all obstacles to follow some inchoate dream. Maybe what actually disappointed her most was that she didn't have any big dreams. The truth was, she was pretty contented day to day, satisfied by what she *had* achieved.

Maybe, she thought ruefully, *I'm just not very exciting, if starting a garden is one of my big dreams.*

A few minutes later, she'd dragged the hose out front and had moved it a dozen times to outline the bed she saw in her mind's eye. She stretched the hose into a curve, but decided a rectangular shape suited the house better. Not until she was satisfied with the dimensions did she start to dig.

Her shovel bit into the sod and sank deep. With triumph, she lifted out the first shovelful, reached down and shook loose dirt back into the hole, then tossed grass and roots into the wheelbarrow.

Tomorrow, she thought, *I'll sneak into the hospital when I know Adrian won't be there and I'll tell the hat lady all about the beginning of my garden.*

A real garden.

She wondered if Adrian Rutledge, buttoned-down attorney, had any hobbies or dreams. Or did he deny that side of himself because it reminded him too much of his mother?

She wondered what *he* was doing with the rest of his day. And with tomorrow.

WITHIN HALF AN hour of leaving Lucy's, Adrian wished he'd lingered. What was he going to do with himself? Hang around the hospital all afternoon and evening?

He did feel obligated to drive straight there and settle

in at his mother's bedside for another uncomfortable, one-sided talk.

She didn't look better. If anything, her face seemed more sunken today, as if the flesh had begun the process of drying up, and he was being given a glimpse of how she'd look when she was laid in her coffin. Adrian wished desperately he could see her eyes and some spark of the mother he remembered.

"I went through your things today," he told her, because the silence was worse than hearing his own voice. "I felt bad, as if I was intruding."

It was rather like that moment in childhood, he realized, when it struck you like a lightning bolt that your parents were regular people, not just Mom and Dad. And you had no idea how other people might perceive them. Heck, you weren't sure who they actually were. So you went looking.

But you were afraid of what you'd find. He had been apprehensive. He still was. He wanted his mother to be the woman he remembered—sad sometimes, yes, confused, too, but also fun and wise and capable of true joy. He didn't want to find out she'd become angry or disgusting in some way or… He didn't know. Someone else. Someone he didn't know and never would.

The mystery of where she'd gone and who she'd become ate at him. There was a reason he had blocked her out all these years. Her mysteries left a hollow in him, too. After walling himself off all those years ago, Adrian didn't like knowing that any part of his deepest self depended on another person.

Lucy Peterson's face flickered before him then, and he wasn't sure why. Maybe because he could imagine her shaking her head and saying, "Of course we all depend on each other!" Growing up in this small town, she'd never known a day without the interconnections of family, friends and neighbors. Maybe that's why she'd come back after college. Thinking she wanted to strike out on her own was one thing; actually wrenching herself free of the web of roots that tangled with her own was another altogether. Probably she needed those to sustain her.

Adrian shook his head, thinking he'd be strangled by those same roots and all the well-meaning people.

"The conch shell is beautiful. Could you hear the ocean in it?" He leaned forward, watching his mother's face for some shadow of memory. "That piece of china, too. I remember when I found it, you telling me the ocean must have washed it all the way from China. Now, I'd just think it was a broken piece of pottery and drop it back onto the beach. But you made me think it was magical. You were good at doing that, Mom. Making ordinary things shimmer, as if they were special." He paused. "I let myself forget the way you did that. You leaving me with Dad, I guess I started seeing things more his way. I'm sorry."

He didn't even know what he was apologizing for. Letting his father have his way? Or the fact that in his grief and anger and guilt he'd *wanted* to forget his mother, who had abandoned him?

Adrian sat silent for a minute, long enough to become aware again of the muted beeps of the monitors, to hear voices and a shushed laugh outside the door, the brisk crepe-soled footsteps of a nurse passing in the hall. But the quiet in here was overwhelming, the few sounds isolated and oddly lonely. Once again, he wished he'd brought something to read aloud.

"Lucy's going to take your books back to the library. I couldn't tell if you'd read them yet or not." He paused. "I met the librarian the other day. Maybe I already told you. She misses you. She says you're her favorite patron. Now she doesn't have anybody to talk about books with."

Was his mother's color becoming worse, too? The word *waxen* had come to him when he first saw her, but now it seemed her skin had taken on a yellow tinge as well. Had the doctor noticed? Did that mean her organs were trying to shut down?

He sat back in the chair, feeling stunned. Wasn't it strange how little prepared he was for the idea that she would die without ever waking up. When he arrived Friday, he'd mostly been in shock. The idea that this frail, white-haired woman lying in the bed was his mother hadn't seemed quite real to him. Maybe it still didn't. But the woman his mother had been before she disappeared had come alive for him again, if only in the reawakening of his memories.

Looking at the prominence of her bones and the pallor of her skin, Adrian thought, *I might not need to move her to a nursing home near me.* She might simply slip away.

There might not be any need for dutiful visits. He'd never done one single thing for his own mother. He hadn't even been the one to find her.

"God, Mom…" His voice came out broken, raw. "If only I'd known…" Without thinking, he reached for her and gripped her nearest hand hard. It was warmer than he'd expected, and smaller than he remembered.

How often had he laid his hand in hers, confident she'd return his clasp, that she *liked* holding hands with him. 'Cause Mom and him were always gonna do something.

A sound tore at his throat, shocking him.

Her eyelids twitched.

Adrian stiffened and stared. A small shudder seemed to move over her face, flaring her nostrils briefly. Behind closed lids, her eyeballs moved. Was she trying to open her eyes?

"How is she?" Ben Slater asked from beside Adrian.

He started violently, then tried to cover up by straightening and rolling his shoulders to loosen the muscles.

"I don't know. Did you see how her face was moving?" It had gone still now, as if to make him a liar. "Her eyelids were twitching and she seemed to be...I don't know, trying to frown or say something or—"

The doctor laid a hand on his shoulder. "It might just have been reflexes, you know." His voice was gentle. "A random firing of neurons."

"I was thinking her color looked worse today," Adrian said.

Dr. Slater stepped closer to the bed. "I can't say I see a change, but we'll keep monitoring her kidney function."

"You don't think she is going to wake up."

"I didn't say that. Were you talking to her when her face became mobile?"

"Yeah, but I've talked to her every time I came."

"It could be the coma is becoming lighter."

Adrian suspected he was being patronized. He could imagine the cherubic doctor patting him again and saying, *There's always hope*.

What kind of hope would they be talking about anyway? he asked himself with a surge of impatience. No matter what, she wouldn't be the mother he remembered, who balanced on a high wire between sanity and a world that was only in her head. The hat lady was a homeless woman who pushed her belongings in a stolen shopping cart and was as crazy as the current administration's monetary policies. If she did wake up, she'd have to be institutionalized.

Maybe what he should be hoping was that she *didn't* wake up, hard-hearted though that was.

For a moment, he let himself imagine his father's reaction if he'd still been alive. He'd be impatient, disdainful, distant. You'd never know this woman had ever meant anything to him. He'd have driven over here to Middleton, looked to verify her identity, made the decision immediately to move her to long-term care, then put her from his mind except to instruct his assistant to pay the bills.

And maybe he'd have been right to be quick, ruthless and unsentimental. Adrian had no idea what, if anything, he was accomplishing here.

The doctor was watching him with kind eyes. "I hear Lucy has been introducing you around town."

"She thought I could learn something about what Mom's life has been like."

"Is it working?"

"Yeah." He pinched the bridge of his nose. "Yeah, it is."

"She was unconventional, at least by Middleton standards, but loved."

"Not by everyone."

Slater shrugged. "There are narrow-minded folks anywhere. Got to have someone to look down on."

It sickened Adrian to know that he would have been one of those people. Oh, he'd have been polite and maybe even given her his pocket change, the way he sometimes did with the bleary-eyed bums on First Avenue in Pioneer Square. Pity didn't rule out disdain.

"It she schizophrenic?"

"It's a good possibility, from what Lucy tells me. I didn't know your mother well. The wife and I go to a different church, and me, I've dedicated myself to whacking a white ball around eighteen holes and sometimes even thirty-six at least five days a week. Our paths didn't have occasion to cross much."

"Can she be medicated?"

"If she comes out of the coma? Sure. Will she become instantly normal? Probably not. Twenty years have made her what she is." He surveyed Adrian keenly. "Try to remember that she's a good woman who has made countless friends, who's a stalwart at her church and at the thrift store. She's well-read. One of the things Lucy told me she appreciates most about your mother is that she notices beauty everywhere, instead of letting her eyes pass over it the way most of us do. Normally we see with new eyes only twice in our lives—once when we're children ourselves, and seeing everything for the first time, and then when we have our own children and see through their eyes. But your mother gave the people who cared about her the gift of seeing afresh. I think some of them like Lucy won't altogether lose it."

Adrian knew exactly what the doctor meant. His mother had never lost the ability to see with wonder.

Adrian had lost it the minute he came home to find his mother gone.

Lost it? His mouth twisted. Or thrown it away?

Or maybe he'd already been losing it, like any boy heading toward puberty. Maybe that was the gulf he'd felt opening between him and his mother: he'd started caring about other people's perceptions. Pretty soon he would have cared more about them than hers, and she would have been left all alone.

However his father had driven her away that summer, he'd only hastened the inevitable.

Dr. Slater moved past Adrian and took his patient's hand, talking pleasantly to her for a moment as if she could hear. His arm blocked Adrian's view of his mother's face.

Slater's voice sharpened. "You're right. Her face is becoming more mobile. Hmm." He stepped back from the railing. "You talk to her."

Adrian stood and reached for his mother's hand again. "Mom, it's me, Adrian. I'm still here. I'm all grown up. I don't look much like you remember me, but I'm the same person." Was he? He shook off the thought. "I can hardly wait to talk to you. Find out about your life. *Maman* has missed you so much. We could fly up there for a visit. She's kept your bedroom the same all these years. Wouldn't you like to see her?"

"Will you look at that?" the doctor murmured.

She seemed to have multiple tics. Her eyelids twitched, her mouth worked, muscles in her cheeks jerked.

"Something's definitely going on." Slater watched her with narrowed eyes. "When were you planning to move her?"

The question jolted Adrian. He should be heading back to Seattle Tuesday afternoon. He'd expected Carol would have a list of assisted living facilities for him to check out then.

Now, he couldn't even remember what his Wednesday appointments were. He hadn't opened a file on his laptop since he got here. He couldn't imagine being able to concentrate if he did.

"Ah…I hadn't gotten that far," he admitted. "I guess I was hoping for a change."

"Good. I'm going to ask that you not move her until we see whether her condition is changing."

Adrian nodded. "Fair enough."

"Thanks." Slater held out his hand and they shook. "I'm going to talk to your mom's nurses, make sure they're keeping a close eye on her. I might check back in later tonight."

"Thank you," Adrian said, his voice gruff.

"You're welcome. Your mom's somebody special." Dr. Slater nodded and left.

Lucy, Adrian thought with a surge of excitement. He should call her. She'd want to know there'd been a change. He pictured her rushing right over to sit beside him.

Then he remembered the family get-together and the fact that she'd spent all morning and the early afternoon with him for his benefit. He couldn't keep expecting her to drop everything.

And all those twitches might mean nothing at all. They might indicate—how had the doctor described it?—the random firing of neurons. Slater might have been pretending to more excitement than he felt, another metaphorical pat on the back. Did med school include classes on dealing with the patients' loved ones?

Forget it. She's responding to you. Keep talking to her.

He pulled his chair as close to the bed as he could get it and still accommodate his long legs, held his mother's hand and talked. Talked until he was hoarse. He started by telling her about himself: his first girlfriend, getting his law degree, the friends he'd lived with through grad school, the first time he'd addressed a jury in a court-room, making partner at his firm. A couple of different nurses came and went, adjusting his mother's pillows and the height of the bed, shifting her slightly, talking cheerfully to her.

He moved on to rambling about anything and everything that entered his head: the Mariners coming close to making the World Series last October, their lousy beginning this spring, a pro bono case he'd taken on a couple of years ago, snippets from the newspaper.

A couple of times her eyeballs moved or her mouth puckered, but eventually he realized he wasn't getting any response. He'd probably worn her out. Deciding to think of her as taking a much-needed nap, he gently laid her hand back on the coverlet and said, "I'm going to go get some dinner, Mom. I'll come back for a little while this evening. You get some rest, okay?"

No answer.

Big surprise.

Adrian stood, stretched and walked out.

He was vaguely surprised to walk out of the hospital to find it was still full daylight. Barely past five o'clock. He hadn't been there as long as it felt. He guessed he'd head back to the bed-and-breakfast, maybe check e-mail, then decide what to do for dinner.

Lucy's house wasn't a quarter of a mile out of the way. He could drive by, see if her car was there. She'd want to know about his mother. He could keep it brief, undemanding.

A block from her house, Adrian saw her car in the driveway. She must have gone out at some point, because it had been moved. Half a block nearer, and he saw her sitting on the front porch steps. She'd been working out front, since the lawn was cluttered with a wheelbarrow, shovel, rake and a heap of what looked like discarded plastic bags.

Then he grinned. She'd dug out that flower bed she had talked about. By the time he pulled to the curb, he could see the newly turned earth. He guessed from the bags she'd dug in manure and who knew what else.

Lucy spotted him before he came to a stop. Alarm widened her eyes and she rose to her feet as he got out of the car.

"Adrian! Is everything okay?"

He'd seen the wince as she stood. She was filthy. Even her face was dirt-streaked. Her hair must have started in a ponytail, but it was straggling out now, a strand sticking to her forehead.

"Fine," he said. "If by that you mean Mom. I stopped by to tell you she's making some facial expressions. I thought for a minute her hand even tightened on mine. It might just be reflexes, but Dr. Slater seems hopeful."

"Really? She's been completely unresponsive. Oh, Adrian!" She glowed. "I was so afraid… Oh, my goodness."

"I thought you might like to know."

Her teeth sank briefly into her lower lip. "Of course I do!"

He nodded toward the dark, turned earth. "Appears you've had a busy afternoon."

"And I look disgusting," she said ruefully, but without the self-consciousness he might have expected if he'd caught any of his former girlfriends in a similar state. "I was just trying to work up the energy to go in and shower."

"It looks good."

"It will when I'm done. I just dug in a ton of manure and peat moss and bone meal. I was planning to go to the nursery in the morning. There's a great one in Sequim."

He rested a foot on one of the lower stairs, enjoying the play of emotions on her face.

"What do you have in mind?"

"A climbing rose, for starters." She turned to survey her creation. "It can climb up the porch railing. And maybe a clematis, too. They can twine together. Then a couple of shrubs. Maybe old roses. I've always wanted to grow some." She laughed. "I already told you that, didn't I? Oh, and perennials, and probably some annuals to fill in this year. It's going to be such fun. I'm awfully tempted to start digging on the other side of the porch, too. Because now it looks unbalanced, doesn't it?"

He had a sudden impulse. "What if I came and helped in the morning? I can't spend all day at the hospital. I don't know much about plants, but I can dig and haul the sod away."

She gazed at him as if he'd gone nuts. "Are you serious?"

"Sure." He felt oddly light. "I could sweat out all my frustrations."

A laugh escaped her. No, a giggle. "Now that you mention it, all that labor *was* therapeutic."

"Will I be depriving you?"

"Something tells me I'm going to hurt in the morning. I think I can do without too much more therapy."

Adrian grinned at her. "You don't hurt right now?"

She made a face at him. "Oh, yeah. Why do you think I was just sitting here?"

"Why don't you shower?" he suggested. "I could take you out to dinner."

"Oh, you don't have to—"

"I was thinking pizza. Unless you don't eat it unless you've hand-rolled the crust from organic, whole wheat flour and canned the tomato sauce yourself?"

"Are you making fun of me?"

"Wouldn't think of it," he assured her.

"Pizza and beer sounds really good, if you don't mind waiting. Um...do you want to come in?"

"I'll just sit out here," he said. From somewhere, he added, "Hollyhocks." At her startled glance, he shrugged in embarrassment. "I was just thinking of Mom."

"The flowers that reach for the sky," Lucy said softly.

"Yeah."

Her smile was as glorious as any rose in full bloom. "Definitely hollyhocks." She crossed the porch and opened the screen door. "I'll hurry."

"Take your time," Adrian told her, and sat on the top step, his back to the newel. Waiting, he felt better than he had all day.

CHAPTER EIGHT

ON THE WAY HOME from the nursery, Lucy cranked up the radio and in happy abandonment sang along with the top ten hits even though she couldn't carry a tune. Her trunk was tied down with a bungee cord, and her backseat was covered with newspapers and buried in a forest of greenery, some of which waved in her vision when she glanced in the rearview mirror.

She was happy. Ridiculously, gloriously, absurdly happy. She tried to tell herself it was because she'd actually accomplished something this weekend that pleased her and not spent it stripping the kitchen floor and picking up a prescription at the pharmacy and grocery shopping and hearing all the latest, trivial family gossip at her mother's on Sunday night.

But she knew she was kidding herself. She was floating on a wave of euphoria because Adrian Rutledge had stopped at her house yesterday and invited her out for pizza. And because, better yet, he was at her house right this minute, not only waiting for her, but also slaving in her yard because he apparently wanted to.

She was being an idiot. He'd be gone soon. Probably tomorrow, and if not then, within the week. He appreciated what she'd done for his mother. He was thanking her. Heck, he might even be a little bit lonely. It could be that he was thinking of her garden, as she had, as something that would be meaningful to his mother.

He was not falling madly in love with her, Lucy Peterson. The plain Peterson sister. Nobody ever had, and he was a particularly unlikely candidate to become the big exception.

But just for today, she refused to listen to reason. She'd had fun last night. For once, they hadn't talked about his mother. He'd listened with incredulous amusement to tales of *her* family instead. He'd asked about other people he had noticed around town, including several of the nurses and Jason Lee, the editor of the *Courier*.

She told him more about Elton Weatherby, the aging, courtly lawyer, and how residents of Middleton had had to drive to Sequim or Port Angeles to find an attorney until the 1950s. That was when Elton returned from law school at the University of Puget Sound and set up practice in his hometown.

Looking stunned, Adrian had paused with his beer stein halfway to his mouth and said, "He's been practicing for fifty years?"

"Most people have been doing whatever they do for close to that long when they retire," she pointed out. "Think about it. You start work as an auto mechanic right out of high school, you don't retire until you're sixty-five, and that's assuming you can afford to retire then, you'd have been working for, um—" she had to calculate "—forty-seven years."

"Good God," he'd said, and swallowed.

"Besides, Mr. Weatherby told me he loves the fact that he meets so many people and hears so many stories. No day is the same as the one that came before, is how he put it."

"Is he planning to keep tottering into court until the day he turns up his toes?" Adrian asked.

"No, he'd like to find someone to buy the practice. Or even a young attorney to bring in to take over. He had bypass surgery last year. Mrs. Weatherby would like them to go to Arizona during the winter. Her arthritis is bad when it gets cold."

This time he shook his head. "Good lord."

Lucy had wondered from his amazement whether he actually liked his job. She'd had the impression he couldn't imagine going into his office every day for nearly fifty years. Of course, he probably wouldn't have to. Clearly, he made plenty of money. He could probably retire at fifty and…and do whatever rich people did. Sail the Caribbean. Lounge on the beach in Cabo San Lucas. Lucy wasn't quite sure. She thought she'd be bored without work.

Turning onto her street, she began to smile. Maybe she wouldn't be bored, not if she had a huge English cottage-style garden to maintain and kids and grandkids to cook for.

Just don't fool yourself they'll be Adrian Rutledge's, an inner voice warned.

Since she wasn't nearly that stupid, she didn't feel any compulsion to argue. Besides, that might not even be the life she wanted.

Adrian's Mercedes was parked at the curb. She pulled in to the driveway and stopped where they could unload most easily.

He'd accomplished an amazing amount while she was gone. The wheelbarrow was currently piled high with sod, but he'd nearly cleared the rectangle under the dining-room window to match the bed she'd dug out yesterday. He was standing looking at it, but turned when she got out.

He was on his cell phone, she saw. She heard him say, "Yeah, I said clear the rest of the week."

Lucy unhooked the cord holding the trunk closed and pulled the first flat of perennials out.

"The Kendrick deposition?" he was saying, his gaze resting on Lucy. "Reschedule." He frowned as he listened. "Yeah, yeah, I'd forgotten what a time you had. Okay, then, have Crawford do it." Pause. "You heard me right."

Lucy set the flat on the grass and went back for another one.

Adrian covered the phone. "Don't carry anything too heavy. I'll be off in just a second." He went back to his conversation. "My mother's condition is…unstable. I don't want to leave until we know more. Crawford's capable of handling the Kendrick case."

He listened, returning short answers that made no sense to Lucy, finally ending the call. "That was Carol. My administrative assistant," he said unnecessarily. He set the phone on a porch step and went to Lucy's car, lifting one of the two climbing roses from the floor of the backseat. When he set it down on the grass, he read the label. "Zepherine Drouhin."

"It's supposed to be really fragrant. I like fragrance."

He nodded acknowledgement and passed her, going back to the car.

Buffeted by a surge of lust, Lucy stayed behind, pretending to be inspecting his work. Adrian Rutledge was sexy in an expensively cut dark suit, and in the polo shirt and khakis he'd worn yesterday. But put him in well-worn jeans, athletic shoes and a plain gray T-shirt that clung to broad shoulders and bared strong, tanned forearms, dishevel his hair, add sweat, dirt and a strong, earthy smell, and her knees went weak. Which made no sense, but she couldn't help herself.

"You went all out," he observed, returning with plant pots encircled in each of his arms.

She managed a cheeky grin. "It was the most fun I've had in years."

He returned the grin, looking years younger than he had when she met him, his teeth a flash of white in a dirty face. "Does that suggest there's something wrong with your life?"

She was tempted to ask if he was talking about sex. If so, it was overrated, in her opinion. Although… Lucy couldn't help wondering if sex with Adrian would be different. Way different.

"There are different kinds of fun," she said with dignity.

"Yeah, there are." His voice was deep. No longer smiling, he just looked at her, his expression thoughtful and…something more.

Lucy looked back. She suddenly had trouble breathing.

Of course, she lost her nerve and began to babble. "You've gotten so much done. I'm really impressed. I wasn't gone *that* long. And I'll bet you don't ache like I do. Obviously, I need to get more exercise."

The corners of his mouth twitched. "I run regularly. But I suspect I will be sore tomorrow. I can't remember the last time I used a shovel."

"So…you aren't going back to Seattle tomorrow?"

"You heard? No. Mom seemed to be reacting because I was talking to her. And Slater asked me not to move her until we can tell what's going on with her."

He couldn't have made it more clear that he *would* be moving his mother, or that he remained in Middleton only because of Dr. Slater's request.

"Yes, that makes sense," Lucy said with forced cheer. "Well, let me finish unloading the car and then I can help you."

"No, you start planting. I'm not far from done."

While she carried the last flat of perennials over, he disappeared around the house with the wheelbarrow to deposit his load in the pile she was now designating as her compost heap. Or maybe it was an eyesore, but at least it was in back by the alley, and it would compost eventually, wouldn't it?

She set the pots out the way she thought she wanted to plant, then rearranged them half a dozen times. Adrian gave advice a couple of times, then once he'd finished amending the soil, helped her lay out the shrubs and perennials she'd bought for his side of the porch, too.

His side. Who was she kidding?

But it was fun having the companionship of someone who had invested as much hard work as she had. He gave his full attention to such problems as whether the half dozen hardy Geranium Johnson's Blue should be sprinkled amongst other perennials or clustered in artful drifts.

A few times, he would look down at one of the plants and say, in an odd tone, "Mom grew that."

He remembered the spiky Siberian irises and the tall Japanese anemones from her garden.

"And peonies," Adrian said reminiscently. "We had a whole row of them on top of a retaining wall along the street. Pink and white and red. It was really something when they were in bloom. Cars would stop in the middle of the street so the drivers could gawk."

Lucy had bought a couple of peonies, one for each side. She was pretty sure they needed some kind of staking, which made her wary of having too many.

They broke off to have sandwiches, which she put together quickly in the kitchen and they ate on the front porch steps. Lucy asked more about his early-morning visit to the hospital. Adrian had been disappointed that he'd found his mother unresponsive.

"Yesterday may have been a fluke. I'll go back this afternoon when we're done here." He glanced at her. "You probably have things to do, but if not—"

"I've been staying away so I didn't intrude," Lucy admitted. "I'd love to come. Except…I really need to shower first."

He looked ruefully down at himself. "Yeah, I'd better do that, too."

Having downed the sandwiches and the apples she'd sliced, they went back to work companionably. When they were done setting every single plant she'd bought into the ground, Adrian insisted on helping her clean up.

Then they stood on the grass and admired the two flower beds.

Looking satisfied, Adrian said, "Give 'em a month or two, and this is going to look great."

He wouldn't be here to see.

Ignoring her hollow feeling, she said, "I think I need some annuals to fill in. There's a lot of bare soil." She frowned. "Maybe we should have put everything closer together."

"What, you don't believe they're going to get as big as the nursery says they will?"

She sighed. "I'm impatient. I want my garden bursting with flowers *now.*"

"You want the equivalent of fast food?"

Lucy laughed at herself. "No, I don't. Fine, you've made your point."

"Isn't watching plants grow supposed to be half the pleasure?"

"I don't know. I've never actually gardened before, except for hanging baskets. I only imagined gardening. Which isn't quite the same."

"Ah." He was quiet for a moment. "Mom used to say something about possibilities."

Lucy couldn't help noticing how much more casually he now said *Mom* instead of *my mother,* in that stiff way he'd had. It was as if she'd become a real person again to him. Lucy was glad about that, if nothing else.

"Well." He stirred. "I'll head to the B and B and shower. Then I'll come back for you. Say, half an hour? Forty-five minutes?"

She nodded. "I'll be ready." When he started to turn away, she stopped him with a hand on his arm. "Adrian. Thank you. I wouldn't have gotten nearly as far without you."

"You know, I actually enjoyed myself today." He sounded surprised. "It felt…"

When he seemed unable to supply a word, Lucy did. "Real?"

"Real." His eyebrows pulled together as he seemed to sample the concept. "Yeah. Most days, I write e-mails, I make phone calls, I file briefs. Nothing you can touch or look at a month later."

A tinge of sadness in his voice made her want to reassure him. "But…you must affect people's lives."

"Do I?" He shook himself. "Definitely time for that shower. I'll see you in a bit."

He strode to his car and got in so quickly, Lucy wondered if he hadn't wanted her to see that he felt even a moment of doubt about his life. But maybe it wasn't that. Maybe he was just determined to shut off any unwelcome reflection.

Lucy gazed once again at her new garden and, for a moment, saw it as it would be, in glorious bloom, not as the bare beginnings it now was. She imagined the hat lady beside her, nodding gently in approval, her new spring hat adorned with a riotous bouquet of silk flowers. In this picture, Adrian was there, too, debonair in a cream-colored linen suit, as if they'd all been to Ascot.

Then, smiling crookedly at her absurdity, she tore herself away and went inside to get cleaned up.

LUCY SEEMED CONTENT to stay with Adrian at his mother's bedside for a couple of hours. She was thrilled by every facial tic and refused to let him dismiss any new activity as random.

She scowled at him. "Dr. Slater didn't really say that."

"Yeah, actually he did. Although that was before," Adrian admitted, "he'd actually seen for himself how expressive her face is getting."

"Well, there you go then." She gave a firm nod, her jaw jutting out as if to tell him she'd keep arguing as long as he wanted.

Of course, he didn't want. Sitting here in the hospital was different with Lucy beside him. She was able to talk to his mother so naturally, anyone listening in would assume she was getting responses of some sort. With her as an example, even he began to get the hang of it.

"You know," Lucy said suddenly, after talking about which old roses she'd bought and why, "none of these bouquets are fragrant."

"What?" Adrian stared at him.

She waved at the pot of chrysanthemums on the windowsill and the two bouquets on a bedside stand. He'd bought one himself downstairs in the gift shop, and had seen from the card that the other was from Lucy and George, the grocer. "Until your mom opens her eyes, she can't see them. But if we brought really fragrant flowers, maybe she could smell them."

What an idiot he'd been. Of course she was right. Adrian wanted to stand right that minute and go drag a florist away from his dinner table to make up a new bouquet.

"Like what?" he asked. "Roses?"

She wrinkled her nose. "Most florists' roses are hybrid teas and might as well be plastic. Oriental lilies—they have a powerful fragrance. No, I know what! Mom has an early lilac. We can cut our own bouquet." She smiled impishly at him. "We can do it tonight. I won't even ask. Mom'll never notice a few missing branches."

God, she was beautiful.

Stunned by the power of his realization, Adrian wondered how he'd been so oblivious in the beginning. No, he knew why—he was used to hothouse flowers, showy and pampered. The women in his world visited their salon weekly for manicures and facials; they applied makeup skillfully, wore three-inch heels and shopped for clothes at Nordstrom or the downtown boutiques. Any pets were elegant purebreds, and the women's cars as expensive as they were.

His gaze moved over Lucy's face, now in profile, sa-

voring her high, curved brow, the wing of her cheekbones, the slightly pointy chin with a hint of a cleft,
the scattering of freckles on skin that had the translu-
cence of a child's. She'd acquired a scratch across one
cheek today, courtesy of Zepherine Drouhin, but she'd
only laughed and wiped away beads of blood onto her
shirt hem.

He wasn't sure what her prized climbing rose would
look like in bloom, but she made him think of a wild
rose—pale pink, perhaps, without complicated whorls,
the few simple petals perfectly arranged on long, arch-
ing canes, the scent elusive and sweet.

Adrian didn't know how it had happened, when he'd
only known her a few days, but he couldn't imagine
driving away from Middleton without planning to see
her again.

*You know people. Lean on them. Find her the per-
fect job.*

What if a restaurant like Veil or Earth & Ocean offered her a job as sous chef? That was the opportunity
she'd dreamed about. Would she follow him to Seattle?

Did wild roses transplant into urban, postage-stamp-
size gardens?

Why not? he thought recklessly. She longed for a life
more sophisticated than Middleton could give her. People here wouldn't change; fifty years from now, they'd
still expect clam chowder on the menu every Friday. As
talented as she was, she deserved better.

And he liked the idea of having her in his life, of
exploring where this peculiar blend of tenderness and
hunger he felt would take them.

"She squeezed my hand!" Lucy turned to him, her

mouth forming a circle of delighted astonishment. "I'm sure she did!"

Adrian smiled at her, relaxing now that he'd figured out a course of action.

Find his mother a place in the best assisted-living facility in Seattle, and Lucy a job at her dream restaurant.

He didn't let himself think about the garden she'd created that weekend, or the café that bore her stamp, or the family that aroused amusement, exasperation and love in her. The family that sustained her.

Middleton wasn't that far from Seattle. She could visit. Maybe even keep the house.

And if she didn't like Seattle… His jaw tightened. Well, maybe he'd find that whatever he felt for her here evaporated in the real world.

"Show me," he said, and leaned forward to see the slender, long-fingered hand of this surprising woman wrapped around the arthritic hand of his mother.

And damned if he wouldn't have sworn the clawlike fingers tightened and clung to Lucy…who was beaming.

"You're coming back to us, aren't you? Thank goodness! We miss you so much. We're waiting, Elizabeth." Her voice had a hitch, softened. "Whenever you're ready."

"Whenever you're ready," he echoed, believing for the first time that she would wake up, that he would have a chance to become reacquainted with the mother who had disappeared from his life so many years ago.

His heart seemed to swell in his chest, and he sat back in his chair.

What would it be like? Having her back? Discovering the history he hadn't understood as a child? Learning, perhaps, to hate his father?

Lucy would listen if he had to talk, he thought involuntarily. He could deal with anything, if she were there.

Damn it, he had to find a way.

ADRIAN INSISTED ON taking Lucy to dinner again that evening, this time at the Steak House.

He seemed…different tonight, she kept thinking. Less tense, more confident, even expansive. She blossomed under the full force of his charm even as she felt wary.

It was relief, she tried to tell herself. She felt a little of that giddiness, too. It was really beginning to seem that the hat lady would come out of the coma and be herself again. And imagine how much stronger the spark of hope must be for Adrian!

On Friday, he'd discovered the mother he thought long dead was alive. He'd spent the past three days recovering his memories of her and at the same time assimilating the likelihood that she would never regain consciousness or know that he had found her. And now…now it looked like she would. Why wouldn't he feel like celebrating?

They waited until dusk to drive to her mother's street. Lucy knew it was silly to sneak in to her own parents' yard and steal lilac blossoms, but she didn't want to knock and have to introduce Adrian to her father and whatever stray aunts or cousins happened to be over, embroiling them both into an explanation of the change in the hat lady's condition.

Everything else in her life had to be shared with the family grapevine; that was the price of having their support. But she didn't want to share Adrian. And especially not what she felt for him, which she was terribly afraid was writ bright on her face to anyone who knew her well.

Like her mother, father or any stray aunts or cousins. Or, God forbid, her sister, who knew her best of all.

Anyway, Lucy could just imagine her father peering at her over his reading glasses, doubt weighting his voice. "Her cheek has a tic? And her eyes are rolling behind the lids, but she isn't opening them? And Ben says this means something?"

That was her father: the Eeyore of the Peterson clan. He always saw the dark cloud on the horizon. She loved him dearly, but she didn't think Adrian needed an introduction tonight.

She had Adrian park three houses down. The neighborhood dated from the fifties, and trees were large and leafed out with spring. Several of the neighbors had large lilac bushes in their yards, too, but none had blooms as far advanced as her mother's.

She and Adrian hurried through a pool of light cast by the streetlamp, then slowed in the dark beyond, peering past a snowball bush in full bloom.

"That's my parents' house," she whispered, indicating the brick rambler.

"You grew up there?" He spoke in a low voice, too.

Lucy nodded. "The lilac is the one by the front window."

The house blazed with lights. As they watched, a figure moved in front of the window. Samantha. Why was Samantha here? Lucy wondered indignantly, and knew the answer. Probably Mom had invited her so she could tell the family all about Adrian. By this time, they must know how much time Lucy was spending with him. She'd seen enough heads turn as cars passed her yard today while they were working.

Pull the drapes, she willed her sister, who instead turned and looked out the window. Lucy gripped Adrian's hand and held him back.

"Wait."

He nodded. She couldn't help noticing that he didn't disentangle his hand from hers.

"Okay, now," she whispered, when her sister turned and disappeared toward the kitchen.

"Is that Samantha?" Adrian murmured in her ear. "I thought she was supposed to be turning down my bedcovers and putting a chocolate on my pillow right about now."

"She's probably already done it."

She'd never asked what he thought of her much prettier sister. He hadn't talked about her beyond mentioning that Sam had told him about his mother's routine. With a pang of jealousy, Lucy speculated on whether her sister poured him a cup of tea and sat down to talk to him every night when he got back to the B and B. Sam was exceptionally easy to talk to. She'd never gone through the suspicious stage as a child that Lucy had. Mom made a point of telling people that even as a baby Samantha had grinned happily at complete strangers. She was a born hostess.

Mom invariably chuckled at that point. "My Lucy, why she glared at everyone at that age!"

Right now, Lucy quit worrying about Sam as she and Adrian hurried across the springy grass and pressed their backs against the brick wall of the house, just as her father walked across the living room. He didn't even glance toward the window. Once he'd vanished from sight, Lucy let out a breath she hadn't realized she was holding.

"Do you have the clippers?" she asked.

Adrian pressed them into her hand, nurse to her surgeon. She couldn't see very well; night had crept upon them from the dusk they'd started in. But she snipped several branches, freezing every time she saw movement inside.

By the time she backed away, it was all she could do not to giggle.

"The front door!" Adrian murmured in her ear, with an urgency that had her dropping to a crouch beside him. He took the clippers from her.

"I'd better get back, Mom." Samantha's voice came easily to their ears.

"You're so busy you can never stay," Lucy's mother complained. "If you're going to have guests seven days a week, you need to bring in some help. Bridget's looking for a job, you know."

"Lucy already hired her," Sam said. "Anyway, I can't afford help yet. Maybe by summer, if business is good."

"I know it will be." They embraced.

Samantha went to her car out on the street without ever looking toward where her sister and Adrian crouched beside the lilac. The front door remained open, spilling light onto the porch and walkway, until Sam was safely in her car and had started the engine. Then Lucy heard her father call something from another room, and her mother begin to answer. The door closed, cutting her off, and Samantha drove away.

Lucy's giggle escaped, and she clapped a hand over her mouth.

"Oh, dear. I should have knocked and told Mom I wanted to cut a bouquet. She wouldn't have minded."

"We don't want her to catch us now. God knows what she'd think."

She gave a hiccup. "Oh, no!"

"Shh!" She could tell from his voice that he wanted to laugh, too. "Come on. Let's run."

They raced across the lawn, Adrian towing Lucy, who clutched her stolen lilac branches in the other hand. Not until they'd reached the sidewalk and passed the big snowball bush that hid them from her parents' house did they stop, their laughter spilling out.

She hiccuped again, and they laughed even harder. It seemed natural to feel Adrian's arm around her, his breath against her cheek.

"You got the flowers?"

"Can't you smell them?" She held the armful up and he breathed in.

"You're a genius."

"Of course I am," she said on another bubble of laughter. Or was it a hiccup?

"More than a genius." His voice had changed, deepened. "I wouldn't be here if it weren't for you."

She went still inside the circle of his arm. "Trespassing on my parents' property?"

"In Middleton. Finding my mother." So quietly she barely heard him. "Finding you."

His hand touched her neck, slid up the column of her throat and lifted her chin. The next moment, his lips found hers.

CHAPTER NINE

WHEN LUCY'S MOUTH immediately softened and parted for his, Adrian forgot where they were. He forgot everything but her.

He crushed her to him, the scent of lilacs rising, and feasted on her mouth. She tasted of the Chardonnay she'd sipped with dinner, of the laugh she'd swallowed barely a moment ago. She was slim and taut and yielding, all at the same time.

Arousal was instant. Every sensation felt heightened: the cool night air, the pillow of her breasts pressed against his chest, the vibration in her throat, the stroke of her tongue. He gripped her hips and pulled her tighter against him even as her arm encircled his neck and she made a whimpering sound.

The blaze of the headlights of an approaching car seared Adrian's eyes through closed lids. He groaned and reluctantly lifted his head.

"Unless we want the whole town gossiping…"

"Oh, no!" she breathed, not the most flattering response she could have made. She whirled and started toward the car, not waiting to see the way his hands dropped heavily to his sides.

He hadn't locked the doors; she was already sitting on the passenger side by the time the car passed them, headlights silhouetting her briefly, and Adrian got in behind the wheel. She sat rigidly, staring straight ahead.

He put the key in the ignition, but didn't turn it. "Did I crush the flowers?"

"The flowers…? Oh." Her head bent as she looked down at them, although he didn't know how much she could see. "No. I held them, um, to the side."

"Okay." He waited.

"Why don't we go to my house?" Lucy spoke in a rush. "I can trim them and put them in a vase. Then if you want you can drop them at the hospital tonight."

You *can drop them at the hospital.* No more *we.*

Adrian had believed himself to be reasonably skilled at the games men and women played. Now, he had absolutely no idea what to say. Hadn't they been working their way toward a kiss? Why did she seem upset?

"You won't come with me?" he asked, baffled.

"Oh, I don't think I'd better. I should never have taken so much time off this weekend. I need to work on my books this evening…." Her voice trailed off.

It might even be true. As a small-business owner, she likely did devote her days off to such tasks as accounting and ordering. But given that he guessed it was now eight o'clock, he wondered how much she'd actually get done tonight.

He nodded anyway, even if Lucy couldn't see, and started the car. "I'm sorry," he said.

"Sorry?" Her head turned sharply.

"That you can't take the time to come. Since this was your idea."

"You'll let me know if…if she responds?"

"I'll let you know." He drove several blocks. "I'm not sorry I kissed you."

"I'm…not sorry you did, either." She sounded so constrained, he couldn't tell what she felt.

"You don't seem happy."

"I just need to…well, think about it. Okay? I mean, you're here for a week. That's pretty temporary."

"Seattle isn't that far," he said mildly, although his hands had tightened on the steering wheel.

"I've had the impression you could hardly wait to see the last of Middleton. You're eager to move your mother." Her voice was even now, so reasonable it ticked him off.

"Give me a little credit," he said, anger edging every word. "I was somewhat in shock when you walked in and announced that the mother I thought was dead had been hanging around this little town for ten years. You think I should have embraced Middleton immediately?"

"You didn't have to be…to be condescending."

"What makes you think I was? You're sure it wasn't in your own mind?"

"Oh, come on. You were blown away to find out that Dr. Slater was actually competent enough to treat your mother."

Her hostility couldn't have been born this minute, Adrian realized in shock. He'd been right when he thought she didn't like him.

"Do you blame me? Small community hospitals don't have neurosurgeons."

"Did you think a small community hospital had a doctor competent to set a broken bone?"

He wrenched the wheel, pulled to the curb in front of her house and braked so abruptly, the seat belt bit into his shoulder. Adrian turned to glower at her. Light from a streetlamp let him see that she was fumbling

onehanded to release her seat belt, and she looked...
panicky.

No. God. On the verge of tears.

"Let me." He reached out.

"No!" She batted at his hand. "I can get it!"

He felt dense. It shouldn't have taken him so long to
realize that he'd scared her. He didn't entirely understand why a kiss would have that effect, but he knew
he wasn't wrong.

"Lucy..."

"What?" she snapped.

He sat very still, trying to make himself unalarm-
ing. "I really am sorry. It was..." *Impulsive* would be
insulting, and not even entirely true. "I've been wanting to kiss you."

There was a moment during which she didn't move.
Then, with a sigh, she sat back in the seat. "No, I'm
sorry. I think I panicked. You're...a little out of my
league."

He stared at her. "What in hell does that mean?"

"You're successful, rich. Hot. I live in some little
town. I cook. I'm nothing special to look at." She let
out another gusty sigh. "And I sound pathetic, don't I?
I don't even mean it. I *like* myself. But I can't possibly
be the kind of woman you usually—"

Adrian kissed her again. Roughly, passionately, and
his fingers shoved into her hair so she couldn't escape.
He let her go as suddenly.

"I don't see it that way." His voice was hoarse.

She gulped. He heard her.

"Oh."

"If you don't like me, say so. But don't put yourself

down. You're an extraordinary woman. What you did for my mother out of sheer kindness puts me to shame."

"That doesn't make me—"

When she stopped, he asked, "What?"

"Pretty," she whispered. Then, louder, "Sexy."

Baffled, Adrian said, "I wouldn't have kissed you if I didn't think you were both." How had she developed such low self-esteem? He tried not to think about his own original assessment of her. He'd been blind. An idiot.

After a moment she nodded. "Okay."

She sounded so damned equable, he could only repeat, "Okay what?"

"I like it that you think I'm pretty and sexy. And that you kissed me. And I'm sorry I was so…so old-maidish about it."

Good God, was she a *virgin?* Was it possible in this day and time?

Not likely in Seattle, but in Middleton…who knew? Adrian examined the idea and discovered that he didn't mind. Mild way of saying that he was getting aroused, thinking of it.

"You sure you don't want to come to the hospital with me?" he asked, when he wanted to say, *To hell with your sister's place. Can I spend the night?*

"Of course I will. I was being silly. Come on, let's put these in water." She flicked her seat belt off and opened the door with no trouble now that she'd calmed down.

He followed her into the house, watched her choose a vase from several in a kitchen cupboard, deftly trim the stems and arrange the spray of lilac blossoms. Their scent filled the kitchen as she worked, so heady he thought, *I'll never be able to smell lilacs again without thinking of Lucy. Of this moment.*

Lucy carried the bouquet to the car and let him buckle her seat belt. As they drove, with occasional streetlamps or headlights illuminating her face, Adrian asked, "Why do you think you're nothing special to look at?"

She was silent for a long time. He began to be sorry he'd asked. But at last Lucy said, "You know Samantha. And my other sister Melissa is a senior at WSU over in Pullman. They're both way prettier than I am. They got the blue eyes and blond hair. And curls! I heard people sometimes say that one or the other was the pretty Peterson girl. It was never me."

She had tried very hard to sound matter-of-fact, as if knowing what people said about the Peterson sisters didn't hurt her, not at all. But he also wondered if all this was in her head, because he couldn't see it, not when he pictured the sister he did know.

Adrian shook his head in disbelief. "Samantha's pretty in that Barbie-doll way. But you... You're classy." He felt inarticulate, rare for him, an attorney skilled at riveting the attention of juries. Maybe he was better in the courtroom than in personal relationships. Usually he could tell a woman she was beautiful and that was all he had to say. But Lucy's vulnerability made it important for him to get this right. "You have gorgeous skin and great cheekbones and a directness I hardly ever see. Maybe most of all, what you did for my mother makes you one in a million. I keep looking at you and thinking—"

He stopped, not wanting to put this into words. His longing was too unformed. She had a capacity for caring greater than anyone he'd ever known. When she loved, it would be completely. He could depend on that love.

He could trust her not to leave him.

Jolted, Adrian hardly heard Lucy ask, "Thinking what?"

That was what he believed deep inside? That no woman would love him enough to stay?

Why not? some voice inside asked. *If your own mother ditched you, how likely is it someone else will stick it out?*

He was usually the one to end relationships. The one who got bored. The one who couldn't imagine waking to that woman's face every morning for the next fifty years.

Or had he made damn sure he never cared enough to be sliced to the bone when she left him?

He pulled in to a parking spot at the hospital, set the emergency brake and turned his head to look at Lucy, who was watching him in puzzlement. Maybe, he thought, he just hadn't met the right woman.

Until now.

Sure. How did he know any such thing? It was this damn town. His head had been spinning since he got here. He shouldn't have canceled his appointments. A few days in Seattle would have given him some perspective. His mother didn't need him. Either she was going to wake up or not. He was deluding himself to think it was his voice leading her out of the fog.

Adrian also knew, looking at Lucy's anxious face, that he was glad not to be leaving Middleton tomorrow. He had close to a week during which he could spend as much time as possible with Lucy, figure out what he felt and where it was going. He had the sudden, reckless realization that he had been as happy today as he could ever remember being.

So to hell with perspective and distance. He'd grab what he could while he was here. Real life would intrude soon enough.

"I keep thinking I've never met anyone like you," he heard himself say. "And I want to figure out what makes you different."

"Hmm." She grinned at him. "You know what they say about the way to a man's heart."

"You can cook," he agreed.

"Wait'll you taste my potato soup."

"I might never want to leave Middleton."

Her smile faded; it seemed as if her eyes became more shadowed. But she said, "Hey, you never know. Shall we go see your mom?"

He agreed and they got out. Walking into the hospital, he had a strange feeling in his gut.

Never leave Middleton? That had been a joke. *Was* a joke. But something told him it was different for Lucy. She flirted with the idea of leaving Middleton, but would she really?

He found that he really wanted to know the answer to that question.

ADRIAN GLANCED UNEASILY around. "I know Middleton is old-fashioned, but, uh, did we just cross some space-time continuum?"

It was the following Saturday night, and Lucy had taken a break to walk him out to his car after he had dinner at the café.

Now she followed his gaze to the teenagers sashaying

down the sidewalk and laughed. The girls wore poodle skirts and ponytails, and the boys had hair greased back.

"Tonight's the Spring Fling at the high school. I'm one waitress short because of it. Some of the kids must be grabbing a bite before they go on to the dance. The theme is always the Fifties. I don't actually know why."

"Wasn't there a high school in Middleton in the 1940s? What did they do then?"

"Heaven knows. Maybe you should ask Elton."

He'd had lunch the other day with Elton Weatherby, Middleton's one and only attorney. Elton had been alone at a table at her café when Adrian came in. He'd waved off Mabel, gone over to Elton and asked if he could join him. Lucy had started out of the kitchen when she first saw Adrian, and had been delighted to hear Elton say, "I hear you're a colleague, young man. By all means! By all means, pull out a chair." He'd swiveled in his chair. "Where's that girl? I've already put in an order. Now, where in tarnation has she gotten herself to? If you haven't tried the soups here, you really should."

"I've been having at least a meal a day here," Adrian had said. "Lucy's soups are damn good."

Smiling, she had gone back to the kitchen and left them to...what? Tell war stories? What *did* two attorneys discuss? Hateful judges and heroic courtroom stands? Did a corporate attorney ever make passionate pleas before a jury? She had no idea.

She hadn't actually thought to query him about what he and Elton had talked about, even though she had somehow spent quite a lot of time with Adrian that week, despite her work schedule. She'd joined him a couple of mornings for breakfast at Samantha's. Sometimes when he came in to eat at the café, she took a break and sat with him for twenty minutes or half an hour. She'd gone to the hospital with him three mornings that week.

And then there was last night, when he'd stopped by at closing and followed her car home. They had sat out on her porch glider in the dark and made out like a couple of teenagers. She'd flushed every time she thought about it today.

She had found herself singing at odd moments all week. It felt so different, having somebody waiting when she closed the restaurant, or calling at bedtime to talk about their days, or choosing his seat in the café so he could see her whenever she popped out of the kitchen. Somebody who so plainly liked to touch her. Just the way he laid a hand on the small of her back to guide her on the sidewalk made her knees weak.

What she was trying very, very hard not to think about was the fact that the week was drawing to a close. She knew he wasn't planning to leave tomorrow, but what about Monday? Wouldn't he have to go back to Seattle at some point? He hadn't said, and of course that was partly because of his mother.

It seemed that each day her coma became lighter. Ben Slater was coming by twice daily. Adrian was spending much of his time at her bedside, reading to her and talking. His voice had become gravelly from overuse.

Lucy would have loved to know what he was telling his mother. He had talked some to Lucy about the years after his mother disappeared, which sounded very sad to her. Despite his confusion and grief and buried anger, he had fallen in line with his father's expectations rather than rebelling. Having been surrounded by nosy, affectionate relatives her entire life, she couldn't imagine growing up in a household as silent as his had apparently been, and so lacking in love.

As far as she was concerned, if he retained any ability to feel love himself, it was thanks to his mom. His father must have been a very cold man.

"Oh, no! There's Uncle Will and Aunt Lynn," Lucy said now, out on the sidewalk. "You don't want to meet them, do you?"

"God, no!" Adrian said fervently, drawing her with him into the dark alcove of the doorway two businesses down from the café. Yvonne's Needle & Thread closed at five every day, which Lucy sometimes envied. Mouth close to her ear, he asked, "How many aunts and uncles do you have?"

"Oh…my mother has two sisters, both married. And Dad has a sister and a brother. That's not too bad."

He drew back to stare at her, although she doubted he could make out her face. "Not too bad? Are you kidding? That's…four aunts and four uncles. I don't even want to know how many cousins you have."

"And lots of *them* have kids, so I have cousins once removed. You're right," Lucy said agreeably. "It's horrible." She rose on tiptoe and cast her arms around Adrian's neck. "That's why I have to lurk in dark corners to get kissed."

"Hard to get by with anything in this town," he muttered, before bending his head to kiss her as requested.

Her brain immediately became as mushy as her knees. Nobody had ever kissed her the way Adrian did. She wanted to believe it wasn't just expertise, that there was some sort of magical connection between them, but the fact that he was really good at kissing sure didn't hurt. And also, a hunger and urgency in the way he held her made her want very, very much to quit being cautious and ask him to spend the night.

But, of course, Samantha might know he hadn't returned to the bed-and-breakfast, and Sam did have a big mouth. Plus, Lucy already ached at the thought of him driving away from Middleton, even if he did promise to call. Right now, she was rather desperately holding at least some small part of herself back. If she made love with him, she was pretty sure the inevitable goodbye would be nearly unendurable.

So she backed away when his hand slid up her side and covered her breast at the same moment as he nipped her lower lip with sharp need.

"I'd better go back to work," Lucy whispered. She was trembling as the cool evening air came between them.

"I'm sorry." He sounded shaken. "I forgot—"

"It's okay." As lightly as she could manage, she said, "It was exciting, sneaking kisses out here with you."

"Can I come by tonight?" he asked with an urgency that stole what little breath she'd regained.

She didn't think she could resist him tonight. Her awareness that this week was almost over made her vulnerable.

"I'm awfully tired tonight." She sounded unconvincing to her own ears. "I really had better go back in."

He let her past, but said, "Breakfast?"

"If I don't sleep in." As if she'd be able to sleep at all, thinking about him. Ready to walk away, she couldn't. "Why don't you come to my house instead? I'll make brunch."

"Do you *want* to cook on your day off?"

"I love to cook," she said truthfully. "It's fun just to please myself. Although I must warn you, my pastries probably aren't as good as Sam's."

His voice had relaxed, as if he'd been afraid she was rejecting him. "Her scones are amazing."

"I'll make muffins," she decided. "I froze some high bush huckleberries last year. And omelets. I can toss in anything."

"All right." He kissed her on the cheek. "I'll see you in the morning. Nine? Ten?"

"Make it ten. It's not brunch if it's too early."

He let her go, then, but she knew he was still standing by his car watching until she went back into the café.

The moment she did, her aunt called to her. "Lucy, dear! Did I miss you outside? My goodness, I haven't seen hide nor hair of you for ages."

Lucy forced a smile and went to kiss the proffered cheeks. "Uncle Will. Aunt Lynn. How are you?"

They told her, of course. Aunt Lynn was Lucy's least favorite aunt. She had a delicate stomach, she always told everyone, and invariably complained after eating Lucy's cooking that, my, she did use spices, didn't she? "I do so much better when food is milder," she would declare, as if everyone didn't know that already and avoid her offerings at family potlucks.

Lucy did like Uncle Will, however, who was a genial man who enjoyed working with his hands and who let his wife do the talking. A plumber, he had refused payment every time Lucy had had to call him. Once, he'd told her the payment in lunch that day was ample. She'd already had a particularly spicy chili simmering when her kitchen sink backed up.

"I miss food with some taste," he'd told Lucy rather wistfully, after his third bowl of chili.

She would feel sorry for Uncle Will, except that she'd seen the way he looked at his wife sometimes, as if he was still madly in love with her. Obviously, he saw a different woman than the rest of the family did.

When Lucy told them she had to get back to the kitchen, Aunt Lynn said, "You'll be at Marian's tomorrow, won't you? We missed you last Sunday. Your sister promised to bring pecan pie, and I'm bringing apple."

With only the tiniest smidgen of cinnamon, she would be sure to mention proudly.

Lucy forced a smile. "Yes, of course I'll be there. Mom put me down for potato salad."

Uncle Will's face brightened. Lucy's potato salad did not taste like his wife's.

Why, Lucy wondered as she returned to the kitchen, did she have this instinctive desire to steer Adrian away from her family? Was she afraid they'd scare him away? Or was it simply that her parents would assume it meant something if she invited a man home to meet them? She didn't know. All she was sure of was that she wanted to keep Adrian to herself. She was ashamed to realize she even hated having to share him with Sam.

If they had brunch together in the morning, would he wonder why she didn't invite him to her aunt and uncle's for Sunday dinner later? They definitely were...well, not dating, but seeing each other. Which would make it natural for her to ask him. If their positions were reversed, she was afraid her feelings would be hurt.

Of course, if she made an excuse and let him go to the hospital without her, maybe he'd never have to know.... Lucy grimaced. Uh-huh. Sure. Sam and her big mouth. It was a surprise *she* hadn't already asked him. But then, not even Sam had any idea how much time Lucy was spending with him.

But everyone in the family did know something was going on. Probably she'd make matters worse if she didn't bring him, especially after she skipped last week's Sunday dinner to spend the day with Adrian. Given that his mother had always been Lucy's "project," as the family liked to put it, they'd expect her to try to make him feel at home while he was in Middleton.

In other words…she really didn't have any choice. Not unless she wanted her nosier relatives to start speculating.

So. She'd invite him, and if he didn't make an excuse and not come, she'd be casual and friendly while they were there. Just like she always was. He wouldn't kiss her in front of her parents and other assorted family members, and once they'd had the chance to really talk to him—read, grill him—they'd lose interest. He'd merely be part of Lucy's peculiar little project.

It wouldn't occur to a one of them that her heart was going to break when Adrian left Middleton for good.

And she definitely wanted to keep it that way.

CHAPTER TEN

SUNDAY DINNER for this family was apparently a command performance. Pretty much everyone showed up, which made Lucy's decision last week to skip it so that she could have him to lunch even more noteworthy. Adrian couldn't imagine being closely related to so many people.

Fortunately, the afternoon was sunny and Lucy's aunt had set long tables out on the lawn. He didn't like to think about being crammed into the downstairs of the modest two-story house with this crowd.

Food hadn't been served yet. Since they'd arrived, Lucy had been leading Adrian from group to group, introducing him to people whose names he wouldn't remember the next time he came face-to-face with them.

The latest cluster included Lucy's mother and the same aunt who had descended on Lucy's house that time he was over. Another woman of their generation was with them.

"Have you met my aunt Lynn?" Lucy asked.

"I don't think so," he said, holding out a hand. He'd seen her, though, he realized; she was the one he and Lucy had dodged on the dark sidewalk last night.

"Lynn Rodgers," she told him. "Lucy's father is my big brother."

Aunt Marian, he seemed to recall, was Lucy's mother's sister instead.

A gaggle of screeching children raced toward them,

parting at the last second to pour around them. He winced and stepped closer to Lucy.

"Are those all cousins?"

A particularly shrill giggle rent the afternoon as the kids sprang up the porch steps and vanished inside the house.

Lucy's gaze had followed them. A frown puckered her forehead. "Mostly. I don't know the redhead. Do I?"

Aunt Lynn's mouth pinched. "I believe Polly let her two both bring friends. I don't know what she was thinking. And then allowing them to behave that way."

"They're just burning off energy, Lynn," Lucy's mother said tolerantly. "They'll all be good as gold by the time we sit down to eat."

"I trust Polly will insist on *that*."

Sourpuss, Adrian thought, even though he rather hoped he wouldn't be seated anywhere near anyone younger than eighteen. If he was lucky, family tradition might put the kids at their own table.

"Goodness, Helen," Aunt Lynn continued, her gaze zeroing in on Lucy's mother. "You must be wondering why you don't have any grandchildren yet."

Her tone was a little smug, leading Adrian to realize that the unfortunate Polly was probably Lynn's daughter. Which meant some of the ill-behaved hellions were her grandchildren.

Lucy's mother laughed. "I'd just as soon my girls got married before they considered becoming parents. And, of course, my children are considerably younger than yours, Lynn."

That stung. Spots of color appeared on the sour-puss's cheeks. "Well, *mine* weren't so eager to wander all over tarnation before settling down. Assuming yours ever do."

With a quick glance at the fire in her mother's eyes, Lucy intervened. "Not fair, Aunt Lynn. Melissa's still in college, and Sam and I are stodgy members of the Middleton Chamber of Commerce. That's pretty settled."

She sniffed. "Until you start families, *I* don't consider you established. Now, if you'll excuse me, I'd best find Polly. Heaven knows what those children are up to inside. Let me apologize in advance if they damage anything, Marian."

To no one's regret, she hustled away.

"Honestly," Aunt Marian said. "How a man as nice as your Owen could have a prune-faced sister like Lynn!"

"Now, Marian," Lucy's mother said without much force.

"She's just awful," Lucy declared, earning two disapproving looks from her mother and aunt. Her chin rose. "I don't care whether you think I should say it. She's just...just..."

As she struggled to find the right word, her mother said, "What will Adrian think, Lucy? Lynn's just..." She cleared her throat. "Just..."

Marian gave a hearty bray of a laugh. "We all know what she is, and so does Adrian. Young man, you probably have a few choice relatives of your own, now don't you?"

Lucy made a quick gesture that came too late. Adrian said evenly, "Actually, my family tree is pretty sparse. Both of my parents were only children, like I am."

"What a shame," Aunt Marian exclaimed. "Not even any cousins?"

The children, he saw out of the corner of his eye,

were streaming out of the house now, reinforced by half a dozen who were slightly older. He flashed on a scene from the movie version of *Lord of the Flies,* with the grimy child actors, half-naked and carrying burning torches. Was it really a shame he hadn't grown up with a passel of shrieking girl cousins, or a bullying boy cousin like the one he saw deliberately trip a smaller boy, who immediately broke into angry tears?

Lucy seemed to be watching his face somewhat anxiously. "They're really perfectly nice kids. They just get a little wild sometimes."

Marian started. "Gracious, what am I thinking? Those scalloped potatoes are going to be creamed potatoes if I don't get them out of the oven."

"Do you need help?" Lucy called to their backs as the two women hurried toward the house.

"No, no." Her mother flapped a hand as she went. "You brought your potato salad. You've done your part."

"Well," Lucy said into the little silence left in their wake, "I think you've met everyone."

God, he hoped so, Adrian thought fervently. Juries didn't intimidate him; extended families did. He'd sometimes wished he had a sibling, but one would have been ample.

He looked at Lucy, whose gaze moved from group to group as if she were doing a mental inventory. Making sure she hadn't skipped Great Aunt Bertha or second-cousin-once-removed Algernon, Adrian suspected. Despite what he feared was going through her head, he enjoyed watching her, with the sunlight picking up shimmers of gold and bronze in her hair and highlighting the freckles on her nose. He didn't recall ever considering anyone's ears pretty before, but hers seemed perfect to him, delicate whorls with lobes that each held a single, tiny diamond.

He loved her neck, too, long and slender, with baby-fine hairs at her nape. He wouldn't mind nuzzling it right now.

"Maybe we could sneak around the corner of the house for a few minutes," Adrian suggested.

Alarm flashed in her eyes. "Are you kidding? There's no privacy around here. Oh. There's Samantha." She sounded relieved as she raised her voice and waved, too. "Sam!"

Sam came, a man in tow. Evidently, he was a cousin of some sort, too, rather than an actual date. He and Adrian exchanged desultory conversation for a minute, then he wandered away.

Letting the sisters' conversation wash over him, Adrian thought longingly of that morning, when he'd actually had Lucy to himself. He'd gotten to watch her cook, which meant he'd had plenty of time to appreciate her back—her tiny waist, encircled with the apron ties, gently rounded butt encased in snug jeans and the flirtatious bob of her ponytail as she moved between mixing bowls and stove.

They had talked, too, arguing politics, sharing musical tastes, trading snippets here and there of their daily lives. An hour had passed, two hours, immensely satisfying in a way in which Adrian wasn't much accustomed. It was something like a gift exchange: here's a bit of me, to which she offered a bit of herself, upon which he gained courage and gave more. Casual, but feeling important. He wanted her, yes, with an urgency he was keeping banked to the best of his ability. But he

also didn't want to ruin whatever was happening between them by pressing her too soon.

He'd never had that worry before, or this sense that
they were creating something delicate and easily dam-
aged. Adrian hoped like hell that whatever it was gained
some solidity soon, both because he'd like to get her
in bed and because he simply had to go back to Seattle. Carol, he knew, was increasingly perplexed by his
lack of interest in ongoing cases. That morning, he'd
dodged a phone call from one of the firm's partners.
He wouldn't get away with hanging around Middleton
for another week.

After brunch, Adrian had left Lucy with a promise
to come back for her at four and gone to the hospital. It
had gotten so that he had a favorite parking spot, and
he knew most of the women who staffed the information desk as well as the nurses on his mother's floor.
Initial suspicion had melted away in the face of his
seeming devotion.

Maybe real devotion, he'd thought, sitting at his
mother's bedside and watching her face twitch as some
kind of impulses fired in her brain. He didn't know anymore. Did he love her? The idea of her? Would he feel an
instant, heartfelt connection when/if her eyes opened?
Or realize anew that this woman was a stranger?

Right now, he was in the eye of the hurricane, so to
speak, over the first turbulent emotions, bemused by
this odd, quiet town, separated from everything familiar in a disconcertingly thorough way given how near
he was geographically to Seattle. Sooner or later, he
was going to be flung back into the necessity of making decisions. The fact that his mother was so clearly

battling her way free of the coma was all that kept him in this peculiar state of suspension.

The weird thing was, he would have expected to be bored and impatient, disdainful of this backward little town and the inhabitants who seemed placidly unaware that the world was passing them by. Ten days ago, he wouldn't have been able to conceive of himself enduring Sunday dinner with fifty or so relatives of a woman he'd barely met himself.

Much less, after watching their bickering, laughter and tolerance for each other's foibles, having the passing thought that it might not be so bad to have a whole bunch of people who actually cared about you even when you screwed up, who embraced even a member nobody actually liked, because she was nonetheless one of them.

He was even starting to understand why Lucy had mixed feelings about the whole family thing—wanting, on the one hand, to escape their nosiness and interference, while on the other finding it hard to pull away.

He quelled a tug of anxiety by reminding himself that Seattle wasn't so far she couldn't come home often. It was a perfect compromise. Surely she'd see that.

Aunt Marian appeared on the back porch bearing a casserole dish and called, "Time to line up!" The women ferried food out to the long serving table while the men and kids scrambled for position. Even Lucy deserted Adrian to help bring out dish after dish.

That was another thing, Adrian realized, making this town feel so backward: there were definite gender roles here that had been mostly abandoned among his friends and contemporaries. He knew couples where neither of them cooked; they ate out or brought home take-out every night. One of his occasional racquetball partners, a bank trust officer, liked to cook and did most of it in his home. Not many people he knew had children; they were too busy building careers to take time out yet, and weren't sure they ever would.

In Middleton, it appeared Lucy and Samantha were the anomalies, women too engaged in their careers to get married or have children. Of course, Lucy's career was cooking and Sam's making a home-away-from-home for people with the bed-and-breakfast. He wondered what people would have thought if the sisters had gone into law or medicine or dentistry instead. Maybe a little less tolerant, a little less certain they'd "settle down" eventually.

But then he noticed the men didn't actually get their food first; their wives edged into line with them, and a few men dished up for their women. Aunt Lynn's Will, Adrian saw, was one of those. From what Lucy had told him, that was no surprise; Will probably simply chose anything bland. But Adrian also saw the way she smiled when she took it, as though—damn it—she really loved him. Go figure.

Lucy joined Adrian in line right before he reached for a plate, and quietly steered him clear of a few dishes.

"Jeri's bean dish is really awful. Most of us take some to be nice, but you don't have to." And, "Emily loves pepper. We haven't been able to cure her of it. Unless you want to clear your sinuses…"

He didn't. There was ample food to choose from, and his plate was soon heaping.

They sat squeezed together between Samantha and the cousin whose name he couldn't remember on one side, and a wheezing grandfather and his live-in nurse on the other. Lucy's side, thank God. She cut up some of the old guy's food for him. Conversation was table-wide and lively, with rejoinders shouted from one end to the other. Adrian found himself laughing more often than he remembered in a long time, sometimes at the absurdity, sometimes at a jab of surprisingly sharp wit.

The squeezed part he didn't mind. Lucy and he kept bumping arms. Her hip was snuggled cozily against his. He could turn his head and find her smiling at him from inches away.

Several assorted children were across the table from them, but Aunt Marian was right; they'd burned off their energy and were well-behaved and even semihu-man. All except one boy, not more than six or seven, who kept squirming and occasionally slipping out of sight under the table. A girl who might have been ten or eleven kept hauling him back up, sometimes while still whispering with the friend on her other side. It seemed she'd had plenty of practice.

"The doctor recommended Ritalin for Jake," Lucy told him, as if reading his mind. "But Jeri is digging in her heels, and I don't blame her. He's just a boy. He's learning to read, he's actually a whiz with numbers, and why should she drug him to make teachers happy, is her theory."

His own father wouldn't have tolerated any behavior approaching hyperactivity, Adrian couldn't help think-ing. He'd have been drugged into submission.

He nodded. "I've read about the concern that drugs like Ritalin are being overused. I had a friend like Jake, and he grew up to be perfectly normal."

Once Tony Brodzinski had started playing sports, he'd been able to use all that restless energy. He'd gone on to play baseball for a couple of major league teams and was currently pitching for the Cincinnati Reds. Adrian hadn't stayed in touch with him, but other friends had.

He told Lucy about Tony, and she said with satisfaction, "Jeri will be glad to hear about him. She can use reinforcement."

On the other hand, Adrian thought, watching the kid bat away his sister's hand, knock over his milk and accidentally poke the boy on his other side in the eye with his elbow, maybe Jake could use a little help.

But his mother appeared, mopped up the mess and soothed the younger boy, issued a stern warning then went back to her seat farther down the table. Jake managed to stay still for the next two or three whole minutes. Adrian hid a grin when he saw the boy's gaze slide sideways to be sure his sister was distracted before he slithered out of sight as quick as a snake vanishing under a rock.

"Mo-om!" the girl complained.

"He is a handful," Lucy said with a sigh.

Adrian had never given serious thought to having children of his own. He'd even said, when friends asked, that he didn't intend to have any. What in hell did he know about raising kids? Great example his own parents had set, the one abandoning him and the other stern, demanding and distant.

But suddenly, sitting there at the long table with Lucy on one side, Samantha on the other, a hyperactive boy bumping into Adrian's legs to escape his sister, who had also gone under the table, Grandpa Peterson cackling at a joke Lucy had just told him, Adrian knew: he wanted children.

It was a strange and bewildering feeling, this sudden sharp need to pass on his genes, his memories, to have a child count on him. Something close to panic clutched him. This was like being on a bullet train, the landscape that might have been familiar blurring because of the speed. So much was changing, so fast. Two weeks ago, he'd been contented with work, friends, condo. Now he wanted…everything. A wife, children, love, maybe even some of the chaos of this big family.

He tried to tell himself he was having a momentary impulse that he'd get over. By the time he drove off the ferry into downtown Seattle he'd have gotten over this idiocy. Lucy, he definitely wanted; all the rest of it, no.

But the panic continued to crawl over his skin like goose bumps, and he knew, deep down, that he really had changed. Lucy had found him. Something so simple, hardly even a huge effort on her part. But because she had found him, he in turn had found her, a woman with an astonishing capacity for love and kindness, thinly veiled by wariness that she'd be hurt. And because she'd brought him here to Middleton, he'd remembered the time before his mother left, when he'd known hugs and silly jokes and a playfulness he'd later had to suppress. He'd remembered being loved, being encouraged to dream.

And now he wasn't sure the man who two weeks ago he had believed himself to be existed at all.

In desperation he thought, *I have to get away. I have to find out if something in the air here is screwing with my mind.*

"Time for dessert," Lucy told him, her smile intoxicating. "I hope you saved room. Sam's pecan pie is to die for."

"What?" her sister exclaimed indignantly from his other side. "Are you telling him my pie will kill him?"

Lucy laughed. "Only from bliss."

Still dazed, he had a slice of the famous pie and a cup of coffee, the old-fashioned kind. Middleton, he had been shocked to realize soon after his arrival, not only didn't have a Starbucks, but it had no espresso stands, either. You wanted a cup of coffee in this town, you made it yourself or you signaled for the waitress at the café or the Truck-Stop Diner outside of town. They did not call black coffee Americano in Middleton. Coffee was coffee, same as it had always been. Fortunately, he liked a plain cup of black coffee, but still. It was another sign Middleton was out of step with the world just down Highway 101.

Pretty much everyone pitched in to clean up, tossing paper plates, covering leftovers and sorting out which bowls and dishes were whose. Lucy clutched her empty bowl when they left after an exhausting round of good-byes.

The sky was a dusky purple that would rapidly darken into nightfall. He guessed the sun was still above the horizon on the other side of the Olympic Mountains, where beachgoers could watch it sink into the ocean. Adrian wondered if Lucy could be talked into running away for a couple of days. He'd love to walk the beach at Kalaloch with her, see her eyes widen in delight when she spotted a perfect sand dollar and lifted it triumphantly from the damp sand. They could sit with their backs to a driftwood log and watch the sunset, the fiery orb seeming to melt as it met the vast arch of the Pacific Ocean.

His jaw tightened. *He* couldn't run away. He had to

go back to Seattle no later than the day after tomorrow. Kalaloch with Lucy would have to be deferred until he'd persuaded her to sell the café and move to his side of the sound.

If she took a job as a sous chef at a high-end restaurant, would she be able to get away? Or would he find himself waiting for her occasional night off? Perhaps a Saturday-morning breakfast, before she left for work? Perturbed, Adrian realized how inconvenient it was that her career involved such long hours that happened not to coincide at all with his working schedule. Even if she was in Seattle, when the hell *would* they see each other?

"Thank you for coming." Seated beside him as he drove, Lucy was looking straight ahead, not at him. "I know a big family gathering isn't your idea of a good time, so it was nice of you."

"I had fun," he was surprised to hear himself say— and mean. "I'm pretty sure I ate more food today than I usually do in a week, but I think I'll survive. And, damn, it was good."

"The Martin women can all cook," she said, sounding pleased. "Now, Dad's side of the family…"

Jeri, who was so fond of pepper wasn't a Martin, he remembered. On the other hand, Aunt Marian's scalloped potatoes were darn near as good as Lucy's potato salad, and an amazing rosemary chicken with pearl onions had been Lucy's mother's dish.

"It's a wonder your father isn't fat."

She chuckled comfortably. "He can eat and eat and eat without ever putting on an extra pound. He and Mom were made for each other."

Adrian stole a glance at her smiling face. He was beginning to believe that Lucy was made for him, but he was far from sure she reciprocated the feeling. He had noticed today that she'd evaded his touch a couple of times when he had lifted a hand to lay it on the small of her back. She hadn't wanted to be claimed in any visible way in front of her family. That didn't strike him as a good sign.

They reached her house, and he braced himself for her to peck him on the cheek and claim to be so tired, she'd better not sit on the porch swing with him tonight.

He pulled into the driveway, set the emergency brake, and turned off the ignition. In the sudden silence his heartbeat quickened. He had the stricken feeling that the next few moments mattered terribly, that she was on the verge of telling him something he didn't want to hear. He turned in his seat to look at her, willing her to say, "It's such a nice night, why don't we sit outside for a while?"

Say it, he willed her. Or, "Would you like another cup of coffee before you go?"

Instead, she took a very deep breath and turned, too, so that she faced him. In the dim light, cast by a streetlamp fifty yards away, he couldn't make out her expression. But her eyes were dark, and he did see her open her mouth as if to speak, close it again, hesitate, then try again.

Her words tumbled out. "Would you like to come in?"

Say, "How about a cup of coffee?" Or, "It's such a nice night…"

He blinked. "What?"

"I know it's late and if you don't want to come in—"

"I want to," he said hastily. "Of course I do." Was she kidding? He'd go anywhere with her.

Now and forever.

God. Was he crazy? He hadn't known her long enough to be thinking things like this.

Her breath escaped in a tiny gasp. "Okay."

Wait. Why was she nervous, if this was merely a casual invitation? And she definitely *was* nervous.

"Is this just for coffee? Or…?"

"Well…" She clutched the bowl as if it were a baby she was protecting with her life. "I was thinking *or.*" She pressed her lips together. "Even though Sam will know if you're even the smallest bit late, never mind stay out all night, and then the whole family will know. Unless I plead with her." Her voice firmed. "I can do that. I'll call her in the morning. Someday she'll want a secret kept, too."

"Why am I a secret?" He had to know, even though his heart was slamming in his chest and all he wanted to do was kiss her.

"Wouldn't *you* want your sex life private from your family? Especially if there were so many of them, and they all liked to gossip?"

"Yes," Adrian admitted. "I would. The sex part. I just don't want you to feel like you have to keep *me* a secret."

He couldn't see her well enough to be sure, but he suspected she was rolling her eyes. "I took you to Sunday dinner, didn't I?"

"Yeah." Suddenly, he didn't give a damn about her family, or their gossip, or about tomorrow at all. He just wanted that giant bowl to not be between them. He unhooked his seat belt and hers. "Let's go in." His voice sounded raw to his ears. "Now."

Their car doors opened simultaneously, but he was faster. They met on her side, the bowl still between them, but who was noticing?

CHAPTER ELEVEN

LUCY'S LAST THOUGHT before he kissed her was, *Please, please, don't let me be sorry I did this once he's gone.*

Then his mouth closed over hers with such raw hunger, she quit thinking at all. Or at least not very coherently. Instead, she kissed him back.

Somehow she held on to that big serving bowl. It even made it inside, if not to the kitchen. The minute the front door closed behind them, Adrian took the bowl from her. She had no idea what he did with it. He was back, impatient and oh, so male, before she could wonder.

They shed jacket and sweatshirt right there in the entry. Then he groaned and pulled her up against him, his hands gripping her buttocks, so that she couldn't help feeling his erection. She flung her arms around his neck. Instead of kissing her immediately, though, he searched her eyes.

"I want you," he said, in an odd, rough voice. "You're sure about this?"

Lucy bit her lip and, after only the smallest of hesitations, nodded. "Just a little nervous."

"Why?"

She thought she ought to warn him. "I'm not very experienced."

He went completely still. "You're a virgin?"

Lucy shook her head. "No, I had a couple of different

boyfriends in college. I was trying to live wild, you see. But…well, it was just a few times, and—" She stopped.

"And?"

"Um…not that exciting."

"Ah." He relaxed. One of his hands moved from her butt up her spine, leaving a trail of fireworks behind it. "We'll have to try to improve on that."

On a burst of nerves and enthusiasm, she blurted, "I did sort of think it would be different with you."

Momentarily his hand paused and his eyes narrowed. "So this is in the nature of an experiment?" That rough, raw quality to his voice was gone; instead he sounded carefully neutral.

She must have annoyed him, Lucy realized, but she wasn't quite sure how. It wasn't an insult to let him know that she assumed he had way more experience and skill in bed, was it?

Feeling a little indignant, she said, "If I'd wanted to experiment, I wouldn't have gone so long without… you know."

"So why me?"

"You're different," she said simply. "I've never felt like I do when you kiss me."

He smiled, all charm and something that made her heart squeeze. "Good," he murmured. "You're different, too."

Of course, she wasn't different at all, unless he meant rustic or unsophisticated. He was just being nice, which she appreciated. And he *did* want her. She couldn't be mistaken about that.

"Bedroom upstairs?" he asked.

"Yes."

"Shall we do this in style?"

"What do you mean—?" She hadn't finished, when he lifted her high and her legs closed in panic around his waist. Her sandals dropped to the floor. She squeaked and grabbed tight. "I can walk!"

"But then I'd have to set you down." With one large hand he kneaded her hip, while the other hand gripped her nape. "And you feel good like this." He captured her mouth with his.

Oh, it did feel good wrapped around him like this. Her hips rocked; he groaned and thrust his tongue into her mouth.

Somehow he did make it up the stairs with her in his arms. He'd wrench his mouth from hers and climb a couple of steps, then back her against the wall and kiss her as if he needed her taste more than he'd ever needed anything in his life.

By the time they reached her bedroom, Lucy couldn't have stood on her own two legs if her life had depended on it. She trembled, aching to have him inside her.

He laid her on the bed and followed her down, planting a knee between her thighs, still kissing her even as his hand slid under her T-shirt. He stroked her belly and closed his hand over her breast, squeezing. Her nipples had hardened and pressed against his palm. If only her bra were front-opening! When she made a sound of frustration, he growled in response and pulled her to a sitting position.

Lucy lifted her arms and let him peel off the shirt, then he unclasped her bra and tossed it aside. She'd never thought much about her breasts; after all, she only wore a B cup. But Adrian looked at her with hot gray eyes that made her feel sexy.

A little shyly, she reached out and tugged his shirt up

in turn. He let her pull it off. He had a glorious chest: broad and powerful without being overmuscled, the dark hair silky under her questing hands. In her curiosity, the urgency had abated, and Adrian seemed willing to let her explore. He touched her, and she touched him. He nuzzled her breasts and suckled them in turn; she kissed his chest and licked the base of his throat where she felt his pulse hammering. Lucy loved the salty taste of his skin and did it again.

He tried to laugh, but she heard the desperation in it. He said, "Maybe the next time," which she didn't understand, and pushed her onto her back. The ache in her lower belly was back, and the feel of him unzipping her jeans was almost unbearable. He pulled her panties off with the jeans.

Lucy couldn't help herself. Her thighs pressed together and her hands went down to cover herself. Adrian laughed again, but shakily. "You're beautiful, sweetheart. Don't be shy."

"I—I can't help it," she whispered.

"Would it help if I take my pants off?"

She might be even more self-conscious, but she nodded anyway, shockingly eager to see him. Adrian pulled back from her far enough to shed his khakis and shoes. Lucy's belly cramped at the sight of him. She was sure neither of her college boyfriends had been anywhere near as large. That should have frightened her but instead was awfully exciting.

He laid down on the bed beside her, on his side facing her. "Touch me," he said, his voice guttural.

Lucy stole a glance upward at his face. His eyes still had that molten look, as if heat burned inside him. He nodded once. She put her hands on his chest again. That felt almost safe. Except that he was very warm, and his heart hammered so hard it seemed to resonate through her. And the way his muscles jumped as her hands moved downward gave her a heady sense of power.

When she finally touched him *there,* his whole body spasmed. Her exploration didn't last very long. All of a sudden he pushed her onto her back and rose above her. "Sorry, sweetheart. I can't take any more."

Somehow *he* was the one exploring now, his hands sliding up her legs, tickling the sensitive skin of her inner thighs. Her legs were splayed wantonly apart with no conscious order from her. When his fingers curled in her pubic hair, her hips rose from the bed in an agony of wanting. He parted moist flesh and stroked, with her gripping his shoulders so hard her fingernails must have been digging in.

The tension rose in her belly, coiled exquisitely tight, driven as much by the sight of the expression on his face as by his touch. "Adrian?" Her voice shook. "I want you. Not just—"

"This?" His fingers drew circles.

"Please!" she gasped.

He made a raw sound and turned away. The sound of ripping made her realize he'd come prepared. Thank goodness. During the drive, she'd thought about asking, then forgot in the enormity of the decision. *She* should have bought some condoms, but she'd have had to drive to Sequim to do it. That was the trouble with a town where everyone knew you.

He was back so quickly she didn't have time to feel anything but gratitude. He stroked her again and again, pressing, pressing… No, not with his hands, they were cupping her face as he looked into her eyes and pushed slowly forward, deeper. Her breath snagged in her throat as he filled her. The sensation was amazing, exactly what she'd needed. She lifted her hips to meet him and breathed a high, "Ooh!" that would have embarrassed her at any other moment.

Every muscle in his back was rigid with restraint. His teeth bared as he paused, buried in her. Lucy closed her eyes, savored the feeling, then rocked just enough to let him know she was ready for more.

He pulled out slowly, then thrust again a little harder, a little faster. It felt so good. No, amazing. Her fingers dug into his back. Out, in, each thrust more powerful, more urgent. His chest vibrated with a groan. Lucy whimpered.

Oh, yes. She felt like a bomb with the spark racing down the fuse toward her body. She could all but see it behind her eyelids, a flare of fire crackling, almost there, almost…

She imploded, a wave of pleasure that thundered through her like a tsunami beyond anything she'd ever felt.

He let go a second later, slamming into her, his body shuddering, a groan escaping against her cheek as he pressed his open mouth to it.

Lucy held on tight and rode the wave, high on it even as it tumbled her dizzyingly over and over.

The tsunami washed out slowly, leaving tingles and ripples in its wake. Lucy lay boneless beneath him, feeling both drained and utterly relaxed and energized all at once. A secret smile curved her mouth.

Now that was an adventure!

Adrian rolled at last, taking her along so that she sprawled atop him. When she lifted her head to look down at his face, he grinned at her. "So. Was it different?"

"Yes! Oh, yes! I had no idea." She marveled. "Was it my fault before? Or the guys' fault?"

He laughed, the skin beside his eyes crinkling, and she could see he felt a little smug. "Sex is rarely as good as that was. Rarely? Try never. What we just did takes…"

When he paused, she filled in silently. *Love. It takes love.*

"Chemistry," Adrian finished. "Something special." *Love.*

As quickly as joy had swelled in her chest, it evaporated, leaving her so sad she hid her face against his neck so that he wouldn't see.

His hand stroked idly down her back, kneading here, teasing there, learning her contours.

"God, I wish I didn't have to go back to Seattle," he muttered suddenly.

Lucy bit her lip so hard she tasted blood. She had an intense inner struggle to master herself, then lifted her head. "Oh? Are you having to go back right away?"

"Tomorrow morning. I've stayed longer than I should." His hand kept moving, pressing harder, imbued it seemed with some of the same tension she now felt. "I'll be back next weekend, I promise, but I have to show my face at the firm."

"Oh. What if your mother…?"

"Wakes up? She'll do it with me or without me." He sounded grim, either because he was convincing himself his mother didn't really need him at all, or because he hated the idea of her opening her eyes when he wasn't here to greet her.

Lucy nodded, wordless, even though she couldn't

imagine being in his position and heading back to work as though the mother he'd sought for over half his life wasn't about to emerge from a coma.

Maybe, she thought doubtfully, he didn't care as much as she'd wanted to believe he did. Maybe he was fighting the fact that he did care more than he was comfortable with.

Or maybe she was being naive. After all, it wasn't reasonable for him to risk his position at the law firm and with his clients so that he could linger indefinitely in Middleton, holding his unconscious mother's hand.

Yes, that was it, she decided. Wanted to believe. He was just being…realistic.

And he did say he'd be back next weekend. So he wasn't cutting and running now that he'd gotten what he wanted from her.

She gave a nod and what she meant to be an accepting smile. He searched her face, his own suddenly taut with…she didn't know. Frustration? Desire? Even anger?

At me? Lucy wondered, before he growled something under his breath and pulled her head down so that he could kiss her with a hunger as desperate as if they hadn't just made love.

It seemed he wanted her again. She hadn't thought people did it again so soon after the first time, but her body responded with startling enthusiasm. She might be heartsick, but oh, she wanted him while she had him here, with her. And he must feel the same, because before she knew it he was swearing and fumbling for another condom, and she was completely ready.

Apparently, Lucy discovered that night, sexual satisfaction was only temporary. And people could not only make love again right away, but they could also do it three times. And, after a little sleep, a fourth time.

Sleep wasn't *nearly* as important as she'd thought it was.

LUCY PUT A brave face on it, but Adrian could tell she was shocked by his departure the next morning. He'd been warning her that he'd have to go, but she'd evidently convinced herself that he would stay at his mother's side however long it took her to wake up.

If she woke up.

His faith was eroding. Yeah, her coma had become lighter. But he'd seen no change in days now. Sure, she twitched and even seemed to flinch from bright light, but did that necessarily mean she hadn't suffered acute brain damage? Reflexes weren't the same thing as the conscious self that made a person individual. Yes, there were stories about people who'd been in comas for months or even years waking up and being themselves again, but they were the exceptions. Newsworthy. What were the chances his mother would be one of them?

Unlike him, Lucy would never give up hope. Her tenacity was one of the qualities that made her so different from anyone else he'd ever known.

That had made him fall in love with her.

She'd insisted on making breakfast. Staying to eat it prolonged the misery of the goodbye, in his opinion, but he couldn't deny her anything. She chattered, and he did his best to respond without being able, an hour later, to remember a single thing either of them had said. He was willing to bet she couldn't, either.

Behind her smile, she looked so forlorn when she walked him to the door, he felt as if someone was clawing his chest open. It hurt, kissing her one more time then walking to his car. He'd wondered briefly if he was having a heart attack.

At the inn, Samantha gave him a look he ignored. He went upstairs and packed, then came down and settled his bill. Her expression relaxed slightly when he reserved the same room for Friday and Saturday night the coming weekend, and he realized she'd been indignant on her sister's behalf.

Middleton barely showed in his rearview mirror before the forest closed around the road, and within minutes he'd arrived at Highway 101. There was the sign: Middleton, 5 miles.

Five miles, and in another universe.

A semi roared by, followed by an RV and a couple of campers. People who'd taken an extended weekend over here on the peninsula, and were now heading home. They probably never even saw the sign for Middleton, or gave a passing thought to who would live out here in the middle of nowhere and why.

How in hell, he wondered again, had his mother ended up here, of all places?

Then he turned onto the highway, and Middleton fell behind him.

FOUR DAYS LATER, it seemed as remote and unlikely as Timbuktu.

Lucy, he missed. Middleton, however, took on a hazy, unreal quality in his mind, rather like the memories he'd been dredging from the distant past that included his mother. They were actual memories, yes; but perfectly recalled? Probably not. They were colored by family tensions, by his mood, by his limited understanding, and ultimately by her disappearance. He couldn't be sure anything had happened the way he remembered it.

The first day or two in Seattle, he felt buffeted by the noise and speed of traffic and the crowds and the urgency with which people strode the sidewalks. He had some trouble concentrating, would find himself gazing out the floor-to-ceiling window in his office without really seeing the cityscape beyond the glass. He kept battling a feeling that nothing around him was real.

By Wednesday, it was Middleton he knew to be unreal. He'd felt a familiar surge of anger at the shoddy research a couple of associates had done in his absence. There was ice in his voice when he told them what he thought and sent them back to do it right. He snapped out orders for Carol to put through calls or check his schedule or find out why information wasn't right where he wanted it when he wanted it. He thought about Lucy sometimes, his chest tight, about his mother less often. Middleton itself, with its old-fashioned air, seemed as illusory as a Wild West town on the Disney lot. For all he knew, residents had engaged in an elaborate conspiracy to bamboozle the big-city attorney. Why they would have bothered, he couldn't imagine, and didn't care. He was back to figuring how quickly he could get his mother moved to an assisted-living facility here in Seattle, and Lucy into his condo and bed.

He called her twice, but both conversations were briefer than he would have liked and stilted. He said, "I miss you," and she said it, too. Otherwise, she told him that no, his mother hadn't opened her eyes yet, although she thought any day it would happen, and that he'd missed the chance to try her famous potato soup today. He was the one with almost nothing to say. She wouldn't get what he'd done all day, he told himself. *You mean she wouldn't approve,* a voice whispered. She would listen with bewilderment if he tried to explain why he was fighting tooth and nail to defend a corporation engaged in unethical practices. So he didn't try, merely said, "Doing my best," when she asked if he was catching up at work.

Friday he worked until 8:00 in the evening. Adrian would have waited to drive over until morning if it hadn't been for thoughts of Lucy. Hell, if not for Lucy he wouldn't have gone at all. He'd fallen so far behind at work, he might never catch up. The last thing he should be doing was heading out of town for the weekend.

But…he couldn't get her out of his head. The café was open and busy tonight, of course, but if he got a move on he could be waiting when she closed.

Mind made up, he packed a bag swiftly and caught a late ferry to Bainbridge. He didn't go up to the observation deck, but got out of his car and leaned on the railing, catching the sea air, hearing the gulls cry and watching the sun drop behind the Olympic Mountains, jagged and white-tipped. For the first time all week, some of the tension left his neck and shoulders, the sharp-edged impatience and drive that kept him going blunted.

The drive felt weirdly familiar this time. It seemed to go more quickly, as if his car leaped eagerly forward. His thoughts kept jumping between work and Lucy, with his mother slipping in occasionally.

Why the hell hadn't Brock returned his call? If he thought he could keep dodging… Lucy's face, dirt-smudged but shining from within as she admired her newly planted flower beds. What kind of bad luck had gotten Judge Roberta Easton assigned to the ParTex case? The damned woman drove a hybrid and was a vegan, for God's sake. What were the chances she'd rule fairly when big business clashed with the Sierra Club et al? Push her into saying something inflammatory. Yeah, that might work. Then he could demand a change of courtroom. His mother, young and pretty, laughing gaily; her face shifting, changing, aging, going still and unresponsive against the white pillow. Beep, beep, beep, life support.

He couldn't remember disliking a client as much as he did Lyle Galbreath, the young CEO of ParTex, accused of sliding around environmental regulations. Listening politely, attentively, his thoughts hidden, Adrian had wondered what it would be like to defend someone he'd known for years, someone who was scared and troubled and heartsick—or, God, actually *innocent.* Someone with a good side and maybe a bad side but also a sense of remorse, who was thinking about something besides profit.

Lucy's voice, rich and expressive, reading Elizabeth Barrett Browning. Tremulous. "I want you." She'd wanted all of him. Would she still want him once she understood that his livelihood was defending scum like Lyle Galbreath? Would she want his heart?

His headlights picked out the sign: Middleton, 5 miles. He turned, darkness closing around his car, the headlights finding only the yellow stripe down the center of the deserted highway and the trees choking it on both sides. It was suddenly like being a kid who'd opened the closet door to find a path leading into a mist-wreathed forest instead of his clothes on hangers. Last time he'd felt reluctant incredulity. This time…he hardly knew. He found himself looking ahead eagerly for the first lights. There was some of the same disorientation, but also a sense of homecoming. He knew every business on Main Street. He'd smile and nod at people coming out of the café, because he'd met them, or knew they were related to Lucy however distantly, or had been kind to his mother.

Did he have time to go to the hospital first? He glanced at his watch. Would they let him in this late? Probably. In a small-town hospital like Middleton, nobody was big on rules.

The café wouldn't close for another fifteen minutes. Lucy would be stuck there for another hour at least. Adrian made up his mind. He had time.

So instead of turning to go downtown, he continued toward the hospital. His foot lifted briefly from the gas pedal when he passed Safeway. He never went by the spot where his mother had been hit without looking, as if he might see a ghostly reincarnation of the accident. Middleton seemed like the kind of place where it might even be possible.

The information desk at the hospital was dark and deserted. Adrian made his way upstairs, remembering his first time here. Only this was different, of course. The nurse at the station looked up and beamed at the sight of him. "Mr. Rutledge! Your mother's been so restless today. I know she'll be glad you're back."

"Do you mind if I go in for a minute?" he asked. "I know it's past visiting hours—"

"Don't be silly," she said comfortably. "Take your time. She doesn't have a roommate you'd be disturbing. I haven't turned out her light yet."

"Thanks."

When he circled the drawn curtain and went to his mother's bedside, he expected her to be sleeping, as the entire hospital seemed to be around them. Instead, to his shock, he found her head turned on the pillow so that she could scowl fiercely at the empty chair. Her mouth worked, as though she desperately wanted to say something.

"Mom?" He reached out and took her hand. "Mom, it's Adrian. Are you all right?"

Stupid question. What did he expect? *Yes, dear, of course I am?*

But she gripped his hand. This time, it couldn't be in his imagination. Her fingers bit into his and her head rolled frantically on the pillow. Restless, the nurse had said. More as if she were just below the surface, fighting her way up.

"Hey. It'll come," he said. "Don't worry."

He kept murmuring nonsense, she kept twitching spasmodically and holding on to him so hard, he was afraid he'd have to all but pry her fingers from his when it came time to leave. Eventually she subsided, though, and he thought she might even be asleep by the time he slipped out. He turned off the light as he went, and told the nurse, "She seems to have settled down."

"Oh, thank goodness. I'll bet she knew you were there."

He felt a pang. She had responded to him. By the time he walked out of the hospital into the night air, however, he'd reminded himself that his mother was unlikely to have the slightest idea who he was if she did wake up. Maybe having anyone at all there holding her hand and talking to her would have calmed her.

With all the businesses closed, he was able to park

right in front of the café. The front door was locked, but Mabel hurried to open it when he knocked.

"Adrian, I didn't know you were coming back today."

"I wasn't sure I could make it." He nodded toward the kitchen. "Lucy in back?"

She smiled. "I'm done out here. Tell her goodnight."

"Will do."

Surprising him, she reached out and gave his hand a squeeze. "I'm glad you came." Then she hurried out, leaving him staring after her. Did everyone in town assume he'd ditched Lucy and his mother both for the bright lights of the city?

Hadn't he come close?

"Mabel?" Lucy's voice came from the kitchen. "Is someone here?"

"Mabel says goodnight." Adrian walked toward the back.

She appeared in the doorway. "Adrian?" Her face lit. "It *is* you!"

She hadn't thought he would show up tonight, either, he realized. He'd have been ticked at her lack of faith, if guilt hadn't niggled at him for the reluctance he'd felt all day. Part of him *hadn't* wanted to ever return to Middleton. He'd been afraid....

Afraid? Of what? Adrian asked himself in shock, but didn't let himself pursue an answer he wasn't sure he had.

"Yeah," he said roughly. "It's me."

He took a couple of long strides; she flung herself at him. His arms closed around her compulsively, hers around him as tightly. His heart cramped, his eyes burned, and he thought, *Am I afraid of this?*

But he had a bad feeling it wasn't that simple.

CHAPTER TWELVE

LUCY LIFTED her head at last. "Have you been to the hospital yet?"

"Yeah." Adrian slowly, reluctantly, loosened his hold on her. "The nurse said Mom was restless. But it was more than that. It seemed as if...I don't know, as if she's fighting something I can't see."

Lucy nodded. "I almost called you this morning. I started to wonder if she can hear us now but can't quite respond. Think how frustrating that would be."

He shuddered, hating to think about her trapped, unable to scream, unable to let anyone know she was *there*. Yeah, *frustrating* was one word for it. "You should have called me."

"But you said you'd come," she said simply.

In complete faith? Or had this been a test? Pass if he showed, fail if he didn't? Didn't she understand that real life couldn't be set aside so easily? Would she close the café for weeks on end because her mother needed her?

Yeah, he realized. She would.

"I'm here." He couldn't tell her how close a call it had been. Especially not when he felt an overwhelming sense of...rightness. Yeah, that was it.

To hell with real life, he thought violently, even as he knew he didn't mean it. Couldn't afford to mean it.

"Yes." She sighed happily and lifted her face.

Funny thing, given the bruising force of their initial embrace, but this kiss stayed tender. He felt a tearing sense of regret at how close he'd come to disappointing Lucy. He hated the idea that anything he did would hurt her.

Rubbing his cheek on the top of her head, he said hoarsely, "Are you almost done in here?"

"Done?" Lucy pulled back, wild roses blooming in her cheeks, her eyes dazed. She blinked. "Oh. You mean the kitchen. Um… Just give me a minute."

"Can I help?"

She shook her head. "I really was almost done."

He picked up this week's edition of the *Middleton Courier* and sat to read the local gossip while he waited for her, his interest only cursory.

The high school boys' baseball team had failed to make the state playoffs, but the coach was optimistic for next year with so many strong players who had been sophomores and juniors this year. Stephanie Marie English had won a Rotary Club scholarship for a college semester in Rome to study art.

Talk about culture shock for a kid who'd never known anything but Middleton.

A memorial service held for Lucille Burnbaum had been well-attended. The old lady had been ninety-eight, Adrian read, and most recently had been a resident at the Olympic Retirement Home. She left an astonishing number of descendants. He was not at all surprised to see that she'd graduated from Middleton High School back in the thirties.

Did anybody ever *leave* Middleton?

Ignoring the chill he felt, since he hoped like hell

Lucy would in fact be willing to leave behind her hometown, Adrian continued to read.

Jeffrey and Ann Peterson welcomed a baby boy, weight six pounds seven ounces. They almost had to be related to Lucy. Good God, how many baby, wedding and Christmas presents did she have to buy?

"I'm ready."

He looked up from the paper, startled at how engrossed he'd become. The kitchen was dark, and she was shrugging on a sweater as she crossed the dining room to him. He studied her as she approached.

Her hair was pulled into a bun, although tiny tendrils straggled after a long day's work. She looked tired, and yet color was still high in her cheeks and her eyes were soft, as though his mere presence made her happy.

His chest hurt again. If this was love, it was damned uncomfortable. Why was he having trouble enjoying the moment, uncomplicated by guilt or a sense of inadequacy or the reminder that he only had until Sunday?

"Good," he said, voice husky.

He followed her home, remembering belatedly that he should have checked in at the B and B. Instead, he took his overnight bag into Lucy's house. He'd claim his room at Samantha's in the morning. If they were really lucky, no one would happen to notice his car parked out front before then.

He gave a grunt of amusement. Yeah, right.

But, hey. Maybe if several relatives chided her about having a man spending the night, it would annoy Lucy enough to give her an added push to make the move to Seattle.

Of course, he had yet to *ask* her if she'd consider moving.

This weekend? Or was it too soon?

Each time he realized what a short time he'd known Lucy, he felt a fresh shock. In his entire adult life, he'd never let anyone be as important to him as she'd become in a matter of weeks.

Inside, she told him somewhat shyly that she needed to take a shower. At her suggestion, he made himself a sandwich and had a glass of milk while he waited. The microwaveable dinner he'd eaten at his desk seemed like a distant memory.

He heard the shower running upstairs, then silence. When she padded barefoot into the kitchen, her face had a rosy hue, her wet hair was loosely braided and she wore a pink chenille robe. The creamy skin and hint of a cleavage revealed at the *V* of the neckline made him wonder if she wore anything beneath the robe. His body immediately tightened.

She smiled at him. "Oh, good. You did find something."

He had to look down at his hand and the remnant of the sandwich to know what she was talking about. "Yeah. Thanks." His gaze swept over her hungrily. "I like you barefoot."

"My toes like it, too." Her eyes were an even deeper blue than usual, suffused with some emotion.

He shoved his plate away and turned the chair, the legs scraping on the floor. "Hey. Come here."

She came to him without hesitation, her cheeks even pinker, but her gaze never leaving his. When she stopped in front of him, he reached up and stroked the smooth, clean line of her throat, continuing down her chest to where the shawl collar crossed. When he untied the robe and slowly parted it, she made no move to resist, only watching his face.

She was naked beneath it, her skin warm and fragrant from the shower, her breasts perfect handfuls, her waist supple and slender, her hips a gentle swell. She quivered with reaction as his hands savored her body.

Adrian had never felt a surge of desire so savage. For a moment he went still, trying to get a grip on himself. "I shouldn't have started this until we'd made it to bed," he said rawly.

"I always did love that scene in *Bull Durham,*" she whispered.

He laughed. At least, he thought he did. With one hand he swept the plate and glass from the table, wincing at the sound of glass splintering. Then he lifted her up, the robe open, and sat her butt on the table. One more sight of her body, pale and pretty and sexier than anything he'd ever seen in his life, and he crushed her mouth beneath his.

Her arms clamped around his neck and she kissed him with hunger as ferocious and undeniable.

"You're beautiful," he heard himself say once, in a voice he didn't recognize. The words *I love you* were there, too, but clogged in his throat. He hadn't said them since he was a little boy, and his tongue didn't know how to shape them.

They got his shirt unbuttoned, but not off, his pants open. If he hadn't carried a condom in his wallet, right there, he wouldn't have had the strength of will to go find one. He tried to let her put it on, but thought he'd explode at the tentative touch of her fingers. With a guttural sound he took over, kissing her the whole while, pushing her back down onto the dining-room table. Her legs locked around his waist as he slammed into her in an act so primitive, he'd lost all ability to reason. Sensation rolled atop sensation: creamy skin, gasps, the sharp edge of her teeth, the hot slick glove of her body.

She cried out, spasming, taking him with her. Shockwaves ripped through him, the pleasure so intense he didn't know how he'd live through it and come out unchanged.

He went still as the waves washed out, still holding her with arms that shook. Suddenly unsure his legs would keep holding him, he wrapped her tight and all but fell onto the chair, Lucy straddling him.

They both gasped for breath. Adrian nuzzled his face against the curve where her neck met her shoulder, breathing in her scent. Lavender, maybe; he didn't know. Something flowery but subtle, something Lucy.

"Did you miss me?" she murmured.

His laugh was far more genuine this time, if also as shaken as he felt. "Oh, yeah. You could say that." He kissed the base of her throat, her pulse skittering against his lips. *I love you.* "I don't want to be without you."

"What?" She pulled back to study him with the startled, wary look of a doe surprised around a bend in the trail.

"Do you think—" he cleared his throat "—you could consider moving to Seattle?"

She was silent for a moment, her eyes searching his. "Are you asking me to live with you?" He could hear the constraint in her voice.

"No." He hadn't known what he was going to say until this moment. "It's probably too soon, but... Ah, I'm asking you to marry me."

"Marry you."

It was killing him that he couldn't tell what she was thinking. "I won't pressure you—"

"Why do you want to marry me?" she asked. "Is it because of…this?" Her glance down encompassed their bodies, half-dressed, flushed with the most intense sex of his life.

"No." He twitched. "Yes, of course, but—" *Say it.* He swallowed, and stepped off into space. "I've never known anyone like you. Anyone with your heart." He laid his fingertips right where it beat, beneath her breast. His voice became scratchy. "I love you."

"Ohhh," she breathed, and suddenly her eyes welled with tears. "I thought— I was afraid—" She pressed her lips together. "I never dreamed—"

"What? Say it."

"That you'd want me forever. I thought this might be…casual for you."

Throat tight, he said, "I'm not a casual man."

"You love me."

"Yeah." He couldn't take his eyes from her face, dominated by those huge blue eyes swelling with tears. "Is there any chance…?"

"Yes!" She laughed even as she cried. "Yes! I think I fell in love with you that first night here, when you looked so stunned."

Grinning foolishly, Adrian devoured the sight of her face. "You'll marry me? You'll at least think about it? I don't want to keep leaving you here. I didn't—" He stopped, stunned by what he'd almost said.

Her head tilted like a curious bird's. "You don't…?"

He tugged her close, so she couldn't see his face. To the top of her head, he finished the sentence. "I didn't like myself without you around." He paused. "I was angry all week."

"Oh, Adrian!" she whispered, wrapping her arms around him and squeezing hard enough to steal the air from his lungs. "I love you. I love you, I love you, I love—"

He surged to his feet and said urgently, "Let's go to bed."

She laughed, even though her cheeks were still wet. "I can walk, you know."

Adrian had the rueful realization that his pants were down around his knees. "I think you'll have to," he admitted, letting her slide down his body to the floor.

She really laughed when she realized what his dilemma was, but he didn't mind. Her laughter never had a bite to it.

"Yeah, yeah," he grumbled in pretend annoyance, and pulled up his pants. The glint of glass caught his eye, and he said, "Ah…I seem to have made a mess."

Tying the belt on her robe, she peered at the dishes and shards of glass scattered on the floor. "I can clean it up in the morning. I don't feel like it right now." She grinned at him. "You can break my glasses anytime you want."

That earned her another kiss, after which she turned out lights as he picked up his overnight bag at the foot of the stairs and went with her to her bedroom.

He detoured to the bathroom to clean up and brush his teeth, returning to her bedroom to find her already in bed, her robe laid over the back of an antique rocking chair.

She smiled at him. "I hope you brought more than one condom."

He lifted a box from his bag. "A man who feels like I do never goes unprepared."

There was that laugh again; no, that giggle, airy and young and heartstoppingly happy.

He had made her happy. Adrian didn't think he'd ever made anyone happy before, outside of triumphs in the courtroom that satisfied his clients.

Somewhere, in the back of his mind, he had the disquieting realization that he didn't want to make Lyle Galbreath happy. The son of a bitch deserved to fry, not to be bailed out to offend again all so that his company could make more money.

That's my job.

He didn't always have to like it.

Maybe tomorrow he'd talk to Lucy. See what she thought. But not now. Now, he was going to make love with her again.

With, he thought, *the woman I'm going to marry.*

He flung his pants over the same chair. Her wide-eyed gaze went to his erection. Then, she lifted the covers to welcome him into her bed.

LUCY AWAKENED IN the morning first to the realization that she wasn't alone in bed; her head was pillowed on a warm, solid chest and she seemed to be draped over a man.

Adrian, she thought sleepily, contentedly. She had no immediate inclination to move. From his slow, deep breathing, it was obvious he was still sound asleep. Heaven knows they'd been up a good part of the night.

He loved her. He'd asked her to marry him.

Joy fizzed in her chest, but it wasn't alone. Puzzled,

Lucy tried to identify the funny mix of emotions that didn't seem to quite blend.

She was happy. Of course she was. She wished—oh, that she was a little more sure of Adrian, that this wasn't some kind of crazy impulse on his part that had to do with his having found his mother, and him being so certain that no one else in the world would have championed her the way Lucy had. It was as if he'd never met any nice people before. He was so utterly convinced she was special in a way she didn't really think she was. Some people gave their lives to helping the homeless, or children orphaned by AIDS, or…abandoned animals, or any of a thousand important causes. All she'd done was be nice to one gentle, confused, lost woman. It had been practically an *afterthought*. Adrian was bound to realize some day that she was actually pretty average. And then what would happen?

Maybe she was the one who needed to gain confidence, she tried to tell herself. He loved her. Why was she so determined to question his feelings, and so quickly? Because she didn't believe in her good fortune, that someone like him really wanted *her*?

But she didn't think that was it. No matter what Adrian said, she'd never be able to think of herself as beautiful. But he had succeeded in erasing some of her certainty that she was the plain sister. Clearly, *he* didn't see her that way, which pleased her immeasurably.

No, the faintly queasy feeling in her stomach, Lucy realized, had more to do with what all this meant. She'd be selling the café and looking for a job working for someone else, because she couldn't imagine that she could afford or had the resources to start a restaurant in Seattle. And…she'd be moving to Seattle, of course.

Adrian had said something about his condo, which meant no garden. Unless they could pick out a house together? A roommate from Lucy's freshman year in college lived in Bellevue, but otherwise she'd be starting all over to create a circle of friends. The idea should be exciting. It *was* exciting! She'd been so sure all her life that she wanted to live somewhere that was more vibrant, more sophisticated. She had been getting awfully set in her ways. What was it she'd thought last week? That she was *contented.* Lucy wasn't sure she liked that word. It sounded middle-aged and stodgy. Wasn't it past time she struck out on a new path, not surrounded by people who'd known her forever? Just think, her family wouldn't be butting in to every decision she made.

Only…what that really meant was that they wouldn't be around at all. They'd keep having the Sunday dinners, but she and Adrian wouldn't make it very often. It was too far to drive more than once a month, tops. And would he want to come at all?

She could still call Sam when she was aggrieved about something, but her sister wouldn't know the people she was talking about. They wouldn't ever have the chance to do a mystery weekend together at the bed-and-breakfast.

Of course, the wedding would be here in Middleton, so she'd be surrounded by family then. And maybe Adrian would take her someplace exotic for a honeymoon. If he could get away from work long enough.

But Lucy felt a peculiar, sinking sensation in her stomach when she imagined herself newly moved into his condominium, and him getting up early and leaving for work. Didn't he say he worked sixty-hour weeks and sometimes more? She would start job hunting, of course, and…she didn't know what else.

Oh, she was being a coward. Imagine, she told herself, him leaving for Seattle without her. Was that any better? Her heart squeezed, and she knew she couldn't bear losing him. This would be an adventure, that's all. She had never planned to stay in Middleton her entire life.

Satisfied, she closed her eyes and snuggled, if such a thing was possible, even closer. She wouldn't wake Adrian up, but she could hardly wait until he did open his eyes. Although she was feeling a little sleepy again.

Lucy was drifting, almost asleep, when the jangle of the telephone ringing made her jerk.

She didn't keep a phone by her bed. Her mother was much too fond of calling before Lucy liked to be up in the morning. She hurriedly slipped out of bed, but saw that Adrian was stirring anyway, blinking and gazing at her with the blank look of someone who hadn't quite placed himself yet.

If it was her mother, she'd kill her. *Especially* if Mom was calling because someone had told her Adrian's car was parked outside her daughter's house all night.

But it wasn't actually that early, Lucy saw, detouring around the broken glass and making it into the kitchen as the answering machine picked up. Lucy hadn't gone to voice mail, because she liked being able to hear who was calling and then decide if she wanted to answer.

"Lucy, this is Dr. Slater. I've already left messages for Adrian on both his cell and home phones. His mother has regained consciousness. I'm hoping you're home and able to make it into the hospital this morning to help orient her. She's pretty confused." He paused. "Give me a call."

Lucy lunged for the phone. "Dr. Slater?"

He'd already hung up.

"Who was that?"

Lucy turned. Adrian was coming down the stairs wearing only jeans. Barefooted and bare-chested, he paused and stretched, his expression one of sleepy-eyed satisfaction.

Still grappling with the news, she said, "That was Dr. Slater. He says…he says your mother has woken up."

Adrian froze a few steps from the bottom. His expression almost broke her heart. For just a moment, he was the little boy who'd come home from the summer in Nova Scotia to find his mommy wasn't there. It was as if he'd heard a sound upstairs, in her bedroom, and hope tore at him even as he knew it probably wasn't her.

He swallowed. "Then I suppose we'd better get dressed and go to the hospital." A muscle in his cheek twitched. "That is…do you have time?"

His courteous question outraged her, but then she recognized it for what it really was: that same little boy bracing himself to do something terribly frightening on his own. Of course he wouldn't plead, but, God, he hoped.

"Don't be silly," she said. "Of course I'm coming. Oh, let's hurry!"

Still looking stunned, Adrian turned and started up the stairs ahead of her.

WHAT IF SHE didn't know him? Never recognized that he was her son, the boy she hadn't seen since she hugged him so fiercely as he was being sent away twenty-three years ago this June?

Adrian moved his shoulders impatiently. She was still his mother. His responsibility. Whether she knew him or not was unlikely to have any impact on the decisions he'd have to make on her behalf. She was mentally ill and unable to adequately care for herself. That was reality. He'd have to find some kind of supervised living situation no matter what.

The wrench in his chest told him he wasn't as dispassionate as he wanted to be. To have found his mother after all these years and then have her fail to remember him… That would hurt.

He could hardly wait to call his grandmother, who was waiting for this moment. She'd taken the news that her long-lost daughter had turned up better than he had feared, saying, "I used to beg God to give me an answer. That was all I asked for. And now I have it."

God, he thought, had chosen to give her more.

Adrian stole a glance at Lucy, who leaned forward as if she could make the car go faster. Thank God for Lucy. No matter what happened, it would be all right with her there. If his mother knew anyone, it would be Lucy.

He took the first spot he saw in the parking lot. Lucy got out as fast as he did, and was ahead of him when they reached the front doors despite his long strides.

"Oh, I can't believe…" she said in a wondering voice, as they went up the elevator.

He laughed in astonishment. "You? You've always believed."

"I think sometimes I pretend."

"You?"

"Well…I am generally optimistic," she admitted.

"Half-full."

"Maybe." No one was at the nurses' station, and they were almost to his mother's room. "But you know," Lucy said, "whether you see a glass as half-full or half-empty, the exact same amount of water is in it."

"I'm not so sure." His tone was peculiar even to his own ears. They had turned into the hospital room, and Adrian's stride checked. His heart was drumming.

He heard his own, childish, self-important voice. *When I get home from school today, Mom and me are gonna plant tomatoes. She says she bets mine grow big as this globe!*

How had Mom been both so sad and so optimistic? Or had she, too, pretended?

Instead of hurrying ahead, Lucy had paused at his side, looking at him in silent inquiry. Seeing his momentary paralysis, she reached over and took his hand, her own so much smaller than his but strong.

He might have hurt her with his desperate grip, but she didn't even wince. For an instant, he squeezed his eyes shut, then gusted out a breath.

"Ready or not," he murmured, and pushed the curtain aside.

CHAPTER THIRTEEN

JUST BEFORE THEY ROUNDED the curtain, Adrian heard Ben Slater talking. "Yes, you're in the hospital. You got hit hard on the head and you've been unconscious."

His tone was infinitely patient, but Adrian guessed he was repeating the information for the umpteenth time.

"My head?" His patient sounded querulous. "Why would they hit my head?"

Adrian's heart lurched. The last time he heard his mother's voice, she'd been waving frantically and calling after the car as it drove away, "Tell *Maman* to let you call me!"

"I will! I will!" he'd yelled back.

Then his father had snapped, "For God's sake, roll up the window."

The curtain swayed as his shoulder brushed it. Adrian came to a stop at the foot of the bed, distantly aware of Dr. Slater, of Lucy still holding tight to his hand, but they were in soft focus at the edges of his vision. What he saw was his mother.

The bed had been cranked up so that she sat nearly upright. She was still too pale, her hair white and unkempt, the IV attached to her hand. But her eyes, the blue only slightly faded from his memory, were open.

With her face now animated, he knew her on a primal level that nearly brought him to his knees.

"Mom," he said hoarsely. *Mommy.*

At the sound of his voice, she turned from the doctor. Her stare was at first uncomprehending, then bewildered; finally he saw alarm then distress that crumpled her face.

"I don't know who you are. Should I?" she appealed to Dr. Slater.

He took her hand and spoke gently. "No. You haven't seen your son in a very long time. He was a little boy the last time you saw him. Now he's all grown up."

"Do I…do I *have* a little boy?" she whispered, studying Adrian furtively.

Disappointment lodged in his throat, making it hard to answer. "Yes. Do you remember? Dad sent me to spend the summer in Nova Scotia with *Maman* and *Grandpère.* You…were gone when I came home. Dad never told me where you went."

"There…there was a little boy." Tears welled in her eyes. "I don't know who he was."

Dr. Slater stepped away, unnoticed. Lucy hung back, letting go of him.

Adrian forced himself to take the last couple of steps, to wrap his hands around the railing. "*I'm* that little boy. Adrian. I grew up."

She searched his face now with a hunger that echoed his own. "You look like someone."

"Dad. Do you remember him? Your husband?"

She shrank back against the pillow, inching away from him. "Am I married? I don't want to be married." Her voice had become more tremulous. "I don't have to be, do I?" she asked the room at large.

Pity gripped him. "No. No, you don't have to be. You haven't been in a very long time. You and Dad got divorced. Do you remember him?" Adrian asked again. "Max Rutledge. He died. I know I look like him."

"You look like someone," she said, in a small frightened voice.

"I wanted to be a ferryboat captain. You took me down almost every day to watch the ferries load and unload. The seagulls would sit on the pilings until the ferry horn sounded, and then they'd screech and soar around it. Sometimes we'd see sea lions. And do you remember the divers? We'd watch their heads bob up."

"It smelled good," she said unexpectedly.

"Yes." Tears burned the back of his eyes, and he, too, could smell the salty, fishy scent of the sound mixed with the exhaust from cars waiting in the ferry line and the aroma of food cooking in the dockside restaurants. For a moment, he wasn't here at all; he was a child again, holding his mother's hand and reveling in the sound of the ferry horn, the sight of water opening between it and the dock, the workers bustling importantly in their bright orange vests as they blocked the wheels of cars and operated the ramp on the dock itself.

Without thought, he held out a hand. His mother slowly, tentatively, lifted her own and laid it in his. It was somehow a shock that his was so large and hers so small instead of the other way around, jarring him from the so-vivid memory. And yet the clasp felt right. They held hands, and they looked at each other, and a knot inside him loosened for the first time in all these years.

"I do remember," she whispered. "That little boy was mine, wasn't he?"

"Yes." He had to clear his throat. "Yes. He was yours."

"But…but who are you then?"

"I'm that little boy, all grown up," he repeated.

Confusion furrowed her brow. "I tried to find him. I know I did."

Choked up, he could only nod.

"I think I tried to go home."

He felt the wetness on his cheeks. "Do you remember your garden? The roses, and the bright blue and purple delphiniums? And your peonies? People would stop their cars to admire the peonies."

"Peonies like manure, you know," she told him. "You have to feed them."

A lump in his throat, he nodded. He did remember. He could almost hear the buzz of honeybees and feel the sun on his face and the carpet of grass he sat on as he watched his mother work in the garden. She often talked, telling him what she was doing and why. He helped her grow seedlings in the small greenhouse attached to the back of the garage. His tomatoes hadn't been quite as big as the globe in his elementary school classroom, but they'd grown fat and red and tasted better than any tomato he'd eaten before or since.

Mom and me grow better tomatoes than anyone, he'd bragged.

"Most plants like to be fed," he said, in a choked voice.

"Do you have peonies in your garden?" she asked.

He used his shirtsleeve to swipe at his cheeks. "I don't have a garden."

Unhappiness deepened every line in her face. "I don't think I do, either. I wish I did."

"Maybe you can again."

Her hand went slack in his. "Who are you?"

He closed his eyes and let her hand go. He was intensely grateful when Dr. Slater stepped forward and said, "You look tired. Perhaps it's time for a nap."

She looked from Adrian to Slater with suspicion and confusion. "Why are you here when I don't know you?"

"I'm the doctor," he said patiently. "You're in the hospital. You hit your head really hard on the pavement."

Lucy came to Adrian's side then. "Elizabeth, I'm so glad to see you awake and talking again. I'm Lucy."

"Of course you're Lucy. Who else would you be?"

Lucy laughed, as naturally as if her sister were teasing her. "Nobody at all. That was a silly thing to say, wasn't it?"

"Yes. I know Lucy," Adrian's mother told the two men.

"Of course you do," Dr. Slater said comfortably.

"Do you have a headache?" Lucy asked.

"I feel…" Her face worked. "I don't know what I feel." She struggled suddenly to sit up straighter and grabbed for the bars. "My cart! Where's my cart? Did somebody take my things?"

"No. No, all your things are at my house. Do you remember crossing the highway to go to Safeway? You were hit by a car. I took everything home to be sure it stayed safe while you got better here in the hospital."

It went on that way: comprehension, bewilderment, all answered by Lucy's steady warmth and reassurance. Adrian backed away from the bed, drained, stunned by how much he felt for this frightened, prematurely aged woman who could summon only fleeting memories of him, her son.

Lucy sent him away to get breakfast. He went back to her place, showered and packed his overnight bag again. About to close her front door behind him, he turned around and went back to the bedroom where she stored his mother's paltry belongings. He picked through, taking a few things he thought might mean something to her.

Ten minutes later, he checked in at the bed-and-breakfast.

As he was signing the book, Samantha watched him with a frown puckering her forehead. The expression was startlingly like Lucy's when she was perturbed.

"Are you all right?"

All right? Adrian didn't know. The ground beneath his feet had shifted.

"My mother regained consciousness. Lucy's at the hospital. I'm going back as soon as I—" For a moment he couldn't remember what he was supposed to be doing. "I don't suppose you're still serving breakfast."

"Not officially, but I'll put something together for you," she said immediately. "Why don't you drop your bag off upstairs and then come to the dining room?"

Samantha's "something" turned out to be scrambled eggs, thick slabs of whole wheat toast smothered in homemade blackberry jam and pastries that melted in his mouth. Adrian ate as if he were starving, which seemed to please her.

He went back to the hospital to release Lucy, who murmured, "Ssh, she's napping." One of the gift-shop volunteers had offered her a ride home, she said. "So you can stay." She kissed him on the cheek, then added, "I'll try to pop in midafternoon, between the lunch and dinner crowds," before she departed. She didn't question the small carton he carried.

His mother's sleep was more peaceful than the coma

had been, although the similarity was great enough that Adrian couldn't seem to tear his eyes from her. Sitting there at the bedside, he couldn't help wondering whether people ever slipped back into comas. What if she never opened her eyes again?

An hour passed. Two. Where the hell was Slater? Adrian wondered angrily.

Having breakfast. Or lunch, as late as it was. Shaving.

Adrian rubbed a hand over his own stubble. Should have done that himself. He didn't want to scare her.

A nurse came in several times, checking monitors. He was touched when she brought him coffee from the cafeteria.

He was taking a swallow of it when he realized his mother's eyes were open. She stayed very still and stared at him with all the alarm of a wild creature cornered.

"You're awake," he said, careful to speak quietly. "You're in the hospital. Do you remember getting hit by the car?"

"I don't want to be in the hospital! I don't like hospitals!" She sat up and grabbed for the bed rail, her gown slipping to bare a protuberant collarbone. "Let me out!"

He hit the Call button, and with the nurse's help calmed his mother.

He had to explain all over again who he was.

"I did have a little boy," she said again, eyeing him with deep suspicion.

"I brought pictures." He opened the carton he'd set at his feet, hoping this was the right thing to do. He regretted having left her driver's license and that long-ago Mother's Day card at his condo in Seattle. But he handed her a school photo of him that she'd kept all these years and watched her stare down at it.

After a moment she lifted her gaze from the picture, examined his face minutely, then returned to the photograph.

"Yes, that's really me," Adrian said.

She looked at the other pictures, including the one of herself as a girl. That one she stared at the longest. Adrian talked, telling her about her parents and the home in Nova Scotia where she'd grown up.

"I can't remember how to get there," she said sadly.

He had to swallow several times before he could speak. "I know."

After a minute he lifted the conch shell from the box and saw her smile. He set it on the bed beside her.

"I always wanted one of those," she confided. "I tried to bring one home once, from Hawaii. But *he* wouldn't let me. He said it was too big." Her eyes clouded with the memories. "I found that one at a garage sale. Imagine! They were selling it for two dollars."

"You were lucky."

"Lucky?" She nodded, stroking the satiny interior. "Sometimes I am, you know."

His heart was damn near breaking. "You were lucky to meet Lucy." Or was he the lucky one, because she'd brought Lucy into *his* life?

"Do you know Lucy?" His mother gazed at him in surprise. "She has me to lunch often. We're good friends."

"I know you are." He smiled at her. "Lucy said she'd be by for a visit this afternoon, between her lunch and dinner crowd."

Her face brightened. "Have you eaten her soup? It's very good."

Adrian agreed that he had. He got her talking about meals she'd eaten at the café, and told her he'd met Father Joseph. His mother confided that she didn't really like to listen to sermons, but she did enjoy the children. "And they need me," she told him with simple satisfaction. Her forehead creased. "This isn't Sunday, is it? Because they count on me."

"No, it's Saturday. And they know you won't be there tomorrow, since you're in the hospital. Some of the other mothers are filling in."

"Oh."

Back and forth. One minute she remembered, the next she was confused. Adrian was handicapped by not knowing what she'd been like before the accident. She hadn't remembered her past, or had professed not to. So, okay; that part might *be* normal for her. But he guessed the present had been in clearer focus for her, or she wouldn't have remembered the classified ads for garage sales and which started on Friday and which on Saturday, that *this* day was Sunday and she needed to be at the church, and so on.

Slater did show up and examined her, then talked to Adrian privately in the hall.

"Her mental acuity is actually quite remarkable considering." He shook his head in apparent admiration, his cherubic face glowing with delight.

"She's still pretty confused."

"Wouldn't you be?" the doctor said simply. "And yes, I feel confident she'll be back to herself in no time, champing at the bit to be out of the hospital."

Remembering her panic, Adrian said, "She doesn't like hospitals."

"If your father did commit her..."

God, yes. This bed, with the railings that looked like bars, might feel like prison to her. "Lucy says that most of the time she refused the offer of places to stay."

"Because she didn't like being obligated?" Slater rocked on his heels, thinking. "Or because she feels trapped if she's indoors for any length of time?"

Adrian shook his head, mute. His own mother, and he knew next to nothing about what was going on in her head.

"Perhaps this is a good time to evaluate her mental-health issues," the doctor suggested. "She might make further improvement on an appropriate drug regimen."

Adrian nodded numbly. "Yes, in a few days."

Slater clapped him on the back. "Give her time before you make any decisions."

Watching him stride down the hall, Adrian thought bleakly, *What choice do I have?* She obviously couldn't take care of herself.

Lucy came again and went, as did Father Joseph, whom she'd called with the news. Adrian used his visit to have a hurried dinner in the cafeteria before returning to his mother's bedside. The nurse greeted him with relief.

"She's agitated when you're gone."

"I keep having to explain again who I am."

She gave him a gentle smile he would once have interpreted as pitying. "But I think maybe, deep inside, she *knows*."

Lucy came for him after she closed the café. By then

his mother was sleeping. He stood wearily, and they both looked down at her.

Lucy's hand crept into his. "Today felt like a miracle," she said softly.

Did it? He moved his shoulders to ease knotted muscles. Maybe. His mother *had* remembered him, if only through the haze of a great distance.

He couldn't claim his memories of her were much sharper. Bits and pieces kept coming to him, but he'd been dismayed to realize how much he had shut out, either to please his father or in self-defense. Most recalled memories were good, but today, as he had patiently explained yet again who he was, he'd suddenly remembered walking in the door from school one day, just like any other day until then, to have her start violently at the sight of him and stare at him with wild eyes. She'd cried, "Go away! I won't listen to you! You're not there. You're not! You're not!"

"Mommy?" he had whispered in fright. "It's me. Adrian. Who are you talking to?"

"Nobody! I won't listen!" Clapping her hands over her ears, she had whirled and run from the kitchen, shutting herself in her bedroom. He had gazed longingly at the phone, wanting to call his father and say, "There's something wrong with Mom." But he hadn't, because… He didn't know why, just that his *job* was to shield his mom from everyone. Even Dad.

Especially Dad, Adrian thought now, in the hospital. He wondered whether she'd been on medication in those days. Whether she'd resisted taking it. Whether his father had been scared for him, coming home after school to her. In his own way, had he thought he was doing the right thing?

Maybe, Adrian thought again. If only his father had talked to him, if not then, later.

"You'll follow me home?" Lucy asked, her hand still in his as they rode the elevator down.

He studied her face. In the harsh white hospital lighting, she looked like she had bruises beneath her eyes. Freckles stood out in heightened relief. Neither of them had slept much last night, and the phone call from Slater had come early this morning.

"You look exhausted."

"I am tired, but—"

"I checked in to the B and B," he reminded her. "My stuff's there. Samantha will expect me."

She frowned at him. "Why did you do that?"

"Because I was trying to protect you from gossip. I'd made the reservations last week, you know."

"I don't care what my family thinks."

They'd reached her car and stopped. Running his hands up and down her arms, which were bare despite the cool night air, Adrian said roughly, "Are you sure?"

"Of course I'm sure," she snapped, just vehemently enough he didn't believe her.

"We're both tired," he said. "Why don't you come to Sam's for breakfast in the morning?"

After a moment she dipped her head, her expression still sulky. "Oh, fine."

He kissed her, feeling extraordinary tenderness. It heartened him that she was prepared to defy her family for him, although he was discovering that he didn't like the idea of their disapproval. He didn't want her to lose more than she had to, only because she'd made the decision to love him.

He drove behind her—stupid as it was, considering

she'd been getting herself home without his protection for years—then pulled to the curb until he saw her unlock her front door, give a wave and disappear inside. He looped back to her sister's, where it appeared everyone had gone to bed. A note taped to the stair newel told him about the snack he could help himself to in the kitchen if he was hungry.

A tired grin pulled at his mouth as he turned that way instead of starting up the stairs. The Peterson sisters did like to feed people.

THANK GOODNESS THE café was closed the next two days. Lucy spent most of them at the hospital with Adrian.

She liked that he'd brought the conch shell to his mother. It was something she'd loved, and was better than flowers, although he did bring those, too. Sunday he called a florist in Port Angeles and had a huge bouquet of peonies delivered. The hat lady cried. When she grabbed her son's hands and pulled him close until his forehead rested against hers, Lucy eased out of the room. She waited for several minutes then wiped tears from her eyes before she went back in.

He did come home with her Sunday and Monday nights both, but wouldn't stay to sleep.

"Sam won't know," she protested one night.

"Yes, she will. She leaves me a snack every night."

"Maybe you weren't hungry. Maybe you got up and left early."

He laughed. "Who'd turn down anything either of you have cooked? And there's no way I'd get up earlier than she does. I swear she's already in the kitchen baking by six."

Lucy made a face. "She always liked mornings."

"But you don't?"

They hadn't actually had a chance to find out things like that about each other, she realized. She didn't know if he was usually grumpy in the morning, or unbearably cheerful, whether he normally needed six hours of sleep a night or nine.

"My alarm never woke me. When I was in high school, Mom always had to yell until she got mad to make sure I was up." She grinned at him. "You notice I don't make breakfast at the café."

That was one of the nice things about those couple of days. His mom tired easily, then the two of them could talk, sometimes quietly at her bedside, sometimes in the cafeteria.

Monday morning Lucy overheard part of a terse phone call he made. He sounded unhappy, and she was a little chilled by his remote expression when he turned and saw her.

"Work?" she asked.

He gave a short nod. "This is not a good time for me to go missing in action."

"Is there ever a good time?"

Adrian grimaced. "No."

Then he changed the subject, and she didn't try to pursue the question of when he would have to go back to Seattle.

The hat lady was better each day, more herself. Of course she was weak from being in bed so long. First she made it shakily to the bathroom; by Monday evening, she was able to walk slowly up and down the hall. She was eating, and even reading after the librarian visited and left her a couple of books.

Lucy could tell Adrian was frustrated that she was

remembering her life in Middleton but not much about before. He wanted to know where she'd been in the intervening years. He wanted her to remember *him* better than she did.

Tuesday morning he came to Lucy's house for breakfast, then they drove separately to the hospital. When they walked into his mother's room and he said, "Hi, Mom," she gave him a surprised glance.

In an upper-crust British accent, she asked, "Who are you?"

He swore under his breath. "I'm your son, Adrian. Don't you remember? Last night you told me what my first word was—"

"Yes, I answered you last night. No, this morning, sir, I say."

He stared at her, baffled. "What in the hell?"

Lucy squeezed his forearm and murmured in his ear, "I think she's Elizabeth Barrett Browning again. The poet?" she said, when he stared uncomprehendingly at her.

"My God. She's crazy."

"Don't say that in front of her." Lucy turned and marched out of the room, aware when he followed. She swung to face him. "I told you what she's like."

"Damn it, even though she's been confused, she's been herself," he all but yelled at her. "Why this? Why now?"

"Because she's getting better."

He shook his head and kept shaking it. "This is *better*?"

"It's who she's been for a long time," Lucy tried to explain.

Intense frustration on his face, he said, "I don't have time for this. I've got to get back to Seattle today."

"Back to Seattle?" Lucy echoed. "You didn't say—"

His expression changed. "I got another call on the way over here. I don't have any choice. I'll try to make it back Friday."

"But…what if she's ready to be discharged before then?"

He gave a short, harsh laugh. "You're kidding, right? I've talked to Slater. I've told him I'll be making arrangements for her."

It was the way he said *arrangements,* so chilly, so… final.

Something heavy settled in Lucy's chest. She felt stupid. She'd built some kind of castle in the air where he was concerned. He'd never been the man she thought he was; he couldn't be if he could stick to a decision he'd made back at the beginning before he'd known his mother at all.

Before he'd known Middleton, and Lucy.

CHAPTER FOURTEEN

SHE'D BEEN AWARE FROM the beginning that Adrian had some kind of nursing home in mind. Of course if his mother hadn't come out of the coma she'd have had to be cared for. Why, Lucy asked herself, hadn't she realized he was going ahead with his plan even as the hat lady recovered?

Still standing there in the hospital corridor, she said, "You're not going to let her stay in Middleton?"

"Living on the street?" He looked at her as if *she* were crazy.

"She did okay," Lucy mumbled. Maybe it wasn't the best solution, she could see why he balked, but she hated the other possibilities, too.

"She won't have you anymore," he said, in the tone of an adult pointing out the obvious to a child. "Wouldn't you rather she was in Seattle where you can see her?"

The pain in her chest was so great, she could hardly breathe. This man staring at her with such impatience seemed like a stranger. Could she really leave Middleton and everyone else in the world she loved to share her life with him? The fact that he hadn't given any thought at all to what would make his mother happiest bothered her terribly.

Would he make decisions like that for her, too? Lucy wondered. Yes, he was taking responsibility. Yes, he was doing what he considered right. All without the slightest hint of compassion or understanding. Was he more like his father than he would admit to being?

"Why are you looking at me like that?" His attention was torn away when the cell phone she hadn't even realized he was carrying rang, and he flipped it open to read the caller's number. Snapping it shut, he said, "I've really got to go. We can talk about this later." He nodded toward the elevator. "Walk me down?"

"You aren't going to say goodbye?"

His jaw flexed. "Miss Browning doesn't even know who I am. She isn't going to miss me."

Lucy lifted her chin. "No, I think I'll stay here with her."

That frustration flashed across his face again. "Think about it. You'll see that I'm right." When she didn't respond, he added a clipped, "I'll call."

Lucy took a step toward the room so that he didn't try to kiss her. Right this moment, she couldn't bear to have him touch her. "Drive carefully."

"I know this isn't ideal...." He frowned, looking like the man she'd first met when she tracked him down in Seattle: impatient, emotionally distant, prepared to dismiss her.

I didn't like myself without you around. He'd paused, then added with seeming reluctance, *I was angry all week.*

Maybe, she thought in a kind of horror, *that's who he really is.*

He said something else; probably repeated, "I'll call."

She stood there and watched him walk away, very likely already putting her and his mother out of his mind.

No, that wasn't fair. He'd said, "I love you."

Tears burning in her eyes, Lucy whispered, "What if I *don't* see that you're right?"

For once, her mother had knocked. When Lucy answered the door, Helen said rather tentatively, "May I come in?"

"You don't have to ask." She tried very hard to wipe all signs of unhappiness from her face. It was bad enough that her mother would ask about the dark smudges under her eyes. She'd hardly slept at all last night.

"I'm not the one who usually barges in." Her mom followed her in and they headed toward the kitchen. They always talked in the kitchen; that's where Martin women felt the most comfortable. "That's your aunt Marian."

"*And* Aunt Lynn. *And* Aunt…"

Laughing, her mother said, "Okay, okay! We don't stand on ceremony in this family."

"Tea?"

"Please." She pulled out a kitchen chair and sat.

Lucy couldn't help remembering what she and Adrian had done on that very table. Biting her lip, she turned her back as she ran hot water into the teakettle. Some things, parents didn't need to know.

"So what's up?" she asked casually, once she'd set mugs out on the counter.

"I think that's my question." Her mother's gaze took in the exhaustion on her face, and more. "I've been worried about you."

Adrian had left only yesterday. How could her mother know to worry?

"Why?" Lucy asked.

"You haven't talked to me at all lately. Even your father guessed you'd fallen for Adrian. The fact that you haven't said anything has made me wonder—"

"Wonder?" she echoed, faintly.

Her mother's voice was gentle. "Oh, whether he reciprocates your feelings. Or whether you're afraid he doesn't."

Just like that, tears were rolling down her cheeks. With shaking hands, she swiped at them. "Oh, Mom!"

Her mother was out of the chair in an instant and had her arms around Lucy, holding her as she cried. "Oh, sweetie," she murmured. "Oh, sweetie, I'm so sorry."

Lucy sobbed until the teakettle whistled, then went to the bathroom to wash her face and compose herself while her mother poured the tea. She'd already carried the mugs to the table and was waiting when Lucy returned.

"How can he be such an idiot?" Helen said furiously, the minute Lucy had sat down. "Not to love you the way you deserve."

"Mom, that isn't it." So quickly, tears threatened again. By sheer force of will, she managed to hold them back. Or perhaps she'd run out of tears. "He says he loves me." She hesitated. "He asked me to marry him, Mom."

Her mother gaped at her. "And you didn't tell me?"

"Everything happened so fast. It was the next morning that his mom came out of her coma and—"

Helen's eyes narrowed. "And you weren't sure you were going to say yes."

"I did say yes." And oh, it hurt to remember her joy. Taking a deep breath, she told her mother everything:

her hopes, her doubts, her fears. "Am I crazy?" she begged at the end.

Her mother's expression was sorrowful. "Are you sure he isn't right about the hat lady? I mean, look what happened to her."

Lucy bristled. "Anybody could have been hit crossing the highway."

"Yes, of course. But you can't tell me you weren't already worried about her. I was shocked to hear that she's only in her fifties. Her diet is terrible, most nights she has no shelter. You've done your best for her, but—"

Her throat closed. "Was it good enough? Is that what you're asking?"

"I'm not suggesting you could or should have done more. Lucy, what you did for her was extraordinary. I'm simply asking if she might not be better off where she's taken care of."

"Can you imagine her in a room in a nursing home? Maybe sharing with someone else. Able to go out only under supervision." Her voice shook. "Those places lock their doors, Mom."

Her mother was silent for a moment, her eyes troubled. "No," she said at last. "No, I can't. She's a little bit like a wild creature. But, unlike you, I can see why Adrian might believe he's doing the right thing."

Lucy slumped. "I can, too. It isn't really his decision that bothers me. It's the way he came to it. He didn't even talk to me, Mom. He'd made up his mind before he got here that first night, and he never even considered changing it. She'd made herself a life here, one she chose. Surely there was a way to compromise."

Her mother held up her hand. "Don't get mad at me. I agree. And I can see why you can't marry a man who won't talk over big decisions with you, and actually *listen* to you."

"Oh, Mom." With no warning, the tears spilled over this time. "I wish I didn't love him!"

Her mother scooted her chair around to Lucy's side of the table so she could once again hold her. "I know," her mother murmured. "I know."

ADRIAN DID CALL that week, although once again he sounded harried and…different. He wasn't her Adrian, he was the impatient, guarded man Lucy had met that first day, when she walked into his office. The one who'd wanted to believe she was lying to him, for reasons she couldn't imagine.

What must it be like, to always assume the worst about people?

She'd have sworn she had discovered who he really was beneath that hard veneer, but now she wondered. He'd been only ten years old when his mother disappeared from his life. A little boy. He'd had over twenty years to be influenced by his father, to take on the habits and mind-set that made him who he was. Probably she'd been naive, even foolish, to believe he could somehow shed those aspects of himself, as if he were wriggling out of his skin and leaving it behind, just because he'd recovered childhood memories, found his mother.

Found me.

He did say, the first time he called, "I know you're upset with me, but you have to look at reality, Lucy."

"We had a real life before you came to Middleton." She tried so hard to sound as calm as he did, but her voice defied her by trembling. "It wasn't so bad."

He was silent for so long, she almost cracked and started babbling, conceding him anything he wanted.

But at last he said, "I'm getting the feeling you wish you'd never come looking for me."

She squeezed her eyes shut, willing herself not to cry. "I didn't say that. I wouldn't. She needs you, and you need her."

"What about you?" he asked softly. "What do you need?"

"For you to talk to me," she whispered, remembering everything she and her mother had said. "To really talk to me."

"What do you think I'm doing now?" he snapped. He sounded ragged, even angry. He muttered something she took as an expletive. "I want to see you, but I can't get away until the weekend. Can we put this on hold until then?"

Did that mean his decision wasn't final? Hope, fragile but still alive, stirred in her. That he might actually listen this time?

"Yes. Okay," she said. "I'm here."

At last, Adrian's voice softened. "I wish I was there with you. Or you were here with me."

Would she have wanted to be there in Seattle with him? Probably home alone in his condo, which she pictured as ultramodern, with chrome and neutral colors and none of the messiness her idea of real life produced. If she were there, they'd still be talking on the phone, because he'd be in his office.

But she knew suddenly she didn't care.

Yes, she had made discoveries of her own these past weeks. Perhaps, in showing Middleton to Adrian, she'd seen it anew herself. However it had happened, she knew now that she loved her hometown. She loved living here, knowing her customers, knowing her neighbors, feeling her family's love and support behind her. If she could, she'd travel—she did want to see more of the world. But she wanted to be able to come home again. Starting all over in a new place wasn't the adventure she'd yearned for. Loving someone, trusting him, taking the risk of giving so much of herself to him, *that* was the real adventure.

And for that, she'd leave Middleton in a heartbeat. If Adrian really was the man she'd fallen in love with, she couldn't imagine wanting to be anywhere he wasn't. She was good at making friends. She could build a satisfying career, pursue hobbies, perhaps talk him into buying a house where she could garden. And he would come home to her every night, however tired, however frustrated by his day. They'd talk, they'd make love, they'd start a family of their own.

Her choice would be him, with no hesitation. If he was the man she wanted so desperately to believe he was.

"I wish that, too," she admitted.

His voice lowered to a rumble. "I'll see you this weekend. I promise. If things work out the way I think they will…" He paused, and she heard a woman's voice in the background. Carol, no doubt.

Carol, who was the one who'd been looking for the assisted-living home for his mother. Carol, who didn't even know the hat lady.

He came back on. "I've got to go. I'll see you this weekend. Friday, if I can get away, otherwise Saturday."

"Yes. Okay."

He didn't say "I love you." Lucy supposed he didn't want to, with Carol standing there.

But, setting down the phone, she found the absence of the words bothered her. It seemed symbolic. The arrogant, hard Adrian Rutledge, attorney-at-law, wouldn't let anybody see him being soft.

Still, he *had* implied that they still had time to talk, that there might be room for negotiation. So she would let herself feel hopeful. Because he did love her. She believed that much.

"You're taking her, just like that?"

Lucy didn't even know why she was in shock. Yes, she did—she'd foolishly imagined that he was promising her something that apparently had never crossed his mind.

When he said, "Can we put this on hold?" he hadn't meant that there was still time to talk about his mom's future. He'd probably thought he could pacify her in person. Or else he hadn't understood that his decision wasn't just about how happy or unhappy the hat lady would be, but was also about him.

This scene had begun playing out last week, and all it was doing now was concluding. She was the idiot, thinking that, because his voice had softened, she'd gotten through to him. Apparently she'd been an idiot all along, believing that once he knew his mother he'd slow down and think about what would give her the best quality of life.

Instead, he scowled at her. "What do you mean, *just like that?* I let you know last night that I was coming."

Yes, he had. She'd found a message on her phone at

home when she got in at nearly midnight after closing the restaurant.

I got lucky and found an opening for Mom at a great place. I've already called Slater. I'll be over in the morning to get her. Meet me at the hospital? Say, eleven?

Too late to call him back, or so she told herself. He couldn't mean it. Or…was there any chance he'd gotten his mom a bed at the nursing home here in Middleton as a temporary measure, and that he wanted to surprise her?

Dumb, dumb, dumb, she told herself now.

"She's going to be so scared."

"More scared than she was living on the street?" He snorted, as if she were being ridiculous. After a pause, he conceded, "It'll be an adjustment."

Her face felt stiff; her voice came out wooden. "Why didn't you just have her transported in an ambulance? Or a helicopter? And saved yourself the trip?"

He moved his shoulders. "I, uh, liked the idea of us riding the ferry together. I thought…she might be excited."

For a moment her heart quivered. The man she'd fallen in love with was still in there. But then she imagined the hat lady in a room at an assisted-living facility where the doors were undoubtedly locked. She would have no freedom at all.

"The place has a garden." Adrian sounded tentative. "Her room looks out on some roses."

Lucy swallowed a lump in her throat. "Can she go out? Maybe take walks?"

She saw the answer on his face. Sucking in a breath,

she told him, "I said goodbye to your mom already. I just waited to—"

"Tell me what you thought?"

She gave a twisted smile. "Something like that."

He reached a hand out to her, his voice gruff, urgent. "Lucy... I know I said we'd talk, but I can't get back until next weekend. Friday night—"

She backed away, not meeting his eyes. "Don't bother."

He flinched. "So in the end this is about my mother."

"No." Lucy shook her head and took one last, agonizing look at his lean face and the turmoil in his eyes. In a choked voice, she said, "It's about you." Then she turned and fled.

Through the haze of tears, she had no idea whether people were staring as she hurried out of the elevator and crossed the lobby then the parking lot. She knew only that Adrian didn't follow.

ALL ABOUT HIM? Adrian thought incredulously. Who was she kidding?

His fingers flexed on the steering wheel as he followed the line of weekend traffic. In the end, it was really all about her. Or maybe it was about his mother. Was Lucy making the point that, while he might be Elizabeth Rutledge's son, she still knew her best?

Feeling sick, he thought, *It's true.* But what in hell did she think he should do? Walk Mom to the hospital door and wave cheerily as she pushed her shopping cart toward the highway then God knows where? She was fifty-six years old. She had multiple personalities. Letting her continue to live on the street wasn't an option.

"I don't know this place." Beside him, Elizabeth's

voice quavered. She gripped the armrest so hard, her knuckles shone white. "Where are we going?"

They hadn't even reached the Hood Canal Bridge, and he'd already repeated himself twenty or so times. But he smiled reassuringly anyway and said, "Remember? We're going to ride on the ferry."

"And then you're taking me home. Right?"

"Don't you *want* to ride on the ferry? Remember when we used to do that? We'd walk on, and go outside so the wind blew on our faces. Well, this time we're driving the car on."

She stiffened. "That doesn't look like a ferry."

The highway emerged from a long curve to reveal the bridge ahead, the broad canal sparkling beneath.

He explained that they still had an hour's drive.

"When will we be home?"

What, in her mind, was home? Adrian wondered. The hospital? One of her hideouts? The church? Middleton in general?

"Remember, I talked to you about the new place you'll be living."

"I don't want a new place." She was definite about that. "I don't think I want to ride on the ferry, not if you won't take me home."

"Remember the accident? You still need extra care. You're not very strong yet, Mom."

"Father Joseph always lets me stay in my room at the church. I can do that. Or Lucy. Lucy would let me stay."

Goddamn it. She probably would. But Adrian couldn't foist his problems on Lucy. Not now, when it was clear she didn't love him. Not really, not the way he'd believed when he had been riding on a powerful wave of hope.

And it wasn't as if she'd ever offered, he realized, his thoughts crystalline and sharp-edged. The anger he clung to was keeping the agony at bay, but it was there, barely hiding around the corner. He focused on the anger, shutting out the grief. Until he got his mother settled, he couldn't afford to break down.

Yeah, Lucy wanted him to find a solution, but she'd never suggested an alternative. Apparently he was supposed to have figured out a perfect answer—which, of course, she already knew, but hadn't shared with him. Maybe it had been a test, one he'd failed. Well, to hell with her, he thought, teeth clenched, and knew he didn't mean it.

"I don't know where we are," his mother repeated. Her frightened gaze swung from the landscape to him. "I want to go back now!"

Gripping the steering wheel so hard he swore the plastic groaned, Adrian explained again. And again. And again.

CHAPTER FIFTEEN

STILL CLENCHING THE steering wheel, Adrian tried to count his blessings. At least his mother was herself today, not Queen Elizabeth or the poet. She was definitely in the here and now. Adrian tried to be glad.

Lucy had packed his mother's pitiful store of belongings into a couple of suitcases, which he suspected she'd bought for the occasion. His mother had already been dressed when he arrived at the hospital, wearing a pretty flowered dress with a wide belt, comfortable shoes and a hat, one of those small oval ones that perched rakishly atop her head, edged by net that dipped over her forehead. It made him think of Audrey Hepburn.

He grimaced. No, if she glanced in a mirror she'd see Elizabeth Taylor, he supposed.

With only another dozen repetitions of the same conversation, they made it to Poulsbo, then onto Bainbridge Island, and finally to the ferry landing. She fell silent briefly when they drove on, the ramp rattling beneath the tires, and the ferry workers directed him to park on one side. Adrian set the brake and turned off the engine, then closed his eyes briefly. His neck and shoulders were so tight, he wasn't sure he could unbend enough to unlatch the door or get out.

After a minute, he said, "Shall we go up? I always liked watching the ferry pull away from the dock."

"We won't get off, will we? We'll ride it over and back, the way we always did. That might be fun."

He unfastened her seat belt and his own, and got out of the car. Panic was building in his chest. What happened when they got to the other side? Would she fight him? How the hell could he leave her at the assisted-living place if she was terrified or crying?

He heard Lucy's voice in his head. *Did you ask* her *what she wants?*

He didn't have to. He knew. She wanted to return to her familiar small-town streets, her familiar routine. Garage sales on Friday and Saturday mornings, the church day care on Sundays, the library, the hair salon, Safeway and the Pancake Haus and Lucy's café.

Grimy, pushing her stolen shopping cart, inviting pity and charity.

Adrian held open the heavy door for his mother. She climbed the steps slowly, holding up everyone else. Once on the passenger deck, she had to sit immediately, looking pale and alarmingly fragile.

Would she be happier at the Middleton assisted-living facility, even if she'd be confined there, too, and he couldn't see her very often?

But Lucy would be there. Not with him in Seattle the way he'd dreamed. Believed she would be.

He realized, as his mother shakily rose and leaned on his arm so they could proceed slowly toward the back of the ferry and the outdoor deck that looked down on the still loading cars and the dock, that he was as bewildered as she was.

He'd caught one of the first ferries that morning, eager to arrive. Of course he'd only see Lucy briefly, but he could kiss her, talk to her, make plans. He'd go back next weekend.

But the minute he saw her, he knew something was wrong. She'd looked at him as if he were a stranger. When he tried to remember all the things she'd said, they blurred.

He did remember one accusation. "I thought you were getting to know *her*. But you never saw her as a person, did you? Only as she related to you."

His mother wrapped her hands around the railing and leaned against it, her head lifted for a minute, her eyes closed, as a breeze toyed with her white curls. She breathed in as though the salty air tasted like fine wine. For that brief instant, apparently oblivious to the chattering family who had joined them out here, she looked at peace.

She had always been fragile. As long as Adrian could remember, he had wanted to shield her from the world. Was that so bad?

"That summer I went to visit *Maman* and *Grandpère* in Nova Scotia, where did you go?" he asked.

Her eyes opened and she turned her head. After a minute, she said in a voice so soft he had to bend closer to hear, "It was a hospital. I think. He said I'd get better."

"Did you?"

"They made me feel so cloudy." Her eyes pleaded with him for understanding. "I wasn't *me*. I don't know who I was. I don't like hospitals."

"Where did you go after you left the hospital?"

Her forehead crinkled in puzzlement. "I tried to go home, but I couldn't find it."

"Home to me in Edmonds, or to your parents?"

The ferry horn sounded, making them both jump.

The gulls cried and swooped overhead the way he remembered from when he was a boy. She looked away,
watching the water churn between them and the dock.
"I don't know. There was someplace I thought I should
go. But I couldn't."

He felt sick, imagining her homeless, frightened,
unable to remember even how to call her own mother.

"I missed you," he said quietly, past the lump in his
throat.

"I thought you were still a little boy. I'm not sure
how you can be my Adrian."

"I am." He smiled at her, although the effort hurt. "I
still love to ride the ferry."

"I think I have to sit down," she said. "If you don't
mind."

"Of course I don't."

He found them a seat inside by the window, and
watched her gaze hungrily out at the sailboats chasing
each other, the barge moving slowly to the south, the
water a bright blue with the sun almost directly overhead.

He could take her on outings. To restaurants and
parks and to the beach. When she was stronger, they
could fly to Nova Scotia. He wondered if she might even
want to stay there, at least for now. Except *Maman* was
a very old woman now, not able to care for her.

But the people in Middleton had. He thought they
might be happy to continue to do so, except for the
grumpy few who had always disdained her, their one-
and-only homeless person.

She wouldn't have to be homeless. He could certainly
afford to rent her a room, or even buy her a house if
she wanted one.

Yes, but could she be trusted to live alone? What if she left a burner or curling iron or God knew what on, or a faucet running? What if she locked herself out on a cold night, or forgot where she lived, or...?

As if Lucy were sitting there beside him, he heard her say, "She's not senile, you know. Do you think that parents would trust her with their children if she were? Or that she could enjoy reading the way she does, and discussing the themes? That she could keep appointments? She's remarkably well-organized, actually. And she has such a good memory for the names of authors whose books she's loved, and perennials and old roses, and historical figures."

Had she said that, when she was trying to persuade him to make a different plan? Adrian wasn't sure.

Suddenly he felt sick. Had he made the right decision? Had it ever been the right one for his mother?

He felt a yawning emptiness inside and identified it. He didn't want to lose her again, and he thought he would if he gave her back to Middleton. But the truth was, she wasn't the mom he remembered anyway. Oh, she was still that, in flickers of memory, but those were overlaid by the life she'd chosen since. One that hadn't been so bad.

Would Lucy have him back if he took his mom home to Middleton? The tearing pain in his gut told him no. It was too late. He'd done something wrong. Or maybe it was just who he was. Nobody since his mother had ever loved him. Why had he believed Lucy could?

But maybe, just maybe, he could make things right for the hat lady.

It seemed symbolic that they were seated to be looking back rather than forward, at the approaching cityscape. Turning his face away from the window, telling himself his eyes burned from the bright reflection of the sun on the water and not from emotion, Adrian thought, *I want to go back, too. I want to be part of a family, part of a town.*

He had responsibilities. Clients.

Did he give a damn about a one of them?

I can't move to Middleton if Lucy doesn't want me.

No, but he could change his life. He could accept the lessons she and his mother had taught.

And…it wouldn't hurt to explore possibilities, would it? In case he hadn't been wrong about Lucy?

Still hurting but also feeling a fragile renewal of the precious hope Lucy had given him, he said, "Mom, I'm sorry I dragged you on this trip."

She smiled sunnily at him. "I'm fine, Adrian. You were right. This *was* fun. Although I am looking forward to going home."

He smiled at her wryly. "I know."

Crazy or not, his mother was on to something. Middleton did feel like home, in a way his expensive Seattle condominium and the city he knew best never had.

Lucy, please find me worthy.

LUCY PEERED AT herself in the mirror from between only slightly puffy lids. The cold washcloth had done its job. Chances were good that no one would notice she looked any different than usual, especially once she got bustling in the kitchen over hot burners.

She'd considered not going in. Shea could have filled in for her, or even Samantha in a pinch. But giving herself something to do was a good thing, and anyway, this was her life. Bleakly Lucy thought, *I chose it.*

She still couldn't quite believe she'd thrown away everything she had ever believed she wanted: a gorgeous man who loved her, the possibility of adventure in the wider world, the chance to escape her overabundant family while still being near enough to see them sometimes. Even the impetus she needed to try out her culinary skills for the benefit of more sophisticated diners.

What kind of fool was she?

But in her heart, she knew she couldn't have made a different choice. Adrian's decision to institutionalize his mother without even exploring alternatives made a mockery of all the times they'd talked about the mother he remembered, a woman who had shaped the man he was despite her absence from so much of his life. That man, Lucy had imagined, could be playful, protective, soft-hearted, impulsive. He would be the perfect father. She'd *seen* him in her mind's eye, out on the lawn spinning a little boy in circles, both of them laughing, his smiling mother looking on.

Dumb, idealized dreams. Because, obviously, he wasn't that man.

She blinked fiercely to keep tears from flooding her eyes again. It was three o'clock and she needed to get going if she was to be ready for the dinner crowd.

She had started down the stairs when her doorbell rang. Lucy's step checked and she frowned. That was odd. Who would be stopping by at this time of day? Besides her family, of course, who had the annoying habit of letting themselves in without bothering with any nonsense—as her aunt Beth put it—like ringing the doorbell.

Puzzled, Lucy opened the door.

Like a mirage, Adrian and the hat lady stood on her

front porch, Adrian tall and so formidably handsome she was cast back to the first time she saw him.

Her throat closed. She was imagining them. Wasn't she?

He cleared his throat. "I'm glad we caught you at home. I was afraid you'd be at the café."

"I…was about to leave."

Expression wary, he was looking at her entirely too closely. He would notice the puffy eyes.

Well, so what! she thought with defiance. He was the one who'd disappointed her. She wouldn't apologize for loving him, or for grieving for what might have been.

"Um…can we come in?"

The hat lady, whose carriage was very erect, even regal, beamed at Lucy. In a very upper-crust British accent, she said, "Your flower beds are lovely! What a talented young lady you are."

"Why, thank you." Lucy smiled at her. "Please. Do come in. May I offer you a cup of tea?"

"That would be nice, but I wonder…" She glanced at the man at her side, then met Lucy's eyes again, some embarrassment in hers. "I dislike asking for a favor, but…I do believe I need to lie down for a bit. My son suggested I might take advantage of your hospitality."

"Of course you can." Lucy resisted the impulse to hug the frail woman. Because, after all, you weren't supposed to touch Her Majesty without permission. "Let me show you upstairs."

The progress was slow. Adrian, watchful, waited at the bottom. The hat lady was worn out by her day. Lucy showed her into the guest room.

"May I?" she asked, and, given permission, unpinned the hat. She helped her guest take off her shoes and lie down, then spread an afghan over her. "Shall I close the curtains?"

"No." Her friend, the Queen of England, smiled, her eyes closing. "I like the sunlight on my face."

Lucy tiptoed out, pulling the door almost closed. For a moment she paused there, afraid to go down and face Adrian.

Afraid to find out she was wrong about why he'd turned around and driven his mother back to Middleton. But putting it off wouldn't change anything, would it? Lucy drew a deep breath and made herself start down the stairs.

He waited at the bottom, one hand on the newel post, his eyes never leaving hers from the moment she appeared at the top.

"Thank you," he said, nodding upward.

"I've always loved her. Did you think I wouldn't welcome her?"

His jaw knotted. "I meant, for not questioning our reappearance. I don't think she ever understood that we weren't supposed to turn around and come back to Middleton."

She stood two steps from the bottom, where she could still look down at him. "Why did you come back?"

"Because I realized you were right." His voice was raw. He wasn't a man accustomed to admitting to faults. "I didn't listen to her. I thought about my responsibilities, not her needs."

A wave of dizzying relief washed over Lucy. She had to grab the banister for support. She had been right about him after all. No, wrong, at least the last time she saw him.

"I'm sorry," she whispered. "For everything I said. I should have trusted you."

"No." He reached out, his hand stopping just short of covering hers. His fingers curled into a fist and he withdrew it, as if unsure whether his touch was wanted. "No," he said hoarsely. "I needed to hear every word. I almost didn't, you know. I was pretty angry when I left."

"I know." Oh, she yearned for him to take her in his arms! But she wasn't sure that was what he had in mind at all. *He* would still be going back to Seattle. Would he ask her again to go?

She had already answered that question for herself. Yes, yes, yes! Even though she had discovered, after a lifetime of chafing at the bonds of family and small town, that she *belonged* here. But she belonged with him, too; him, most of all. Perhaps, like Dr. Slater's wife, she could persuade Adrian to retire to Middleton someday.

She had hurt him, though, and he was a proud man. He might never ask again. He might not want her.

"I had to explain over and over where we were going," he said. "But nothing I said sunk in. Mom just kept asking whether we were going home after we rode the ferry."

"And so you decided to bring her."

He grimaced. "And thus we're, uh, imposing on you. Do you need to go to work? I can stay here with Mom, or take her over to your sister's once she wakes up."

"What do you have in mind?" Lucy asked. "I mean, for your mom?"

"Well, that depends." He rubbed the back of his neck, as if to ease tension. "Don't you have to go? I could come back tonight to talk to you, when you get home. Or tomorrow."

"Let me see if I can find someone to fill in for me."

She left him standing there and went to the kitchen, where she made a swift phone call. Then she returned and said, "I'm off the hook until Tuesday. Let's sit down."

He nodded and followed her into the living room, where he hesitated until she sat on one end of the sofa, one foot curled beneath her. He chose the other end, close enough that she could see how rigidly he held himself, the strain on his face, the tight line of his mouth.

"I may buy her a house. Or rent her a room, depending on what you think's best."

Oh. He wanted only to talk about arrangements for his mother.

Lucy nodded, as if considering the options.

"Or perhaps, ah, something like a mother-in-law apartment." Even his voice sounded stifled, with a soft burr. Only his eyes were vividly alive, searching her face. "Depending on you."

Not on what she thought best, but *her.* Hope swelled painfully in her chest.

"What do you mean?" she asked carefully.

"I love you. I didn't just bring my mother back. I brought myself back."

Tears overflowed, and she launched herself at him. "Oh, Adrian! This has been the worst day of my life!"

His arms closed around her with bruising force, and he pressed his cheek against the top of her head. "*God.* I was so afraid—"

When he broke off, she pulled back slightly so that

she could see his face. The vulnerability there wrenched her heart.

"I thought…you hadn't really loved me. Believing that was easy. Or maybe I never quite believed you did. After my mother left me—"

"You never felt loved again," she said slowly, shocked despite herself.

"Felt?" His face twisted. "I don't think I was. My father…I doubt he knew how."

"Oh, Adrian." Lucy kissed him slowly, sweetly, tasting her tears and knowing he would as well. "*I* love you."

He made an inarticulate sound that vibrated in his chest then kissed her back, his mouth hungry. Passion was there, but the desperation with which they held each other had another cause entirely.

"Can you stay tonight?" Lucy asked, when she could. "I don't care if your mother's in the guest room…."

"I can stay. If you mean it." Her next kiss apparently reassured him. It was a minute before he could continue. "I can stick around until Monday—"

"Really?" She drew back again. "You've missed so much work."

"I'm quitting," he said flatly.

Shaken, Lucy shook her head. She had to have heard wrong. "What?"

"If you want to stay in Middleton, I'll buy Weatherby's practice if he's really prepared to sell. If you don't—"

She interrupted him. "But…you can't possibly *want* to give up being a partner in a major Seattle law firm so that you can…well, defend Bill Bartovich when he gets in a drunken brawl at the tavern."

He actually grinned at her, so handsome he took her breath away. "I thought Middleton had real crime."

"Of course it does. Sometimes. But…mostly, you'd probably be drawing up wills and refereeing property disputes and—"

"Defending drunken loggers?"

"Yes."

He was still smiling, so much tenderness in eyes she'd once considered chilly, Lucy thought she could die happy right that minute. "What you mean is, I could take care of the legal concerns of my friends and neighbors. Instead of defending corporate scum in court."

"Surely you don't feel that way about all your clients."

Adrian made a quick, impatient gesture. "No. Of course not. But I've had increasing doubts lately. Especially—" he cupped her face "—since I met you. I've been…jealous. I want what you have. Family. People who care."

Her eyes filled with tears again.

With his thumbs, he gently brushed the tears away. "If you want to move to Seattle—or anywhere at all—that's okay, too. I'm still quitting the firm. I want to do something different with my life. We can make provisions for Mom."

She couldn't seem to quit crying, even though now her nose was running, too. "Are you sure? I do want to stay here, but not if you'll be unhappy—"

"Never." He pulled her close and let her weep happily against his shoulder. "I was kind of hoping you'd say that. Middleton seems to have cast its spell on me. I like the idea of raising our kids here."

Lucy wept some more. Eventually, she left him long

enough to wash her face and blow her nose. She didn't dare even peek at the mirror. He loved her; he wouldn't care that her face was blotchy and puffy and horribly unattractive.

When she returned to him he kissed her as if he hadn't noticed how she looked at all. Lucy found that amazingly satisfying.

Finally, with her cuddled up to him, he said, "On the ferry I flipped through some real estate booklets. I saw a house for sale here in Middleton. A big old place with a carriage house that's been turned into an apartment."

"Oh!" She sat up. "The Andrews house. I've seen the For Sale sign. It's amazing. But…can you afford it?"

"Sure," he said in surprise. "Or we could stay here. Do you own this house?"

Lucy shook her head. "I rent from my uncle Will. Of course he'd never kick me out."

"Do you mind moving? Right after you started your dream garden?"

"No. Oh, no." Darned if she wasn't near to tears again. "I can start again. And that garden will be my own."

Adrian nodded. "I asked you once before, but I think I need to do it again. Will you marry me, Lucy Peterson?"

"Yes. Yes!"

They kissed, and they held each other, and they murmured confidences. He told her that they'd had to wait nearly forty-five minutes in the ferry line on the other side, and he'd gotten the paperback copy of *The Fellowship of the Ring,* with its yellowed pages, out of the trunk and started reading it to his mother.

"She was too tired to go up top once we did get on

the ferry, so she took a turn reading to me during the crossing."

"Was it worth the wait?" Lucy asked.

He was silent for a moment. "Yeah. It was pretty gripping. And sitting there, with my mom reading to me, after all these years..." His voice roughened. "Isn't it funny, when you think you have everything you need, and then you discover you didn't. Here I am with my mother, and you, and someplace to call home."

Her chest hurt, she loved him so much. Lucy nodded. "And I have you, and I've found out I don't want to leave home after all."

She could hardly wait to tell the hat lady that miracles happened every day.

* * * * *

We hope you enjoyed reading

IN BED WITH HER BOSS

by *New York Times* bestselling author

BRENDA JACKSON

and

RICH MAN'S FAKE FIANCÉE

by *USA TODAY* bestselling author

CATHERINE MANN

Both were originally Harlequin® series stories!

Harlequin Desire stories feature sexy, romantic heroes
who have it all: wealth, status, incredible good looks…
everything but the right woman. Add some secrets,
maybe a scandal, and start turning pages!

Powerful heroes…scandalous secrets…burning desires.

Look for six new romances every month
from Harlequin® Desire!

Available wherever books are sold.

The Lassiter family lawyer has some surprise news for one stunning woman…

She looked prettier than a painted picture come to life. Yep. Trouble with a capital *T* if he didn't get his mind back on business.

"After you learn the details of your share of the Lassiter fortune, you'll be able to buy me dinner next time." *Next time?* Man, he was getting way ahead of himself, and that was totally out of character for his normally cautious self.

Hannah looked about as surprised as he felt over the comment. "That all depends on if I actually agree to accept my share, and that's doubtful."

He couldn't fathom anyone in their right mind turning down that much money. But before he had a chance to toss out an opinion, their waiter showed up with their entrées.

Logan ate his food with the gusto of a field hand, while Hannah basically picked at hers, the same way she had with the salad. By the time they were finished, and the plates were cleared, he had half a mind to invite her into the nearby bar to discuss business. But dark and cozy wouldn't help rein in his libido.

HDEXP0414

Hannah tossed her napkin aside and folded her hands before her. "Okay, we've put this off long enough. Tell me the details."

Logan took a drink of water in an attempt to rid the dryness in his throat. "The funds are currently in an annuity. You have the option to leave it as is and take payments. Or you can claim the lump sum. Your choice."

"How much?" she said after a few moments.

He noticed she looked a little flushed and decided retiring to the bar might not be a bad idea after all. "Maybe we should go into the lounge so you can have a drink before I continue."

Frustration showed in her expression. "I don't need a drink."

He'd begun to think he might. "Just a glass of wine to take the edge off."

She leaned forward and nailed him with a glare. *"How much?"*

"Five million dollars."

"I believe I will have that drink now."

Don't miss
FROM SINGLE MOM TO SECRET HEIRESS
Available May 2014
Wherever Harlequin® Desire books are sold.

Desire

Powerful heroes…scandalous secrets…burning desires.

Save $1.00 on the purchase of

FROM SINGLE MOM TO SECRET HEIRESS

by Kristi Gold

available May 6, 2014,
or on any other Harlequin® Desire book.

Available wherever books are sold, including most bookstores,
supermarkets, drugstores and discount stores.

Save $1.00

on the purchase of
FROM SINGLE MOM TO SECRET HEIRESS
by Kristi Gold
available May 6, 2014
or on any other Harlequin® Desire book.

Coupon valid until July 1, 2014. Redeemable at participating retail outlets
in the U.S. and Canada only. Limit one coupon per customer.

52611403

Canadian Retailers: Harlequin Enterprises Limited will pay the face value of this coupon plus 10.25¢ if submitted by customer for this product only. Any other use constitutes fraud. Coupon is nonassignable. Void if taxed, prohibited or restricted by law. Consumer must pay any government taxes. Void if copied. Millennium1 Promotional Services ("M1P") customers submit coupons and proof of sales to Harlequin Enterprises Limited, P.O. Box 3000, Saint John, NB E2L 4L3, Canada. Non-M1P retailer—for reimbursement submit coupons and proof of sales directly to Harlequin Enterprises Limited, Retail Marketing Department, 225 Duncan Mill Rd., Don Mills, Ontario M3B 3K9, Canada.

U.S. Retailers: Harlequin Enterprises Limited will pay the face value of this coupon plus 8¢ if submitted by customer for this product only. Any other use constitutes fraud. Coupon is nonassignable. Void if taxed, prohibited or restricted by law. Consumer must pay any government taxes. Void if copied. For reimbursement submit coupons and proof of sales directly to Harlequin Enterprises Limited, P.O. Box 880478, El Paso, TX 88588-0478, U.S.A. Cash value 1/100 cents.

5 65373 00076 2 (8100)0 11911

® and TM are trademarks owned and used by the trademark owner and/or its licensee.
© 2014 Harlequin Enterprises Limited

NYTCOUP0414

REQUEST YOUR FREE BOOKS!

2 FREE NOVELS
FROM THE ROMANCE COLLECTION
PLUS 2 FREE GIFTS!

YES! Please send me 2 FREE novels from the Romance Collection and my 2 FREE gifts (gifts are worth about $10). After receiving them, if I don't wish to receive any more books, I can return the shipping statement marked "cancel." If I don't cancel, I will receive 4 brand-new novels every month and be billed just $6.24 per book in the U.S. or $6.74 per book in Canada. That's a savings of at least 22% off the cover price. It's quite a bargain! Shipping and handling is just 50¢ per book in the U.S. and 75¢ per book in Canada.* I understand that accepting the 2 free books and gifts places me under no obligation to buy anything. I can always return a shipment and cancel at any time. Even if I never buy another book, the two free books and gifts are mine to keep forever.

194/394 MDN F4XY

Name _____ (PLEASE PRINT)

Address _____ Apt. # _____

City _____ State/Prov. _____ Zip/Postal Code _____

Signature (if under 18, a parent or guardian must sign)

Mail to the Harlequin® Reader Service:
IN U.S.A.: P.O. Box 1867, Buffalo, NY 14240-1867
IN CANADA: P.O. Box 609, Fort Erie, Ontario L2A 5X3

Want to try two free books from another line?
Call 1-800-873-8635 or visit www.ReaderService.com.

* Terms and prices subject to change without notice. Prices do not include applicable taxes. Sales tax applicable in N.Y. Canadian residents will be charged applicable taxes. Offer not valid in Quebec. This offer is limited to one order per household. Not valid for current subscribers to the Romance Collection or the Romance/Suspense Collection. All orders subject to credit approval. Credit or debit balances in a customer's account(s) may be offset by any other outstanding balance owed by or to the customer. Please allow 4 to 6 weeks for delivery. Offer available while quantities last.

Your Privacy—The Harlequin® Reader Service is committed to protecting your privacy. Our Privacy Policy is available online at www.ReaderService.com or upon request from the Harlequin Reader Service.

We make a portion of our mailing list available to reputable third parties that offer products we believe may interest you. If you prefer that we not exchange your name with third parties, or if you wish to clarify or modify your communication preferences, please visit us at www.ReaderService.com/consumerschoice or write to us at Harlequin Reader Service Preference Service, P.O. Box 9062, Buffalo, NY 14269. Include your complete name and address.

ROM13R